*Make time for friends. Make time for **Debbie Macomber**.*

Dear Reader,

This book is dedicated to the friends of my youth. Each one played a special role in my life. Diane, Kathy and I went through all twelve years of school together, and we stay in touch to this day. Carol joined us in the fifth grade, and she and I still manage to get together from time to time—we laugh a lot. Cheryl came into my life in the seventh grade. Then there's Jane (my best friend through high school), Judy, Cindy, Bev and Yvette. We all met in high school and we continue to see each other. Friendship is like that. Lives and times may change, but true friends remain; they're somehow always part of us. I'll admit that we're having our fortieth class reunion this year (hard to believe though that is), so it seems fitting to mention their names.

I'll admit something else. At a recent reunion, Jane and I decided to look up our old boyfriends. We didn't have any luck finding them—both had moved—but we sure had a good time trying. Like Susannah, we didn't know what we'd say other than "Hi. Remember me?" (We weren't actually convinced they would…)

I hope you enjoy *Susannah's Garden*—a celebration of friendship, the pleasures of recognising that growing up brings with it some difficult choices and decisions. The middle years, especially, can reverse the dynamic of the parent-child relationship, as Susannah discovers and as I did, too, with my own parents.

Debbie Macomber

Debbie Macomber

Susannah's Garden

MIRA is a registered trademark of Harlequin Enterprises Limited, used under licence.

Published in Great Britain 2011
MIRA Books, Eton House, 18-24 Paradise Road,
Richmond, Surrey, TW9 1SR

© Debbie Macomber 2006

(Originally published 2007 in UK as *Old Boyfriends*)

ISBN 978 0 7783 0416 6

58-0511

MIRA's policy is to use papers that are natural, renewable and recyclable products and made from wood grown in sustainable forests. The logging and manufacturing processes conform to the legal environmental regulations of the country of origin.

Printed and bound by
CPI Group (UK) Ltd, Croydon, CR0 4YY

For my friends all through school,
as we remember the paths we took,
and didn't take.

Jane Berghoff McMahon, Judy St George Senecal,
Cindy Thoma DeBerry, Diane DeGooyer Harmon,
Cheryl Keller Farr, Kathy Faith Harris,
Bev Gamache Regimbal, Yvette Dwinell Lundy

and

Carol Brulotte

I

Vivian Leary stood motionless at the corner of the street, her eyes darting from side to side. She had no idea where she was or how she'd gotten lost. After all, she'd lived in Colville her entire life. She should know—*did* know—every square inch of this town. But the last thing she remembered was going out to collect the mail and that must have been hours ago.

The street didn't look familiar and the houses weren't any she recognized. The Henderson house at the corner of Chestnut and Elm had been her marker, but it was nowhere in sight. She remembered that the Hendersons had painted their place white with green shutters. Where was it? she wondered, starting to feel frantic. *Where was it?* George would be upset with her for taking so long. Oh no, how could she have forgotten? George was dead.

The weight of grief settled over her, heavy and oppressive.

George, her beloved husband, was gone—taken from her just two months short of their sixtieth anniversary. It had all happened so fast....

Last November, her husband had gone outside to warm up the car before church, and a few minutes later he lay dead in the carport. He'd had a massive heart attack. The nice young man who'd come with the ambulance had told her George was dead before he even hit the pavement. He sounded as if this was supposed to comfort her. But nothing could have eased the shock, the *horror,* of that dreadful morning.

Vivian blinked hard, and despite the May warmth of eastern Washington, a chill raced up her bare arms. She tried to extinguish her growing panic. How was she going to find her way home?

Susannah would know what to do—but then she remembered that her daughter didn't live in Colville anymore. *Of course* Susannah wasn't at home. She had her own house. In Seattle, wasn't it? Yes, in Seattle. She was married with two precious children. Susannah and Joe's children. Good grief, why couldn't she think of their names? Her grandchildren were her joy and her pride. She could picture their faces as clearly as if she was looking at a photograph, but she couldn't recall their names.

Chrissie. The relief was instantaneous. Her granddaughter's name was Chrissie. She was born first and then Brian was born three years later. Or was it four years? It didn't matter, Vivian decided. She had their names now.

What she needed to do was concentrate on where she was—and where she should go from here. It was already starting to get dark and she didn't want to wander aimlessly from street to street. But she couldn't figure out what to do next.

If there'd been any other pedestrians around, she could've stopped and asked for directions to Woods Road.

No...Woods Road had been her childhood address. She hadn't lived there since she was a schoolgirl, and that was before the war. For heaven's sake, she should be able to remember her own address! What was wrong with her?

The place she was looking for was the house she and George had bought almost forty-five years ago, when the children were still at home. She felt a mixture of fear...and shame. A woman of eighty should know where she lived. George would be so frustrated and impatient if he ever found out about this.... Only he'd never know. That didn't make her feel any better, though. She *needed* him, and he wasn't there to help her, and that filled her with anxiety so intense, she wrung her hands.

Vivian started walking again, although she wasn't sure where she was headed. Maybe if she kept moving, if she concentrated hard enough, the memory would eventually return to her.

Her legs tired quickly, and she sighed with relief when she saw a bench by the side of the road. Vivian couldn't understand why the city would place a nice wooden bench there—not even near a bus stop. It was a waste of taxpayers' money. If George knew about this, he'd be fuming. He'd been a public servant all those years, a superior court judge. A fine one, too, a man of principle and character. How proud Vivian was of him.

Still, she was so grateful for somewhere to sit, she wasn't about to complain. George had freely voiced his opinions about matters of civic responsibility and what he called city hall's squandering of resources. While she listened to her husband's views, she didn't always share them. She had her own thoughts when it came to politics and things like that, but she usually didn't discuss them with George. That was something she'd learned early in her marriage. George always wanted to convince everyone of the superiority of *his* ideas and he'd argue until he wore people down. So when her views differed from his, she kept them to herself.

Sitting on the hard bench, she glanced about, hoping to find a landmark. Oh my, this was a busy street. Cars whizzed past, their lights blinding her until she felt dizzy. She wasn't nearly as tired now that she was sitting. That was good, because she needed to think. Thinking was important. She hated forgetting basic facts, like her address, her phone number, people's names. This happened more and more often now that George had died, and it frightened her.

Perhaps if she closed her eyes for a moment, that would help. She'd try to relax, clear her mind, since all this worry only made her memory less reliable.

It was chilly now that the sun had gone down. She should've brought a sweater but she'd been working in the garden earlier and it had been hot. Her irises were lovely this spring, even though her garden was in sad shape. For years, it had been a source of pride and she hated the way it looked these days. She did as much as she could, but so much else needed to be done. Weeding, pruning, planting annuals… After dinner she'd decided to do some watering and remembered that she hadn't collected the mail. That was when she'd gone out, planning to walk to the neighborhood mailbox. And now here she was, lost and confused and afraid.

That was when Vivian sensed someone's presence and opened her eyes. Joy coursed through her veins as she stared, wondering if her mind had betrayed her.

"George?"

Her husband of fifty-nine years stood beside her, shadowed under the nearby streetlight. His smile warmed her and she straightened, eyes wide open, terrified he'd disappear. George had come to help her, come to save her.

"That *is* you, isn't it?"

He didn't answer but stood there plain as could be. He'd always been such a handsome man, she thought, admiring his broad shoulders and his confident posture.

They'd been high school sweethearts and known each other their entire lives. Vivian felt she was the luckiest girl in the world when George Leary asked her to marry him. They'd been apart for nearly three years while he was fighting in Europe. Then he'd gone to college to get his law degree on the G.I. Bill. That time of struggle had paid off, though, and after a few years of private practice, he'd been invited to join the bench. George had been the one and only love of her life and she missed him terribly. How like him to come to her now, in her hour of need.

Vivian reached out to him, but George backed away. She dropped her hand abruptly, biting her lower lip. No, of course—she should've realized she couldn't touch him. One couldn't touch the dead.

"I'm lost," she whispered. "Don't be angry with me, but I can't find my way home."

He smiled again and she was so relieved he wasn't upset

with her. She'd forgotten things before he died, too, and sometimes he got frustrated, although he tried to hide it. She'd even stopped cooking but that was because she'd forgotten so many of her recipes. The ones in cookbooks were too hard to read, too confusing. But George never complained and often heated soup for both of them.

Vivian felt she should explain what had happened. "I went to get the mail and I must've decided to go for a walk, because when I looked up I wasn't anywhere close to the house."

He stretched out his hand and she got to her feet.

"Can you take me home?" she asked, hating how plaintive and helpless she sounded.

He didn't answer. Then she realized that dead men couldn't talk, either. That was all right; she didn't care as long as George stayed with her. Six months it had been since he'd died and every one of those months had seemed an eternity.

"I'm so glad you came," she whispered, trying to hide the way her voice cracked with emotion. "Oh, George, I miss you." She told him about the garden, even though she knew she was rambling. He'd never liked it when she talked too much, but she was afraid he'd have to leave soon, and there was so much to tell him. "George, I'm sure Martha is stealing. I just don't know what to do. I watch her like a hawk when she comes to clean, but still I find things missing. I can't let her rob me blind, and yet I hate to fire her after all these years. What should I do?" She hadn't really expected him to answer, and he didn't.

Then, suddenly, she saw the house. They were on Chestnut Avenue, where they'd lived since 1961. She walked laboriously to the front door, holding on to the railing and taking the steps one at a time. When she looked up to thank George for helping her, her beloved husband had vanished.

"Oh, George," she sobbed. "Come back to me…please. Please come back."

2

Susannah Nelson dumped the leftover broccoli salad into a plastic container and shoved it inside the refrigerator, closing the door with unnecessary force. Brian, her seventeen-year-old, had mysteriously disappeared after dinner, leaving her with the dishes. She shouldn't be surprised. He had a convenient excuse every night to get out of doing his assigned chores.

"Is something bothering you?" her husband asked from his perch in the family room. Joe lowered the newspaper and all Susannah could see were his dark brows and his eyes behind the steel-rimmed reading glasses.

She shrugged. "I don't suppose you've noticed, but this is the third night in a row that Brian hasn't done the dishes," she said, more sharply than she'd intended.

"I'll do them," he offered.

"You shouldn't have to do that," Susannah told him. "Nor should I."

Joe set the newspaper aside. "This isn't about Brian, is it? You're upset about something else."

"Well, I *am* annoyed about the way he's been skipping out on chores, but you're right, that isn't everything." What concerned her most was her inability to identify a specific reason. She'd been on edge for weeks, feeling vaguely dejected.

It didn't help that she'd dreamed of Jake again last night. Her high school boyfriend had been making nightly appearances, and that unsettled her as much as anything. Susannah was happily married and despite the abrupt ending to her teenage romance, there was no good reason for her to dwell on Jake. Her marriage had survived the crises that any successful marriage does. Her children were nearly grown; her daughter was in college, ready to start her own life. Brian had summer employment, working for a construction company, and would earn enough to pay his own car insurance. The school break would officially begin in a day's time, and she'd be free for nearly seven weeks. Why, after more than three decades, was she dreaming of Jake? It made no sense whatsoever. There he was, big as life, filling her head with memories of a long-lost love.

"School's almost out," Joe reminded her. "That should cheer you up."

He was right; it should. Today was the last day of classes and her fifth-grade students had been overjoyed at the prospect of summer vacation. Susannah was equally ready for a break. Maybe for more than a break—a change. What kind of change, she didn't know. She supposed she could think about it over the summer—after tomorrow, anyway, when she'd be finishing her paperwork.

"You've been restless since your father died," Joe commented in a mild voice. He glanced at her across the family room. "Maybe you should talk to someone."

"You're saying I should talk to a counselor?" She hated to think it had come to this. Yes, her father's death had been a shock, but at the time her grief had seemed... formal. Almost abstract. As though she'd mourned the *idea* of losing a father more than the man himself. She'd never gotten along with him. They'd tolerated each other, at best. As far as Susannah was concerned, her father was dictatorial, overbearing and arrogant. The moment she turned eighteen, she couldn't get away from him fast enough.

"He was your father, Susannah," Joe reminded her gently. "I know the two of you weren't close, but he was still your father." He removed his glasses. "In fact, maybe that's why you're feeling like this. Now that he's dead, there's no opportunity to settle your differences—to work things out."

Susannah shook her head, dismissing the suggestion. Her relationship with her father had been difficult. Complicated. But she'd accepted that reality years ago. "This has nothing to do with him."

Joe looked as if he wanted to argue, but she didn't let him. "Yes, his death was unexpected, but he *was* eighty-three and no one lives forever." The truth of the matter was that while they weren't completely estranged, they rarely spoke. That didn't seem to bother him any. Over the years, Susannah had made occasional efforts to bridge the gap between them, but her father seemed incapable of deepening their relationship.

Whenever she'd phoned or visited, Susannah talked to her mother. George Leary was a decent grandfather; she'd say that for him. Both Chrissie and Brian thought the world of her father. As for her—well, it was better to not think about the way he'd interfered with her life, especially during her teenage years. Yes, she was sorry he'd died, especially so suddenly, but she discounted the possibility that his death was the cause of this discontent she felt. If she was going to blame anyone, it would be Jake. But it wasn't as though she could mention this to Joe, her husband, her wonderful husband. *Hey, honey, I've been thinking about another man lately.* That wouldn't go over too well, no matter how understanding Joe was.

Her husband continued to study her. "Even though you don't agree," he said slowly, "I suspect your father's death had a strong impact on you. Don't you remember what it was like when my parents died?"

She did remember and was embarrassed to admit that she'd grieved for her father-in-law more than she had her own dad. When Joe's mother died ten months later, they'd both been devastated. It had been a rough time for them as a family. Susannah had envied Joe's close relationship with his parents when her own, particularly with her father, was so distant.

"Of course it was a shock to lose my dad," Susannah went on, "but I don't think this mood—"

"Depression," Joe inserted. "Low-grade, garden variety depression."

"I am not depressed." Even while she denied it, she knew Joe was right.

Her husband raised his eyebrows. "If you aren't depressed, then what is it?"

Joe was a solid, strong, self-assured man. Honorable.

After twenty-four years together they'd grown accustomed to each other, so alike that they often ordered the same thing from a menu, read the same books, voted for the same candidates. She didn't understand how she could lie beside him in the same bed night after night and dream about another man. This wasn't like her. Not once in her entire marriage had she even *considered* looking at another man.

She'd be crazy to risk her marriage by searching for a high school fling. The episode with Jake was long over. She hadn't seen or talked to him since she was seventeen, and that was…oh, more than thirty-three years ago now.

Joe replaced his glasses after polishing the lenses on his shirt. "You've had a lot going on in the last six months. Your father's death, your fiftieth birthday, a demanding year at work and everything else."

He wasn't telling Susannah anything she didn't know. Perhaps those *were* the reasons for this discontent, this need to find out about Jake, but she doubted it. Even gardening, her passion, didn't soothe her—or distract her. While she was quick to deny that anything was wrong, Susannah felt certain it all went back to her high school boyfriend and the way their relationship had ended. What she needed was *closure*—that irritating, overused word. And yet nothing else quite explained it. Jake was an unfinished part of her life, a thread left hanging, a path not taken.

In that sense, her father's death *had* triggered her unease, her recurring memories of Jake, since George was the one responsible for breaking them up. As always, he'd been so sure he knew best. The problem was that he sat on his high and mighty judgment seat in court during the day and didn't step down from it when he came home to his family at night.

Susannah refused to dwell on thoughts of her father, refused to let herself nurture these negative feelings toward him. But tonight, for reasons she didn't understand, her memories of Jake wouldn't leave her alone.

"It might be a good idea for you to spend a few weeks with your mother this summer. Perhaps then you'll find some resolution concerning your father."

"Maybe," Susannah agreed, although she didn't really believe it. They'd already decided she should visit Vivian once the summer holidays started, to check up on her and assess the situation.

The phone pealed in the distance, but neither Joe nor Susannah hurried to answer it. With a teenager in the house, there was no need.

Brian stuck his head out his bedroom door and shouted her name at an ear-splitting decibel. "Mom!"

Susannah wanted to ask him who it was, but he'd retreated into his bedroom so fast she didn't have a chance. Walking over to the kitchen phone, she lifted the receiver and waited for him to hang up.

"Hello."

"Susannah, is that you?"

The female voice was familiar, but she couldn't immediately place it.

"It's Martha West. I'm sorry to bother you."

"Oh, that's okay." Susannah tensed. Martha had been the family housekeeper for years. The only reason she'd be calling was to tell her something had happened to her mother. "Is everything all right with Mom?" The last time Martha phoned had been with the news that Susannah's father had dropped dead of a heart attack.

"She's just fine," Martha assured her. "I did want to

talk to you, though, before you drove here. Vivian mentioned that you planned to visit soon and, well…" She hesitated. "There's no easy way to say this." Again she paused. "Susannah, your mother seems to think I'm…taking her things. I hope you know I'd never do anything like that. I swear I had nothing to do with those missing teaspoons."

"Teaspoons?"

"Your mother accused me of taking four of her matching teaspoons when I was there to clean this afternoon."

"Martha, I know you'd never do anything like that." The woman was completely trustworthy.

"I would hope not," she blurted. "And let me tell you that if I *was* going to steal, it wouldn't be teaspoons."

"Makes sense."

"Then she said I hid her purse. I searched for an hour and found it tucked behind the sofa cushions. When I showed it to her, she said I was the one who'd put it there."

Susannah groaned. "Oh, Martha, I'm so sorry."

"I don't know what's wrong with her," the housekeeper said, sounding exasperated. "Nothing's been the same since your father died. One day she's her normal self and the next, well, I hardly know her anymore. She asked me why I'd take her things. I would never! You know that. Teaspoons? She believes I walked away with her teaspoons and God help me, even though I looked everywhere, I couldn't find them. But I didn't take them!"

"I'm sure you didn't. I'll talk to her," Susannah promised.

"So she hasn't said anything to you about me supposedly stealing her things?" Martha asked.

"No." This was a half truth. In their last conversation,

her mother had said she wanted to have a talk about Martha once Susannah arrived. Susannah had assumed that the housekeeper was planning to retire. As it was, Martha cleaned the house only twice a week now. She was getting on in years, too.

"I'll talk to her," Susannah said a second time—although she had no idea what she'd say.

"Please do, and if you can't convince her that I'm an honest and loyal employee then…then maybe I should look for work elsewhere."

"Don't do that," Susannah pleaded. "Give me a chance to get to the bottom of this."

"Good." Martha seemed somewhat appeased.

"I'll be in touch when I get there," Susannah said.

After a few words of farewell, Martha ended the conversation and Susannah replaced the phone.

"What was that all about?" Joe asked as he refolded the evening paper.

Susannah sighed deeply and told him.

"You did say your mother seems awfully forgetful these days."

Susannah nodded. "I talk to her almost daily, but there's only so much information I can get over the phone." She sighed again. "Mom keeps telling me the same things over and over, but I thought that was simply old age. Maybe it's more than that." Many of her friends faced similar concerns with their aging parents.

"What about asking one of her friends?" Joe came into the kitchen and stood beside her. Gazing down at her, he clasped her shoulders, his eyes serious.

She looked up at him with a resigned smile. "I'll give Mrs. Henderson a call. She's been Mom's neighbor for years."

After finding the Hendersons' phone number, Susannah reached for the phone again. When the initial greetings were dispensed with, she was quick to get to the reason for her call. "I'm worried about my mother, Mrs. Henderson. Have you talked to her lately?"

"Oh, yes," Rachel Henderson told her, "she's often out puttering in her garden—not that she gets much done."

"How is she…mentally?" Susannah asked next.

"Well, to be honest, she just hasn't been herself since she lost George," the neighbor said thoughtfully. "I can't say exactly what's going on…but I'm afraid something isn't right with Vivian."

"How do you mean?" Susannah asked. Joe walked over to the coffeepot and poured himself a mug while watching her.

She knew. Deep down, Susannah had known for weeks that her mother was having problems. She'd sensed changes in Vivian even before her father's death.

"I realize you talk to your mother a lot and I don't mean to be putting my nose in where it doesn't belong. Al said I should mind my own business, but then this evening…"

"What happened this evening?" Susannah asked, suddenly nervous.

"I'm sure you're aware that Vivian hasn't adjusted well to losing your father."

"I know." Her mother was often weepy and sad, talking endlessly about George and how desperately she missed him. Susannah had driven across the mountains to visit over spring break but had only been able to stay four days.

Vivian had clung to her, pleaded with her to remain in Colville longer, but Susannah couldn't. Driving there and back meant the better part of two days, and that left only one day to prepare for school.

Susannah had tried to talk her mother into moving to Seattle, but Vivian had stubbornly refused to consider it. She didn't want to leave Colville, where she'd been born and raised. Her surviving friends all lived in the small town sixty-three miles north of Spokane.

"Something happened this evening?" Susannah repeated, wanting Rachel to get to the point.

"I know this may shock you, but your mother asked me to help her find George."

"What?" Susannah's eyes shot to Joe. "She thinks my dad's alive?"

"She claims she saw him."

"Oh, no," Susannah muttered.

"She was wandering down the street, looking confused. I got worried, so I went after her. Then she started talking all this nonsense about George—how he brought her home and then disappeared. When was the last time you saw her?"

"March." Susannah knew she needed to visit Colville more often, but she hadn't been able to make it during the last few months. Between Brian's sports, other commitments, including a teaching workshop, and social engagements, there hadn't been a single free weekend. Guilt felt like a lead weight dragging her down. "I planned to drive over this weekend. School's out for the summer and I'm going to spend a couple of weeks with Mom."

"That's wise," Mrs. Henderson said. "She's lost weight, you know."

Her mother was barely a hundred and ten pounds when Susannah had seen her in March.

"I don't think she cooks anymore," her neighbor went on.

During her visit, Vivian had asked her to make dinner every night. Susannah hadn't minded and the shelves certainly seemed to be well stocked. Although Susannah had noticed a number of gourmet items her mother had never purchased before. Like fancy mustards. And sun-dried tomatoes in pesto, which Susannah had used in a pasta sauce.

"You mean she isn't eating?" Susannah clarified.

"Not much, as far as I can tell. I keep inviting her over for dinner, but she refuses every time. I'm not the only one she's refused, either. She seems to be holed up in the house and barely comes out, except to work in her garden."

"But…why?" Her mother had always been social, enjoying the company of others, hosting parties for George and their friends.

"You'll have to ask her that."

"But on the phone she talks as if she sees you quite a bit," Susannah said. It wasn't like her mother to lie.

"Oh, yes, we chat over the fence, but I swear…" Mrs. Henderson paused. "Sometimes I'm not sure your mother knows who I am."

"Oh, dear." This was what Susannah feared most. Her mother was losing her memory, and it seemed due to more than the erosion of old age.

"Another thing," Mrs. Henderson said, hesitating again.

"Go on," Susannah urged.

"The other day when I went to check on her, I found

her sitting in the dark. Turns out she forgot to pay the electric bill. She felt embarrassed about it, and I don't think she'd like me saying anything to you, but I felt you should know."

Susannah groaned inwardly. These were the very things she'd worried about. Bills unpaid, the stove left on, meals and appointments forgotten.

"Not to worry," Mrs. Henderson rushed to add. "I helped her get it straightened out and her lights are back on. Like I said, she told me you'd be visiting soon and I thought I'd talk to you then, but this business with her seeing George—now, that's got me worried."

It worried Susannah, too. She wished Mrs. Henderson had contacted her earlier. "I tried to talk to Mom about moving into assisted living when I was there in the spring."

"Yes, she told me. It upset her something fierce that you were going to kick her out of her own house."

"She said that?" Susannah's stomach tightened. She was hurt that her mother would even think such a thing, let alone voice it to a neighbor.

"Yes, but quite honestly, Susannah, I don't feel she should be on her own any longer."

Susannah should've insisted back in March, but she hadn't felt she could take her mother out of her home so soon after a major loss. She'd had enough upheaval in her life. Evidently it'd been a mistake not to act sooner.

Susannah ran one hand through the soft curls that had fallen onto her forehead.

"It might be best if you came right away," Mrs. Henderson suggested. "I would've phoned you myself, but Al said I should keep out of it. Seeing that you phoned me, well, I figured I'd better tell you what's going on with your mother. I hope that's okay?" she asked anxiously.

"I'm grateful you told me," Susannah said. "I'll drive over as soon as I can make arrangements."

After a brief farewell, Susannah replaced the receiver. Joe leaned against the counter, still watching her, coffee mug in hand.

"I'm afraid it's worse than I thought," she said, answering his unspoken question. "Apparently she's wandering around the neighborhood looking for my father."

Joe released a low whistle. "You're going over right away, then?" Originally Susannah had intended to wait for the weekend.

"I guess that would be for the best." Then, thinking out loud, she added, "I don't have any choice but to put her in an assisted-living facility."

"I agree."

Susannah pinched the bridge of her nose, dreading the approaching confrontation. Her mother would fight her on this. She didn't doubt that for a minute.

"Do you want me to go with you? Perhaps the two of us will be able to talk some sense into her."

Susannah shook her head.

"You're sure?" He frowned as though disappointed. "You were wonderful when my parents died, Suze. I want to be there for you."

For a moment Susannah was afraid she'd cry. "No...I need to do this on my own. I've decided," she said, the idea taking shape in her mind as she spoke, "that I'll stay in Colville for a while." Although it was crazy to even con- sider the idea, she might be able to find out where Jake was living. She had to talk to him, had to find out what had happened and why. Susannah *knew* her father had something to do with the breakup; she just didn't know the details. Maybe, once she learned the truth, she could put an end to this fantasizing about Jake.

"Okay." Joe sighed heavily. "But after you convince her to move, you'll have to make a decision about the house."

Susannah hadn't even thought of that. All at once the task seemed overwhelming.

"How long do you think it'll take?" Joe asked.

She didn't meet his eyes while she contemplated spending time in Colville. "Three weeks should do it, I imagine. Possibly a month."

"That long?"

"It isn't going to be easy to talk my mother into leaving her home," she said. "And there's the matter of arranging assisted-living accommodation for her. And cleaning the house. Whether I decide to rent it or put it on the market, either way it'll need to be cleared out."

"I could help. Brian, too."

"No, I can manage." She appreciated the offer, but she wanted to spend time with her mother—just the two of them. Not only that, she had a private agenda concerning Jake, an agenda she couldn't confide to her husband. She had to resolve *that* problem on her own. If Joe and Brian were there, she'd be torn between her present and her past. "Perhaps on the weekends, if you want." As a dentist, Joe couldn't change his appointment schedule at the last minute.

"Brian and I have our fishing trip scheduled for next weekend, but we can cancel that."

"No, don't," she protested. It was hard enough for the two of them to find time together.

Joe nodded. "Then we'll try to come one weekend after that." He put down his coffee mug and glanced at her, a half smile on his face. "I have a feeling you're going to learn a lot more than you expected from all of this."

Susannah suspected he was right.

CHAPTER

3

Chrissie Nelson shoved the last of her clothes into her suitcase and looked anxiously out her dorm room window. Jason was late. He'd promised to be here by ten to take her to the airport. School was over and the dorm was mostly deserted. She'd be flying out of Eugene, where she attended the University of Oregon, to Seattle for the summer. The end of the school year didn't thrill her, mostly because she'd be leaving Jason behind. She wasn't like some of her friends, eager to return home. In fact, Chrissie dreaded the emptiness that lay ahead.

Pushing her long straight blond hair over her shoulder, she suppressed a deep sigh. Her roommate, Katie Robertson, had left the night before, and so had several of her other friends. Jason had driven Katie to the airport, but Chrissie's flight wasn't until today. He'd stopped by the dorm after he'd dropped Katie off; he and Chrissie had gone out for a farewell drink and he'd promised to meet her in plenty of time for her 11:30 flight. When he'd picked Katie up, he'd arrived with two hours to spare—*and* he'd waited with her at the airport. Chrissie had a niggling sensation that he'd been more solicitous than necessary....

That made it sound as if she was jealous and she wasn't. Jason had never given Chrissie the slightest reason to doubt his devotion. He was simply thoughtful. Latching her suitcase closed, she grunted as she lifted it off the mattress with both hands and set it on the floor.

The problem with going home for the summer was that she didn't have a job. And at this late date, the prospects of decent employment were slim to none.

She was almost twenty and still tied to her parents. Chrissie hated that. The idea of being at home for the next eight or ten weeks—and dependent on her parents for spending money—depressed her. She preferred to stay in Eugene, but her part-time job on campus had ended with the semester. Next year everything would be different; Chrissie intended to make sure of that. This would be her last summer in Seattle. She was an adult, and she wanted to live her own life.

As soon as she got home, she planned to tell her parents that she was moving out of the dorm. Two other girls had invited her to live off-campus with them in a small house. They'd divide the rent, and it would be much cheaper than living at the university for a third year. It would be a good experience, she'd tell her parents, plus it would save them money. She was perfectly capable of managing on her own. Her father would listen to reason, but she wasn't sure she could count on her mother.

Jason's Honda Civic pulled up to the curb. Chrissie leaned out the window and waved. He climbed out of his car, glanced up and smiled, then waved back. "I'll be right there," he called.

That was typical of Jason—always considerate. She felt fortunate to be with him. They'd met on a blind date and he'd impressed her the moment they began to talk. They had a lot in common, but that didn't mean they were alike. Far from it. Jason, a law student specializing in accounting law, was about as conservative as they came. His grades were high and his work habits disciplined and methodical. Chrissie, on the other hand, was carefree and fun-loving, and something of a procrastinator. The problem, she'd decided, was that she worked best under pressure. Term papers were written the night before they were due. What other people failed to understand, she often explained righteously, was that she'd been thinking about the subject for weeks, gathering the needed data. Starting it early wouldn't have improved the end product.

Jason never left anything to the last minute and her delay tactics exasperated him. Still, they were crazy about each other. He did occasionally try to change her ways—and vice versa. At least he didn't constantly complain about her study habits like her parents did. Her grades weren't any worse in college than they'd been in high school. Okay, they weren't *great* but she never got less than a C. The major reason she'd decided on college was because all her friends were going. Everyone just expected her to continue her education, and she hadn't come up with anything she'd rather do.

She stayed more because of the social life than the academics—the parties and the boys. Jason, with his wide muscular shoulders, could have been a football player, but sports were of little interest to him. He dressed for class as if he were going into an office, wearing sweaters and slacks in the winter and short-sleeve shirts and Dockers in the summer. His hair was conservatively cut, above the ear. Basically, he was every mother's dream. Her dream, too, although she would never have expected to fall for a guy like him.

On that first date with Jason, she'd tried to find the beast within, striving to break through his proprieties, with limited success. She was convinced there was a bad boy inside him waiting to emerge and Chrissie wanted to find him. Jason certainly didn't object, and while they were different they were also good together. He appreciated her spontaneity and lightheartedness. She liked the fact that he was reliable and thoughtful. And although they might argue about everything from politics to movies, they had an enjoyable time making up afterward.

Needless to say, her parents were thrilled with him, and who wouldn't be? He was as close to perfect a boyfriend for their daughter as they could hope for. She and Jason hadn't talked about marriage yet, but it wouldn't surprise her if he gave her an engagement ring at Christmas.

Jason came into her room and heaved the heavy suitcase into his arms. Grunting and panting, he maneuvered it down the stairs—no elevator in her building—while she carried her backpack and purse.

When they reached the bottom, Chrissie cast him a woebegone look. "I wish I didn't have to leave."

"It'll be fine," he said without meeting her eyes. But that

could've been because he was busy hoisting the suitcase into his trunk.

Still, his offhand remark startled her. "It will?" She found that hard to believe.

"I'll miss you like crazy, but before we know it you'll be back."

His cavalier attitude was completely unexpected. She wanted him to feel as bereft as she did; obviously he didn't. Eyeing him closely, she wondered if she was reading more into his comment than warranted. She didn't want to sound like a whiny ten-year-old, but she was taken aback by his response.

She decided not to overreact. "You're right, of course. Besides, I can come and visit you over the Fourth of July."

"You can?"

"Sure, why not?" she asked.

"Don't you want to save your money for school?"

She shrugged, as if financial concerns were of little significance. She'd assumed he'd leap at the suggestion. Apparently not. A moment later, Jason took Chrissie by the shoulders and astonished her by kissing her long and hard. Normally, he frowned on public displays of affection, but today nothing about him was the same. She reveled in his moist lips molding to hers as he held her close. "Next summer..." she whispered.

"Next summer?"

"I'll find a way to stay in Oregon."

"Good." With that, he placed her backpack carefully beside the heavy bag and shut the trunk.

"First things first," she said as Jason opened the passenger door.

He hesitated, looking puzzled.

"I have to convince my mother to let me move out of the dorm before I talk to her about staying in Eugene next summer," she elaborated.

"You really have a thing about your mother, don't you?"

"What do you mean?" Chrissie flared.

"You always seem worried about what she's going to say."

His observation irritated her. "That's not true." She didn't want to argue, but he'd totally missed the point.

"You just said you had to get your mother to agree that you can rent with Joan and Katie," he murmured. "For the last week, ever since final exams, you've been complaining about going home and having to deal with her. Not once did you mention your dad."

"My father is the more reasonable of the two." She was furious that Jason would even suggest she had a problem with her mother.

"From what I understand, it's fairly common, you know? Mother-daughter conflict, I mean."

"Really?" Chrissie said coldly as she climbed into the passenger seat and without waiting closed the door. She fastened the seat belt while Jason walked around to the other side of the vehicle.

"You and your mother seem to have these underlying issues," he said when he got into the car. He inserted the key into the ignition.

She stared at him, annoyed that he was pursuing the subject. "Are you trying to start a fight?" she asked, refusing to be drawn into one.

Jason turned to her, then gradually smiled. "Not really. Are you?"

"No."

"Good." He pulled away from the curb.

"You don't act as if you're going to miss me all that much," she said, and immediately wanted to swallow her words. They made her seem insecure and she wasn't.

"What makes you say that?"

"Nothing." She shook her head.

"Is it because I didn't encourage you to fly down for the Fourth of July? If so, the reason—aside from not wanting you to spend the airfare—is that I already have plans."

"You do?"

"My parents asked me to visit them and I said I would."

It didn't escape Chrissie's notice that he didn't invite her to join him and his family.

"Are you glad I'm leaving Eugene?" she asked. She knew he'd be staying; he was fortunate enough to have a full-time summer job with a big law firm. His family lived in Grants Pass, a couple of hours away.

Jason sighed as if she were behaving like a difficult child. "Forget I asked," she snapped. "It was a stupid question."

"Yes, it was," Jason said. He gripped the steering wheel with both hands. "Why are you being so sensitive?"

He was right; she was overreacting, even though she'd vowed not to. "Maybe I don't want to go back to Seattle for the summer. Maybe I'd rather be here with you instead of trapped in a house with my mother for the next ten weeks." The moment she mentioned her mother, Chrissie realized she'd said the wrong thing.

"Why don't you talk to her, then?"

"About what? My relationship with her? My mother's so caught up in her own world that she can't be bothered with me."

Jason stopped at a traffic signal. "I'm sure that's not true."

"How would you know? You only met her once." Chrissie had brought Jason home at Easter and he'd spent three days with her family. The visit had been a success on all counts.

As they'd pulled out of the family driveway, Chrissie had basked in her parents' approval. Both of them had liked Jason immensely.

"You have wonderful parents, Chrissie," he said now.

"Yes—but my mother's going to make my life hell this summer. She's upset with me for not having a job, although she'd never come right out and say so. Instead, she'll find a hundred different things to criticize."

"I thought you were going to look for a job over spring break," Jason reminded her.

"I was, but I got busy—the time just slipped away. Don't you start on me, too."

"Chrissie…"

"You have no idea what this summer's going to be like."

"Oh, come on, Chrissie. It's not—"

"Let me give you an example," she broke in, "and this is based on experience. Mom will ask me to clean the bathroom and I will. Then she'll come in after me and scrub the sink all over again. This is her way of letting me know that I didn't meet her high standards." The summer stretched before Chrissie like one long exercise in tolerance and patience. "If she didn't like how I cleaned the sink, you'd think she'd just say so, but oh, no, not my mother."

Jason muttered something noncommittal.

"Brian has a job," she continued. "Mom's already mentioned that fact about fifty times. He's working for a construction company."

"You're making too much of this."

"I don't think so," Chrissie muttered. "What she's *really* saying is that if I'd looked for a job like she wanted me to over spring break, I'd have one waiting for me now." She could imagine the constant barrage of digs that lay in store for her. Her mother couldn't bear the thought of Chrissie being idle all summer, so she'd threaten to line up babysitting jobs for her. Babysitting at almost twenty? In Chrissie's opinion, that was cruel and unusual punishment.

"She seems to believe that finding temporary employment is easy. I suppose I could get a job at a fast-food place, but even those aren't as available as they used to be. Besides, I don't want to spend my summer asking someone if they want fries with that."

"Well…" He clearly wasn't interested in arguing with her.

"As a last resort, my dad will leap to the rescue and offer me a pity job."

"A what?"

"He'll bring me to his office and I'll be reduced to doing menial tasks, for which he'll pay me minimum wage." She sighed. "It's going to be a dreadful summer. I can tell."

"It'll be fine," Jason countered absently.

Chrissie doubted he'd even heard her. His mind certainly wasn't on her; that much was apparent. She looked at him and frowned, unsure what to think. Something had changed between them. She could feel it—had felt it from the moment he arrived. Jason had never been late before.

"Is everything all right?" she asked, then added, "Between us, I mean."

He glanced at her and shrugged. "Sure. Why shouldn't it be?"

Instinct said otherwise. "You drove Katie to the airport last night, didn't you?"

"You know I did."

Chrissie noticed that his hand tightened around the steering wheel. What had happened between him and Katie the night before? She didn't mention how long he'd spent at the airport. Originally she was supposed to tag along, but Katie had a lot of stuff and it would've been a tight fit in a small car, so she'd stayed behind. That, apparently, had been a mistake.

Nothing had happened, she told herself. Chrissie couldn't believe Jason would do that to her. Besides, Katie was one of her best friends. They planned on renting a house together in a few months. The last thing Katie would do was steal Jason away from her.

No, neither of them would betray her, Chrissie thought firmly.

The rest of the drive was completed in an uncomfortable silence.

Jason drove up to the curb at the airport and Chrissie climbed out as soon as he came to a stop. Without a word, Jason jumped out and opened the trunk, heaving her suitcase onto the ground.

"The summer will go fast," he said with false cheerfulness. "You'll be back here in no time."

"Right," she agreed with the same fake exuberance. "No time at all."

Jason nodded. "I'll call you soon."

She nodded, too, and dragged her bag onto the sidewalk. "I guess I'd better get inside."

"Have a great summer."

She tried to smile. "You, too."

He leaned forward and kissed her, but it fell short of just about every other kiss they'd exchanged. She was afraid she was losing Jason and it broke her heart.

CHAPTER

4

Susannah wasn't looking forward to this trip back to Colville. The eastern Washington community was like small towns all over the country. Her eyes went immediately to the town clock, which featured a statue of a frontiersman, as she drove through the city center. Colville with its JCPenney store on Main Street was the big city to many of the smaller communities surrounding it. There was a traffic roundabout now, but while she was growing up, Colville had the only traffic light in Stevens County.

It was small-town America at its best.

And its worst.

The drive took seven hours with a brief lunch break. As Susannah rolled into the outskirts of town, her tension grew. She turned the music up louder, trying to lose herself in the insistent beat of the Rolling Stones. The first building she passed was the Burger King restaurant, which had closed its doors. It was probably the only franchise in the entire chain to go out of business. The bowling alley came next. The sign out front listed the special of the day as a breakfast of two eggs, toast and coffee for $2.99—up from the $1.99 of her childhood. That had been the special for as long as Susannah could remember.

She drove past Colville Mortuary, which had once been owned by her uncle Henry, who was long dead now. Susannah had grown up with hordes of cousins, none of whom had settled in the area. They, too, had no reason to stay in Colville.

As she continued down Main Street, she felt a growing sense of dread. Getting her mother into an assisted-living complex wasn't a prospect she relished. This anxiety, however, resulted from more than the difficult task that awaited her. When Susannah left Colville for college, she'd never looked back. Oh, she'd returned any number of times over the years, but whenever she did, the familiar depression returned, too. Part of that had to do with her brother's death; he was killed in a car accident the year she turned eighteen. She was in a French boarding school at the time, and her father's phone call had come in the middle of the day. A call from America was sure to be bad news. And it was. It'd been the worst news of her life. Her brother, older by three years, had died in a crash on a notoriously bad curve just outside Colville.

Susannah's world changed forever that day. If her brother's death wasn't devastating enough, her father had refused to fly her home for the funeral. She never forgave him for that. He'd been the one who insisted on shipping her off to France in the first place. Then, while she was so far from home, her whole life had collapsed. Susannah was never the same afterward. Her parents had never recovered, either.

It seemed to her that whatever happiness her parents had shared vanished after Doug died. Joy fled from their lives, leaving their marriage stark and empty. That was Susannah's perception, although her mother had a different version of events, a version Susannah considered a case of denial. But then, how could Vivian have stayed with her husband if she'd been honest about her unhappiness—and his role in it?

When Susannah had returned from her year away, she could barely tolerate living in the same house. After she left for college, she didn't even consider moving back.

Doug's death wasn't the only reminder she brought with her. She couldn't come here and not think about Jake Presley—especially now that he'd invaded her dreams on a nightly basis. Any number of times over the years she'd wondered about him, but never more than in the last few months. The sweet tenderness of her first love had been ruined by her father, too.

Susannah wanted to believe that Jake was happy, a husband and father, and successful in whatever field he'd chosen. It'd taken her a long time to get over him—but she had. Or so she'd thought.

Shaking her head to clear her mind, Susannah slowed her car to the reduced thirty-five-mile-an-hour speed limit. She passed Benny's Motel and the Safeway store where her mother had shopped for fifty years. The four-block-square City Park was behind the motel. Farther down the street was Ole King Cole's restaurant. Every year on Mother's

Day, that was where her father took her mother for dinner. Either there or Acorn's.

Refusing to be ambushed by the past, Susannah forced herself to stare straight ahead. When she reached the end of Main, she ventured up the hill toward Chestnut Avenue and her childhood home.

The light was on, although it was barely five o'clock in the afternoon and summer-bright. Susannah pulled into the driveway and turned off the engine. The screen door opened instantly, as if her mother had been standing on the other side waiting for her arrival.

The house, built in 1960, was constructed of brick. At the time it had been one of the new ranch-style homes, among the most elaborate in town. It had four bedrooms, one of which her mother used for crafts, plus a finished basement with rec room and laundry.

And the garden. Her mother's beautiful garden. Vivian liked to sit there in the cool of the evening and read or knit. Her father had installed lighting on the back deck for that very reason.

"Susannah." Vivian held out her arms as Susannah climbed from the car.

Bounding up the front steps, she was shocked to see how frail her mother had become, especially in such a short time. She appeared to have aged ten years since Susannah's visit in March. Mrs. Henderson was right; Vivian had lost weight, so much that her clothes hung on her. The belted housedress bagged at the waist and her stockings were wrinkled and loose. Susannah wrapped her arms gently around her mother and felt immersed in guilt. She should've come sooner, should have realized how poorly her mother was doing.

"I'm so glad you're here," Vivian said.

"I'm glad I'm here, too," Susannah told her. Joe would be fine without her for a few weeks. The children, too. But Susannah's mother needed her.

"Come inside," Vivian urged. "I made iced tea."

Susannah slipped her arm around her mother's narrow waist and together they walked inside. She was surprised to see a few newspapers scattered on the steps, still in their protective plastic sleeves. This was unlike her meticulous mother.

The house was much as she remembered it from her last visit. The chair where her father had watched television every night sat empty. The crocheted doily pinned against the back was still in place.

Even in his retirement, the television wasn't allowed on before the five o'clock news. The judge had decreed it and no one dared question his decisions, least of all her mother. Susannah wondered if Vivian watched daytime programs now that her husband was gone. She suspected not. Old habits die hard.

The kitchen table was set with dishes and silverware. "You didn't make dinner, did you?" Susannah asked.

Her mother turned from the refrigerator and frowned. "You told me not to."

"I was planning to take you out to eat, anyplace you want."

"Oh, good. I was afraid I did something wrong."

"No, Mom, you didn't do anything wrong."

Her smile seemed so fragile, so tentative. After all these

years of marriage she was lost without George. Her dependence on him had been absolute, Susannah thought. She blamed her father for that more than she did her mother.

"Sit down and tell me about the children," her mother said, pulling out a chair at the kitchen table for Susannah. The round oak table was an antique now and the chairs along with it.

Stepping over to the counter, her mother filled tall glasses and brought them to the table. Then she sat down, looking expectantly at Susannah.

Susannah sipped her tea. "Brian has a summer job in construction. He's thrilled and the money is excellent."

Her mother smiled with approval. "And Christine?"

"Joe's picking her up from the airport this afternoon."

Her mother's smile faded. "She was away?"

"At school, Mom. Chrissie's coming home from college for the summer."

"Oh, of course. Chrissie's away at school now, isn't she?"

"That's right. She's about to enter her junior year."

"She has a summer job, too?"

Susannah should have anticipated the question. "No. Not yet, but I'm sure she'll find one." This was wishful thinking on her part.

Her mother nodded. "Yes, she will. She's such a beautiful young girl." Susannah's gaze drifted into the dining room, where Vivian kept family photos on the buffet. Chrissie's high school graduation picture stared back at her. Her daughter's long blond hair, parted in the middle, flowed down over her shoulders as she smiled into the camera. Susannah's own high school graduation photograph, taken after her return from France, was positioned next to that of her daughter. Her hair had been long and blond then, too, but curlier than Chrissie's. It had darkened over the years and was now a light shade of brown. These days she kept it short and styled. In her graduation picture, Susannah wore a cap and gown and held her diploma, tilted at an angle as if it were a cherished scroll. It was all for show.

"Chrissie's so much like you at that age."

Susannah's gaze flew back to the photographs. Frankly she didn't see the resemblance. Her daughter was nothing like her in temperament or in looks. At almost twenty, Chrissie still had a lot of growing up to do.

"It's in the eyes," her mother continued.

Susannah looked again, partly, she supposed, in the hope that her mother was right. For the last year or so, Susannah and Chrissie had been at odds. Not for any particular reason, but over a succession of little things. Susannah felt that her daughter didn't take life seriously enough. She didn't put much effort into school and tended to waste time lounging in front of the TV, indulging in long conversations with her friends and sleeping in until noon. Chrissie should have summer employment, but instead of going on a job search, she'd frittered away her spring break, convinced she could charm herself into employment when it suited her.

"Your hair was that blond when you were young," her mother said wistfully.

Susannah didn't want to disillusion her mother, but Chrissie's pure blond color came courtesy of an expensive salon.

"The minute Joe's mother set eyes on the baby, she told us Chrissie looked exactly like her aunt Louise," Susannah commented. Joe had rolled his eyes, but Susannah did see a resemblance. Not then, of course, but more recently.

"She's still at school?"

"No, Mom, Chrissie's flying home. Joe's going to the airport to pick her up."

"Oh, yes, you said that, didn't you? I forget sometimes."

"That's all right, Mom, we all do." She gave her mother's hand a reassuring pat, then stood. "I'd better bring in my suitcase."

"You'll stay more than a day or two this time, won't you?"

"Yes, Mom, I'll stay."

A smile brightened her mother's dull eyes. "Good. I hoped you would. I've been so lost without your father. And now Martha's left me, too!" She slipped her hand into the pocket of her dress and removed a tissue to dab her eyes.

Martha had quit! Susannah groaned inwardly as she walked out of the house and opened the trunk of her car. She brought in a large suitcase; assuming she'd be in town for a few weeks, she'd packed more than her usual overnight bag.

Susannah carried her suitcase down the hallway to her childhood bedroom, which remained exactly as it had when she'd lived at home. Her desk was still there; her chair, too. The heavy blue drapes were the same, although faded, and the lighter blue shag carpeting looked terribly dated now. She couldn't imagine why her parents had never updated their home after she'd graduated from college. It was as if they'd been stuck in a time warp for the last thirty years. There'd certainly been money to make changes.

"I saw a friend of yours last week," her mother said, coming to stand in the bedroom doorway, watching Susannah as she unpacked.

"Who?" Susannah had few friends in town. She'd attended her ten-year reunion, but had felt awkward and out of place. She'd been married to Joe for three years then, and the two of them had stayed at each other's side. Susannah hadn't returned for subsequent reunions. She didn't know these people anymore. Because she'd been away for the last year of school, she hadn't even graduated with them, not officially.

"Just a minute," her mother said and closed her eyes, forehead creased in thought. "Carolyn!" she said triumphantly. "You remember Carolyn. Carolyn Bronson." Her mother paused. "She said you should phone her sometime."

"Carolyn Bronson?" Susannah couldn't believe it. Carolyn had been her best friend and the richest girl in Colville. They'd gone to France together. Her father owned the mill that employed nearly forty percent of the town—or had at one time. With the changes in the lumber industry, Susannah didn't know how the yard had fared.

"You were good friends with her, right?"

Susannah nodded. "But I haven't seen Carolyn in years." Carolyn had been the one friend from Colville she'd stayed in touch with for a while. Then they'd grown apart and their correspondence had dwindled down to an annual Christmas card. About twenty-five years ago, Susannah's card had come back stamped: MOVED—NO FORWARDING ADDRESS. She hadn't heard from Carolyn since. Her mother had read in the paper—she regularly studied the obituaries—that Carolyn's parents were both gone. Susannah hadn't realized Carolyn was back in Colville.

"Carolyn was so excited when I told her you were coming to town. She said she'd love to see you."

"Did she happen to mention if she was married?"

Vivian shook her head. "She didn't say, but I think she would have if she was, don't you?"

Carolyn had married shortly after college; it had lasted barely a year. To the best of her knowledge, Carolyn had never remarried. Susannah wondered if the experience of that divorce had left her friend cynical about marriage.

"I remember her mother," Vivian murmured, pinching her lips. "She always acted as if she was better than the rest of us." Carolyn's mother had been a war bride from Paris, and in retrospect Susannah thought she'd never really adjusted to life in a small American town. Carolyn had been an only child, and her mother had insisted her daughter attend high school in France. She and Susannah were friends all through grade school and junior high, and then Carolyn had left for a boarding school just outside Paris. They'd written for a while, but their letters became infrequent as they each made new friends.

Later Susannah's father had sent her to the same school. Carolyn had been her salvation.

It was Carolyn who'd cried with her when she learned of Doug's death. Susannah had been inconsolable and desperate to get home. But that wasn't to be. She was convinced she wouldn't have survived the rest of that horrible year without her best friend.

Back in the United States, they'd attended separate colleges but stayed in touch. That special bond had lasted through Carolyn's failed marriage. Then Susannah met Joe and they'd married and the friendship had slowly come to an end.

"I'll call her after dinner."

"Oh, she gave me her number. It's unlisted." Her mother seemed flustered for a moment and then relieved. "I remember now, I put it in my purse so I wouldn't lose it."

"When did Carolyn move back to Colville?"

Her mother blinked several times, as though this was something she should know and didn't. "I don't...remember. I don't recall if she told me." Changing the subject, her mother motioned toward the chest of drawers. "Should I clean out the drawers so you'll have some place to unpack your things? Your father put stuff in there."

"No, Mom, don't worry about it."

Vivian nodded, then shuffled away, presumably to change clothes.

Susannah finished her unpacking. Then, taking the cell phone from her purse, she sat on the edge of the bed and punched the number that would dial her Seattle home.

Her son answered on the second ring.

"Hello, Brian."

"Hey, Mom. How's Grandma?"

"She's fine. Is your father home yet?"

"Yeah. Chrissie's here, too. We've already had a fight over who got to use the phone." He lowered his voice and it sounded as if he'd cupped his hand around the mouthpiece. "Apparently she's on the outs with Jason and she's in one bitch of a mood."

"Static," Susannah said automatically. That was the term she used whenever her children or her students spoke in an unacceptable way. She'd picked up the habit as a fifth-grade teacher. Her kids might consider her old-fashioned, but she didn't allow them to use foul language, insulting labels or bad grammar, and that wasn't a rule she planned to change. She said the word *static* in order to give the child an opportunity to correct his or her mistake.

"One hell—heck of a mood," Brian amended, "but she's been a real you-know-what since she walked in the door."

Susannah sighed. "Let me talk to your father."

"All right." She heard Brian shout in a voice loud enough to shatter glass. "Dad! It's Mom."

"Mom." Chrissie was on the phone first. "I thought you'd be *here*."

"I'm sorry, Chrissie. Grandma needs me right now."

"Well, I need you, too. You should've let me know."

"I'm sorry you're disappointed…."

"Dad isn't any help."

"Did you and Jason have a falling out?"

A half-second pause. "Brian told you?"

"Yes." Susannah could imagine her daughter sending her brother a dirty look.

"How dare he!"

"Chrissie…"

"I wanted to talk to you. I don't know what's wrong, and I think—oh, I don't know, but I'm afraid Jason's interested in someone else."

"Did you ask him?"

Chrissie hesitated. "Not directly. I probably should have. He hasn't phoned yet and he said he would."

"Chrissie, you just got home. Give him a chance."

There was a lengthy silence and Susannah sighed again.

"I'm sorry, sweetheart," she murmured. "I guess all you can do is wait and see."

"You liked Jason, didn't you?"

"Very much." God willing, her daughter would one day marry a man like Jason. Not anytime soon, of course. "You're upset now, but sleep on it and everything will look better in the morning."

"I wish you were here," Chrissie whined. "Why didn't you take me with you? I love Grandma and I'd like to spend time with her, too."

"I needed to get to Colville as quickly as possible." Leave it to Chrissie to make her feel even guiltier. She was tired. School had drained her and nothing about her life felt right.

"Dad said I had to cook dinner," Chrissie muttered. "He said that without you here, I'm supposed to take over meals."

"I'm sure Dad would find that helpful." And since her daughter wasn't working, she could do something around the house, Susannah thought but didn't say.

"He wants me to be his galley slave."

"One meal a day, Chrissie, is hardly slave labor."

"I had plans for tonight."

Susannah didn't want to get into an argument with her daughter. "Let me talk to your father."

"All right, but tell him he's being totally unreasonable."

Susannah rolled her eyes toward the ceiling, grateful to have escaped her daughter's theatrics. Half a minute later, Joe got on the phone.

"Hi," he said. "How was the drive?"

"Great. I listened to music the entire way."

"Did it help?"

His real question was whether she was still depressed. "I think it did," she said without a lot of enthusiasm, "I'll be okay in a week or so." She prayed that was true.

For a moment it seemed as if he hadn't heard her. "Do you intend to visit your father's grave?"

"Why should I?"

"Susannah, don't get all bent out of shape. It was just a question."

"You know how I feel about him."

"All right, fine." He paused. "I still think you might find some answers in Colville."

She bit her lip. "I might." But the answers she needed weren't to the questions he assumed.

"I hope you do, Suze."

Susannah didn't know how to respond to that. Telling Joe her mother was waiting, she ended the conversation and turned off her cell phone. When she glanced up, Vivian stood in the doorway, wearing her church hat and winter coat. "I found Carolyn's phone number," she said proudly, holding a small slip of paper.

"Mom, you don't need your coat. It's almost eighty degrees outside." The temperature had flashed from the Colville State Bank as she'd driven through town.

"I don't?"

"No. Where would you like to go for dinner?" Susannah asked, assisting her mother out of the heavy coat. She hadn't changed her dress, and Susannah found her a light sweater to wear instead of the coat.

"Wherever you want, dear."

"No, you decide, Mom."

Her mother's face fell. She seemed uncertain and a bit confused. "There's always Benny's Café, I suppose."

"Would you rather go to Acorns?" she asked, knowing that was the place her father would have chosen.

Her mother's smile was instantaneous. "I've always loved their oysters. No one in town does them better."

"All right, Mom, that's where we'll go."

"And when we get back, you'll phone Carolyn."

"Yes, Mom, I'll phone Carolyn tonight."

CHAPTER

5

Carolyn Bronson was thrilled to hear from Susannah Leary—no, Susannah Nelson. Naturally, she'd *hoped* Susannah would phone, but for reasons that were hard to explain, she hadn't expected her to. It'd been years since they'd last talked, twenty-five years at least. Decades. Now as she drove into town to meet her, she peered through the windshield looking for the tavern the men from the mill frequented most. Less than a mile down the road from Bronson Mill, it was the only place she could think to suggest.

When Susannah called an hour ago, they'd had so much to say that it took nearly thirty minutes to get off the phone once they'd agreed on a place to meet. They had a lot of years to catch up on, and neither of them wanted to break the connection.

The tavern was on the road that led to Colville, where the old A & W drive-in had been when they were growing up. It'd been converted into a pub and it seemed as good a meeting place as any.

Carolyn thought it was a shame that she'd been back in Colville for over five years and this would be the first time she'd stepped foot in the most popular watering hole for miles around. Even driving below the speed limit, she nearly went past it. She smiled at the name of the tavern. *He's Not Here.* That was actually pretty clever.

Although Carolyn had visited her parents often, she hadn't looked up old friends. Her high school years had been spent in a boarding school in France, at her mother's insistence. Carolyn feared she'd been a bitter disappointment to her delicate French mother. Brigitte had tried hard to teach her grace and charm and what she called the art of being a woman. But, while she'd scored top grades academically, Carolyn had failed to meet her mother's expectations in all other respects, and took after her father's side of the family. The lumberjack side.

She'd always been astonished that her parents had gotten together at all. They'd met in Europe during World War II and her mother had become a war bride. More than once Carolyn had wondered if her mother had ever regretted her choice of a husband, whether she'd resented being forced to live in Colville. Brigitte was like an exotic orchid stuck in a row of sturdy sunflowers.

There were plenty of spaces in the parking lot at the tavern. The light inside was dim and she wasn't sure she'd recognize Susannah. Her own hair, still chestnut but streaked with gray, was even longer now than it had been when they were teenagers. She wore it pulled away from her face in a thick braid that fell haphazardly over one shoulder.

She had on black jeans and a light summer jacket, which was what she generally wore to the mill. When necessary, she donned more feminine attire, but that wasn't often.

She found a booth and slid onto the polished wooden bench to wait. Only a minute or two after she'd arrived, Susannah came through the door, saw her and immediately headed in her direction. Carolyn would have known her anywhere. Susannah hadn't changed a bit. Oh, perhaps she was a few pounds heavier, but not many, and she wore her hair shorter these days. It was a shade or two darker, as well. She had on white linen pants and a teal sweater with large white flowers on the front.

Her childhood friend sat down across from her in the booth, facing the door. "My goodness, when did they get a Wal-Mart in Colville?"

Carolyn couldn't remember. There'd been news of it coming for a year or two before the store was actually built. "I came back five years ago, and it was already here."

"That long? Really? Funny, neither Mom or Dad said anything about it." She dragged in a deep breath. "You look fabulous. It's great to see you."

"You, too." Carolyn meant it. She'd always regretted that they'd lost contact. "How's your mother?"

Susannah set her purse on the bench beside her. "I'm afraid she's worse than I realized."

"I'm sorry," Carolyn said sympathetically.

Susannah leaned back against the hard wooden booth and sighed. "I took her to dinner, and half the time she thought I was my aunt Jean, who's been dead for fifteen years."

"Oh, no."

Susannah laughed softly. "I didn't mean to start talking about Mom. She's a sweetheart, but ever since my dad died she's been confused and—" As if catching herself doing it again, Susannah shook her head. "First, I want to know how we missed seeing each other all these years."

Carolyn shrugged, unwilling to tread through time and examine the might-have-beens, especially those of the last few years. "I don't know. I was so caught up in what was happening to my family, it was all I could do to deal with that. I moved back just before my father died. He'd been sick for quite a while, and the business had gone downhill."

"I wondered about that."

"When I took over, the mill was on the brink of going under. It's taken every minute of every day to get back on track, so I haven't done much socializing."

"In other words, you've had no life."

Carolyn nodded. "That pretty much sums it up."

"How's the mill doing these days?" Susannah straightened, a smile on her face. "I have to tell you I'm *very* impressed that you're running such an important business. I had no idea."

"We're solvent and growing." Carolyn didn't mean to brag, but the mill was thriving at a time when many others were shutting down. Investing wisely, making the most of foreign trade opportunities and her management skills had brought Bronson Mills from the verge of closing its doors to becoming a major player in the state.

"What about you?" Carolyn asked. "Were you in town a lot?"

Before her friend could answer, the waitress came for their order and they each asked for a Diet Coke.

Susannah waited until she'd left before answering. "I didn't come to town very often—two or three times in the last five years. Until recently, Mom and Dad drove over to the coast to visit me. Dad died last November."

Although Susannah mentioned her father's passing without apparent emotion, Carolyn detected a small quaver in her friend's voice. Her own father had been dead several years now, but she continued to feel his loss each and every day.

"You lost your mom, too, didn't you?" Susannah asked.

"Mom died of cancer about two years ago," Carolyn said, and while her death was equally painful, Carolyn felt that her mother was ready and, in fact, had welcomed death. Her life had been nothing like she'd dreamed, filled with disappointments and disillusionment. And without her husband, she lost whatever contentment she'd managed to find. Brigitte had not succeeded in making many friends or developing interests of her own; that was something Carolyn didn't like to think about.

"Dad died of congestive heart failure," she added. It was a horrible way to die. Carolyn was grateful she'd been with him those last months. They'd always been close, but they'd drawn even closer as the end of his life approached.

When Carolyn first returned to Colville, she'd assumed she'd be selling off the mill, but during the last months of her father's life, she realized she couldn't let go of her heritage. The mill had been in the family for three generations, and now it was hers. Owning Bronson Mills, she'd discovered, was even more of a responsibility than it was a privilege.

"I'm sorry," Susannah murmured.

"Losing my dad was hard," Carolyn admitted. "The two of us were tight. After I'd been here awhile, I began to feel that no matter where I lived, this town, this place, was my home."

"Do you like it—running the mill, I mean?"

Carolyn smiled, embarrassed to admit the depth of her feelings about the family business. "I love it. I didn't think I would. The only reason I got my MBA was to please Dad, but I promptly took a job in Oregon working with Techtronics. I enjoyed it and advanced to a management position. I'd just been offered another promotion when I got the call from Dad."

"The call?"

Carolyn would never forget that phone conversation. "His whole life, Dad never asked a single thing of me." Unlike her mother, who seemed to be consumed by demands, most of which Carolyn was incapable of fulfilling. "He asked me to come home. He needed me. I put in my notice the next day, packed up and headed for Colville."

The waitress returned with their drinks and for a moment they were silent.

"I wish I knew how to help Mom," Susannah said thoughtfully. "I know I'll have to move her, but convincing her of that's going to be hard."

Carolyn didn't envy her friend the task. "What are you planning to do with the house?"

"Once I know Mom's comfortable, I'll probably put it up for sale. Assisted living is expensive. I was shocked when I made a few phone calls and found out exactly how much it costs. Dad provided for Mom, but their largest asset is the equity they have in the house. There's no question that I'll have to sell it, and the sooner the better so I can invest the money."

"What about taking her to Seattle, to a facility near you?" That seemed more logical to Carolyn.

"I wish I could get her to budge, but she refuses. Her friends are here—even though she hardly ever sees them— and things are familiar to her. Plus, the housing fees are more reasonable on this side of the mountains than in Seattle."

"At least you still have your mother," Carolyn reminded her. "When mine died, I had this gut-wrenching revelation that I was an orphan. All alone in the world. I was almost fifty years old and I kept thinking I wasn't ready to be an adult. Sounds ridiculous, doesn't it?"

"Not at all," Susannah said. "I feel the same way. I hate having to make decisions about my mother without Doug to talk to." She swallowed visibly. "It's not fair. My brother should be helping me with this. Doug should *be* here."

Carolyn bent her head to hide her reaction to hearing his name. A twinge of pain passed through her. His death had hit her hard.

Susannah stared into the distance. "I miss him. My brother died thirty-two years ago, and I still miss him." She lowered her eyes to her drink and swirled the straw around, clinking the ice cubes against the glass. "Doug and I should be dealing with this together."

Carolyn didn't want to talk about Doug. "You're still married, aren't you?" she asked. "That's what your mother said when I ran into her."

"Oh, yes... Joe and I have been together for almost

twenty-five years. We have two kids, both nearly grown. Joe's a dentist and I teach fifth grade."

"I always thought you'd marry Jake." As Carolyn recalled, her friend had pined for him the entire nine months she'd spent in France. She'd waited endlessly for his letters. In the beginning he'd written, but he'd stopped after the first few months. Then Doug had been killed and Susannah had gone into a deep depression.

A faraway look came over her friend. "I always believed I'd marry him, too…." She ended with a shrug. "He'd moved by the time I returned from France. I tried to find him but I never could. I wonder what happened to him—why he left and why he didn't come back."

Carolyn was furious with him for abandoning Susannah when she'd needed him most. She remembered how Susannah had asked around for him after their return. But he was gone; his family, too.

"My last time with Jake was horrible," her friend continued, seemingly lost in her thoughts. "I sneaked out of the house, and we met in my mother's garden. We sat on that stone bench, behind the trellis. It was always so romantic there, and it smelled so lovely." She raised her eyes to meet Carolyn's. "Jake wanted me to run away with him and I didn't have the courage to do it. I was only seventeen. I said no. In the morning my parents drove me to Spokane to catch a flight to France."

"And you never heard from him again?"

"Other than those few letters after I left, nothing."

Carolyn leaned closer. "You did the right thing. Can you imagine how you'd feel if your daughter eloped at that age?"

Susannah smiled. "That certainly puts things into perspective, doesn't it? My daughter is as headstrong as I was and more than a handful. She's almost twenty and insists she's an adult, but she acts more like a teenager."

Susannah brought out pictures of her children and showed them to Carolyn. Chrissie and Brian were very attractive, and so was Joe, Susannah's husband, in a solid, appealing way. Although she'd never met him, Carolyn had a positive feeling about Joe—about all of Susannah's family. She rarely admitted it, but she would've liked a husband and children of her own. It hadn't happened. The divorce had devastated her, and she'd buried herself in her work in an effort to forget. Before she knew it, she was forty and then her father got ill.

Still, most of the time she didn't mind being alone. Better that than marriage to a man like her ex-husband, whose repeated infidelity had undermined the little confidence she'd had. In fact, she was shy and always had been. She'd learned to overcompensate in other areas and was an effective manager. Few would guess how difficult it was for her to communicate with a man socially.

Susannah slipped the photos back inside her purse. When she glanced up, she seemed to study Carolyn, then said, "You look happy."

Her friend's assessment surprised Carolyn. But Susannah was right. Only recently she'd found herself singing as she dressed for work. The sound of her own voice had caught her off guard and she'd stopped abruptly, wondering what there was to be so excited about. She'd realized then that it wasn't anything in particular. She was content and had become secure in herself. Yes, every now and then she entertained regrets, but she suspected everyone did. The business was running at a profit and that would have pleased her father beyond any of her other accomplishments. The mill was once again Colville's main employer and as the mill went, so did the town. She had reason to be proud. The family business had given her a sense of purpose; it was in salvaging Bronson Mills that she'd truly forged her identity.

"What about you?" Carolyn asked, wondering about her friend's marriage. "Are you happy?"

"Of course," Susannah answered quickly, perhaps too quickly. She reached for her Coke. After a moment, she said, "The truth is, I've been depressed and out of sorts for the last few months. Joe says this all goes back to losing my father, but I disagree." She glanced up. "I…" She hesitated, looking mildly embarrassed. "I've been thinking a lot about Jake."

"Really?" Carolyn watched her friend closely.

"It started a little over three months ago. I haven't told anyone—I can't. Not even Joe… Out of the blue, Jake came to me in this…this stupid dream. I can't even tell you what it was about. From that moment on, he's been on my mind almost constantly, and now he shows up in my dreams practically every night."

Carolyn didn't know what to say. "He's probably married, don't you think?"

Susannah nodded. "It's flirting with danger, but I want to find him."

"And do what?"

Susannah frowned. "I don't know yet. Ask him, I guess, why he never wrote me after Doug died. Ask him why he moved and didn't tell me where he'd gone. I keep thinking about what would've happened if I'd run away with him that night."

Nothing good was Carolyn's guess, but presumably Susannah knew that.

"I don't suppose you've heard if he's living in the area?" Susannah asked, her eyes alight with hope.

Carolyn didn't. "No, but then I don't know everyone in town."

Susannah pushed the hair away from her forehead. "Like I said, I haven't told Joe about this. I feel so guilty, as though I've been unfaithful, but I haven't done anything. I wouldn't risk my marriage over this. I'm just curious, you know?" She looked nervously at Carolyn.

"And you want to find out what happened to Jake."

Susannah slowly nodded. "Yes. I want him to be happy and to let him know that I am, too. I'm not interested in starting an affair." She smiled. "As Erma Bombeck once said, I don't have the underwear for it."

Carolyn laughed.

"I can't believe we're having this conversation. I have to tell you it feels good to discuss this crazy idea." She paused, staring into the distance. "All I want is five minutes with Jake. Even a phone conversation would satisfy my curiosity. Is that so terrible?"

"No." Carolyn understood, but although she didn't say it, she agreed with Joe. Susannah's discontent—apparent in this sudden urge to find her high school boyfriend—was somehow connected to her father, to his death. She knew that the relationship between Susannah and her father had been a difficult one; this was a huge loss in Susannah's life, whether she accepted that or not.

Once more her friend made a circular motion with her straw setting her ice cubes clinking. "You were always the kind of friend I could talk to. I would never have made it through those last five months in France without you."

"We were good friends," Carolyn said simply, thinking *Maybe we can be again.*

The waitress came by and they ordered fresh drinks. "I should head back to Mom," Susannah said reluctantly, "but I don't want to leave. Talking to you has really helped. I don't feel nearly as guilty or alone as I did earlier. Thank you for that."

"Do you know how long you'll be in town?" Carolyn asked. Her friends were few, and she had little life outside of the mill. She gardened, fed the deer that ventured on to her property, did a bit of needlepoint and worked fifty- or sixty-hour weeks. That was the sum total of her activities.

"I'll be here for three or four weeks," Susannah told her. "It all depends on how things go with Mom."

The waitress returned with their Diet Cokes.

Carolyn picked up her drink. "If you get a chance, stop by the mill and I'll give you the grand tour." It would be fun to show her friend the improvements she'd made, even if Susannah didn't understand their importance.

They talked for another fifteen minutes, and Susannah tested her French, which after all these years was surprisingly good. Carolyn remained fluently bilingual. Toward the end, Carolyn's mother had spoken exclusively in her mother tongue.

"I remember that my conversational French improved according to how much wine I drank," Susannah said, laughing.

Carolyn grinned. "Mom made me learn French as a

child. I grew up speaking both languages." She rarely used it now, but she certainly didn't regret having the ability.

"Have you gone back to Paris since high school?" Susannah asked.

"A few times. My grandparents died in the war and I only had one aunt, who never married. My mother didn't want me to lose my heritage and I'm grateful for the time I had there, but my life is in Colville." Carolyn knew why her mother had insisted she study in France. She'd been hoping her daughter would meet a nice French boy and fall in love with him. Unfortunately, Brigitte hadn't realized how closely the nuns watched over their charges at the boarding school. Any chance of meeting boys inside—or outside—those convent walls had been virtually nonexistent.

Susannah checked the time. "It's nine o'clock. I'd better go. Mom's probably waiting up for me." She took a deep breath, then said, "I've made arrangements to take her to visit a couple of assisted-living facilities tomorrow."

"She doesn't know yet?"

Susannah shook her head. "I thought I'd broach the subject over dinner, but I couldn't do it. Mom was so pleased to have me with her and so excited about going out to a restaurant, I didn't have the heart to upset her."

"She misses your father, doesn't she?"

"Dreadfully. Which is understandable—they knew each other their entire lives. Mom's completely at loose ends without him, but that's not the worst of it." Susannah shook her head. "As we were driving back to the house, Mom got very quiet. She said she had something important to tell me. She claimed that my father had come to her earlier this week." Susannah closed her eyes for a few seconds. "Her neighbor had already told me about this. But to hear Mom describe it..."

"She's missing him so much that her mind must be conjuring him up," Carolyn suggested.

"That was my reaction at first, too, but then Mom told me he walked her home. This wasn't some momentary visit, some trick of the mind. Her hand nearly left bruises on my arm, she was so adamant. My mother says she spent at least half an hour with my father."

Shocked, Carolyn couldn't come up with anything to say. Except that Mrs. Leary was obviously in bad shape, and Susannah already knew that.

CHAPTER

6

The next morning, Susannah walked through her mother's garden, seeking a moment of peace. It was something she often did at home during the summer, wandering through her own garden, assessing the state of her flowers, inhaling their fragrance, making plans for the day. She noticed that Vivian's plants and flowerbeds were in reasonably good condition—better than she'd expected.

Afterward, she returned to the house for coffee, hoping there'd be some milk or cream. She opened her mother's refrigerator and was appalled at what she found. The cheese had grown moldy. A tomato had shriveled up and shrunk to half its original size. Containers filled with leftovers crammed the shelves, most of them several days, if not weeks, old. Along with that, Susannah saw a number of small tinfoil packages; she assumed these were bits of meat. She had no intention of finding out. Almost everything should've been discarded long ago.

The coffee perked in the old-fashioned pot behind her. Of course she hadn't discovered the carton of milk she'd wanted but the door of the fridge held many small bottles and jars, some of them unopened. Just how many types of mustard could one woman accumulate? Susannah counted twelve different varieties—at least eight more than she'd seen during her visit in March.

"I didn't hear you get up," Vivian said, coming into the kitchen. She tied the sash of her housecoat around her waist. Susannah noticed that her mother had taken to shuffling her feet, as if her slippers were too heavy for her. She took tiny steps and looked so much older than she had even a few months ago.

"Good morning, Mom," Susannah said cheerfully.

Her mother brought down a cup and saucer from the cupboard and set them next to the coffeepot. "Did you sleep well?"

"Very well."

Her mother nodded. "Do you need something?"

Susannah glanced back inside the refrigerator and remembered her father shouting at her as a kid to close the refrigerator door. "I was looking for milk," she said.

"I have lots of milk." Vivian seemed surprised that Susannah hadn't found it. "I'm positive I got some just the other day."

Susannah moved a number of plastic containers onto the counter and sure enough, an unopened milk carton rested at the back of the top shelf. Bringing it out, she placed it on the table and reached for her cup. The smell alerted her the moment she opened the milk. When she saw that the expiry date was over a month ago, she dumped the thick, lumpy liquid down the drain, running water to lessen the foul odor.

"What's wrong with it?" Vivian asked.

"It's gone bad."

Her mother's face twisted with displeasure. The narrowed eyes and pinched mouth was an expression Susannah remembered well from her childhood. It was the same frown she got when she'd misbehaved.

"I think we should take that carton back to Safeway and demand a refund. They sold me spoiled milk."

"Now, Mom…"

"It's just like those big chain stores to take advantage of a widow. Well, I won't stand for it."

"Mom, it's too early in the morning to get upset. Drink your coffee and we'll talk about it later." Susannah figured it was pointless to explain that Vivian had bought the milk six or seven weeks ago and then forgotten all about it.

As her mother poured coffee from the sterling silver coffeepot, her hand trembled. Susannah had to bite her lip to keep from stepping forward and taking over. When Vivian finished, she sat down at the kitchen table, seeming rather pleased with herself. Susannah could only suppose it was because she'd managed without spilling a drop.

"I had a nice visit with Carolyn Bronson," Susannah commented, as she joined her mother at the table.

"Who, dear?"

"Carolyn Bronson. Remember, you saw her recently and she gave you her phone number? We met last night at the pub where the old A & W used to be."

"Oh, yes, of course. How are her parents?"

Susannah found this sporadic forgetfulness frustrating—and sad. But if she reminded Vivian that both Mr. and Mrs. Bronson had died, she might upset her. In any event, she had more pressing subjects to discuss. She decided to be intentionally vague. "I'm not sure, Mom."

"Mrs. Bronson is a funny one." She leaned closer to Susannah and lowered her voice. "She's always putting on airs because she's French."

"Carolyn was one of my best friends all through school," Susannah said mildly.

"I tried to be friendly," her mother continued, ignoring her remark. "Went out of my way, in fact, but apparently I wasn't good enough for the likes of Brigitte Bronson."

"Carolyn sent you her best."

"She was a sweet girl." Vivian sipped her coffee and again Susannah noticed how her mother's hand trembled as she lifted the cup. "Unlike her mother..."

Susannah didn't want to get involved in a mean-spirited conversation about Brigitte, but she knew what Vivian meant. Although nothing was ever said, Susannah had always had the impression that Carolyn's mother didn't approve of their friendship. As an adult, she was able to analyze those feelings, understanding that Mrs. Bronson was a woman whose unhappiness made her cold and resentful.

Susannah waited until her mother had finished her first cup of coffee before she brought up the subject of assisted living. "You must be rambling around this house all by yourself," she began casually.

Her mother stared at her. "Not at all."

"Are you lonely?"

A soft smile turned up the edges of Vivian's mouth. "I was until your father came back to see me."

"Mom—" Susannah bit off words of protest. She was afraid that her mother had lost her grip on reality and grown comfortable in her fantasy world.

Vivian studied her as though waiting for Susannah to comment on her father's visit.

"Actually, Mom," Susannah said, gathering her resolve. "There's something we need to discuss."

"What is it?" her mother asked.

"Mom," Susannah said, praying for the right words. "I'm concerned about you being here all alone, especially now that Martha's quit."

"Don't be," she said, calmly dismissing Susannah's apprehensions. "I'm perfectly fine."

"Would you consider moving to Seattle?" That would solve so many problems, but even as Susannah asked she knew it was futile.

"And leave Colville?" Her mother appeared to mull it over, then shook her head. "I can't. Much as I'd love to be closer to you and the grandchildren, I won't leave my home."

Susannah knew that change of any kind terrified Vivian.

"Doug and your father are buried here," her mother went on.

"Mom—"

"My friends are close by."

Most of whom were dead or dying, but Susannah couldn't bring herself to mention it. "I'd be able to visit far more often," she offered as enticement, hoping against hope that her mother would see the advantages of moving.

Vivian sipped her coffee and allowed the cup to linger at her lips a moment longer than usual, as if she was considering the prospect again. Slowly she shook her head. "I'm sorry, dear, but this is my home. Seattle is way too big a city for me. I'd be lost there."

Susannah reached across the table and took her mother's fragile hand. "That's something else we need to discuss. Mom, I'm afraid this house is too much for you."

"What do you mean?" An edge sharpened her voice.

"I worry about you here all alone, trying to cope with maintenance and—"

"Nonsense."

"Who'll shovel the sidewalk when it snows?"

"I'll hire a neighborhood boy."

"What would you do if a water pipe broke?"

"The pipes aren't going to break, Susannah. Now stop being difficult."

Susannah didn't feel *she* was the one who was being difficult. The more she thought about the problems faced by an elderly person living alone—especially an elderly person losing her memory—the more worried she became.

"I don't know why you'd want to come all the way from Seattle to talk such nonsense to me," Vivian said in a querulous voice.

Susannah remembered what Mrs. Henderson had said about her attempt to discuss assisted living back in March. That had probably influenced today's response—if Vivian even remembered the earlier conversation. Regardless, Susannah had hoped that by pointing out a number of practical issues, she could get Vivian to realize on her own the advantages of moving into an assisted-living complex. Clearly that approach wasn't going to work.

"Mom, I think we need to sell the house."

"What?" Vivian banged her cup against the saucer, her eyes wide. "For the last time, Susannah, I am *not* leaving my home. I am stunned that you would even suggest such a thing."

"Mother—"

Without another word, Vivian stood, deposited her cup and saucer in the sink and disappeared down the hallway to her bedroom, muttering as she left.

Susannah planted her elbows on the table, and cupped her ears with her hands. She closed her eyes, silently praying for wisdom. She hadn't expected this to be easy, but so far she was getting absolutely nowhere.

After Vivian had dressed, she came back into the kitchen. Ignoring Susannah, she collected a straw basket and clippers. The garden was in full bloom; irises and roses were two of Susannah's favorites and they were in abundant display along the white picket fence. The lilacs were pruned and shapely, and their heady scent drifted through the open window.

Given her mother's limited endurance, Susannah had been surprised to discover that the garden looked quite good, although the fence was a disaster. The paint had faded and one entire section tilted precariously. Her father would never have allowed that to go unfixed for more than a day. He was a stickler for order, at home and in the courtroom.

"I thought I'd clean out the refrigerator," Susannah said, making a peace offering.

Vivian kept her shoulders stiff as she pulled on her gloves. "If that's what you want to do, go right ahead."

"Mom." Susannah walked toward her. "We still need to talk."

"Not about me moving. That subject is closed."

"I need to make sure you're safe and well."

"I don't know why you're so concerned all of a sudden. Besides, I'm getting stronger every day." The back screen door slammed as Vivian walked out of the house.

Susannah sighed heavily. She didn't want this to dissolve into a battle of wills between her and her mother.

It took her forty minutes to clean out the refrigerator. She discarded all the containers; the contents of some were impossible to determine. Among the identifiable remains, she found old tuna fish, green-tinged cottage cheese, rotting fruit and vegetables. Her mother saved every scrap and bit. Rather than leave this garbage to smell up the kitchen, she wrapped everything in plastic and carried it outside to the receptacle by the garage.

As she returned to the house, Susannah noticed that the shelves on the back porch were filled with dozens of senseless items. Her mother must've kept every plastic container she'd bought in the last six months. Piles of aluminum trays were neatly stacked, not for recycling, but for some future use. As a daughter of the Depression era, her mother tended to save everything, but it had never been this bad. Even empty toilet paper rolls were carefully piled up.

"Mom, what do you intend to do with all this stuff?" Susannah asked.

Her mother looked over from where she stood in her garden, a hose in one hand, and shrugged. "I'm saving it."

"For what?"

"I don't know yet." She paused. "I never snooped around *your* house."

"I'm not snooping. Everything's out in plain sight."

"Do I question what you save and don't save?"

Susannah had to agree that she didn't. She went back to the kitchen and wiped the counters. This wasn't how she wanted the visit to go, but she couldn't delay the inevitable, either.

"Would you like to ride down to the grocery store with me, Mom?" she asked when Vivian entered the house.

Vivian put one long-stem red rose in a vase and set it in the center of the table. "My lettuce is coming up nicely," she said with satisfaction. "So are my herbs. Rosemary's my favorite, you know."

Susannah nodded. "Maybe we could take a drive around town when we're finished our shopping." She strived to make this sound like an enjoyable outing.

Vivian hesitated, as if she wasn't quite ready to forgive her for their earlier argument. "That would be nice," she finally agreed.

Together they drove to the Safeway. Vivian slipped her arm through Susannah's as they crossed the parking lot and Susannah had the distinct feeling it was because she needed help maintaining her balance. This was also a silent message to let her know all was forgiven now.

They loaded the cart with food Susannah hoped would tempt her mother's appetite. She bought macaroons, her mother's favorite cookie. Asparagus, Ritz crackers and other treats Susannah knew her mother wouldn't purchase for herself. She quietly put back a jar of Russian mustard Vivian had placed in the cart, but kept the olives.

They left the air-conditioned comfort of the store. The sun was out in full force and at ten o'clock it was nearly seventy-five degrees.

"It's going to be a hot one today," Susannah said as they transferred their groceries to the trunk of her car.

Her mother responded with a half smile. "I'm sorry, Susannah, but I wouldn't do well in Seattle. I know you're disappointed, but I can't leave Colville. This is my home."

A lump momentarily filled Susannah's throat. "I know, Mom. I don't want to take away your home. Please understand that I only want what's best for you."

"I'm the one who knows what's best for me."

"Of course you are. Assisted living doesn't mean you'll lose your independence. I—"

"Assisted living? Why bring *that* up?" Cutting her off, Vivian climbed inside the car and locked the door.

"Well, I guess that's that," Susannah said under her breath. She finished unloading the groceries, closed her trunk and parked the cart.

Opening the driver's side door, she slid into her vehicle. "It wouldn't hurt to take a look, would it?"

Her mother refused to answer.

"Mom, please don't be so stubborn."

Vivian turned her head away and gazed out the passenger window. In all her life Susannah had never seen her mother behave quite like this. Susannah had always viewed her mother as a subservient and obedient wife, the passive partner in that marriage. She couldn't remember her mother going against her father's dictates even once. Her father, the judge, ruled the home and his family. What he said was law.

Thinking about it now, Susannah marveled at the fact that, despite her father's authoritarian ways, Vivian often managed to get what she wanted. The methods she employed were never direct. Vivian was a master manipulator, and that was clearer in retrospect than it had been at the time.

Now Susannah was compelled to be equally indirect. "I thought we'd go for a short drive," she said pleasantly. She turned on the ignition and the air-conditioning kicked in, flooding the car with an influx of hot air until it gradually cooled.

Vivian remained quiet.

"You didn't tell me there was a Wal-Mart in town," Susannah said in conversational tones. "Want to go?" Her mother had always loved shopping.

"Oh." Vivian smiled then and the tension eased from between Susannah's shoulder blades.

Instead of going back to the house to drop off the groceries, Susannah detoured and drove past the first of the assisted-living facilities she'd contacted. It was a modern complex that resembled a nice hotel, with balconies and a fountain in front of the circular driveway.

Susannah didn't say anything, but slowed as they drove past.

"You apparently don't know your way home anymore," her mother said, ice dripping from every word.

"Oh, I know where Chestnut Avenue is," Susannah murmured. She shook her head. Vivian had never been to the assisted-living facility, but she knew exactly where it was located.

"I don't want that milk to spoil."

"It won't." Susannah turned and drove toward the house.

In less than five minutes, Susannah was unloading the car. She put the refrigerator items away and left the rest of the bags on the kitchen counter, afraid that if she delayed too long her mother might change her mind.

"You ready?" she asked.

"For what?" Her mother blinked as if confused.

"We're going to Wal-Mart, remember?"

Vivian studied her, apparently not sure this was something that interested her.

Yeah, right, Susannah thought. She had trouble hiding a smile as the two of them went back to the car. The Wal-Mart parking lot was nearly full. This time her mother didn't slide her arm through Susannah's, but after a few steps she clasped Susannah's elbow.

"I don't think I've seen this many people since the Fourth of July parade," Vivian said as the blue-vested store greeter steered a cart toward them.

"Payday at the mill," the woman said, commenting on Vivian's remark.

Carolyn was doing well this season, Susannah mused as she allowed her mother to push the cart. Having something to hold on to helped Vivian keep her balance.

They'd started down the first aisle when Susannah heard someone call her name. She turned to find a tall, slightly overweight woman watching her. It took a moment to realize who this was.

"Sandy? Sandy Thomas?"

"Susannah Leary?"

They broke out laughing at the same time. "My goodness, it's years since I saw you." Sandy's eyes sparkled with unabashed delight.

Sandy had been a good friend, the kind of person who always saw things in a positive light. They'd kept in touch after graduation, and Susannah had served as a bridesmaid in Sandy's wedding when she'd married Russell Giddings, the local pharmacist's son.

"I didn't know you lived in Colville," Susannah said.

"Russ and I have been back for ages."

Susannah smiled at Vivian. "You remember my mother, don't you?"

"Yes, of course. Hello, Mrs. Leary."

"Hello, dear. You were Susannah's friend, right?"

Sandy nodded.

"My daughter's trying to move me out of my home," Vivian announced, loudly enough for several heads to turn in their direction.

"Mother!"

"Well, it's true." Vivian leaned against the cart. "You think I don't know what you're doing?"

"My mother's living over at Altamira," Sandy said. "And she loves it. She told me she was sorry she waited so long to move."

Susannah smiled her gratitude.

Vivian crossed her arms in defiance. "I'm not leaving my home, and that's all there is to it."

Sandy shared a sympathetic look with Susannah. "Let's get together soon," she suggested.

Susannah shrugged, unsure what to tell her. Getting Vivian settled was her top priority. "I'd like to," she began, "but…"

"I'm in the phone book, so call me." Sandy squeezed her elbow, letting Susannah know she understood.

She would have welcomed the opportunity to visit with Sandy. They'd become friends after Carolyn was shipped off to boarding school. Sandy had been with her the night Jake had first asked her to dance.

A tingle of happiness went through her at the memory. They'd gone to a school function after the football game—a dance in the high school gym. Jake had been at the game, too, with Sharon, another girl from their class. He'd been talking to the players on the sidelines. Susannah had just started her junior year and Jake was a recent graduate. He worked at the mill and had stopped by the dance—without Sharon. Several of the senior girls flirted outrageously in hopes of getting his attention. Susannah thought he was the cutest boy in the universe, but she was convinced she didn't have a chance with him. She was only sixteen; he was nineteen.

When Jake had crossed the gym floor and held out his hand to her, she'd nearly keeled over in a dead faint. He didn't say a word as he drew her into his arms for a slow dance.

When the music faded, he'd looked into her eyes, smiled softly and touched her cheek with his index finger. Then, again without speaking, he walked away. If Sandy hadn't come and collected her from the dance floor, Susannah figured she would've stood there like a statue with everyone dancing around her.

Oh, yes, Susannah definitely wanted to get together with Sandy. And not *just* because she'd have a chance to talk freely about Jake.

"This is a good price for—"

Her mother's voice cut into Susannah's musings. "It is," she agreed automatically, although she didn't have a clue what Vivian was talking about. Suddenly—impulsively—she faced her mother. Jake's name hadn't been mentioned in over thirty years and it was time for answers.

"Mom," Susannah said. "Do you know whatever happened to Jake Presley?"

"Who?"

"Jake Presley, my boyfriend in high school."

"He wasn't that singer, was he?"

"No, Mom," Susannah said. "That was Elvis."

"He's dead, isn't he?"

She nodded. "I'm asking about Jake Presley. He used to live in Colville, remember?"

Her mother considered the question. "What did his father do?"

"He worked at the mill." Susannah strained her memory, but she couldn't recall his first name. Jake had been an only child. His mother had run off when he was four or five and he lived with his father.

After a moment, Vivian shook her head. "Sorry, I don't remember any Jake Presley."

"That's all right," Susannah said and struggled to hide her disappointment.

"I'm sorry." Her mother seemed genuinely apologetic.

"It's all right, Mom," she said again.

Only it wasn't.

Vivian had turned on the Food Channel, pen and pad on her lap as she wrote down recipe after recipe. Puzzled, Susannah watched her mother. As best as she could figure, Vivian hadn't cooked a meal in months.

Susannah hadn't brought up the subject of assisted living since this morning, but she was biding her time. Getting her mother to be reasonable would require some inventiveness.

"Mom, I'm going to call Joe and the kids," she said, getting up from the sofa.

"Okay." Her mother's eyes didn't waver from the television screen.

Susannah walked into the kitchen and picked up her cell phone, which she'd left on the table. She sat down and hit the first button on her speed-dial. Pressing the phone to her ear she waited. Three rings passed before Chrissie answered.

"Hi," her daughter said, sounding more cheerful than she had in their last conversation.

"It's Mom."

"Oh." Her voice flattened. "How's Grandma?"

"Okay. What about you?"

"All right, I guess."

"Don't act so enthusiastic."

"Dad's making me cook dinner again," Chrissie muttered. "He said I couldn't make anything that came from a box."

"Your father and I are trying to avoid processed foods as much as possible."

"He wants me to create a menu for his approval. Can you *believe* it? I spent two hours in the kitchen this afternoon. This is my vacation, too, and now I'm stuck at home and bored out of my mind."

Susannah didn't remind Chrissie that if she had a job, none of this would be happening; she knew her words wouldn't be appreciated any more than her advice would.

"I haven't heard from Jason." Her daughter's depression and frustration were evident even over the phone.

"I'm sorry, sweetheart."

"No wonder he was so eager for me to go home. It's just that—oh, never mind, you wouldn't understand."

"Are you sure you've read the situation correctly? Why not just wait and see?"

"Yes, I'm sure," she fumed. Her daughter made a scoffing sound. "I *knew* something was wrong the minute he came to take me to the airport. A woman knows, Mom. Something happened between him and Katie, and I think it's been going on for a while. I didn't pick up on it until that day, and now I'm furious with him and Katie."

Susannah had no idea what to say, so she added another lame, "Wait and see. It might not be as bad as you think."

"Oh, yes, it is." Chrissie groaned in derision. "The situation here isn't helping, either."

"What do you mean?" Susannah asked.

"You wouldn't understand," Chrissie repeated. "You're with Grandma and I'm stuck here. Thanks a lot, Mom. Thanks a *lot*." Having said that, she slammed down the phone and screamed for Joe.

A minute later her husband picked up the receiver. "Hi, Suze," he said. "How's Colville?"

"Growing. There are so many changes I can hardly keep track. I took Mom shopping and she practically bought out the shoe department at Wal-Mart."

She heard his gentle amusement. "I wondered where you got your penchant for shoes." Shoes had always been Susannah's weakness.

"How's it going with your mother?" he asked.

"Not good." She described how her mother had embarrassed her in front of Sandy.

"She feels threatened," Joe said. "You would, too, in similar circumstances."

"Maybe, but…"

After spending an entire day with her mother and witnessing how easily she tired, Susannah was more concerned than ever. They'd had to stop frequently for breaks; once Vivian had even taken a brief nap on a pull-out sofa in the furniture department, with Susannah standing anxiously by.

"I don't know how to handle this. The minute I bring up the subject of assisted living, she gets defensive and angry."

"Did you mention the phone call from her neighbor?"

Susannah straightened. "No. But maybe if Mrs. Henderson and I both talked to her, Mom might listen."

"She might think you're ganging up on her, too."

Her husband had a good point. "You're right, she probably will. I'll tell her about the phone call first and if I have to, I'll bring in Mrs. Henderson."

"Did you take her to tour any of the facilities?"

Susannah sighed in discouragement. She hadn't even gotten close. "I drove past one, and Mom made some sarcastic remark about not knowing the way home."

Joe chuckled. "She's got quite a stubborn streak."

"I don't remember her being like this. My mother was the soul of tact and graciousness, and all of a sudden she's—" Susannah didn't finish. She noticed a movement out of the corner of her eye, and turned to look. To her horror, she found her mother in the hallway, listening in on her conversation. Lowering the phone, she whirled around. "Mom?"

With a sheepish look, her mother walked into the kitchen. Susannah didn't know how long she'd been standing there, but suspected it had been quite a while.

"Joe," Susannah breathed, shocked that her mother would stoop to eavesdropping. "My mother was standing in the hallway, listening to our conversation."

"I'm not leaving my home," Vivian said loudly, "and you can't make me."

"Susannah?" Joe's voice rang in her ear.

"I'll call you later."

"Okay." She heard the drone of the disconnected line from her cell phone before she clicked it off.

"Mom, I think we should talk," Susannah said, gesturing for Vivian to join her.

"Not if you're going to say what I think you are." Her mother started to back out of the kitchen.

"Aren't you curious about why I drove over here earlier than I'd originally planned?"

Her mother hesitated. "A little."

"Sit down, Mom." Again Susannah motioned toward the other end of the table.

"I'll miss my show."

"The Food Channel runs the same episode in the morning, and before you say anything, it's perfectly all right to watch television in the middle of the day."

Her mother's eyes narrowed, and her expression seemed to say she wasn't sure she should trust her daughter. This wasn't the way Susannah wanted to begin such a crucial conversation. Instead of arguing further, she leaped into it. "Martha phoned me in Seattle, and I talked to Mrs. Henderson, too."

Her mother sat down on the chair, her posture straight, her eyes filled with defiance. "All right, tell me what Rachel's saying behind my back. As for that Martha, she's not to be trusted."

"Mother, Mrs. Henderson is your friend." She'd intercede for Martha later.

"She's jealous of my garden. She always has been." Her mother crossed her arms defensively. "Her gladioli and irises never do as well as mine. Her roses, either."

Susannah intended to avoid *that* issue, in case it turned

into another War of the Roses. "Mrs. Henderson called because she was worried about you. So is Martha. Your friends are concerned."

A sheepish look came over Vivian. "You'd be lost and confused, too, if you lost your husband of fifty-nine years."

Susannah said nothing.

"I will die in this house, Susannah. It's my home. It's where I belong. I am not moving."

The situation was impossible. "Mother, please listen because I need you to hear me."

"I *am* listening. I just don't like what I'm hearing."

"I talked to Dr. Bethel a few days ago, and he agrees it's time for you to make the transition to a facility." Susannah had called him the morning of her departure, wanting not only his assessment but any ammunition he could provide.

Her mother gasped, as if her longtime physician had betrayed her. "I don't believe it!"

"Please don't make this any more difficult than it already is. I've made appointments to tour Altamira and Whispering Willows tomorrow."

"Then you'll go by yourself, because I refuse to be part of it."

A crescent-shaped moon was tucked in a corner of the sky as Vivian sat in her garden, a wad of tissue in her hand. She couldn't sleep. The wind-up clock George had used for years had ticked relentlessly at her bedside as she counted off the hours. Soon it would be daylight and she had yet to fall asleep. It felt as if everyone she knew and trusted had turned against her, including her own daughter. She'd once considered Rachel Henderson a friend, but no longer.

Even Dr. Bethel and Martha. She wished she could talk to George; he'd know what was best. But he'd only come to her that one time.

So Vivian had decided to sit outside. Whenever she shut her eyes, all she could think about was the fact that she was going to lose her home. Susannah wanted to move her in with strangers. She *couldn't* leave Chestnut Avenue.

She was old and had lost so much already. She'd buried her husband and her only son. All she had left was her daughter, her house, her things. A lifetime of everything that was most important surrounded her in this home. All her pictures. Her furniture. The crystal vase that had belonged to her grandmother, whose mother had brought it from Poland. Vivian treasured it. Her flowers had never looked more beautiful than in that vase….

Perhaps worst of all, Susannah was asking her to give up her garden. This was almost more than she could bear. There was comfort in her garden, in its beautiful colors, its scents….

Tears welled in her eyes and she rested her head against the back of the garden chair and swallowed a wail of grief. Susannah would do it. She'd seen that glint in her daughter's eye. She'd seen the determined set of Susannah's mouth. Even as a child, Susannah had been stubborn, often to the extent of foolishness, defying George at every turn. Her only living child would haul her off to an asylum, all the while declaring that it was for Vivian's own good.

Exhausted, she finally closed her eyes and slowly rocked, letting the gentle movement lull her into a state of relaxation.

"Vivian."

Someone was calling her. A quiet voice far off in the

distance. Was it in her mind? Or was it real? Vivian strained to hear. It was her George; she knew that much. George struggling to come to her, struggling to cross the great divide.

Vivian's heart rate accelerated as she opened her eyes. "Yes, George, I'm here—I need your help." She hurried to tell him everything. "Susannah wants to move me into an assisted-living facility. What should I do... Tell me, what should I do?" She waited but no one answered.

"George, please! I need you to tell me what to do."

Her cry was met with silence. She peered into the shadowed corners of the garden but saw no sign of him.

Sobbing openly now, Vivian began to rock back and forth but found little solace. She closed her eyes again, and it was then that she heard a single word float past her, soft as a whisper.

One word that would change her world. One word that told her what she had to do. One word from George. She'd asked and he'd answered.

George told her to go.

Chrissie Nelson stared at the silent telephone and cursed it for the umpteenth time that day. No one had phoned, not even her best friends. Everyone was either vacationing or working, and she was trapped at home and she hated it.

Getting a job, any job now, was pointless and nearly impossible. She couldn't even work at her father's dental office, not that she really wanted to. She'd done that the previous summer and it hadn't gone well. Okay, so maybe she wasn't as reliable as he thought she should be; apparently he was still annoyed about the days she'd disappeared after lunch, because he hadn't offered her a part-time position this summer—not even as a last resort. Her job, he said, was cooking and cleaning, and he was supposedly paying her. He didn't have enough money in his account to give her what she felt this was worth.

Chrissie would much rather be with her grandmother. She'd always been close to her Grandma Vivian, and she hadn't seen her since the funeral and everything had been so upsetting then. Grandma had been so brave when the family left. Chrissie remembered seeing tears running down her grandmother's face as the family car pulled out of the driveway and then she'd started crying, too. It'd been so hard to leave her behind. Chrissie's heart ached for her—and all at once she knew what she had to do. She had to go to her Grandma Vivian. That was where she wanted to be, where she *needed* to be. Somehow she'd find a way.

Determined now, Chrissie reached for the phone and dialed her grandmother's number in Colville. After four rings she assumed no one was home, but just as she began to hang up, her mother answered.

"Hi, Mom, it's Chrissie." She forced a bright cheerful note into her voice.

"Chrissie. You're lucky to catch me. I was outside watering Grandma's garden."

"What's going on?" she asked, wondering how to lead into the subject of joining her mother.

Her mother seemed preoccupied. "Grandma and I just got back from visiting assisted-living places."

"Grandma went willingly?" So progress had been made.

"Your grandmother was willing to listen to reason this morning."

"That's good, isn't it?"

"Very good. This is difficult for her. I don't know what made her change her mind but whatever it was, I'm grateful."

"Where's Grandma now?" Chrissie asked.

"She's lying down at the moment, thinking everything over."

In other words, she was taking a nap.

"I had a great idea I wanted to talk to you about, okay?" Chrissie hated sounding like a little kid afraid of being refused, but she sensed that her mother wasn't going to like this idea.

"Sure. What is it?"

"Dad mentioned that you were planning to rent Grandma's house or maybe sell it right away."

"Yes." Her mother seemed reluctant. "It's one of the nicer homes in town and I'm not sure it would be wise to bring in renters, especially since we won't be able to keep an eye on the place." She seemed to be thinking out loud, weighing her options.

"Either way, you're going to have to pack everything up, right?"

"True."

"So you could use some help."

Her mother didn't answer immediately, which probably meant she'd caught on to where Chrissie's questions were leading. She might as well get directly to the point. "Can I come to Colville?" Her mother's hesitation was long enough to raise Chrissie's hackles.

"You don't want me there, do you?" she asked hotly.

"That's not it."

"I can help, you know."

"Yes…"

"Then tell me why I can't come. It's boring around here and everyone I know either has a job or is on some fabulous vacation while I'm a prisoner in this house scrubbing toilets." That wasn't an exaggeration, either. "Don't you think it's time you hired a housekeeper?"

"Your father did," her mother reminded her in a mild voice. "You."

"Very funny," Chrissie muttered. "*Very* funny."

"Your father needs you there."

"No, he doesn't," Chrissie argued. "No one does. This summer is a complete waste. I want to be with you and Grandma." Her throat started to tighten up and she made an effort to hide how miserable she was.

"And do what?" her mother asked.

Chrissie sighed. "I already told you. Help pack stuff and spend time with Grandma."

"But everything has to be sorted. I'll have to decide what to keep, what to sell and what to give away. I don't think my mother's capable of doing any of that, so I'll be the one making those decisions. I've got to get your grandmother moved, too." Her mother sounded overwhelmed by it all.

If that was the case, Chrissie couldn't understand why she balked at her offer. "Well, then, I can be with you when you do it."

"This isn't a vacation, Chrissie. This is hard work."

Sometimes her mother could insult her without realizing it. "I *know* that. I can help, Mom. What do you think—I'll watch television all day? This is a difficult time for you and Grandma."

"It really is." Her mother's voice quavered a little. "I had no idea it would be so difficult."

"Moving Grandma?"

"Yes…"

"Then I can come?" The pleading tone was back, but Chrissie didn't care. She felt it was her right to be with her grandmother.

"Let me talk to your father first."

Chrissie clenched her teeth, not knowing what to expect from him. It would be just like her dad to insist she stay in Seattle. She couldn't; she absolutely couldn't do that. If she had to deal with her brother and father all summer, she'd go crazy. But that wasn't even the issue. Her grandmother needed her and so did her mom, and she needed to be with them. No, the decision was made. Chrissie was going to Colville whether she had permission or not.

CHAPTER

9

The house was eerily quiet as Susannah settled in front of the television. After four very long days, the move was complete. Her mother was about to spend her first night at the assisted-living complex. This single day had felt like an entire month.

The movers had arrived at eight that morning, eager to get the truck loaded. By the time everything had been set up in her tiny four-hundred-square-foot apartment, her mother was exhausted. So was Susannah.

The staff at Altamira had been wonderful. The forms were all signed and delivered, financial arrangements made and Dr. Bethel had given his written instructions. Once her mother had agreed to the move, it was as if everything had fallen naturally into place. In fact, they were fortunate that there'd been a unit available. Another sign, in Susannah's opinion, that this really was meant to be.

It was dark now, after ten, and Susannah should be more than ready to collapse into bed, but her mind wouldn't stop spinning. The house was a shambles. Drawers open, cupboards, too. The floors were littered with remnants of her mother's life and, in many ways, Susannah's own. Emotion was close to the surface and grew closer with every minute.

Susannah realized she should phone her family and then go to bed, but sleep would be impossible. Nor did she feel like escaping into mindless television. She stood and wandered aimlessly from room to room, thinking she should sort through a few things, start packing what had been left. But her back hurt and her heart hurt and she'd never felt more alone.

The whole situation was just so painful. Yes, she knew it was the right decision for all involved—but then why was she feeling this relentless guilt?

The phone rang and she glanced at it, not sure she was up to answering. Her father had believed caller ID was an unnecessary expense so she could only speculate who'd be phoning this late at night. It was probably her daughter, but Susannah didn't have the energy to cope with more of Chrissie's entreaties and complaints. Turning away, she decided not to answer. Then she changed her mind and impulsively grabbed the receiver.

"Hello." She kept her tone as level as possible.

"Hi, it's Carolyn. I'm sorry to call so late but—"

"Carolyn." Susannah didn't bother to disguise her relief. "How'd the move go?"

Susannah leaned against the kitchen wall and wrapped the long cord around her elbow. Her father hadn't believed in cordless phones, either. "Pretty well—except that Mom hates it already. She put on a good front but I could see how unhappy she was."

"I tried phoning a couple of times, and I wondered when there wasn't any answer."

"I stayed with Mom until she went to bed." Susannah stared out the dark kitchen window as she tried to make sense of all the emotions churning inside her. "I couldn't make myself leave. Mom seemed so small and broken—as if her life was over." Tears sprang to her eyes. "I was aware that the move would be difficult for her, but I didn't realize how hard it would be for me." She couldn't restrain a low sob, and it embarrassed her. Susannah wasn't the type of woman who gave in to tears easily and yet here she was, an emotional mess.

"Is there anything I can do?" Carolyn asked.

Susannah was grateful for her friend's sympathy. "No... it's just that I feel so awful about doing this to Mom, even though I know it was necessary." She paused. "I don't want to be the one making these decisions."

"I was on my own with my mother after Dad died," Carolyn reminded her. "Trust me, I know how hard this is. I didn't need to move Mom into a facility, thankfully, but sometimes I wonder if she might've done better with other women her age." Abruptly changing the subject, she added, "The reason I phoned was to see if you could come for dinner one night next week. Thursday works best for everyone else."

"Everyone else?" Susannah repeated. "Who's everyone?"

"I ran into Sandy Giddings and she mentioned seeing

you at Wal-Mart, so I invited her, along with Yvette Lawton and Lisa Mitchell. Is that okay?"

"Of course!"

Sandy, Lisa and Yvette had been Susannah's best friends through high school. "I didn't know you'd been friends with them, too."

"We're acquaintances more than friends," Carolyn explained, "but I want to connect with the community and this seemed a painless way to get reacquainted."

"It sounds great. Thanks for setting everything up."

"Girls' night out," Carolyn said.

Susannah could use a night to relax with old friends. Although she'd lost touch with these women, she felt excited about seeing them again. Carolyn might need to reconnect with the community, but Susannah needed to connect with her past. That had become clear to her. Sandy, Yvette, Lisa and Carolyn were part of her personal history.

She and Carolyn chatted a few minutes longer and afterward she felt much better. She sat in front of the television again, flicking through channels, but she still couldn't concentrate. Then she went to bed, but it was a long time before she slept.

Her dreams were filled with memories of her childhood, of her mother baking cookies and serving as her Camp Fire Leader. She dreamed of summer walks with her father, going for ice-cream cones—always strawberry for her, vanilla for him. As a judge, he was a community leader and to her, he'd seemed the most wonderful man in the world. Her opinion had changed when she entered high school and she'd discovered how dictatorial and unreasonable he was. She dreamed of the yearly Easter egg hunts she'd participated in as a kid and swimming in the local pool with her friends.

The next morning, the sun shining in her bedroom window woke Susannah. It was a pleasant way to wake up, especially when the clear, bright sunshine was accompanied by the sound of birdsong. She showered and dressed, and made a pot of coffee, drinking her first cup outside. Before leaving to visit her mother, she watered the plants, lingering among the roses for a few minutes and marveling anew at her mother's energy. Vivian might have let other things go, but she'd maintained her garden. Then she loaded the car with a few odds and ends for her mother's new home and headed out.

When she reached Elm Street, Susannah surprised herself by taking a left instead of a right and drove up the road that led to the cemetery. She hadn't been to her father's grave since the funeral. Why she felt the urge to go now, she couldn't say. Perhaps it had to do with her dreams, with her need to revisit the past.

She parked near the entrance—the only car there—and walked between the grave markers to where she'd stood almost seven months earlier. As she moved across the lawn to her father's grave, she remembered his casket being lowered into the ground. The headstone was in place now, her mother's name on the marble slab beside his, along with Vivian's date of birth, followed by a blank space to note her mother's death.

Susannah stood, feeling stiff and uncomfortable, on the freshly watered lawn. "Hi, Dad," she said, her voice a hoarse whisper. "How's it going?" She snickered at this weak attempt at conversation. From her early teenage years, she'd never really had much to say to him. It wasn't any easier now that he was six feet under.

"Mom says you're the one who told her to go into assisted living." Yesterday, her mother had made a point of letting Susannah know the reason for her sudden change of heart.

Susannah slid her shoe over the grass, which was slick and moist beneath her feet. "I suppose I should thank you for that."

Biting her lower lip, she walked two grave markers away but didn't read the names on them. She wanted to leave, to walk back to her car and drive off, but for some reason she couldn't make herself do it.

"You know, Dad, you weren't the easiest man to live with. Mom went along with whatever you wanted, but not me. I know we would've had a better relationship if I'd given in to you, but…I couldn't."

In many ways her father was a tough man, rigid and often uncompromising. He had to be, sitting on the bench, dealing with lawbreakers and…well, lowlifes. Not surprisingly, her father had become emotionally distant, more so after Doug's death.

As clichéd as it seemed, George Leary had favored his only son. After her brother died, it was as if the sun had permanently disappeared from her father's world. Their relationship had been strained before her brother's fatal car accident, but had deteriorated even further afterward. The truth was, her father hadn't loved her as much as he had Doug.

Susannah gasped at that realization, pain spiraling through her. She clenched her hands into tight fists. That was it, although she'd never acknowledged it before. Doug, his precious son, was dead and she'd been a damn poor replacement.

With Doug's death, this branch of the Leary family had died out. Her uncle Henry had never married; Uncle Steve died on D-Day. That left only Doug to carry on the family name and he was gone. Gone, too, were her father's dreams.

She was fifty years old and it had taken her this long to figure it out. In one of their recent conversations, Joe had suggested Susannah make an appointment with a counselor to help her deal with her father's death. At the time she'd dismissed the suggestion. Today, however, she was beginning to think there might be some benefit to discussing her feelings.

"When you died, I thought that if we'd had a chance to talk...to sort everything out," Susannah whispered, "it would've been better for us both. I wanted to tell you how sorry I was and now...now I wonder if it would've done any good. You were so set in your ways, so self-righteous."

Tears streaked her cheeks and she brushed them aside, angry that her father still had the power to reduce her to this. "I wanted to talk to you, but I know that was impossible."

She circled his grave site, years of anger and frustration building to a fever pitch. "Not once in all the time since I returned from Paris did we have a decent conversation. Didn't that bother you? I was your only surviving child. Didn't you want to *know* me?"

Standing over the grave, she closed her eyes and waited for the ache in her heart to abate. "I wonder if you noticed how rarely Joe and I came to Colville. Did you ever wonder why? No, I don't suppose you did."

Susannah had remained dry-eyed during her father's funeral. Joe claimed her father had loved her deeply, but Susannah believed otherwise. She'd stayed strong for her mother, or so she'd told herself. Now she realized she hadn't allowed herself to grieve, not for the father he'd become or the father he could have been—the father she remembered from early childhood. She couldn't break down for fear that once she started, she might not be able to stop.

As Susannah walked to her car, she was emotionally spent. She battled sorrow and tears, and regretted coming here.

When she reached her parked car, she leaned against the passenger door, trying to compose herself before going to visit her mother. She wasn't up to it this morning. Instead she'd tackle the house, packing what she could, and making some of the decisions that had to be made.

As she got into the car, it occurred to Susannah that she hadn't visited Doug's grave in years. She almost began to cry again as she thought about her brother, who was just a week over twenty-one when he died.

On the way to the cemetery, Susannah had driven around the very curve where his car had gone off the road. From what she'd subsequently learned, he'd been doing in excess of seventy miles an hour when he hit the guardrail and slammed into a tree. Her one wish was that he hadn't suffered. She couldn't bear it if he had.

Susannah needed a few minutes to locate her brother's grave. She wondered again why her father hadn't been buried next to his son. Instead, Doug was five rows up.

Presumably all the grave sites close by had been sold. That must have frustrated her father.

To Susannah's astonishment, lovely pink roses and purple lilacs were arranged in a vase by the headstone. She knew her mother had routinely visited the grave that first year, her grief nearly overwhelming. But to the best of her knowledge, Vivian hadn't been to the cemetery recently and if she had, she would've left flowers at her husband's grave, too.

Susannah crouched down and fingered the delicate petals. The roses, still buds, hadn't been cut more than a few hours ago. She stood and glanced around, wondering if whoever brought them was nearby. As far as Susannah could see, she was alone.

Despite everything she'd told her father, Susannah had little to say to her brother. She smiled down at his grave, blew him a kiss and returned to the car, determined to leave and not come back for a long, long time.

From the cemetery Susannah drove to Safeway, where she picked up packing boxes. Then, feeling she owed her mother a visit, she decided not to postpone it, after all, and drove to Altamira. Her mother sat in her tiny apartment, waiting for her. The minute Susannah walked in, Vivian stretched out her arms, her eyes pleading.

"What took you so long?" she asked in a faltering voice. "I was afraid you weren't going to come."

"I wouldn't do that," Susannah assured her. Taking the fragile, bony hand in her own, Susannah knelt so that the two of them were at eye level. "How did you sleep last night?"

"I didn't. Not a wink."

"Too much noise?"

"No...yes. I don't know and the food here is terrible. You don't expect me to eat cold eggs and dry toast the rest of my life, do you?"

"Mom, give it a chance."

"I hate it already. I know your father thinks I should be here, but I'm telling you right now, Susannah, I want out."

"Two weeks," Susannah reminded her. "You promised me you'd give it your best shot for two weeks."

Reluctantly her mother nodded. "Yes, I know, but I can tell you this isn't going to work."

Susannah prayed with all her might that her mother would change her mind and soon. Because there were no other options.

"Where are my clothes?"

"Mom, we already brought your clothes, don't you remember?"

"What about my purple dress? I need that dress, Jean. You didn't give it away, did you?"

"No, Mom."

"Jean, oh, Jean, what am I going to do?"

Susannah had to bite her tongue to keep from correcting her mother. "I brought everything you asked for."

"I'd be more comfortable if we brought over your father's chair, too," she said next.

Susannah had been afraid of this. "Mom, there isn't room for Dad's chair in here."

Her mother gave a quick shake of her head. "There's plenty of room. I'll just move a few things around and we can set up my sewing machine in the corner."

Her mother hadn't sewed in years. Decades, even. But all Susannah said was, "I'll see what I can do."

"And bring me my books, too."

"I will, Mom." Apparently she was being sent off to do errands. "Did you meet any of the other tenants this morning?"

Vivian lowered her voice. "This place is full of old people. I'm telling you, Susannah, I don't belong here. I swear everyone's at least eighty."

Rather than try to persuade her mother to give the facility a chance, Susannah left to do the errands Vivian had decreed. She was adamant that Susannah find her purple dress, but Susannah couldn't remember seeing one in her mother's closet.

Emotionally drained, she went back to the house. She unlocked the front door and propped open the screen as she dragged in the boxes.

Halfway into the living room, she paused and looked around. Everything looked exactly as she'd left it, but something didn't *feel* right. Except she didn't know exactly what. Standing in the middle of the living room, she felt a chill creep down her spine. She was imagining things, she told herself. And yet...

Drawing in a deep breath, she ventured cautiously into the kitchen.

"Is anyone here?" she cried out.

No one answered.

"Hello?"

Again there was no response.

Heart pounding, Susannah moved from room to room. As far as she could see, nothing was amiss—until she reached Doug's bedroom. Her mother had kept it in pristine condition, hanging his high school graduation picture on the wall, along with an array of ribbons from track meets and other sporting events. They were missing, each and every one of them. For some sick reason, someone had broken into the house and stolen her brother's high school memorabilia.

No matter what the future held, Susannah knew she could never let her mother find out about this.

CHAPTER

10

Susannah didn't know what to make of this strange theft. The fresh flowers on her brother's grave added to the mystery. Then to find that someone had gone through Doug's high school things... It wasn't only his ribbons that were missing, either. A couple of other things—a souvenir from Disneyland, a Beatles album, seemingly unimportant mementoes of his too-short life—had simply disappeared. Perhaps her mother had given them away, but Susannah doubted that. Anything of Doug's was precious and treasured by both her parents.

Years ago, Brian had asked if he could have Doug's old baseball cards and her father had refused. Susannah had fumed about that for weeks. Now they appeared to be missing, as well.

Doing her best to ignore the nagging worries, she packed what was left in her mother's closet, which took most of the afternoon. She put aside a few additional outfits for Vivian, although the purple dress did not come to light. Her one real find was an old journal her mother had started in 1951, shortly after Doug was born. The fake leather front had cracked over the years. It had a tiny lock without a key, but Susannah tested the fastening, and it sprang open as if waiting to share its secrets.

She held the open book in her hand for the longest time, wondering if she dared read it. Deciding it would be an invasion of her mother's privacy, she set the palm-size diary on the dresser.

More than likely her mother didn't even remember that she'd kept a journal. But then her mother remembered the oddest things.

By the time she'd finished clearing out the closet, packing clothes and shoes into boxes for Goodwill, Susannah was ready for a break. Her mother hadn't worn any of this stuff in years, but she'd only scraped the surface—there were two chests of drawers in the bedroom, plus shelves, a dresser…. This wasn't promising.

The phone rang just as she was about to make herself some tea.

"Mom!" her daughter cried. "Where's the curry powder?"

"What do you need curry for?"

"A recipe," Chrissie said. "I was watching a show on the Food Channel and I decided to make curried chicken but it calls for curry powder and I'm supposed to add it *now*."

Susannah refrained from mentioning that curried chicken obviously needed curry power and she should have gotten it out earlier. "Look on the shelf next to the refrigerator."

"I already did. It's not there. This is *important,* Mom. Dinner will be ruined without it."

Chrissie's tone suggested that the world would come to an end if she didn't locate the curry powder within thirty seconds.

"Try the next shelf up. If I have it at all, it'd be there."

"Okay." The word was smothered as if Chrissie had pressed the receiver against her shoulder.

Susannah could hear tins and bottles being shuffled around, followed by an exclamation of victory. "Thanks, Mom. See ya." With that, the phone went dead.

"Glad to be of service," Susannah muttered as she set the phone back in place. This was the first display of enthusiasm she'd seen from Chrissie since her return home. Joe hadn't given a definite answer to their daughter's request about visiting Colville, but apparently Chrissie had accepted the fact that she was needed at home. That was fine with Susannah. While she'd welcome help with the house, Chrissie would be a distraction, too.

As she put on water for a pot of tea, Susannah felt a sense of pride that her husband and children were managing without her. Her kids were maturing, assuming more responsibility.

Sitting at the kitchen table a few minutes later, with her tea steeping, she remembered the old diary she'd discovered. It'd been buried in a hat box, tucked away years ago and forgotten. Still feeling guilty about her interest, she brought it out of the bedroom and set it on the table next to the ceramic teapot and tiny pitcher of milk.

Susannah stared at the diary, afraid she might learn things about her parents she'd rather not know—and yet she was intensely curious. It wasn't hers to read, she reminded herself. This was her mother's private property. Then Susannah remembered that her mother had read *her* diary. Shortly afterward, Susannah had been shipped off to boarding school. Turnabout was fair play, she decided, squelching the guilt.

She opened the book and saw that her mother had used a fountain pen to record her thoughts. It was a five-year diary with only a few lines for each day. Vivian had maintained it faithfully through those years, as if not entering the day's activities would've been wasteful. The blue ink had darkened but remained completely legible. As always, Susannah admired her mother's penmanship, the beautifully rounded letters sloping gently to the right.

April 3, 1957
George took Doug to his Little League practice and then pitched balls to him for an hour afterward. It did my heart good to see how much my husband loves his son and how much Dougie loves his dad.

Susannah recalled how often her brother and father had practiced together. She'd felt a little left out and... unimportant.

June 20, 1957
I talked to George again about going to nursing school, but with the children so young he feels my place is here at home. I tried to tell him that lots of women are working outside the home these days, but he wouldn't listen. I know I'd be a good nurse. George

is right, although I can't help wishing I'd gone into nursing school instead of marrying so young. But with the war...

Susannah frowned. Her mother had wanted to be a nurse? This was news to her. In all her years of growing up, Susannah couldn't recollect one word about her mother having—or wanting—a career, nursing or otherwise. Everything had centered on her father and his role as a judge.

Now that she thought about it, however, Susannah remembered how tender and caring her mother had been anytime she or Doug was sick. When he was ten, Doug had broken his arm in a tumble from his bicycle. It had been a bad break, but their mother had remained calm and gotten Doug to the hospital, where he'd required immediate surgery to have the bone reset. Her mother was a natural caregiver, and yet this one desire had been denied her.

Upset by what she'd read, Susannah flipped the pages to another section.

November 11, 1958
Both children have tonsillitis. The doctor thinks we should schedule surgery as soon as possible. This seems a somewhat drastic procedure to me. I worry about what might happen. I've read everything I could find at the library and was unsettled more than reassured. I talked to George after dinner, but his mind was on a court case. I don't think he heard a word I said. He says I worry too much. Perhaps I do, but surgery, especially for Susannah, who's so easily susceptible to ear infections, concerns me.

As it turned out, Vivian had been right. After the procedure, Susannah had developed an infection and ended up in the hospital for five days. Her memory of that time was cloudy. She did have a vivid image of her mother sitting by her bedside, holding her hand throughout the ordeal.

Distressed, Susannah put the journal aside and poured her tea. Her hand trembled slightly as she added milk and stirred. After the first sip, she reached for the diary again. The next entries all described mundane events—shopping trips, housecleaning, planting bulbs in her garden.

Susannah put down the diary and held her teacup in both hands as she considered what she'd read. In retrospect, she felt she shouldn't have looked at her mother's journal. Only that morning, she'd been bemoaning the fact that she'd never really known her father and now she was learning that she didn't really know Vivian, either.

After a dinner of peanut butter on toast, Susannah drove back to Altamira to see her mother.

"Good evening," Rose, who manned the front desk, greeted her as she walked in the door.

"I'm not arriving in the middle of dinner, am I?"

"Goodness, no. Dinner is served at five."

Susannah knew that, but she'd been so involved with the diary she hadn't noticed the time. The main meal of the day was at twelve, with a light supper in the afternoon.

She saw that several of the residents had congregated in the main room off the entry and an older gentleman sat at the piano, playing Broadway tunes. Five women, two in wheelchairs, nodded their heads to the music. Another wheelchair-bound woman had fallen asleep.

Susannah was sad that her mother wasn't in the audience.

It would help if Vivian made an effort to meet the others, but so far she hadn't revealed the slightest bit of interest or cooperation.

Determined to do everything within her means to help Vivian adjust, Susannah walked down the long carpeted hallway to her mother's suite. The door was closed. She tapped lightly but didn't wait for a response before stepping inside.

Vivian sat in her favorite chair in front of the television, her back to Susannah.

"You can take the tray," she muttered, apparently assuming that Susannah was an assistant.

Susannah glanced at the tray, still waiting on a small table near the door. As far as she could tell, Vivian hadn't touched her dinner.

"Mom."

"Oh, Susannah…" She twisted around in her chair. "I thought it was the girl."

"You haven't eaten."

Her mother rose awkwardly to her feet, keeping one hand on the back of the chair for balance. "I wasn't hungry."

"Why not?" Susannah eyed the minestrone soup and fruit plate and found them artfully displayed. The meals at Altamira were good, and nothing like the institutional food one would expect.

"I'm just not," Vivian grumbled. "Your father told me I should move here, but I don't like it."

"Sit down and I'll bring your dinner," Susannah suggested.

She set up a television tray once Vivian had returned to her chair. As soon as she was settled, Susannah brought her the fruit plate. "I'll warm up the soup in the microwave," she said.

To Susannah's delight, her mother ate every bit of her meal. Soon afterward the assistant arrived and removed the tray. For the next hour, Susannah and her mother sat side by side and watched two game shows in silence.

"Mom," Susannah said when *Jeopardy* ended, "I didn't know you wanted to be a nurse."

Her mother's gaze slid to hers. "Who told you that?"

"I, ah...I came across something you'd written. While I was packing up the rest of your closet," she explained quickly, gliding over the fact that the "something" had been her mother's diary.

"I did consider it at one time," Vivian admitted, reluctance in her voice.

"Why didn't you?" Susannah felt disappointed for her mother but tried not to let it show.

Vivian considered the question. "Your father didn't think it was a good idea, and he was right. A few years after that, George was appointed to the bench and our lives changed. He had a civic responsibility and I did, too."

"You would've been a wonderful nurse," Susannah said, careful to hide her emotions.

Vivian gazed at her thoughtfully. "Perhaps I would. Your father and I talked about it more than once, especially before he accepted the appointment. He realized his new role in the community would be almost as demanding on me," she continued. "He asked me to stay home while you children were young. I agreed. That wasn't the time for me to pursue a career, and then later, well...later I made the decision to stand with him, to be his helpmate. Being available to George and supporting his career was more important to me. It meant I was available to you children, too."

"Do you have any regrets?"

Vivian smiled. "Not even one. Everyone makes choices in life, Susannah. Your father earned a good living, and we were fortunate that I didn't need to work. I saw it as a blessing—and I still do. I volunteered at the blood bank, you know, and I was able to work in my garden."

Susannah wasn't so sure *blessing* was the appropriate word.

"Your father and I were partners. You were always so eager to paint him as a villain and, my dear, he was never that. George was a good man, a loving husband, a wonderful father."

Susannah swallowed her arguments. The family *was* fortunate that Vivian could be home for them all. If she'd ever felt cheated about not going into nursing, it had never showed. But Susannah felt cheated for her, and the opportunity she'd lost.

CHAPTER

The afternoon was cool and breezy as Carolyn arrived back at the mill, parking in her assigned spot. She'd attended a very successful meeting in Spokane with a buyer from a major hardware chain, and all that remained now was finishing up the relevant paperwork.

Her long single braid stretched halfway down her back, swaying as she walked. She wore an unaccustomed suit, a plain navy one with a straight skirt and classically styled jacket. With her white shirt and flat black pumps, Carolyn's "go to meeting" outfit was complete. She couldn't wait to peel off the panty hose. Since she never had any idea what to do with her hair, she'd left it in its usual braid. She could only imagine what her fashionable mother would think if she could see her now. When it came to the feminine arts, Carolyn had failed miserably. The second she got to her office, she changed into jeans, boots and a cotton shirt.

Gloria, her personal assistant, had obviously left early for some reason. That was fine, since she put in whatever hours the job—and Carolyn—required.

As soon as Carolyn finished with the paperwork, she planned to head home herself, since she had company coming for dinner. Inviting Susannah, Sandy, Lisa and Yvette to the house was a giant leap into the public sphere for her. Carolyn had never socialized much; because of her position as Colville's main employer, it was risky. Her father had often cautioned her about getting too close to any one family. Still, none of those women was associated with the mill in any way.

With her responsibility to the business always in mind, she'd kept mostly to herself since her return, forgoing friendships. At times she was lonely, but a sense of duty had been bred into her. She didn't resent her position; she took it seriously. This mill contributed significantly to the local economy, which meant the decisions she made affected the town as a whole.

Paperwork done, Carolyn walked into the yard, where the lumber was stacked ten feet high. Sprinklers continually kept the wood wet and cool. A fire could do massive damage, and every measure was taken to protect the raw lumber. The year before, she'd purchased a new lumber stacker for the cut wood, one that minimized operating costs. With new machinery in place, including the stacker, her goal was to produce approximately 50,000 cubic meters of quality lumber annually. No small goal, but she'd set her sights on that figure and had everything she needed to make it a reality.

When he saw her, Carolyn's plant manager, Jim Reynolds,

hurried toward her with a clipboard in his hand. She relied on Jim, who was directly below her in the chain of command. He was much more than her manager; he was her right-hand man, with a drive and ambition that matched her own. Thanks to his years of working at the mill, the men respected his judgment—and respected him. Carolyn didn't make a move without consulting Jim first.

Ten years younger than Carolyn, he was tall, muscular and tanned from all the time he'd spent outside. He was happily married and had three kids, two of whom were about to enter college. Jim was a dedicated, honorable man. Carolyn was grateful that he worked for her and paid him a salary that was commensurate with his value to the business.

"How'd the meeting go?" Jim asked as he approached.

"We have a deal."

"Hey!" Jim nodded approvingly, giving her a thumbs-up. "Congratulations."

Jim knew as well as she did that this new plywood order would carry them through the summer. It was the first time Carolyn had cracked this hardware chain. She started to relate the details when he interrupted.

"We nearly lost Grady Simpson this afternoon."

"What happened?" Carolyn was instantly concerned. Grady had worked at the mill when her father was still alive. He was close to retirement age and had always been a solid employee.

"Heart attack."

"Is he going to be all right?"

"Looks like it."

Relief flowed through Carolyn.

"But he would've been a goner if it wasn't for the quick thinking of that guy who does the landscaping."

Carolyn knew he worked for Kettle Falls Landscaping, the company she hired for the upkeep of the gardens here and her yard at home. She'd used them for the past three years and they'd done an adequate job. She'd never had any complaints, but the new gardener, who'd started about four months ago, was exceptional. He was conscientious, hardworking and punctual; equally important, he understood plants. No one had done a better job on her yard than Dave Langevin. He'd impressed her enough for Carolyn to ask his name.

"You'd better begin at the beginning," she said.

"Grady was on the stacker when he keeled over. God only knows what might've happened if that guy hadn't been mowing the lawn." The office had a small yard with some shrubs and basic flower beds, which required routine maintenance. "Before anyone else realized what was going on, this guy—Dave's his name—got to Grady."

"I know Dave Langevin," Carolyn said casually.

Jim finished the story, succinctly describing what had happened. "He administered CPR until the paramedics arrived. The EMT said Grady would've been dead without Dave's help."

Carolyn hadn't seen the landscaping truck in the parking lot. "Has he left? I'd like to thank him."

"I thought you might, but he said he had some other work that needed to be done today. As soon as he saw that Grady was in good hands, he went back to mowing the lawn and took off shortly afterward."

Carolyn would seek him out later and thank him. "It sounds like you had an exciting afternoon."

"We did," Jim concurred wryly. "But I can live without that kind of excitement."

Carolyn agreed. "I'll have Gloria check on Grady so you can let everyone know how he's doing." Gloria, her assistant, was about as organized as they come. Her father had drilled into Carolyn the importance of surrounding herself with competent employees, and it was probably the most valuable lesson he'd taught her.

Jim revealed a hint of a smile. "Gloria's already on it."

Carolyn should've guessed as much.

"Grady might need heart surgery later," Jim said, "but for now the danger has passed."

"I'm grateful for that," she said as she headed toward her car.

"Gloria's arranged for flowers to be sent and she's taken care of the insurance stuff." He gestured toward the office. "She left early to meet Grady's family at the hospital."

"Good. I wondered where she'd gone."

"You can always count on Gloria," he said warmly. Reverting to a more businesslike tone, he added, "I'll have an accident report on your desk first thing in the morning."

"Thanks." Carolyn turned back, deciding to spend another half hour at the office. Her dinner preparations were under control and her house was clean. "If you see Dave before I do, would you tell him I'd like to talk to him?"

Jim smiled and promised he would.

Carolyn had been walking on air after closing the deal, but this near-disaster had brought her back to earth fast enough. Strolling beside Jim, she'd almost reached the office when he commented, "I've seen Dave around and I like his work ethic."

"I do, too." She didn't mention that her yard at the house hadn't looked this good in years.

"I offered him a job."

That had been Carolyn's intention. She was grateful for his quick action in saving Grady's life; his decisiveness and commitment made him the kind of employee she wanted at the mill. Whatever she invested in training him would be worth it.

"He thanked me for the offer," Jim continued, "but said he liked his current job just fine. I told him what his starting wage would be and I'm sure it's more than he's making now, but he wasn't interested."

Carolyn didn't know whether she should be disappointed or gratified on behalf of her garden. She was pleased with the work he was doing, but surprised that he'd walked away from a job offer that would likely double his income.

She shrugged. "It's his choice."

"I think he drifts around a lot," Jim said. "I asked him where he was from and he told me he'd been living in California, and before that, Arizona and that he picked fruit in Yakima for a season. I've met men like him before. They don't put down roots."

Carolyn nodded, inhaling deeply. Ponderosa pine and fir scented the afternoon air. As a child, she'd loved the smell of her father's clothes. Now her own shirts carried the same woodsy fragrance. To her, it was more enticing than the most exotic perfume.

They turned the corner just as the whistle blew. All

around her the crew shut down their machines and, within moments, the buildings and yards emptied as men sauntered past, their black lunch boxes in hand. She enjoyed the sound of their talk and laughter, and the fact that they acknowledged her with nods or waves.

Carolyn ended up staying for an extra hour. She finished reading through her e-mail, checked on Grady's condition—which was improving—and then closed her computer before going home.

As she made her way down the long driveway, she noticed the landscaping truck parked outside her house. The bed was loaded with beauty bark, which Dave Langevin had begun spreading over her flower beds. Carolyn was pleased to see him.

She parked in the garage, then stepped out of her vehicle and walked toward him.

Dave was a middle-aged man with dark hair, callused hands and deep-set dark eyes. He wore nondescript work clothes and a big straw hat that shaded his face. As she drew closer, he thrust his shovel into the earth and leaned against the handle.

"I didn't realize you'd be here," she said.

He wiped the back of one hand across his brow. "Your housekeeper said you were having dinner guests, and I wanted to get this beauty bark spread before they arrived."

It was thoughtful of him, and unexpected. "Thank you," she said simply, feeling a bit awkward. "And thank you for your help this afternoon at the mill. Jim told me what you did."

Dave seemed almost embarrassed by her praise. "No big deal."

"I doubt Grady thinks that. Jim said you saved his life."

Dave stared down at the ground, then pulled out the shovel. "Better get back to work," he said tersely.

"I understand, but I wanted you to know I appreciate what you did. Thank you again, Dave."

He seemed surprised that she knew who he was. For a long moment, he held her gaze. "You're welcome... Carolyn."

Just the way he said her name made her look at him again, really look at him. When she saw that her scrutiny unsettled him, she turned and hurried into the house. The oddest sensation settled in the pit of her stomach. The last time she'd felt anything like this had been the day she'd met her husband, her long-divorced husband. There'd been a powerful physical attraction between them and she felt the same thing now, with this man. This groundskeeper who'd let it be known that he was a drifter. She was attracted to Dave Langevin. It was an uncomfortable sensation, one that left her vulnerable and alarmed. At her age and in her position, she couldn't afford to be interested in romance. And yet, there was something about him.... Responsibility, common sense—and lack of time—won out, otherwise she would've invited him in or found an excuse for him to linger. But knowing her dinner guests would be coming soon saved her from making a fool of herself.

Despite her wariness, Carolyn studied Dave from inside the house. After ten or fifteen minutes, he walked over to his pickup truck and stored his equipment on the passenger seat. He opened the driver's door and then, as if aware of her surveillance, he paused and looked over his shoulder at her.

Embarrassed, Carolyn ducked away from the window

and into the shadows, mortified that he'd caught her watching him.

Touching the rim of his large straw hat, he climbed into the truck and drove off. As he rumbled down the driveway Carolyn couldn't shake the feeling that—if she were to allow it, if she were to seek it—Dave Langevin would be interested in her, too.

Susannah no longer felt sociable, but it was too late to cancel out of dinner with Carolyn and the others. Dreading the evening, she sat at the table in her mother's kitchen and tried to relax. Vivian hadn't had a good afternoon and Susannah felt guilty about leaving her, guilty for having read her mother's private thoughts and then questioning her as if she had the right. Susannah blamed herself for Vivian's melancholy mood, which seemed to reflect her own dissatisfaction with life. She'd made a mistake in reminding her mother of unattained dreams; a bigger mistake was bringing it up again today.

She'd mentioned searching for Jake to Carolyn but she'd done nothing, fearing…she didn't know what. Fearing, she guessed, what she might feel once she found him. If she found him. It was quite possibly the most inane idea of her life and still she couldn't let it go, couldn't get the thought of him out of her mind.

Because she was dissatisfied with her own life, Susannah had questioned her mother about the choices Vivian had made. She should've known better. Her mother had grown even more irritable than she'd been last night, claiming that Susannah was looking for excuses to vilify her father.

That simply wasn't true. All she'd wanted her mother to do was acknowledge the truth. Twice, in two different journal entries, Vivian had written about her desire to enter a nursing program and both times she'd been thwarted by George. Now her mother insisted a nursing career hadn't been that important.

Because of Susannah's questions, it had been an awkward visit; she felt bad about that. Later Vivian had refused to eat her dinner and lain down for a nap instead.

The rest of Susannah's day had been spent working. She'd rented storage space and started taking packed cardboard boxes to the unit for safekeeping until she decided what to do with the house. More and more, Susannah realized her mother was incapable of making even the most mundane decisions. Like everything else, this would be up to her. In a midday phone conversation, Joe had suggested that renting storage space might be the best solution for now. He was right and Susannah had immediately called to arrange it. She appreciated the advice but felt he didn't understand the emotional difficulties she was facing.

Susannah was not only dealing with her mother, she was sorting through a lifetime of accumulated *things*. It seemed her mother had never discarded a single dish or piece of clothing, and her father wasn't much better. For decades, she'd largely avoided her father and now, every time she opened a drawer, there he was. The memories of her teenage years made her uncomfortable. Because he was a judge, he felt he could dictate everyone's life, whether he had a gavel in hand or not.

After talking to her husband, Susannah found she was annoyed with him, too, unreasonable though that might be. He was in Seattle, living his normal, predictable life, and she was stuck in Colville. She didn't *want* to decide what to do with Aunt Sophie's handknit bedspread or her father's stamp collection. It was easy for Joe to sit at home and make helpful suggestions, she thought bitterly. Susannah knew he was only trying to be supportive, but at this point she doubted there was much he could do or say that would satisfy her—and that bothered her, too. Almost overnight she'd turned into someone she didn't know or like. Even spending time in her mother's garden hadn't calmed her the way it usually did. In fact, she'd come away irritated all over again. How was it that her mother couldn't manage the simplest of household tasks and yet kept her garden in pristine condition? It was as if Vivian had let everything slide except her garden—her life, her appearance, her mind were just about gone, but not her garden. No, not her precious garden.

Sitting at the kitchen table, Susannah buried her face in her hands. She was upset with her father and her husband, and now she'd added her mother to the list, and Doug, too. If her brother were alive, she wouldn't have to cope with all these painful decisions alone. She knew it was a fruitless thought, but she couldn't stop feeling that way. She wished she could be seventeen again, before the year that changed everything. The year of Doug's death and Jake's disappearance. If she was, she wouldn't think twice about eloping.

More than that, she'd leap at the chance. Oh, to be young again, to be in love with the fervor and intensity of youth. Only this time, she'd defy her father, stand up to him and run away with the man she loved.

At six-thirty, Susannah pulled into Carolyn's long gravel driveway and, as if by magic, her unease left her. She'd loved this house as a young teenager. Tucked against the foothills, it had a lush green lawn that sloped down from the tree line into a soft meadow. Many a late afternoon had been spent with Carolyn, listening to records in her upstairs bedroom and looking out her window, watching the deer graze.

The house itself was a brown-shingled two-story with a sweeping porch across the front. A profusion of roses bloomed in the beds nearby. It was a shame that Carolyn's mother and her own had never become friends, since they'd shared a love of gardening. A large cement patio was positioned on the right-hand side of the house, complete with a set of matching outdoor furniture.

Susannah parked by the three-car garage and reached for her contributions: a package that contained the makings for a Caesar salad and a bottle of wine she'd picked up at the grocery store on her way out of town. She felt a twinge of guilt about bringing something store-bought, but between packing up the house and visiting her mother, there hadn't been time to prepare anything.

The front door was open and the screen unlatched when Susannah approached.

"Come on in," Carolyn called from the kitchen.

Susannah walked inside. Her friend was assembling an

appetizer plate of cheeses, fresh green grapes and crackers, which sat on the marble counter.

"I brought wine," Susannah said, holding up the bottle of white zinfandel. She placed the bag of Caesar salad fixings on the table.

"Great." Carolyn motioned toward the cupboard. "Wineglasses are on the top shelf. And you'll find a bowl in the bottom cupboard."

Susannah quickly prepared her salad. She'd begun setting out wineglasses when the sound of two car doors closing interrupted her.

A moment later, two of Susannah's high school friends walked in together, each carrying a dish and a bottle of wine. From the way Lisa and Yvette looked around, it was clear they'd never been inside the house. Susannah came forward to meet them, and as soon as they saw her, they both started screeching with delight.

Once they'd put the desserts and the wine aside, Susannah was wrapped in a giant hug and questions were tossed at her in quick succession.

"How long will you be in town?"

"Where have you *been?*"

"Why weren't you at the last reunion?"

Before she could answer one question, another presented itself.

"Give her a break, will you?" Sandy Giddings said as she entered the house. She plunked her bottle of wine and a pan of homemade brownies on the kitchen counter. Carolyn brought a huge spinach salad out of the refrigerator and tossed it, letting it wait on the table beside Susannah's.

"I thought we'd eat outside," she said. Carrying the cheese

platter, she led the way to the sliding glass door that opened onto the patio. The round table was covered with colorful place mats and the umbrella positioned to block out the setting sun.

The five women chatted and laughed nonstop through the appetizers, followed by a dinner of salads, creamy stroganoff with buttered noodles and fresh green beans. They lingered over their desserts—Sandy's rich chocolate brownies, berry pie and warm apple crisp with ice cream. Then they cleared the table and returned outside with their glasses of wine, comfortable in the waning sun.

"This is so much fun," Yvette said with a contented sigh. "I can't tell you the last time I had a ladies' night out."

"Me, neither," Sandy chimed in.

They pulled their chairs into a small circle as they caught up with each others' news.

"So you've got two children?" Lisa asked, looking at Susannah.

She nodded.

"I love your ring," Yvette commented. "Is it from your husband?"

Susannah's gaze dropped to the emerald. "Joe got it for me on our twentieth anniversary."

"Ben and I go way back, too," Yvette said, tossing her long blond hair over her shoulder. "But I didn't get an emerald ring on *our* anniversary."

Susannah laughed and then frowned. The last she'd heard, Yvette had married Kenny Lincoln shortly after high school. "I thought you and Kenny—"

Yvette interrupted her. "We divorced two years later. Kenny got into drugs."

"I'm sorry." Susannah didn't want to dredge up unpleas-ant memories.

Yvette raised her eyebrows. "I knew he was experiment-ing with the stuff when we got married, but turned a blind eye to it. The last I heard, he was doing time in Shelton."

Susannah couldn't imagine the athletic Kenny Lincoln behind bars.

"Thankfully I was smart enough to get out of the mar-riage before we had kids. Then I married Ben in 1978."

They paused and sipped their wine.

"Jake Presley was your high school sweetheart, wasn't he?" Sandy asked Susannah.

Funny that Jake's name would come up so easily. The truth was, she didn't want to think about him. Not right now. Not when he'd been with her for weeks, taking over her dreams and her thoughts. "Yes," she said simply.

"Didn't he go out with Sharon Nance?" Lisa asked.

"They broke up," Yvette reminded her.

"Right." Lisa nodded at the memory. "As I recall, she wasn't too pleased about it, either."

Sandy glanced at Susannah, her expression puzzled. "So what happened to Jake? Where is he now?"

Susannah shrugged casually. "I don't really know. He moved the year I was in France."

"You've got to be kidding," Yvette said, clearly taken aback by the news. "Didn't he write?"

"In the beginning, but it didn't last long."

"But I thought—"

Before she'd left for France, Susannah had told her friends that when she returned she'd be marrying Jake. It had sounded wildly romantic and she'd meant it. Except that when she came home, Jake was gone.

"I tried to find him," Susannah admitted.

"What about his dad?" Lisa asked. "He must've known where Jake was. Or did he leave, too?"

"As far as I can tell, they both moved out of town." She raised her wineglass to her lips. Feeling warm and relaxed, she murmured, "I wish I knew where he went and why he never answered my letters." She sighed. "When I was seventeen, I was so sure that Jake and I were meant to be."

"The path not taken," Lisa said. "I think about that sometimes, you know."

"Okay." Susannah pointed at Lisa with her wineglass. "What's yours?"

"My untraveled path?" Lisa looked away in embarrassment. Slowly she shook her head, as if she regretted bringing up the subject.

"Come on," Susannah urged. "You've got one. We all do."

"What about you?" Sandy asked Carolyn.

Carolyn hesitated, then said, "Yeah, me, too."

"I'll tell if you do."

Everyone turned to stare at Carolyn, who didn't seem especially confident. "You tell first and then maybe I will."

Susannah reached for the half-filled bottle of white zinfandel and replenished Carolyn's glass. "Oh, you'll talk."

They giggled as if they were sixteen again.

"Go on," Susannah said. "Lisa, you start, okay?"

Lisa's face reddened. "You'll think I'm an idiot."

"We won't," they all insisted.

Again Lisa looked away, then picked up her wineglass

and drank the last two swallows. When she'd finished she set the glass down. "You probably all think it's some dark secret and it isn't. I just wish I'd gone to college, but I didn't have the marks to qualify for a scholarship."

She stared out into the distance, but Susannah was convinced that she wasn't watching the deer that wandered timidly down into the grassy meadow.

"My dad said if anyone in our family went to college, it would be my little brother. He was the one who'd be supporting a family, not me."

"Don't you just cringe every time you hear someone talk like that?" Susannah muttered. "I mean, it's such a dated idea but I'm sure it still exists."

"The thing is, I could've gone. In my heart of hearts I know that Mom would've fought to get me into a community college if I'd asked. Instead, I got a job with the telephone company, where I still work."

"What did you want to be?"

"That's just it," Lisa explained. "I don't know, but I wanted the chance to learn and discover who I am. All I needed to do was tell my mother how badly I wanted to continue my education, and yet I didn't say a word."

"Why not?" Carolyn asked. "Did you ever figure out what held you back?"

Lisa nodded. "I've thought about that a lot over the years. Mainly it's because I was eager to get out on my own and be independent. If I took the job with the phone company, I'd have the freedom to make my own decisions about life. I wanted out of the family home and I didn't want to be under my parents' control anymore. I realize now that I wasn't gaining nearly as much as I was giving up."

"What about your brother?" Susannah asked. She vaguely remembered Lisa's little brother. "Did he go on to college?"

Lisa nodded. "He attended the University of Washington for one year and flunked out."

Susannah groaned.

"The irony is that I'm the sole support of my family. Bill died of cancer five years ago, and now it's just me and the kids. In another year it'll be me alone."

They were quiet as they all took this in.

"Your turn," Lisa said, turning to Yvette.

"You already know the path I took. More of a detour, really. I wish I hadn't married Ken. When I think back, I knew it was a mistake, but I was so young and naive that I went ahead with the wedding, anyway."

"That's what I did," Carolyn said. "I married the wrong man."

"So is Jake Presley the path you didn't take?" Lisa directed the question to Susannah.

Susannah leaned back in her chair and thought about her life. Despite her youthful love for Jake, she hadn't married the wrong man. Joe was a good husband and she had a good life. She loved her family, her home, her garden. She enjoyed teaching—but then why was she counting the years until retirement? Still, that was a question for another day.

"I'm not sure," she hedged, and then decided she should be honest with her friends. "Yes, I guess he is." She was silent for a moment. "Recently I sometimes wonder if I should've married Jake."

"I thought you said you didn't know where he was."

"I don't mean after I returned from Europe, but before." She glanced around and saw that her four friends were staring at her with wide, questioning eyes. Smiling, she sipped her wine. "The night before I left, I sneaked out of the house to meet Jake. He begged me to drive to Idaho with him so the two of us could get married." She'd had no idea that would be the last time she'd ever see him.

Her friends squealed with shock. Everyone had heard about young lovers who'd done exactly that. There was no waiting period in Idaho, and it was possible to go to a justice of the peace and be married by morning.

"You told him no?" Yvette seemed to find that hard to believe even now.

"I think every girl in school was half in love with Jake Presley," Lisa confided. "He was such a bad boy, and there wasn't one of us who wouldn't have given our eyeteeth to tame him."

Susannah's voice was filled with regret. "I tried to get him to wait, but it didn't work." All she had to do was close her eyes to remember how handsome Jake had looked in his black leather jacket. He was the epitome of cool.

"You never, ever heard from him after you came back? Not even once?" Lisa asked.

"I hoped he'd search for me, but he didn't," Susannah confessed. At least not that she knew of. Susannah wouldn't put it past her father to lie about Jake. All through college she'd waited, certain Jake would find her, certain he loved her, certain that eventually they'd be together. When she reached her mid-twenties, she gave up and married Joe.

The silence nearly undid her. "I have a wonderful husband, don't get me wrong," she rushed to add. "My kids are great and almost grown up. This is the best time of my life."

She didn't quite believe her own words, even though everything she'd said *should* be true. Chrissie and Brian would soon leave and establish their own lives—but just as she was about to relinquish one responsibility, she faced another.

Her mother needed her, depended on her. It felt as if Susannah had gone back to the days when her children were young, only in this instance the child was her mother.

"Carolyn," Susannah said, getting to her feet, eager now to change the subject. "Let me help you with the dishes."

"Nonsense."

"Remember Mr. Fogleman?" Sandy asked softly. Up until now, she'd remained suspiciously quiet. Susannah sat back down.

"The algebra teacher?" Susannah recalled that he'd been strict and unbending. She'd barely pulled a B in his class her junior year. One good thing about living in France was that she hadn't ended up in another of Fogleman's algebra classes.

"I had the biggest crush on him."

"Mr. Fogleman?" Lisa gasped. "Old Fogey Fogleman?" She thrust out her wineglass. "I need a refill."

Carolyn grabbed the wine bottle to replenish her goblet.

"I used to leave notes on his windshield."

"You didn't?"

Sandy blushed. "Really risqué notes."

"You *signed* them?" Yvette shrieked out the question.

"Not on your life." She laughed. "He knew, though."

"How?"

Sandy cupped her mouth with her hand to hide a smile. "He gave me an A—when I deserved a D."

"Are you joking?"

"I'm not." She took a big gulp of wine. "Mom said a man

called and asked for me shortly after I graduated and deep down I feel it must've been Mr. Fogleman."

"What makes you think that?" Susannah noticed that the others had leaned forward, listening intently.

"Mom said it was a rather strange phone call. It almost seemed as if he was happy I wasn't home."

"Whatever happened to Mr. Fogleman?" Lisa wanted to know.

"He transferred to Spokane High School after that one year in Colville."

"You should look him up," Lisa urged.

Sandy shook her head. "I'm a happily married woman, or at least I was until tonight."

More giggles followed. "Good grief, here we are pining after the missed opportunities of our youth," Carolyn said.

"We're all around fifty and we're still afraid," Lisa added.

Only she wasn't, Susannah realized. "I don't know why I didn't look harder for Jake," she said, angry with herself.

"Your dad would've had a conniption," Carolyn reminded her.

"True, but by then I wouldn't have cared. I was eighteen and I could stand up to him."

"What about now?" Yvette asked. "What would you do if you ran into Jake now?"

That gave her pause. "I…I don't know."

"*I* know," Carolyn insisted. "I'd march right up to him and ask why he stopped writing to you!"

Susannah laughed with her friends, but she had to wonder what she'd do if she did meet Jake again after all these years.

Susannah arrived home from Carolyn's house at close to midnight. The evening had given her exactly the infusion of energy she needed. The discontent she'd been feeling for months was affecting her marriage—and that might be one of the reasons she'd started to dream about Jake.

Susannah sincerely hoped this time apart would revive her relationship with her husband. But right now, pleasantly tired and with her spirits high, she didn't want to think about her mother or Joe or anything else. She unlocked the front door and stepped into the dark house. Even before she turned on the light, she froze, instinct taking over. Flipping the switch, she quickly surveyed the room. Someone had been in the house. The first thing she noticed was that the pillows on the sofa weren't the way they'd been left. Her mother had always propped them against the sofa's arms. Before she'd gone to Carolyn's, Susannah had moved them to the top of the sofa. Both were back where her mother used to keep them.

She felt the same eerie sensation she'd experienced the day she discovered Doug's high school track ribbons were missing. With absolute certainty, Susannah knew that once again someone had been inside the house. Every cell in her body relayed that message.

Susannah remained motionless, studying the immediate area for additional signs of an intruder. Her relaxed mood evaporated as her senses went on high alert. Her ears strained for any sound, but she heard nothing.

Other than the sofa pillows, nothing appeared to be out of place. Perhaps she was being unnecessarily suspicious or overdramatic, but she distinctly remembered moving those pillows. It'd been a small act of defiance, foolish really. And yet it provided evidence that there'd been an intruder. While Susannah was with Carolyn and her friends, reminiscing and sipping wine, a stranger had entered the house. Another thought suddenly occurred to her.

Whoever it was might still be inside.

The faintest of sounds—the creak of a floorboard—came from the direction of the hallway. Susannah's heart began a staccato beat that slammed against her chest. Her mouth went instantly dry.

Whoever had broken into the house was *still there.*

Hands shaking almost uncontrollably, she searched her purse for her cell phone and nearly groaned aloud when she remembered she'd kept it in the car to recharge the battery.

Before she could decide on the best course of action, the bedroom door opened.

Terror gripped her. Dashing to the door, Susannah had her hand on the knob, ready to bolt, when a sleepy voice called out from behind her.

"Mom?"

Susannah whirled around. "Chrissie?"

It was her daughter!

"Where were you?" Chrissie rubbed the sleep from her eyes. "Why didn't you answer your phone?"

Susannah hurried over to hug her daughter but had more than a few questions herself. "What are *you* doing here?"

"I came to help you with Grandma," her daughter said, covering her mouth in an attempt to hold back a wide yawn. "What time is it, anyway?"

"Midnight."

"Where were you so long?"

"With friends." Setting down her purse, Susannah walked into the kitchen and turned on the light. The message signal on the answering machine was flashing. "I think we both need to sit down and talk about this."

"I tried to let you know I was coming," Chrissie said.

The flashing light was proof enough of that.

"You didn't answer your cell phone, either."

"It's charging in the car."

"You didn't even look at the phone when you got in?"

Susannah shook her head. It hadn't occurred to her to check. Since she'd spoken to Joe earlier in the day, she hadn't expected to hear from him again.

"How'd you get to Colville, anyway?" Susannah had one car, Joe another and Brian drove a clunker to and from work.

Chrissie's smile wasn't as confident now. "Carley Lyons phoned this morning and said she was driving to Spokane. I

figured if I was that close, there had to be a way to Colville.
Carley said I could get a ride with her if I paid half the gas
and I did."

"Then how did you get from Spokane to Colville?"
Susannah had a feeling she wasn't going to like the answer.

Chrissie's shoulders heaved. "It wasn't easy. Carley
dropped me off at the bus depot. There are some really
creepy-looking people there, you know. Besides, the next
bus to Colville wasn't until the weekend."

Susannah nodded, waiting for the rest of the story.

"Then I thought of John Mussetter. He moved to Spokane
a little while ago. You remember him, don't you? Really,
how many Mussetters could there be in the phone book? I
called him and he said he'd drive me to Colville if I paid for
his gas and time. I agreed to give him all the money I had
with me, which wasn't as much as he wanted, so I told him
you'd pay him the rest and then you weren't here, so I owe
him fifty dollars."

The story just got worse. Susannah resisted the urge to
scold her daughter. She had other concerns. "How'd you get
into the house?" After that episode with Doug's missing
ribbons, Susannah never left without double-checking the
doors and windows.

Chrissie grinned. "I know where Grandma hides the
spare key in case anyone needs to get in."

Susannah frowned. As far as she could recall, her parents
had never hidden a key for easy access.

"Years ago Grandma showed me the place." She
smiled at Susannah. "I was praying like crazy that the key
would still be there behind the brick and it was," she said
triumphantly.

As youngsters, Susannah and her brother had found a

loose brick in the back of the house. The key fit behind it perfectly. Looking at the bricks, no one would suspect anything was hidden there. Susannah had completely forgotten about it and was surprised to realize their hiding place might still exist.

"I put it back," Chrissie assured her.

Deciding she needed a cup of tea, Susannah stood and filled the kettle, putting it on the stove to boil. "Your father knows you're here?"

Chrissie didn't answer right away. "He found out when he came home from work. I left him a note."

"Chrissie!"

"Mom, it was awful without you. Besides, I wanted to be here in the worst way. I love Grandma and I want to be with her. And you, too," she added as if in afterthought. "All Dad and Brian cared about was having me cook and clean for them. I was their slave. Even when I tried to make interesting dinners they complained. Okay, so the chicken curry didn't turn out like the one on the Food Channel, but at least I tried."

Susannah remembered her husband's reaction to the recipe, but Chrissie was right; she was making an effort and clearly it wasn't appreciated. She was right, too, about being close to her grandmother. It might be a real help to have her daughter here, if for no other reason than the closeness Vivian shared with her granddaughter.

Chrissie sat back in the chair and braced her bare feet against the edge so that her chin rested on her knees. Her hair fell forward, obscuring her face. "I phoned Jason this morning."

"Oh?" Considering how adamantly Chrissie had insisted

she didn't want anything more to do with him, this was no small concession. "How'd it go?"

"Bad. He said he wasn't seeing Katie, but I don't believe him. He also said he thought it'd be best if we broke up. That's fine by me—all he had to do was be honest." She sounded nonchalant but Susannah suspected that was merely a pose.

Susannah patted her daughter's forearm. "I'm sorry, sweetheart."

Chrissie shrugged as if it wasn't important, but Susannah could tell that she was hurt.

"Don't be mad at me for coming. Please, Mom, I just had to get away. I needed to talk to you and it isn't the same over the phone. I promise I won't be any trouble."

After the last few days of frustration and backbreaking work, Susannah welcomed the help—and the company.

"Actually, I'm glad you're here."

"You are?" Chrissie sounded so relieved. She tried to hide the fact that she had tears in her eyes. "How's Grandma doing? I'm really worried about her without Grandpa."

Susannah struggled with her own emotions. "She's not adjusting as well as I'd hoped."

"How do you mean?"

"Mom's doing everything she can to make sure she's miserable." Every conversation involved a litany of complaints. The food tasted terrible, the people were unfriendly, the rooms were too cold, and so on. Susannah had stopped listening.

"My being here will cheer her up," Chrissie stated with such confidence that Susannah believed her. "The thing is…"

"What?"

Chrissie sighed audibly. "I don't think Dad's going to be happy about the way I left."

That was no doubt an accurate prediction of Joe's feelings. Susannah suspected some of those messages were his. "Don't worry. I'll square it with him." She turned to her daughter. "As for you, now that you're here, I expect you to work."

"Sure." Chrissie gave her a tired smile. "Thanks, Mom, you're the best."

The sad part was that Susannah didn't feel she was the best at anything. Certainly not at being a daughter or a wife. Not even being a mother...

CHAPTER

14

Vivian was delighted when her granddaughter showed up the next morning. She'd just finished her breakfast—the eggs were cold and the bacon greasy so she hadn't taken more than a single bite of each.

She was getting ready to work outside in her garden when Susannah and Chrissie tapped at her door. Not her garden, she reminded herself. She didn't live in her home anymore. For a moment, she was overwhelmed by a sense of loss.

"Hi, Grandma."

With the way her memory had been acting up lately, she felt obliged to ask, "Did I know you were coming?"

"No, Grandma, this is a surprise."

Vivian hugged the girl and was astonished at how tall Chrissie had become since her last visit. When was that? Three or four years ago? "Such a beautiful young woman," she murmured, pressing her hands against Chrissie's cheeks, studying this girl she loved. But her granddaughter *wasn't* a girl anymore, she was a woman. The realization stunned her. "You look wonderful."

"You look great, too." Chrissie's arms were gentle around Vivian, as if her granddaughter was afraid to crush her. Vivian didn't remember being that fragile. She was, though. She'd changed, become feeble. Frail. What terrible words.

"I can't find my gardening gloves." Vivian was irritated. Her biggest worry about moving into this place was thievery. Hired help was not to be trusted; even Martha, who'd worked for her for years, had turned into a thief. Obviously, someone had walked off with her gardening gloves. They were her favorites and well used. Why anyone would take them was beyond her.

"Mother, what do you need gardening gloves for?" Susannah asked.

As much as she loved her daughter, Vivian swore Susannah could annoy her faster than anyone on earth. Ever since she'd arrived this morning, Susannah had tested Vivian's patience. "So I can trim my roses," she said slowly and deliberately.

Susannah's response was just as slow and deliberate. "Mother, the roses are at the house."

"I *know* that." And she did. She remembered exactly where her roses were.

Susannah cast a look at Chrissie. "But you're *here*."

"My roses need trimming and I'm determined to do it." Vivian wasn't letting anyone near her roses, especially Rachel Henderson. Her neighbor was no more trustworthy than anyone else.

Another glance passed between Susannah and Chrissie, but it was too hard for Vivian to read the look they'd exchanged.

"I could take Grandma back to the house," Chrissie suggested, "so she can work in her garden."

"Would you like that, Mother?"

This was the most ridiculous question Susannah had asked her yet. "Yes, of course I would."

"Okay, Grandma, then let's get you a sweater."

"What about my gloves?" Apparently both Susannah and Chrissie were willing to ignore the fact that someone in this abominable place had stolen her favorite gardening gloves.

"They're at the house, Mom, on the back porch. The pruning shears are in the garage."

"I know where those shears are." She hated to sound so impatient, but at times Susannah treated her as if she didn't have a brain in her head. Yes, she had a few problems with her memory now and then, but that didn't mean she was incapacitated.

"I'll get my jewels."

Susannah and Chrissie exchanged glances again.

"You don't expect me to leave this room when anyone could walk in and take my jewelry, do you?"

"Mom..." Susannah seemed about to argue with her but then she didn't.

That was good, because Vivian had no intention of leaving her pearls behind, not when someone could easily steal them. She retrieved her brown purse, where she kept her favorite necklace, and looped the straps tightly over her arm.

She put on a sweater—she was often cold these days—and reached for her red "everyday" purse.

"When I'm finished with the roses, I'll take you both to lunch. My treat." If she stayed here much longer she'd starve to death. In all her life, Vivian had never tasted blander food. These people obviously didn't know the purpose of a salt shaker or a spice rack.

She locked her room, tested the knob three times, and then they headed for the front door. Susannah stopped to talk to Rose, who ran the desk. Fortunately the staff wore name tags. She wished everyone did. It would help her remember the residents' names. Several had introduced themselves, but for the life of her she couldn't recall the name of a single one. Yes, everyone here ought to wear a name tag.

The instant they stepped into the house, Vivian felt distressed. Furniture had been moved and there were dishes stacked on the kitchen counter. Then when she walked outside, she was in for another shock. "Someone's been in my garden," she blurted. The roses were trimmed and there wasn't a single weed in sight. Everything was tied up and clipped back. There was almost nothing left for her to do. Someone had been in her garden, and it could only have been Rachel, her neighbor.

"Mother," Susannah said, placing an arm around her shoulders. "The garden is lovely."

"Yes, it is," Vivian muttered. She'd come to recognize her daughter's tone and she didn't like it one bit. Just the way she said *mother* told Vivian Susannah thought something was wrong with her.

After ten minutes or so, Susannah disappeared inside the house, probably to make more calls on that little phone of hers. Vivian shook her head hopelessly—Susannah seemed to be making a big mess of things. Frankly, she'd taught her daughter to be a better housekeeper than this. But wanting to maintain the peace, Vivian said nothing.

She wasn't sure how long she and Chrissie worked outside, puttering about, moving a few annuals—when had she put those begonias in? She really couldn't remember. Vivian noticed Rachel Henderson peering through the window a couple of times, but she tried to ignore her. The minute that busybody stuck her nose out the door, Vivian intended to tell Rachel to keep out of her garden, otherwise she was contacting the police.

"I'm hungry," Vivian announced after a while. It was the first real hunger she'd experienced since her daughter had moved her to that godforsaken facility. It was a good feeling. She'd lost interest in food, although heaven knew the best television these days was on the Food Channel.

"I'm ready for lunch, too," Chrissie told her, straightening.

All they had to do now was collect Susannah. Vivian knew where she wanted to go for lunch. Le Gourmand was new to Colville, and Vivian had heard that they served an incredibly good chicken salad. Her mouth watered just thinking about it. She missed going out for lunch; many an afternoon she'd lunched with her two best friends, Barbara and June, but they were both gone now, God rest their souls. George, too.

"They have outside seating," Vivian said as Susannah held open the car door.

"Who does, Mother?"

"Le Gourmand."

"Is that where you'd like to go for lunch?"

Silly girl. She'd already said so. Sometimes she swore

Susannah simply didn't listen. "Yes. It's such a nice afternoon, let's eat outside."

"That sounds perfect," Susannah said, helping Vivian into the front seat.

Vivian struggled with the seat belt. The car manufacturers made them so hard to reach these days. If not for Chrissie's handing it to her, Vivian would've needed to be a contortionist.

"It's new, but apparently their chicken salad is excellent. They add chopped walnuts."

"Le Gourmand has been around for ten years," Susannah said.

"Yes, I know." They did a nice lunch business, but were closed for dinner.

Thankfully there were plenty of empty tables on the patio. Vivian watched as Susannah went inside to place their order. Vivian remembered that she wanted to buy their lunch, but all of a sudden she couldn't seem to find her purse. She twisted around in her seat, and her heart started to pound hard. George would be so upset if she lost her pearls.

"What's wrong, Grandma?" Chrissie asked.

"I don't know what I did with my purse."

Chrissie leaned close and whispered, "It's on your lap, Grandma."

Her relief was immediate. The red purse lay there, as peaceful as a sleeping kitten.

"Your brown purse with the jewelry is in the trunk of the car, remember?"

Actually, that little piece of information had slipped her mind. She was grateful for the reminder, although she wished Chrissie hadn't shared it with the entire world.

"Here comes Mom now."

Susannah took a seat at the small round table. Vivian appreciated the umbrella that had been tilted to shade her face from the sunlight.

"Our order should be ready in a few minutes."

"Did you get my tea?" Vivian asked, but her question was drowned out by the roar of a truck engine as it pulled to a stop at the intersection. A long-haired young man turned to look at them. His window was rolled down and his dark hair fell into his face. He needed a shave, too. His tanned elbow rested on the window ledge, and he hadn't bothered to put on a decent shirt that morning. Instead, he wore a sleeveless T-shirt. While Vivian assessed him, he was making eyes at Chrissie. Such flirting was inappropriate and she was about to warn Chrissie when she noticed that her granddaughter seemed to be enjoying it.

He nodded in Chrissie's direction and to Vivian's horror, Chrissie nodded back. Vivian pursed her lips. He started to say something, but his gaze slid to her and he changed his mind, as well he should.

She needed a few minutes to recognize the young man, but her brain provided the answer the second he looked at her. It was Troy Nance, a known troublemaker.

The light turned green and Troy drove off with a burst of noise and exhaust.

"Who was that, Grandma?" Chrissie asked.

She hesitated, wondering if she should tell Chrissie, and then decided she would. Susannah's daughter was a sensible young woman and would see that Troy was completely unsuitable.

"He's the son of that girl you went to school with," Vivian told Susannah.

"I went to school with a lot of girls, Mom."

"I can't remember her name."

"What's *his* name?" Chrissie pressed.

"Troy Nance."

"Sharon Nance's son?"

"Yes." Of course. Sharon hadn't been married, so she and her son had the same last name. Although hers might be something different now…. Vivian shook her head; she couldn't even imagine who the boy's father had been. Whoever he was, he certainly hadn't stayed in the picture long.

"I haven't seen Sharon in years."

Not that Susannah was likely to cross paths with the other woman. The last Vivian had heard, Sharon was working at the Roadside Inn on the outskirts of town. She was the kind of woman George often saw in his courtroom—the kind of woman he described as trouble looking for a place to happen.

"He's cute," Chrissie murmured.

Susannah's eyes flew to Vivian's and this time the two of them traded a look. Vivian knew what that look meant, too.

It said Chrissie wasn't as levelheaded as Vivian had assumed and Susannah was well aware of it.

15

When Susannah took her mother back to Altamira, she could see that Vivian was exhausted. Still wearing her sweater, Vivian sat in front of the television and automatically put her feet up. Within minutes, she was sound asleep and snoring softly.

Susannah and Chrissie quietly left the room after securing her mother's purse with the jewelry in the bottom dresser drawer. As soon as they were out in the parking lot, Chrissie turned to her and said, "Grandma hardly looks the same anymore."

"I know. She's gone downhill so fast it's frightening." The difference was noticeable even to Chrissie, who tended to be self-absorbed, as were most girls her age.

"What do you want to do now?" Chrissie asked as Susannah unlocked the car door. Chrissie couldn't bear not to have something planned—usually something social. But she seemed genuinely willing to help. With Chrissie there,

Susannah hoped to finish packing up her parents' house more quickly than she'd expected, but the girl would probably wear her out, too.

"I need you to help me finish loading everything up and into the storage unit," Susannah explained. Cleaning out each room was a tedious and heartbreaking process.

"I suppose that would be all right." Chrissie didn't sound enthusiastic and Susannah didn't blame her.

They went to Safeway, where the manager had set aside half a dozen cardboard cartons. Collecting boxes had become part of Susannah's daily routine. Her favorites were the reinforced ones used for fruit. Twice a day, Susannah would take whatever had been boxed up to the storage unit. The boxes were labeled and would wait there, neatly stacked, until she decided what to do with them. When that would be, she didn't know. She'd merely deferred many of these decisions. She still had to figure out what she should keep, what should go to the kids, what could be donated to charity. Susannah was afraid she might discard something she would later regret.

When they pulled up in front of the house, she noticed a smartly dressed woman sitting in a car across the street. When they climbed out of the Crown Victoria and opened the trunk to remove boxes, the same woman emerged from her car.

"Hello," the tall brunette said with a warm smile as she crossed the street. "I'm Melody Highland." She peeled a business card out of a small gold case and thrust it at Susannah. "I work with the Colville Real Estate Company. I understand you're going to be putting your mother's house on the market soon."

Listing it now would be premature; Susannah realized she wasn't quite ready to take that final step. She accepted the card and was about to tell the real estate agent that, but before she could say a word, Melody continued.

"Colville Real Estate has an impeccable reputation in the community. I've been with the firm eight years and I'm their top salesperson."

"Congratulations." Susannah couldn't think of any other response.

"I have several clients who'd be interested in a home such as this in a well-established neighborhood."

Susannah stared at the card. Curious, she looked up and asked, "How did you get my name?"

Melody smiled. "Colville is a small town. Word gets around."

"Was it Mrs. Henderson?"

Melody hesitated and her cheery facade disappeared. "Actually," she said with reluctance, "I heard about you through the storage unit place. They sometimes give me tips on possible listings."

That explained it, and Susannah was more than a little offended by this cozy sharing of private information. "Well, I'm afraid I'm not ready to list the house."

"Perhaps I could be of service in some way?"

"Thank you, but no." Susannah wasn't going to let this woman push her into acting before the time was right.

"Do keep my card. I know we can get top dollar for your parents' home."

Susannah nodded, slipping the business card into her pocket. "Thank you for stopping by, but we really need to get back to work now."

"No, I should be the one thanking you," Melody Highland said smoothly. "I look forward to doing business with you in the near future."

Susannah and Chrissie started toward the house.

"Can I check with you in a week or two?" Melody called just as Susannah reached the front steps.

"I'd prefer to contact you when I'm ready."

"No problem," Melody said and marched back across the street to her car.

Susannah waited until she'd driven off, then set down two of the boxes. "My goodness. She was eager, wasn't she?"

"I guess," Chrissie muttered, seemingly amused. "I'll bet she's already got clients lined up to look at the house. I can imagine how those potential buyers would react if they saw the place now."

They walked into the house and Susannah had the feeling she'd made a lucky escape. She wondered how many other real estate agents she'd have to fend off before this ordeal was over.

"Where would you like me to begin?" Chrissie asked, standing just inside the living room. Hands on hips, she surveyed the area. Five days after moving her mother out, Susannah had made only a small dent in what needed to be done.

"What about the bookcase in the living room?" she suggested. When she had time, Susannah wanted to go carefully through all the titles. Her father had been an avid reader and there might be some first editions in his collection. Those books would be something to hand down to Brian one day.

"Okay." Chrissie grabbed a box. "I'll start there."

Many of her mother's personal things had been taken to her new apartment, but her father's office remained untouched. Until now, Susannah had avoided it, but she couldn't put it off forever.

Knowing her dad, he'd kept meticulous records. She'd have to sort through every file and drawer. Maybe she should wait until she was better able to deal with it emotionally. No—this couldn't wait. She pulled out a stack of files and had just started to go through one of them when Chrissie called her.

"Mom!" she shouted. "Come here quick."

Susannah hurried out to the living room. "What is it?"

"Look!" Chrissie cried, brandishing a fifty-dollar bill. "It fell out of this book when I took it down from the shelf." She held up a history of the Second World War.

"Good grief." Susannah realized there might be more money stashed in other books.

Chrissie reached for a second volume. Holding the book upside down, she splayed it open and two more bills fell onto the carpet. "Twenty-dollar bills," Chrissie said. "These books are *full* of money."

Susannah groaned. She didn't know who had placed the bills there. It could've been either her mother or her father—perhaps both of them. Recently her mother had grown so distrusting of everyone that she'd started hiding things all over the house.

"Be sure and check inside each book," Susannah said. This was going to slow them down even more. "Maybe I should help." Having to examine each volume individually would be time-consuming.

"This is like a treasure hunt," Chrissie said excitedly, taking down a copy of *Gone With the Wind*.

Before Susannah could respond, the doorbell rang. She wove her way through the cartons littering the room. If it was another real estate salesperson, she wouldn't be nearly as polite as she'd been the first time.

She opened the door to a woman in her late sixties, possibly early seventies. "Hello, Susannah," she said pleasantly as if she expected Susannah to recognize her immediately.

Susanna didn't know this woman from Eve.

"I'm Eve Sutter."

Eve? God does have a sense of humor, she thought with a glimmer of amusement. "I'm sorry, should I know you?"

"I'm sure your mother's mentioned my name. We're dear, dear friends."

Susannah couldn't remember her mother ever mentioning anyone named Eve. Not wanting to be rude, she held open the screen door so the other woman could come inside.

"I heard you'd moved Vivian over to Altamira," Eve said as she stepped into the house. "It's a lovely facility, isn't it?"

Susannah nodded. She didn't have time to waste with social chitchat. "How can I help you?"

"Oh, I came to help *you*," Eve said, sounding surprised, again as if Susannah should intuitively know the reason for her visit. "I understand how difficult it is to pack up an entire life. I'm here to offer my assistance."

"That's very thoughtful, but…" Susannah was about to explain that she didn't require this woman's assistance; however, she wasn't allowed to finish.

"I'm sure there's far more here than your mother wants

or needs." Eve scanned the room, leaning to one side as she glanced down the long hallway that led to the bedrooms. "There are a number of things I'd be willing to take off your hands. We wear the same size, I believe."

"Ah…"

"With so much to do, you must be looking for helping hands and here I am. Now, where should I start?" Eve pushed up her sleeves in anticipation.

"My daughter and I have everything under control, but thank you." Susannah walked over to the door and point-edly held it open.

Eve's head reared back as though she'd been insulted. "Of course. Well, I'll stop by later with a bucket of chicken and—"

"We already have dinner plans." Susannah opened the screen door, feeling less and less civil. If this so-called friend of her mother's was a friend indeed, Susannah dis-trusted her.

Eve nodded, smiled sweetly and walked out the door. Susannah closed it with a decisive bang.

"Can you *believe* that woman?" she yelped, her voice rising in outrage.

"Mom…"

"It's like the vultures have started circling overhead. First, that real estate woman and now Eve, my mother's *dear* friend," she said sarcastically. "Whom I never heard Mom mention even once."

Chrissie laughed, but to Susannah this was no laughing matter.

"Come on, Mom, lighten up. She didn't mean any harm."

Susannah disagreed. Eve whatever-her-name was nothing but a freeloader.

The phone rang and they looked at each other, startled. Then Chrissie rushed into the kitchen to answer. Susannah suspected it was Joe; they'd spoken that morning, and he was unhappy with Chrissie, but Susannah had smoothed the waters. Although she didn't approve of her daughter's deception, she was grateful for her presence.

Chrissie was gone for several minutes. In the meantime, Susannah had unearthed another fifty dollars and packed up an entire row of books. Then—of all things—she found four teaspoons hidden behind the out-of-date encyclopedia. The very ones, no doubt, that Martha had supposedly stolen. Which reminded her—she needed to call Martha.

"You won't believe who that was."

Judging by the happiness in her daughter's eyes, Susannah's first guess was Jason, but she'd let Chrissie tell her. "Who?"

Chrissie nearly skipped over to the bookcase. "It was the guy in the pickup."

"What guy?" Susannah asked before she remembered.

"Mother! The guy this afternoon. He figured I was related to Grandma, so he took a chance and called the house. He asked me out."

Susannah was horrified. "You're not going, are you?"

Chrissie laughed as if she assumed Susannah was joking. "Of course I'm going. This is the most exciting invitation I've had in months. I'm well over eighteen, so it's not like I have to ask your permission."

Yes, indeed, the vultures were out in full force.

* * *

Carolyn checked her watch and when she saw it was noon, she leaped out of her chair.

"Carolyn?" her assistant asked as she hurried past.

"I thought I'd go home for lunch today," she said, not stopping to answer questions. Her heart pounded as she reached her truck and got inside. When she'd started the engine and backed out of her parking slot, she happened to catch her reflection in the rearview mirror. Her face was flushed and she was nibbling on her lower lip, which was a habit from childhood. She released her lip as if hearing her mother chastise her, switching between French and English. The words still rang in Carolyn's ears these many years later.

It was all that talk last evening about the paths not taken, she reasoned. Carolyn hadn't contributed much to the discussion. When she'd gone to bed, she'd lain awake most of the night, thinking. There'd been a number of different paths in her life—the ones she'd taken and others left unexplored. One stretched before her now.

Dave Langevin.

She hadn't been able to get him out of her mind. Her mother would be *furieuse* if she knew that her daughter was attracted to a lawn-maintenance man. Since her twenties, Carolyn had lived a solitary life. Thoughts of a relationship, any relationship, were best ignored. She was a woman in a world usually populated by men, and she didn't have the time or inclination for romance. It'd been easy to ignore the fact that she was a woman until she met Dave. When she looked at him, for some unaccountable reason, she felt alive again. In the beginning she'd tried to ignore the attraction, ignore the way he made her feel. It was uncomfortable at best and downright embarrassing at worst. She'd told no one. Really, how could she?

As she turned into her driveway, she realized her timing was perfect. Just as she'd hoped, Dave Langevin was working in her yard doing her regular maintenance. He'd been there on an unscheduled visit the day before, adding beauty bark to her flower beds. Right now he was mowing the grass. With the sun beating down, he'd removed his shirt, and his sun-bronzed torso glistened with perspiration. So intent was she on watching him that she nearly drove off the road. When it came to running the lumber mill, Carolyn was capable, competent, in charge. When it came to male-female relationships outside of business, she felt inept, clumsy and completely tongue-tied.

She parked her vehicle inside the garage and with trembling hands went into the kitchen, where she prepared a ham sandwich and added some coleslaw and pickle slices, although she didn't have the appetite for even a mouthful. After carrying it onto the patio, she sat down and made a show of eating.

Dave had his shirt on now and was pushing the mower to the side of the house, close to the patio.

"Hello again," she said as if it was the most natural thing in the world for her to hurry home in the middle of the day. "You're getting to be a regular fixture around here."

"I hope I'm not disturbing your lunch."

"No. Would you care to join me?" While she might sound casual, nothing could be further from the truth.

"Sorry," Dave said, flashing her a grin. His teeth were white and even. "They don't pay me to dine with the clientele."

"How about a glass of iced tea?" she asked next.

He hesitated and then nodded. "I'd appreciate that."

In her eagerness to get him a glass, she nearly toppled her own chair. Rushing into the kitchen, Carolyn drew a deep breath in a futile effort to slow down her hammering pulse. Inviting a man to join her for lunch was so out of character that it felt as if she'd done something illegal.

She'd thought about little else all day. As she dressed that morning, she'd been putting together a plan of action. She wore her hair down instead of in her customary braid and opted for a white blouse with a lace collar rather than the cotton plaid that was her general uniform. Her jeans and boots were the same, but nothing else seemed to be—including her mind. Gloria had noticed her change of outfit right away and might have made some remark if not for the look Carolyn sent her.

"Do you take it sweetened or unsweetened?" she called through the screen door.

"Unsweetened."

She managed to pour the tea, then took it outside and handed it to him. Dave thanked her with a nod. He hadn't buttoned his shirt, and she had a hard time not staring at his muscular chest. A light mat of sun-bleached hair caught her attention. She felt like a schoolgirl, mesmerized by the sight, and resisted the urge to press her palm against his heart to see if his pulse beat as erratically as her own.

Dave drank the tea without stopping, then pulled off his hat and wiped his forearm across his brow.

"That tasted great. Thank you."

Carolyn didn't know what to say next. Her tongue felt stuck to the roof of her mouth. "You're not from around here, are you?"

He shook his head. "I came up from California."

"I lived there for a while. Which part?" she asked, trying to make conversation, anything that would let Dave know how much she wanted to be his friend. No—*more* than his friend.

"Here and there. I moved around a lot."

Her heart sank. In other words, he wasn't interested in telling her.

But then he surprised her. "I lived in the Fresno area for a time," he muttered.

"How'd you get up here?" she asked, trying again. It was a bit awkward, the two of them standing there, making stilted conversation. She gestured toward the chair. Dave declined, shaking his head.

"I don't stay in one place for long," he said. "I was never one to put down roots."

"What about family?"

"Don't have any." Sadness darkened his eyes and he looked away.

"None?" she repeated slowly.

"None."

"What about a wife?" It was a bold question and she felt astonished at her own audacity in asking it.

"I was never married."

"Never." Carolyn could hardly believe it.

"Like I said, I wasn't one for roots."

She wondered what had happened to this man that kept him from living a normal life. Then it came to her. He'd been in prison; he must have been. It was the only thing that made sense. He preferred not to discuss his past. He hadn't settled down anywhere. He was attractive and appealing and vital, yet he'd never married.

"What about you?" He spoke softly, almost as if he regretted asking the question.

"I'm divorced."

"Children?"

"No… My marriage ended a lot of years ago and well, I never—you know—I never met anyone else."

"That's a shame," he said in a low voice.

She swallowed tightly. "You?"

"I don't have children, either." He retreated a couple of steps, apparently uncomfortable with the information he'd shared. "I should get to work."

Carolyn stepped back, too.

"Thank you," he whispered.

"For what?" she asked.

He didn't answer right away and set the empty tumbler carefully on the table. "The tea," he said.

Carolyn had the distinct impression that his appreciation went beyond a glass of cold tea.

16

"I'm glad you came by," Susannah said as she held open the front door for Carolyn late Saturday afternoon. She'd dreaded the thought of spending the evening alone. For the second day in a row, Chrissie had gone off with Troy Nance. Much to her consternation, her daughter seemed utterly enthralled by him.

Susannah had disliked Troy on sight, and every meeting since had confirmed her negative opinion of her former schoolmate's son. She didn't like the way Troy looked at her daughter, either, as though he was salivating over some tempting delicacy on a restaurant dessert platter. As far as she could determine, he was unemployed, smoked, drank and generally lived on the edge. She was afraid drugs might be part of that scenario, too.

"I brought dinner," Carolyn said, holding up a plastic grocery bag. "A few goodies that'll help us remember our time in France."

Susannah guessed it was a baguette, soft cheese and sun-dried tomatoes in seasoned olive oil. And, of course, Carolyn would include a bottle of red wine. As schoolgirls they'd spent many a weekend afternoon in the Loire Valley, enjoying a repast just like that. Those picnics had always included chaperones, but they'd been fun all the same.

When Carolyn left Colville as a high school sophomore, she and Susannah had been good friends. But during that year in the French boarding school, they'd truly bonded. Susannah wasn't sure why they'd let their relationship erode in the decades that followed.

"Sun-dried tomatoes?" she asked and closed her eyes in ecstasy.

"Plus fresh bread and chèvre."

"My favorite." Her stomach rumbled in anticipation.

"Did you think I'd forget?"

"You didn't have to do all this," Susannah said, although she was relieved to stay home. After an entire day of physically demanding labor, she was content to relax, enjoy this feast and simply talk.

They sat across from each other at the dining room table, and drank wine out of plastic cups. The bread, cheese and tomatoes were served on paper plates.

"Where's Chrissie?" Carolyn asked.

Susannah slowly shook her head. "She met Troy Nance yesterday and they've barely spent a minute apart since then." Okay, that was an exaggeration, because Chrissie had helped Susannah for most of the day. She'd been to visit Vivian, as well. But when she was with Susannah, she'd talked nearly nonstop about how wonderful Troy was.

Carolyn didn't say anything but from her frown, Susannah

deduced that her friend's opinion of this young man was the same as hers.

"What do you know about him?" she asked.

Carolyn shrugged. "Not much. He worked at the mill, but he didn't last long. We have a drug-testing program—because of all the heavy equipment—and once Troy heard about that, he stopped showing up."

Just as Susannah had feared, he seemed to be involved with drugs. Carolyn's story implied as much.

"I don't understand what Chrissie sees in him," she said. That was putting it mildly. "She recently broke up with her boyfriend from school and I suppose she's still feeling hurt."

"Then Troy must be balm to her wounded ego."

This was Susannah's take on the situation, too.

Carolyn sipped her wine. "You've probably figured out that his mother is Sharon Nance. She's been married two or three times over the years, but still goes by Nance."

Susannah did remember Sharon and while they'd never been friends, they'd been cordial. Sharon was hot-tempered as a teenager and had an unsavory reputation. At the age of thirteen, she'd bragged she was dating twenty-year-old men. By comparison, Susannah had lived an innocent existence. Sharon came from a single-parent home—a rarity in those days. Her mother had worked as a barmaid and now, so did Sharon.

Susannah sighed heavily, disappointed in her daughter's fascination with Troy. "I assumed that one date would clue Chrissie in to the fact that Troy is no prize."

"So she went out with him last night?"

Susannah nodded and swallowed a sip of wine. "She was

home early enough, before midnight, and claimed she'd had an amazing time—her word. But I don't think she'd tell me if she hadn't."

"Why not?" Carolyn reached for a slice of bread and then for the cheese.

Discouraged, Susannah leaned back in her chair. She'd failed Chrissie in this situation and wasn't proud of what she'd done, especially because she knew better. "I tried to warn Chrissie about Troy, but I might as well have saved my breath. It was a mistake to say anything because now she's determined to prove how wrong I am."

"I don't think Troy's into hard drugs, if that's what concerns you," Carolyn said.

That was reassuring. But Troy definitely looked like a recreational drug user, and leaving his job at the mill confirmed it. "I talked to my husband and he said we've done our best raising Chrissie and at almost twenty she's capable of making her own decisions."

"And you agree?" Carolyn asked, skewering Susannah with a look. "Never having had children, I wouldn't know."

"The thing is, I don't, either," Susannah muttered. It would've been so nice to spend these weeks with her daughter, just the two of them. They'd been getting along well, and the last thing she wanted now was to be at odds with Chrissie over a young man who'd be in and out of their lives within a few days.

"What I'm finding so difficult is *all* of this," Susannah said, gesturing around her. "I'm packing up my parents' lives and discovering all these bits and pieces of my own life. For instance, Mom saved the first baby tooth I lost. I also came across a file she kept with all my school papers from first grade on. She saved everything, and I do mean everything."

Carolyn nodded. "I know what you mean. I didn't pack up my mom and dad's stuff, but I moved into their home. Everywhere I turned I was confronted by memories. It was a little eerie at first, you know?"

Susannah did. Speaking of eerie... She leaned forward, wondering if she should say anything. "I didn't mention this to Joe because I don't want to alarm him. Someone's been in the house recently."

Carolyn paused, her glass halfway to her mouth. "Someone's broken into the house?"

"No, that's the crazy part. There's been no obvious break-in and nothing of value is missing. Well, some old sports ribbons and baseball cards. A few other things." She paused. "It's happened more than once."

"Are you spooked?" Carolyn asked.

"Yes, and it's driving me crazy. Who would do that and why?"

"Any idea?"

Susannah just shook her head.

Carolyn nibbled on her bread and cheese. "Do you think the spirit of your father is still here?"

"No." The thought appalled Susannah. "That's not it at all. This is...different." Susannah grew quiet in an effort to put her feelings into words. "Thursday night after meeting with you and the others, I came back here and the moment I stepped inside the house, I knew someone had been here."

"Wasn't that when you found Chrissie had arrived?"

"Yes, but I still think it's more than that. True, Chrissie

was there—but I sensed someone else had come in, too. And I'm pretty sure it happened again, maybe even today. That makes three times I know of. This afternoon, I saw that some of my father's papers were missing. I'd just started going through his files and I'd left some stuff on his desk. Then it turned up missing. Gone."

"You're *sure* you didn't toss it?"

"I'm positive. I know it was there and then it wasn't."

"I believe you."

Her friend was silent after that. "Anything on your mind these days?" Susannah asked.

Carolyn's gaze flew to hers, and her face immediately reddened.

"Carolyn?"

She blushed even more profusely, but didn't respond.

"Tell me."

She finally began, "There's this guy…."

Susannah should've known it had to do with a man. "What guy?"

"I'm embarrassed to say anything. His name's Dave. He's with Kettle Falls Landscaping and he maintains my yard and the area outside my office. I can't stop thinking about him. At work I catch myself staring out the window, hoping for a glimpse of him."

"What's the problem? Is he married?"

She shook her head. "No, he says he's never been married. I think…I think he might have a criminal record."

"Surely there's some way you can get that information."

"I already looked on the Internet," Carolyn said, then blushed again. "I couldn't find a thing."

"Do you suppose he's using an alias?"

"I don't know." She shifted as if uncomfortable.

"What makes you think he's been in prison?" Susannah asked gently.

"Nothing, other than the fact that he's so private and much too beautiful never to have married or had a family."

Susannah smiled at her friend's use of the word *beautiful*. She didn't consider men in those terms, but apparently Carolyn did.

"Yesterday afternoon as he left my house, I saw him glance at me—he didn't know I could see him. Ridiculous as it sounds, I got this happy, excited feeling because he was thinking about me. I'm not sure if that's true, but I *felt* it." She brought one hand to her mouth. "I'm too old to have these kinds of feelings."

"As long as you're breathing, you're not too old. It's wonderful that you've met a man who makes you feel alive."

"That's not all he makes me feel." Two red spots brightened her cheeks. She sighed. "It's not a good idea to get involved with him."

"Why not?" Susannah protested. She knew Carolyn, and her friend didn't give her heart away lightly. "You deserve happiness. It's hard enough to find without erecting unnecessary roadblocks."

Still, Carolyn looked uncertain. "I don't know what to do."

Susannah could understand her dilemma. "Why do anything? Just let it happen."

After a moment, a slow smile spread across Carolyn's face. "Maybe I will," she whispered. "Maybe I will."

Sunday morning, Susannah, Chrissie and Vivian attended
the second service at Colville Christian Church, where
Susannah had gone from early childhood. Several people
greeted Susannah and Chrissie and offered Vivian warm
hugs.

During the sermon, her mother held her Bible in her lap.
She appeared to be following intently, running her finger
down a page in the Book of John. Pastor Nichols was
preaching from the second chapter of James, but Susannah
didn't have the heart to correct her.

Chrissie fidgeted throughout the service. As soon as the
organist played the closing benediction, she hurried toward
the door. She was waiting impatiently by the car when
Susannah and her mother got to the parking lot.

Susannah drove her mother back to Altamira, and led
Vivian into the dining room for lunch. The fact that her
mother was joining the other residents for meals was

progress. Until Saturday, Vivian had insisted on eating in her room. Susannah wasn't sure what had convinced her mother to reconsider but she suspected it had something to do with the fees charged to deliver meals.

Once they were back in the car, Chrissie glanced anxiously at Susannah. "You wouldn't mind if I took the rest of the day off, would you?"

Before Susannah could say anything, her daughter added, "Troy and a bunch of his friends are going to Lake Roosevelt to ride Jet Skis. He invited me along."

"Ah…"

"It's Sunday. You weren't planning on packing today, were you?"

As a matter of fact, Susannah had decided she could use a day off. Their morning had gotten off to a late start with church. Her mother would probably rest for most of the afternoon.

Susannah hoped to spend time with Vivian later to discuss some of the decisions that had to be made. Vivian's mental capabilities were clearly diminished, but Susannah felt the need to talk everything over with her, although it usually turned out to be a token effort.

"You don't mind, do you, Mom?" Chrissie pressed.

"I suppose that would be all right." She didn't bother to disguise her displeasure that Chrissie was seeing Troy Nance again.

"You don't like Troy, do you? You don't even know him, but you've already judged him."

"Chrissie…"

"I'm almost twenty years old, for heaven's sake! I'm

going to the lake this afternoon, whether you like it or not. Troy's picking me up in twenty minutes."

Chrissie's mind was already made up and Susannah wondered why her daughter had bothered to ask in the first place. The struggle between approval and independence seemed to be a difficult one for her.

Sure enough, a few minutes later Troy drove up to the house. He climbed out of his truck as Chrissie dashed out the front door and down the front steps to join him.

Susannah stood at the living room window, her mouth pursed with disapproval. She watched Troy grab Chrissie around the waist, then drag her to his side as if staking claim to her sleek, young body. Troy's older pickup truck was scratched and dented, but the sound system seemed to be top of the line. It was loud enough to rattle the living room windows.

The couple disappeared, leaving a trail of exhaust in their wake. Her instincts told her he was trouble. Where that trouble would lead her daughter, Susannah was afraid to guess.

With Chrissie gone, the house seemed unnaturally quiet. Susannah figured she had maybe two hours during which to work or relax before returning to Altamira. She roamed around the house, looking for an unchallenging task, something that would help pass the time. She would've called Joe, but he and Brian had gone salmon fishing for the weekend. Joe said he felt it was important that he bond with his son, in the same way Chrissie and Susannah were doing.

Some bond. Despite Susannah's best efforts, most of her and Chrissie's conversations since Friday afternoon had revolved around Troy. And most of that was Chrissie defending him.

Walking down the hallway, Susannah paused in the doorway to her father's office. The old mahogany desk with the filing cabinet in one corner still needed to be cleared out. Her father had been dead for seven months now and other than the drawer she'd emptied, that desk was exactly as she'd seen it the day of his funeral.

Susannah sighed wearily. There seemed to be no better time to tackle his desk than now. She sank down in the chair where her father had routinely sat to pay bills. Opening the top drawer, she scooped up the first group of file folders. They turned out to be for the various utilities, in alphabetical order, followed by a file for the bank. It was filled with mortgage statements.

The house had been paid off long ago, but every statement could be easily located had anyone asked. She couldn't imagine where he'd kept the last forty years of cancelled checks and knew without a doubt that she'd stumble on them sooner or later. When she did, they'd be categorized by day, month and year.

The desk would take her about two hours, she estimated, prepared to assume the task. With the shredder, a Christmas gift from her and Joe several years earlier, to one side, she sorted through each file.

There seemed no good reason to hold on to all this paperwork. She flipped through the folders, giving them a cursory inspection, then shredded the contents. It was when she reached the last files in the top drawer that she discovered one marked Colville Natural Gas.

That gave her pause, since her parents' house wasn't heated by natural gas.

Sensing that she wouldn't like what she found, she opened it to examine the contents. The first sheet appeared to be a letter of some kind, dated January 1973. Susannah's gaze slid to the bottom of the page. She gasped.

She quickly scanned the text, and her outrage exploded when she realized what she was reading. She vaulted to her feet.

Her father had paid Allan Presley to leave Washington State—with Jake. In exchange for five thousand dollars cash, Mr. Presley had agreed to move a minimum of five hundred miles from Colville. Allan Presley had accepted this cash with the understanding that he and Jake would not only leave Colville, but never return.

Even with the evidence in her hands she couldn't accept that her father would commit such an act of betrayal. She knew Jake's father needed money. As young as she'd been at the time, Susannah remembered Jake's concerns about his father's financial problems. Knowing Allan's hand-to-mouth existence and his weakness for the bottle, her father had offered him money. He'd paid the Presleys to get Jake out of Susannah's life. Because his father had agreed to this blackmail—and that was precisely what it was—Jake had honored his father's word. Although he loved her—and Susannah believed that with all her heart—he'd walked away.

Susannah crushed the sheet of paper in her fist as she fought to control her emotions. She'd *known*. A part of her had always known it would be something like this. Her father had been desperate to keep Jake out of her life, desperate enough to send her to Europe. Desperate enough to manipulate Jake's life, Allan Presley's life and that of his only daughter. It was maddening. No, it was more than that—it was wrong.

Unable to keep this to herself a minute longer, Susannah grabbed her purse and headed out of the house, taking the signed contract with her. She'd smoothed out the crumpled paper, which was now neatly folded in her purse.

Her irritation had settled down but her stomach continued to roil as she found a parking space in front of Altamira. She hoped her mother had managed to rest, because Susannah needed answers and she needed them now. This letter wasn't the only thing she'd uncovered. There'd been some odd withdrawals from his bank account, too.

To her surprise, Vivian's door was open when she arrived. She walked in to see another woman visiting her mother.

"Susannah," Vivian said, her eyes smiling with happiness. "Look who's come to see me."

"Hello," Susannah said, entering the small apartment. Whoever this woman was, she didn't recognize her. She could only hope it wasn't another "friend" like Eve. "I'm Susannah Nelson, Vivian's daughter."

"Sally Mansfield," the woman said. She was about the same age as her mother, but seemed more…alert. More aware.

"I'm a friend of your mother's cousin Judy from California. Lloyd and I were passing through the area twelve or thirteen years ago in our motor home and we went to see your parents. We'd had such a good visit with them when they drove out to California several years earlier."

"That was the year…" Whatever was on Vivian's mind didn't quite make it to her tongue.

"You had a grandson born that year," Sally prompted.

"Yes, yes, the year Brian was born. Remember? Dad and I took a road trip to California that summer."

Susannah did recall a summer excursion, but she'd been busy at the time, with a toddler underfoot and a new baby. Her parents so rarely traveled that whenever they did, it was memorable.

"At any rate, Lloyd and I liked this area so much when we visited that we sold everything in California and moved to Washington. We bought property about twenty miles west of here." Her mouth turned down for a moment. "I'm afraid we got so involved with our place and our traveling that we just sort of…lost touch with your parents."

"Oh."

"Lloyd died five years ago and I've been alone ever since. I moved into Altamira two years back. I was absolutely delighted to learn that your mother's living here now."

"I think the world of Sally," Vivian said, grinning shyly at the other woman. "I can't tell you how pleased I am that we've met up again."

"No more pleased than I am." Sally gently squeezed Vivian's hand. "I hope you're coming down to the fireplace room for the ice-cream social this evening."

Vivian nodded eagerly. "I wouldn't miss it."

This was exactly what Susannah had prayed would happen. She'd wanted her mother to find a friend so she wouldn't feel isolated. Here was Sally, and already Susannah noticed a crack in her mother's defenses.

The three chatted amiably for several minutes before Sally yawned and announced it was long past her naptime.

"I haven't had my nap yet, either," Vivian echoed.

Susannah walked Sally to the door and whispered her gratitude. "I'm so glad you sought out my mom. She needs a special friend."

Sally's tired eyes shone with humor. "We all do. Now, don't you worry about your mother. I'll keep an eye on her for you."

"Thank you," Susannah said fervently. "Oh, thank you."

By the time she returned, her mother was in her favorite chair, feet propped up, her head resting against the cushion. She'd closed her eyes.

"I'll leave soon, Mom, but I have a question first."

Her mother's eyes slowly opened. "What is it, dear?"

"Do you know anything about this?" She handed her mother the creased letter.

Her mother read it quickly and frowned. "I don't understand. What is this?"

"It's an agreement between Allan Presley and Dad," Susannah said.

"That singer again?"

"No, Mom. Allan Presley is Jake Presley's father. Remember, Jake was my high school boyfriend?"

Her mother nodded, but didn't look convinced.

"Dad paid Mr. Presley five thousand dollars to move Jake out of Colville."

Vivian shook her head. "Your father would never do anything like that."

"Mom!" Susannah cried and because she was so upset and restless, she started pacing. "You're holding the evidence. Look at that sheet of paper and you'll see Dad's signature and Mr. Presley's."

"That was a lot of money in—" she glanced at the date "—1973." Her mother's frown deepened. "Where would your father get that kind of money?"

"I don't know."

Her mother sighed. "He was very good with money. He was such an intelligent man."

Susannah was in no frame of mind to think positive thoughts about her father. "It was underhanded and cruel…. I could hate Dad for this."

"Now, Susannah…"

The distress in her voice must have broken through to her mother. Vivian eased her legs from the ottoman and leaned toward her. She stretched out her hand. "You're upset."

"Yes. I'm very upset."

"But everything worked out for the best. You married Joe and you have two beautiful children. You and Joe have done so well."

"Yes, I know, but I could've had a good life with Jake, too. I loved him, Mom, and it kills me to find out how my own father manipulated us." She struggled to make her mother understand why this was important. Yes, she did have a husband and family—a husband and family she loved—but she'd never know what she might have had with Jake. She'd taken the path that led to Joe because the path she would have chosen, Jake's path, had been closed to her. By her father.

"Oh, dear, do you think I was involved?" Vivian asked and then answered her own question. "I don't know, I might've been, but I have to say it doesn't sound the least bit familiar. That was a lot of years ago."

Susannah felt sick to her stomach.

"I'll tell you what, dear," her mother said with the utmost sincerity. "I'll speak to your father about this the next time he visits."

"Mom..."

"George will remember. He was always good with details. He'll remember and when he tells me, I'll let you know."

Susannah wanted to weep.

CHAPTER

18

At nine Chrissie still wasn't back, and Susannah was growing increasingly worried. She phoned home, but Joe and
Brian hadn't returned from their fishing trip yet. Not that
Joe would've been able to do anything even if he *had* been
there. The longer she paced and fretted, the more irritated
she became. This date of Chrissie's was supposed to be an
afternoon outing.

Still, Chrissie was almost an adult and Susannah had
no choice but to allow her to make her own decisions.
Nevertheless, Susannah had a bad feeling about this.

At nine-thirty, she phoned Carolyn. It wasn't only Chrissie
on her mind. The letter she'd discovered in her father's filing
cabinet that afternoon continued to bother her. She needed
a friend, someone who'd listen and sympathize.

Carolyn answered before the second ring.

"Are you busy?" Susannah asked.

"Not particularly, why?"

"Want to meet at He's Not Here? I need to talk."

"Sure."

Susannah was grateful for a friend willing to meet her at a moment's notice. As soon as she hung up the phone, she grabbed her purse and car keys. If Chrissie returned while she was out, fine. Maybe it wouldn't be such a bad thing to let her daughter worry about *her* for a change.

The parking lot outside the tavern was almost empty. Susannah chose a booth and ordered a Diet Coke while she waited for Carolyn, who showed up a few minutes later. She slid into the seat across from Susannah.

"What's up?" she asked, getting directly to the point.

Susannah pulled the letter out of her purse, and in as few words as possible, told her what it was about. Then she added, "I went to Mom to see if she knew anything."

"Did she?"

Susannah sighed. "Well, if she ever did, she's forgotten it now." More and more Susannah realized that her mother had slipped into a fantasy world and had trouble identifying what was real and what wasn't.

"Do you honestly think your mother would tell you even if she did know?"

Susannah couldn't be sure and made a dismissive gesture. "She promised to ask my father the next time he visits."

Carolyn gave her a worried look. "Oh, dear."

"Oh, yes." She rested her chin on her hand. "I said that was a good idea and that I'd be eager to hear what Dad had to tell her. What else could I say? Sometimes, it's like my own mother is a stranger to me."

Carolyn nodded and ordered a glass of merlot when the

waitress swung by. "I imagine there are days when Vivian's a stranger to herself."

Susannah suspected that was true. Her mother didn't understand what had changed or why. At least some of the time, she recognized that her husband of nearly sixty years was dead, but at other times—because she needed him, because it comforted her—she brought him back to life.

"I can't begin to tell you how frustrating and painful it is to learn that my father would do something like this," Susannah cried, brandishing the letter. Her voice shook with emotion; she felt betrayed and sad and wronged all at once. "I didn't think he could hurt me anymore after he died, but...he did."

"So what are you going to do about it?" Carolyn asked.

"Do? What *can* I do? That was over thirty years ago. It isn't like I can turn back the clock."

"True, but..."

Susannah's eyes widened as the possibilities came to her. In her excitement she half rose from her sitting position. "I could find Jake," she whispered. She'd been toying with the idea for weeks and hadn't acted on it because...because she was afraid. Now she saw that she had the perfect justification, a real reason to seek him out.

Carolyn didn't immediately endorse the idea. "You're married," her friend reminded her. "Jake probably is, too. Are you sure this is a box you want to open?"

Susannah recalled the ancient Greek story about Pandora and her box of troubles—as Carolyn had no doubt meant her to. "I don't know...."

"Why is it so important to find Jake?" Carolyn asked next. "Think about it, Susannah."

"Because we were both betrayed by our parents," she said. "His father sold him out and my father offered Mr. Presley the one thing he couldn't refuse. Can you imagine how much money five thousand dollars would've been to a man like Allan Presley?" It hurt to *know,* to have proof, that every bad thought she'd ever had about her father had turned out to be true. He was cunning, devious, heartless. "That wasn't the only large check he wrote, either," she blurted out.

"What do you mean?"

Susannah slouched down in the booth. She hadn't intended to say anything, but now that she had, she felt relieved. "As I was going over Dad's bank statements, I found that he'd withdrawn several large sums of money through the years. All the checks were made out to cash, so there's no way of tracing what he did with the money."

"Investments?" Carolyn suggested.

"If so, I didn't find any evidence of it."

"What about vacations?"

Susannah shook her head. "My parents rarely traveled." In fact, she didn't think her mother had flown more than a couple of times in her entire life. That driving trip to California was probably the only long vacation they'd ever taken.

Carolyn was very quiet. "There might be another reason."

"What?" Susannah had been angry and upset with her father all day. His reasons for withdrawing so much money and doing it in such secrecy were incomprehensible to her. Susannah knew that, until recently, her mother had hardly ever written a check. She had no knowledge of managing finances or how her husband spent their money. She hadn't considered it her sphere of duty; it was his, while she handled household routines and entertaining.

Carolyn hesitated, and when she spoke her voice was low. "I mentioned that my father asked to talk to me before I moved back to Colville, didn't I?"

"You said he wanted you to take over the business."

"He did, but there was another reason. An equally important one." She straightened, avoiding Susannah's eyes. "You might have guessed that my parents' marriage wasn't a good one."

Susannah had wondered about it. She made a noncommittal sound, encouraging Carolyn to continue.

"Mom never adjusted to life in Colville. She hated it here and felt trapped, but almost everyone she loved had been killed in the war. My dad couldn't leave her. He wouldn't do that, so he made the best of it until...until I left home and then, well, he fell in love with someone else."

"Your father had an affair?"

Carolyn nodded. "Lily was his secretary for twenty years and his lover, too."

Susannah couldn't imagine why her friend would be telling her something so painful and so private. Unless... "You think my father...had a mistress?"

"I don't know, but it might explain where the money was going."

"Thousands upon thousands of dollars," Susannah whispered, shocked as she considered the possibility.

"Dad genuinely loved Lily," Carolyn said. "When he

knew he was dying, he called me home. He wanted me to look after her when he was gone."

Susannah was appalled. "I can't believe he'd ask that of you."

"It wasn't easy for me, but I did it because I loved my father. I'm fairly certain Mom never knew. Or if she did find out, she never let on."

"What happened to Lily?"

Uncharacteristic tears clouded her friend's eyes. "She died last year. When I got to know her, I loved her, too. She was more of a mother to me than my own. I buried her next to my father. It was what he would've wanted."

"And your mother?"

"She's on his other side."

The idea of her father having another woman was inconceivable to Susannah. But then, she was quickly learning that she really didn't know him. Not once had she suspected that he'd paid off Jake's father. Just thinking about it made the anger race through her again.

"I'm going to find Jake," she insisted. "I refuse to let my father get away with this. I don't care if he had a mistress. I don't want to know. But I do care about finding Jake. I'm going to put his name in the computer and see what comes up." There had to be Web sites that let you search for missing people.

"What about Joe?" Carolyn asked.

For a moment, she'd conveniently pushed all thought of her husband and his likely reaction from her mind. It was easy to do, easy to pretend he wouldn't disapprove. He was in Seattle and she was here in Colville, and they had never seemed so far apart.

"He'll understand," Susannah said. Then, she added, "I won't tell Joe, not unless I actually find Jake." Why upset him for no reason?

"Do you want my opinion?" Carolyn asked.

Susannah contemplated the question. She was interested in what her friend had to say, and at the same time she feared that Carolyn would tell her to drop this before she got in too deep. That would be good advice; unfortunately it wasn't what Susannah wanted to hear.

"You're going to tell me to let go of this." Susannah wished she could. But she *had* to talk to Jake, if for no other reason than to apologize for her family's mistreatment of him.

"Not necessarily. What I want you to remember," Carolyn said, leaning back and sipping her wine, "is that time in France."

"You think I can forget? That year everything changed for me."

"I recall how you waited and waited for a letter from Jake. For weeks on end you defended him, made excuses for why he didn't write and then after a while you didn't talk about him anymore. It seemed like you no longer cared."

"Of course I still cared, but I had other things to think about!"

Carolyn agreed with a nod. "Doug."

"I'd lost my brother and not hearing from Jake didn't seem important after that—but I did ask about him when I got home. With no success, and now we know why."

Carolyn grew quiet again, then shook her head briskly, as if to chase unhappy memories away. "We're both reacting to the discussion we had with Sandy, Yvette and Lisa the other night."

"Both?" Susannah raised her eyebrows.

"I...I decided to extend my flower beds at the house." Her friend blushed as she said it.

"And you requested that landscaping guy," Susannah finished.

Carolyn gazed down at her wine. "He's going to stop by tomorrow afternoon to give me an estimate. I know I'm being obvious, but, Susannah, I can't stop thinking about him. It all started with that silly conversation and now I'm wondering where it'll end—for you *and* for me."

Susannah wondered, too. "All I know is that Jake's been on my mind for weeks, even before I learned what my dad had done. I'm determined to find him, only...only..."

"What?"

Susannah sighed morosely. "I don't have a computer here."

"I do," Carolyn said, as if it was understood that she'd help. "Come back to the house with me. I'll log on to a couple of search engines and see what we can come up with."

A surge of energy shot through Susannah. She hadn't slept well the night before and was emotionally drained after confronting her mother this afternoon. Her concern for Chrissie wasn't doing anything for her peace of mind, either.

"You want to do that now?"

"I don't see why not," Carolyn said. "I'm pretty much a night person, anyway."

After paying the tab, Susannah followed Carolyn down

the narrow country road. The night was dark, with moon and stars obscured by clouds. The porch light cast a friendly, welcoming glow.

When they arrived, Carolyn unlocked the door and turned off the alarm. She led Susannah into the house, to one of the back bedrooms, which she'd converted into a home office. As soon as she flicked on the light, she settled into the desk chair and reached for her mouse. Within minutes she was logged on to the Internet and making her way through search engines with the confidence of someone who used computers regularly.

Although Susannah had access to a computer at school and at home, she was rarely online. There was only one computer in the house, and Brian hogged it most evenings. For her, the computer was a tool, and she didn't have the leisure time to explore its research or recreational potential.

Susannah got a second chair, pulled it close to the desk and sat down, more than happy to let Carolyn do the work.

After several minutes, Carolyn leaned back with a satisfied grin. "Bingo."

"You found him?" It couldn't possibly be this easy.

"I can't be sure, but didn't you say his father's name was Allan?"

Susannah nodded.

"Here's a Jacob Allan Presley. That sounds promising, doesn't it?"

"Very promising." Susannah couldn't remember Jake's middle name, but it made sense that he'd share his father's.

Carolyn's smile was contagious. "There's only one way to find out. Phone him and see."

"Now?"

"You might want to wait until morning," she suggested, smiling.

Susannah was too excited to sit still. After all these years, all this wondering and regretting, it had taken nothing more than a few strokes of the computer keys to locate Jake.

CHAPTER

19

Late that evening, Vivian woke, and instantly her heart was weighted down by the events of that afternoon. Rarely had she seen Susannah more upset. But whatever Susannah believed, Vivian knew George would never do anything to hurt his children. There must've been some misunderstanding.

The room was dark, but her eyes quickly adjusted to the lack of light. She sat up in bed, trying to make sense of what Susannah had told her. If only George would come to her again. Then she could ask him about all this. He'd explain everything, and Vivian would be able to tell Susannah and her daughter would understand.

Except that George hadn't come and she'd waited as long as she could before falling asleep.

Her husband was the one who'd assured her that moving into the assisted-living center was the right thing to do. Yet not once since she'd arrived had George come to visit. Now she was lonely…and disappointed.

Laying aside the sheet, Vivian reached for her robe and slipped her arms into the long sleeves. Her balance wasn't as good as it used to be. She had a cane, but hadn't wanted Susannah to know how much she sometimes needed it, because her daughter would make a fuss. Consequently Vivian hardly ever used it in front of her family. She needed her cane now, though, and retrieved it from the umbrella stand in the corner.

She hobbled around the darkened apartment from her bed to the living room chair. She couldn't remember where the light was…. But it seemed George always came to her at night, so perhaps if she sat up and waited for him, he'd know how badly she needed to talk to him.

The dark and silence lured her, and it demanded effort not to drift back to sleep. Her head sagged to one side, startling her into wakefulness. Jerking upright, she felt her heart beat frantically until she remembered she was waiting for George. She had something important to ask him—only she couldn't quite remember what. She reassured herself that she'd recall it in a moment.

She tried really hard to think. Her question had to do with Susannah; that much she knew. But George still didn't come.

In an instant Vivian realized why. He must have forgotten she wasn't living at the house anymore. He was probably there now, wondering where she'd gone. He must be terribly worried. There was no help for it; she'd have to go to him.

Leaning on the cane, she raised herself to an upright position and was breathing hard by the time she was standing. Slowly, she shuffled toward the door. It felt as if someone had strapped ten-pound bags of flour to her feet. Lifting them and walking normally seemed impossible. Each step was a struggle, but she wasn't deterred.

Opening the door, she looked both ways and didn't recognize a thing. Heaven only knew where she was now. George would be upset with her.

Moving as fast as she could, she stepped into the hallway. Long and dimly lit, it resembled a hospital corridor, but Vivian knew that couldn't be right. She wasn't wearing a hospital gown and she didn't see any medical personnel. That didn't mean much, though, not these days. All the hospitals were understaffed. No one respected the sick. Old people were left to their own devices.

With labored steps, Vivian started down the hall. No one seemed to be around.

"You're up early."

Not seeing anyone, Vivian stopped and glanced around.

"In here."

She turned toward the sound of the voice and found an elderly man standing next to a pool table. He wore a housecoat and had a pair of crutches. One crutch rested along the side of the gaming table. This was some fancy hospital, if it was a hospital.

"Who are you?" she demanded.

"George."

"No, you're not." She was furious that some man would try to pass himself off as her sweetheart. "I know my husband, and you're not him."

"You're not my wife, either, but my name is still George."

Vivian stepped a bit farther into the room. "I'm looking for him."

George nodded and using his crutch as a pool cue, aimed at the black ball in the center of the table. With an ease that amused her, the ball rolled toward the corner pocket and slid effortlessly inside.

"Good shot."

"I've had plenty of practice."

Vivian began to leave the room. "Very nice meeting you, but I need to find my husband."

"Good luck," he said, waving his crutch at her.

Vivian continued down the hallway. This was a hospital, all right. She recognized the nurses' station. It was deserted at the moment, which was probably for the best. Vivian didn't want anyone to stop her.

Two doors opened to the outside. This area was well lit and, supported by her cane, she started out. To her surprise, no matter how hard she pushed at one door and then the other, they wouldn't budge.

"They keep the doors locked," George said from behind her. He leaned heavily on both his crutches now. "No one can come in or go out until after eight in the morning."

"That's ridiculous!"

"Yup. That's how they do things around here."

She was being held prisoner. "This is an outrage. I'm telling my daughter."

Using both crutches, George swung forward. "Won't do you any good. That's just the way it is. What's the matter, can't you sleep?"

Vivian was tired and confused. "I need to talk to George. I told my daughter I would. She's going to be so disappointed that I didn't see him." This burden was almost more than she could carry.

"Why don't we sit down and you can tell me all about it. I'm a good listener and my name is George."

"But…"

"You can tell your daughter that we talked it over, and then you'll both feel better."

Vivian wasn't sure that would work. Susannah had been so rattled. Doing what this George suggested would be cheating, but she'd promised Susannah…. Only she couldn't quite remember what she needed to find out.

"Have we met?" she asked, wondering if George was someone she should know. He must be; she'd met so many people through the years.

"Not until tonight. I take meals in my room. You're new, aren't you?"

She frowned. "Fairly new." That seemed like a safe answer.

"So, do you want to sit down and talk for a bit?" He gestured with his crutch to the room off the lobby, the one with the massive stone fireplace. It was cozy and inviting, with a number of chairs and a sofa. A piano took up one corner and a bookshelf the other.

"Will it help?" she asked.

"It might," he told her.

Since she couldn't get out of here, Vivian decided she might as well talk to this George. That was the best she could do for now.

Shuffling her feet, moving awkwardly, she made her way into the room and sat down in the big overstuffed chair next to the fireplace.

George used his crutch to push aside the ottoman in the

chair next to hers and carefully eased himself down. "How long have you been here?" he asked.

Vivian shook her head. "I can't rightly say. My daughter insisted I come." She should've fought harder, she mused, and wished she had. "I didn't want to leave my home, but George told me I should."

"Where is he?"

"Calvary Cemetery."

Her newfound friend bent forward and stared at her, as if seeing her for the first time. "Dead, is he?"

Vivian nodded. "But he visits."

"I see."

Vivian hadn't told many people and thought perhaps it was a mistake to trust this man with her secret.

George studied her through half-shut eyes. "Your husband only comes when he feels like it?"

She didn't know exactly how to explain. "He comes when he can. I need to ask him about Susannah. She's our daughter and she was upset this afternoon about something her father did."

"You told her you'd discuss it with him?"

"Yes, but George didn't come and I'm afraid she'll think even worse of him." She was embarrassed to admit to this stranger that her husband and daughter hadn't always seen eye to eye.

"What's the problem?"

Vivian rested the cane between her knees and planted both hands on top. "That's just it—I don't precisely remember. He did something."

"Out of love?"

"Of course! George loved his children. There's only

Susannah now…. Our son was killed years ago. I'm afraid George was never the same afterward."

"I'm sorry for your loss."

Tears welled up in Vivian's eyes. "It wasn't the same with us, either…after we lost Doug."

"I'm sure it wasn't."

The tears ran down her face and she used one hand to wipe them away.

"Now, you listen," George said gently. "You tell that daughter of yours that you talked to George—and you did."

Vivian sniffled. She was willing to listen, but only because she was growing desperate. "What should I say?"

"Tell her that whatever your husband did was for her own good."

"Are you sure about that?"

He nodded emphatically. "Sure as anything. Will you do that?"

Vivian said, "Yes," in a small voice.

"Good." George gave her a satisfied grin. "Now, I think it's time we both went back to our rooms."

Already Vivian felt better. Susannah would, too, as soon as they had a chance to talk.

CHAPTER

20

On Monday morning, right after her first cup of coffee, Susannah reached for the kitchen phone. With her fingers trembling and her heart beating frantically, she pounded out the long-distance phone number Carolyn had gotten off the Internet.

In less than a minute she learned that this Jacob Allan Presley wasn't the boy she'd once loved. The retired telephone lineman who lived in Texas simply told her that the country was filled with Presleys. He wished her luck in locating the Jake she was searching for and that was the end of that.

She replaced the receiver, figuring she was going to need a lot more than luck.

"Any reason you're looking glum?" Chrissie asked twenty minutes later as she strolled into the kitchen in her shortie pajamas. Without waiting for a response, her daughter walked over to the coffeepot and automatically grabbed one of the few mugs that hadn't been packed.

Not wanting to discuss the matter, Susannah shook her head and cradled her cup with both hands as if it was a source of needed comfort. This was not the way she wanted to start her morning. It was barely after eight and she was already depressed.

"Troy asked me to ride into Spokane with him this morning," Chrissie said. She opened the refrigerator and took out a small carton of cream; standing there with the door still open, she added it to her coffee. She returned the cream and closed the door, all without glancing in Susannah's direction.

Chrissie was spending the day with Troy *again?* Objections stumbled over the tip of Susannah's tongue, but she bit them off. "Oh?"

"Yeah!" From the way Chrissie answered, Susannah could tell that her daughter wasn't asking permission. It was a foregone conclusion that she intended to go.

"What time did you get in last night?" As soon as the words were out, Susannah realized the question would have been better left unasked.

"I'm not a child." The disdain in Chrissie's voice wasn't even slightly disguised.

Rather than argue, Susannah pointed out the obvious. "I assumed you were in Colville to help me."

"I'll do my share. Don't worry about it." With that, Chrissie walked out of the kitchen, clutching her mug of coffee.

Susannah might not be a contender for any Mother of the Year award, but she knew her daughter and suspected

Chrissie was up to no good with Troy. Chrissie was definitely feeling guilty about *something*. Susannah didn't want to consider what, although several possibilities loomed large.

After taking a moment to collect her thoughts, Susannah walked down the hallway to Chrissie's room. Tapping on the door, she opened it and found Chrissie cross-legged on the bed. She was staring blankly into space and didn't acknowledge her mother.

"Are you feeling okay?" Susannah asked, leaning against the doorjamb.

Chrissie kept her gaze trained away from Susannah. "Why shouldn't I be?"

Susannah shrugged. "You don't usually snap at me this early in the morning."

"You don't usually drill me about my friends, either. I'm sorry you don't like Troy, Mom. But I do. In fact, I like him a lot. He's not like any other boy I've dated. He's a man, and I'm tired of dating boys."

Chrissie had that right; Troy was certainly no Jason O'Donnell. It was clear to Susannah that Troy's attention was giving her daughter a way to cope with the pain and rejection she felt because of Jason. This wasn't a good situation and she needed to tread lightly, but before she could even suggest that Jason might be a factor, Chrissie said, "You aren't going to give me a hard time about driving into Spokane, are you?"

Susannah didn't have any choice other than to let her daughter go. She didn't like it, but she didn't have the energy to fight Chrissie. Joe seemed to think their daughter was old enough to make her own decisions. Although she usually agreed with him, in this instance she didn't. Still…

"Are you sure this is what you want to do?"

"Yes," came her instant reply, "and before you say anything about Jason and me, you should know this has nothing to do with him. Jason was a boy. Troy is a man."

Susannah opened her mouth, but the disdainful look was back in her daughter's eyes. "You aren't going to guilt me into staying," Chrissie muttered. "This is the first fun I've had all summer."

Susannah didn't understand why everything had to be about fun. Chrissie would experience a rude awakening when she discovered that there was more to life—that fun was meant to be a diversion, not the main activity.

"I'm not really that much help packing up Grandma's stuff, anyway," Chrissie added, as if that excused her behavior.

Without another word, Susannah walked out of the bedroom, gathered up clean clothes and quickly showered. Afterward, feeling refreshed, she dressed and blow-dried her hair and decided to talk to Chrissie again, but it was too late. Her daughter had already left the house.

So much for that.

At nine-thirty Carolyn phoned. "Was it him?" she asked after the briefest of greetings. Her enthusiasm for this project was just the solace Susannah needed, especially after her initial caution about looking for Jake.

"No," Susannah said. "Someone altogether different."

"I have a little time this morning. If you stop by the mill, I'll do some checking on the computer here."

"Will I get a chance to meet the lawn-maintenance guy

you mentioned? You did say he'd be mowing the grass outside your office, didn't you?" she said mischievously.

"No." Carolyn's response was adamant. "And no."

"I'll try not to be too snoopy." A renewed sense of hopeful anticipation filled her. "I'll be there in about an hour." Susannah felt like dancing as she hung up the phone.

She hurriedly ate a piece of toast, then drove to Altamira to see her mother. Vivian was tired and listless, insisting she'd spoken to George, who'd apparently visited in the middle of the night. The conversation delayed her an extra ten minutes while her mother repeated word for word the entire exchange with her dead husband. When Susannah finally left the complex, Vivian seemed grateful to return to her morning nap.

On her way out the door, Susannah made an appointment with the nurse. She felt it was time to discuss the state of Vivian's mental health.

From the assisted-living complex, Susannah drove directly to the mill. She parked in front of the office in the vacant visitor's slot next to Carolyn's truck. As she parked, a battered pickup pulled out. It *had* to be the lawn guy. She tried to get a look at him, but failed.

Carolyn was waiting for her in the outer office.

"Who was the guy I just saw leaving?" she asked casually. "In the beat-up blue truck."

"That was Dave," her friend said, glancing around self-consciously.

"Any reason he stopped by?" She wanted to hear every single detail. "You told me he wasn't working here today."

"He came to get an update on Grady, the man who had a heart attack last week." She paused, taking a deep breath.

"I'm supposed to meet Dave later this afternoon to go over some ideas for my new flower beds." Carolyn said this stiffly, as if she regretted ever commenting on her plans. Then she got up from her desk and closed the door.

"You really are keen on him, aren't you?" Susannah asked.

Carolyn hesitated. "Is it that obvious?"

"Not really, but I know you."

She exhaled sharply. "Call me a coward, but I've decided against the new flower beds. I...don't think I'm going to go through with it."

Susannah had hoped that Carolyn's attraction to Dave would overcome her shyness and her fears.

Carolyn sat down at the computer. Purposely changing the subject, she said, "Like I told you, I had a few extra minutes this morning and logged on to the Internet. I found six other Jake Presleys." With her eyes on the computer monitor, she reached for her mouse and hit the print icon. The hum of the printer started immediately.

"Six!" Susannah felt exhilarated, despite her nagging concerns about Chrissie.

Leaning back in her chair, Carolyn gazed up at Susannah. Her eyes narrowed slightly. "So how's everything with you this morning?"

Susannah merely shrugged.

Carolyn gestured for Susannah to sit down, which she did.

"When we were in France," she said, "I could always tell when you were unhappy. You get this look I can read a mile away."

Susannah couldn't see any reason to hide what was

happening. "Chrissie and I had an argument this morning," she confessed. "She's spending the day with Troy. He's driving into Spokane and she's tagging along."

"They're together again?" Carolyn straightened, frowning slightly.

"That's not all. I went to see Mom before I came here." She mentally reviewed the disturbing conversation. "Mom insisted she talked to my dad again last night. Apparently he had an important message for me. She claims my father loved me deeply. Mom said Dad would never do anything to hurt me. He wanted her to tell me it was because he loved me that he got rid of Jake." Susannah found it impossible to keep the sarcasm out of her voice.

"Ask your mother to have him check up on my parents," Carolyn teased.

"Very funny."

"You notice I'm not laughing all that hard. In a few years that could be us, you know."

Susannah sighed. "I know."

The phone rang, reminding her that the mill was a busy place.

Carolyn grabbed the sheets from the printer tray and handed them to Susannah. "Good luck," she said.

"Thanks. I'll see you later." She walked out the door with a little wave. The fact was, Susannah already had an alternative plan, although she was keeping it to herself for now.

One thing was certain—she intended to find Jake no matter what it took.

CHAPTER

21

None of the six Jake Presleys on Carolyn's list turned out to be the Jake Presley from Colville. Susannah and Carolyn spent Monday and Tuesday evening trying various Internet search engines, but to no avail. When she wasn't on Carolyn's computer or the phone, searching for Jake, she was making detailed notes about her father's cash withdrawals from the bank statements she'd found.

At least every other year, and sometimes more often, he'd made these withdrawals, some large and some not. She also discovered that her father had taken frequent trips out of town. Not once had her mother mentioned these trips. They generally weren't more than a day or two. Business trips, noted in an odd sort of journal her father kept. All he'd written down was the name of a city and a cash amount. In checking the bank statements against the journal entries, she saw that the money withdrawn was the same amount as listed in this pocket-size journal. The largest ones she made special note of.

August 23, 1973—Dallas, Texas—$13,000

March 2, 1978—San Francisco, California—$15,000

October 22, 1980—Boise, Idaho—$10,000

April 19, 1993—Portland, Oregon—$12,000

If these were investments, as both Joe and Carolyn had suggested, she couldn't understand why the withdrawals were made in cash. Two possibilities occurred to her, and they seemed to take clearer shape with every day. Besides Carolyn, the only person she dared discuss them with was her husband. Her biggest fear was that, like Carolyn's father, he'd had a mistress and was traveling with her. That night at the bar, she'd told Carolyn it didn't matter to her if he'd had a lover or not. But it *did* matter. For her mother's sake, she told herself.

Wednesday morning, Susannah woke to learn that Chrissie had already left the house. A quickly scrawled note was propped up against the coffeepot announcing that— surprise, surprise—she was with Troy. In less than a week, her daughter and that shiftless bum had become practically inseparable.

Susannah had a lot on her mind and wanted to talk to Joe about it. She reached him at home, having breakfast. After a brief greeting she launched into her concerns.

"The more I study my father's bank accounts, the more convinced I am that he was either being blackmailed or that he had a mistress."

"Susannah, you don't honestly believe your father would put up with a blackmailer, do you?"

It seemed incomprehensible to her. As far as she knew,

her father hadn't backed away from anything in his life. He didn't tolerate weakness in anyone, especially himself. He was a hard man, difficult to live with, difficult to know.

"I can't really picture him being blackmailed," she agreed. "Then maybe he had a mistress." That idea seemed the more likely of the two.

"What about gambling?" Joe suggested.

"In Boise, Idaho?"

She'd thought of that, too. If her father had made cash withdrawals and flown to Vegas, it would add up, but he hadn't. Instead, he'd listed areas not known for that particular form of entertainment.

"It had to be another woman," she insisted now.

"I don't see it," Joe said. "Your father wasn't the kind of man who'd cheat on his wife."

"I would never have thought Carolyn's father was the type, either." While the two men weren't good friends, they were associates through the service clubs in town. And they were well enough acquainted for George to get the information he needed to send Susannah to the same French boarding school as Carolyn.

"You're far too willing to find fault with him," Joe stated.

"I am not. I have the evidence right here."

"Cash withdrawals and cryptic notes about cities. That isn't evidence."

"He was hiding *something,*" she argued.

"I agree with you there. But you might never learn what it was. Why is it so important? Don't you have enough to do?"

"Yes. In fact, I have far too much."

"You're not getting much help from Chrissie, are you?"

She rested one shoulder against the kitchen wall. Her father had been too cheap to buy a portable phone but he could waste ten thousand dollars on God knows what. "She's spending the day with Troy again."

"Send her home," Joe said. "If she isn't helping you, which is the reason she claimed she was going to Colville, then send her back here."

"I probably should," Susannah said.

"Then why don't you?"

She sighed. "The thing is, Chrissie's good with Mom." No matter how much time she spent with Troy, her daughter made a point of visiting her grandmother every day. Vivian thrived on Chrissie's visits, and proudly introduced her to the other residents. Chrissie's presence at Altamira relaxed Vivian and gave her something to look forward to. Her mother was beginning to adjust and even to socialize, and Chrissie was, in part, responsible for that.

"Susannah…"

"Sorry," she murmured into the phone. "I was just thinking about Chrissie. I don't like Troy or the fact that she's spending so much time with him. But I think she'll come to see for herself what he is." Chrissie was immature, but Susannah still had hope that her daughter would recognize the truth about this new boyfriend of hers.

"You're all right?" Joe asked.

"I'm fine," she assured him.

"No recurrence of someone mysteriously breaking into the house?"

"None." Against her better judgment, she'd mentioned the incidents to Joe a few days earlier.

"You'd tell me if there were?"

"Yes, of course!"

"There seems to be a lot going on in Colville. Maybe I should cancel Friday's appointments and visit."

"Don't be ridiculous," Susannah said. "I really am fine. Chrissie is, too." They spoke for a few more minutes and then hung up with Joe promising to call that night.

Still feeling troubled, Susannah walked outside and into the garden her mother had loved. Even with the burden of packing, she tried to spend a little while tending it every day. Being in this lovely, quiet space usually calmed her, in the same way it had her mother. She wandered between the rows of blooming allium, which resembled giant purple dandelions with the heads growing four to five inches in diameter. The gladioli were in bloom, too, and the lilies, their scent perfuming the air. She sat on the stone bench near the small rose arbor and closed her eyes, raising her face to the sun.

When she got up to go inside, she noticed Rachel Henderson in her backyard with her cat in her arms. The tabby, named Mr. Bojangles, had free rein of Rachel's yard and those adjacent to it. Even though Vivian had frequently complained about her neighbor, she'd never said a word against Mr. Bojangles. Mrs. Henderson waved from the other side of the fence and, smiling, Susannah waved back, but didn't stop for conversation. She wasn't in the mood to chat.

The sun was glorious and the sky a pure, bright shade of blue. She hadn't seen her mother since yesterday and before she resumed packing, Susannah decided to visit. Maybe they could take a stroll around Altamira's beautifully tended gardens.

Perhaps it was her frame of mind, but instead of driving straight to the assisted-living complex Susannah went to the cemetery. On her last visit, she'd been so angry with her father—and at the time, she hadn't known half of what she knew now. For reasons she couldn't explain, she walked over to her brother's grave.

The first thing she saw as she crossed the lawn was the display of flowers that marked the site—a display that was similar to the one she'd seen earlier, with roses again and peonies instead of lilacs. The roses had bloomed now. She couldn't imagine who'd brought flowers to Doug's grave.

She missed her brother terribly—more in these last seven months than in all the years he'd been dead. Glancing at the flowers, she realized she wasn't the only one who missed him. She wondered if the person who'd come to visit had also broken into the house and taken his track ribbons. A long-lost love, perhaps. He'd been dating a local girl when he was killed. She tried to remember the girl's name. Pauline? Peggy?

Patricia! Her name was Patricia Carney. Susannah couldn't help wondering if Patricia still carried a torch for him after all this time. That was a distinct possibility, Susannah mused, bending down to run her fingers over his grave marker.

An hour later, after visiting her mother, who'd been tired and unresponsive and uninterested in a walk, Susannah was back at the house. She continued packing, concentrating on the kitchen and dining room. When she'd taken two carloads to the storage unit, she stopped for lunch, although she wasn't really hungry. She hadn't had much of an appetite for days.

And she knew it was because of Jake.

As she sat at the kitchen table, nibbling at a cheese sandwich, she returned to the half-formed idea she'd had yesterday, when she'd visited Carolyn at the mill. *Hire a detective.* With her limited resources and experience, plus her lack of computer skills, she needed professional help if Jake Presley was ever to be found.

Fortunately, she hadn't packed up or thrown out the Spokane telephone directory. She dug it out of the drawer and flipped through the Yellow Pages until she came to the listing for Private Investigators.

A quarter-page advertisement with a giant magnifying glass caught her attention. The name on the advertisement was Dirk Knight.

She had to bolster her courage to make the call. All the while she was punching out the number, Susannah prayed she was doing the right thing.

"Dirk Knight." The detective himself answered on the first ring. Susannah was afraid this might not be a promising sign. Either he was sitting at his desk with nothing to do, which wasn't a high recommendation. Or he couldn't afford office staff. Or both. His quick response flustered Susannah.

"Hello?" the gruff voice continued.

Drawing in a deep breath, she forged ahead. "Hello, my name is Susannah Nelson and I'm calling to inquire about the possibility of locating someone."

"A missing person?"

"Not exactly missing. This is an old friend I knew over thirty years ago."

"A high school boyfriend?"

"Well…"

"A relative?"

"No—no, it isn't anything like that. This is someone from my hometown that I knew as a teenager." Susannah added a few of the pertinent details.

"I'll need a thousand-dollar retainer."

"A thousand dollars?" Susannah swallowed a gasp. That was out of the question. "Thanks, but no thanks." She replaced the receiver and went down the list alphabetically, calling each P.I. listed.

Twenty minutes later, Susannah had an appointment with a woman named Shirl Remington for three o'clock that same afternoon. This woman, too, required a retainer—in fact, every one of them did. From the detective novels Susannah had read, she should've expected that.

Even with the appointment scheduled, she had some doubts, but she refused to let this go. Making an inquiry didn't cost a dime, so she could at least look into the possibility, see what she'd get for her money.

At ten to three, Susannah located the Spokane address and discovered the agency was in a residential neighborhood. She parked at the curb, rechecked the address, then strode up to the house.

A woman answered. She was tall, willowy and very young. Susannah suspected she wasn't a day over thirty. "You must be Susannah," she said, stepping aside to invite her in.

"Yes." Susannah nodded for emphasis, nervous and unable to hide it.

"Sit down." The woman gestured toward the French doors leading to an office off the living room.

Susannah sat on the edge of a chair and fidgeted with the zipper on her purse as she waited for the other woman to walk behind the desk, sit down and reach for a pad and pen.

"How exactly can I help you?" Shirl asked.

Heaving a giant sigh to ease her nervousness, Susannah explained the situation as straightforwardly and honestly as she could. As she spoke, the private detective took notes. Her long brown hair repeatedly fell forward and she repeatedly pushed it back, looping it around her ear. Susannah tried not to be irritated by that. Why didn't the woman just wear it in a ponytail?

"You wouldn't happen to know Jake's social security number, would you?" Shirl asked hopefully, flinging back her hair as she looked up.

"No." Unzipping her purse, Susannah withdrew two sheets of paper. She unfolded them and slid them across the desk. "These are all the Jake Presleys my friend and I found on the Internet. I've talked to each one personally and can verify they aren't the Jake I knew."

Shirl nodded. "Good. No need to go over ground that's already been covered."

Susannah began to relax. Despite Shirl's distracting gestures with her hair, she liked the no-nonsense manner in which the woman conducted business. After a few more questions, Shirl laid down her pen.

"Is there anything else you can tell me that might help me locate your friend?"

Susannah couldn't think of a single thing. Then she remembered something she hadn't thought about in years. "Yes," she cried. "Jake had a benign tumor as a kid. He had to have it surgically removed and has a thin scar on his left side about two inches below his waist. In front," she added.

Her face turned twenty shades of red as she realized the other woman would guess how and when Susannah had viewed Jake's scar.

Thankfully the private detective didn't comment but merely noted this latest bit of information. Then she looked up again. "As I said over the phone, I'll need a thousand-dollar retainer."

Susannah swallowed and opened her purse. No one would consider the job for anything less than a thousand up front. If she was going to get the answers she needed, she had no choice but to spend the money.

"You take credit cards, don't you?" she asked in a suddenly hoarse voice.

"Yes, I do," Shirl said, smiling across the desk at her.

With shaking fingers, Susannah withdrew her credit card and handed it to the private investigator.

Now all she had to do was find a way to tell her husband.

22

Carolyn stayed late at the mill. Production had closed down for the day and the crew had left the yard. The work site was uncharacteristically quiet. During the day, the office, too, was filled with constant activity; everything changed the minute the whistle blew, signalling the end of the working day.

By late afternoon, she was alone with her thoughts. Alone, period, and that was how it would stay.

Coward that she was, Carolyn had contacted Kettle Falls Landscaping and left a message canceling the additional work she'd ordered for her front yard. She'd be foolish to pursue a relationship with Dave Langevin. This attraction she felt unnerved her. She wasn't good at relationships; her failed marriage proved it. Her father hadn't done well in choosing his life partner and she hadn't, either. But unlike him, she wasn't willing to have an affair. Besides, how would it look for the owner of the mill to be seen with a yard man? That was a snobbish reaction, she knew, but it was what many townspeople would say and she couldn't ignore that. She had a duty to her family name. A duty to the community. Getting involved with Dave would only lead to unnecessary complications. Complications she could live without.

Carolyn had accepted this responsibility long ago. Rather than dwell on how structured her life was, she tackled the paperwork piled on her desk. Because she was constantly interrupted during the day, she generally stayed late two or three nights a week to deal with memos, requests and other paperwork that demanded concentrated effort. Some of this she could have handed off to her personal assistant, but she didn't and wouldn't. Here, in these quiet moments, she gained needed perspective on the business. She tracked orders, kept an eye on inventory, became aware of any staff problems and more.

The still of the late afternoon slipped away. She worked steadily until eight. Then, sitting back in her chair, she turned off her computer and collected her purse, ready to call it a day.

After locking the office, Carolyn waved a friendly good-bye to Nolan, the security guard, and headed toward her vehicle, enjoying the warm evening air. Summer was her favorite season. Here it was, the end of June and it was still light. Maybe that was why she resisted the idea of going home. She decided to visit Susannah, instead, and was driving in that direction when she passed He's Not Here.

The local tavern was a regular hangout for many of the mill workers. A few cars were scattered across the parking lot now, but by this time most of the work crew had gone home to their families.

Then she saw it. The battered truck that belonged to Dave Langevin. Her heart started to beat erratically. By now he would've gotten word that she'd cancelled the extra work. He'd know what that meant. She couldn't help wondering if he was disappointed.

Almost without volition, Carolyn found herself turning into the lot. She sat in her truck for at least five minutes trying to figure out what to do. Her hands were clammy, her stomach was jumping with nerves, and her heart raced. It felt as if a simple decision—whether or not to go inside— was one of the biggest of her life. Swallowing hard, she climbed out of her truck and walked toward the tavern.

The darkened windows barred the sunlight, and it took Carolyn's eyes a moment to adjust. She stood inside the entry and glanced around, looking for Dave.

The place was less than half-full and she saw him right away. He sat at a corner table, his back to the wall, nursing a beer. He glanced up and for the most fleeting of seconds, their eyes met.

Slowly, Carolyn stepped farther inside. The jukebox played a Reba McEntire ballad, and the scent of beer hung in the air. A few men sat at the bar and on the opposite side three or four others were involved in a noisy darts game. One couple, well past sobriety, clung to each other on the tiny dance floor.

Carolyn slipped into a booth that looked directly toward the table where Dave sat. The aching way he made her feel seemed to intensify. It was as if everything female within her sprang to life whenever she was near him. She'd assumed those feelings had disappeared years ago, after her divorce. But Dave Langevin's mere presence had revived them.

Although they'd occasionally talked, she knew next to nothing about him. He'd revealed little of his past, little about himself. He was always courteous and polite. He'd never even touched her and yet she felt his touch every time he looked at her.

"What can I get you, sweetie?" the barmaid asked, strolling up to the booth with a tray in one hand.

"I'd like a beer," Carolyn said, needing fortification. "Whatever you have on draft." A cold beer would taste good after a long, hot day. On an empty stomach the alcohol would likely affect her more quickly, in which case she could order something to eat before she went home.

The woman returned with a frosty mug. The foam spilled over the sides of the thick glass as she thumped it down on the lacquered wood table. Carolyn took a long swallow. It went down just as smoothly as she'd hoped.

When she'd finished half her beer, she began to feel relaxed. With open curiosity she studied Dave, who didn't seem embarrassed by her interest. He met her gaze and slowly smiled. Her heart smiled back and her lips followed before she grew flustered and looked away.

After a few minutes, Dave stood up and seemed to be walking straight toward her. When he walked past her booth and over to the jukebox, she started to breathe normally again. The first tune, the same Reba ballad that had been playing when she arrived, echoed through the room. Then he went back to his table, pausing in front of her booth for just an instant. Just long enough to let her know he'd wanted to ask her to dance, but changed his mind. The *very* way she'd changed hers…

By the third number, a slow love song, Carolyn was ready to leave. She'd made a mistake in coming here. All she'd done was embarrass herself.

At that moment, Dave rose from his chair, his eyes holding hers. With her pulse nearly going crazy, she watched as he came toward her.

Had her life depended on it, she couldn't have looked away. Everything and everyone else in the tavern became a blur.

"Would you like to dance?" he asked in a low voice, offering his hand.

There wasn't anyone else on the dance floor; the drunken lovers had apparently gone home. She nodded and stepped out of the booth. When she placed her hand in his, Dave smiled down at her. The warm sensation of his touch rocked her, but she tried not to let it show.

Without another word, he led her to the other side of the room. When his arms circled her waist and he brought her close, Carolyn slid her hands up his chest and left them there.

The music played, but they barely moved as they continued to gaze at each other. Carolyn felt the strong, steady beat of his heart.

The electricity between them was volatile, threatening to burst into flames with the slightest provocation. Carolyn felt it with every breath she drew. The desire to slip her arms around his neck and urge his mouth to hers nearly overwhelmed her. She wanted him so badly that she closed her eyes, certain he'd see what she was feeling—certain she'd act on it if he did.

The music stopped and a full minute passed before Dave let her go. When his arms fell away, she released the pent-up tension in a long, deep sigh.

"Thank you," he said.

All she could do was nod.

Together they returned to the booth. He waited until she was seated, then went over to the bar, paid his tab and walked out the door.

Carolyn retrieved her purse and slapped twenty dollars on the table. Unwilling to wait for her change, she hurried after him.

At first she didn't see Dave. The sun had set and the last light was disappearing at the edge of the sky. Then she found him, standing next to his pickup, the door already open.

"Dave," she called out, moving toward him. She didn't know what she intended to say, but she knew she couldn't just let him leave.

He didn't answer, but waited for her to join him.

Carolyn approached him, more confused and uncertain with every step. As she came closer, she stared up at him, lost in her feelings.

All she really had to do was look in his eyes and see the tenderness there, the longing. No man had ever looked at her like that. Not even her husband.

Without a word, Dave lifted his hand and held it to the side of her face. His skin was callused and rough against hers. Carolyn closed her eyes and leaned into his palm, moving gently against it. Had she been a kitten, she would have purred with the sheer pleasure of his touch.

"You did the right thing," he murmured. It seemed to take great effort for him to speak.

"I did?" she asked, not fully understanding what he meant.

"I'm a drifter... I never stay in any town for long. You wanted me to work on your garden, but it was more than that and we both knew it."

She blushed and lowered her gaze.

"You also know it isn't a good idea for us to get involved."

"I don't feel that way anymore," she whispered.

He gave a deep, shuddery sigh. "I thought it was for the best—us not seeing each other, I mean."

"Is it?" she asked boldly. "Is that what you want—to walk away from this...feeling?"

He didn't answer her for a long time. "You tempt me, Carolyn, more than you know, but I can't... It wouldn't be right."

"Why not?"

He hesitated. "I get restless. I always do. After a while, I move on. It's just the way I am." His eyes pleaded for understanding. "I don't want to hurt you and I know I would."

"Isn't that a decision I should make?"

He shrugged. "Perhaps."

"Are you afraid?" she asked him.

He glanced away and nodded. "I'll break your heart."

"At least I'll know I have one." Carolyn hadn't realized it was in her to be so honest or so daring.

"I don't want to hurt you," he said again.

"I'll risk it," she whispered.

When he didn't respond, Carolyn decided she might as well own up to the truth. "The only reason I came to the bar tonight was because I saw you were here."

He sighed as if that was what he'd suspected. "The only reason I came was because I thought you might stop by."

Carolyn smiled; she couldn't help it.

"You shouldn't be seen with me. I'm a yard man, and you're—"

"I know who I am." She loved the way he cared about her, wanted to protect her. But appearances no longer mattered and the opinions of others had become irrelevant.

His thumb grazed her lips, and his smile was sad and brief.

That was when she knew that whatever was happening between them should be explored. Susannah was right—it was time Carolyn took a chance. An attraction this strong was a gift to be treasured, a joy to be savored.

"Thank you for the dance," he said. He kissed her ever so gently, his mouth barely touching hers.

He started to climb into his truck, but Carolyn stopped him. "Come to my house Friday night after work."

He seemed about to refuse, but then he smiled. Nodded.

Carolyn stepped back, watching as he drove off. *What had she done?*

After learning Patricia Carney's married name from Sandy, Susannah picked up the telephone directory, which still lay on the kitchen table, and looked up Doug's old girlfriend. She lived in Kettle Falls with her husband and family. Patricia Carney, now Anderson, remembered Susannah and invited her over. Welcoming the distraction and hoping for some clues, Susannah agreed to meet her.

Patricia didn't resemble the girl Susannah recalled. She'd gained quite a lot of weight, and her lovely chestnut hair had turned a salt-and-pepper gray. With many exclamations of pleasure, Patricia led Susannah to the back patio of her cozy rambler.

"I can't tell you how surprised I was to hear from you," Patricia said as she pulled out a chair for Susannah. The pinewood table was covered with a red checkered cloth. Two glasses and a tall pitcher of lemonade sat on a tray, waiting to be poured. There was also a plate of still-warm oatmeal cookies. The patio was surrounded by lush green-ery, including dogwood and lilac bushes, and an array of blooming lilies, peonies and roses. A large vegetable garden took up a good part of the backyard.

What Susannah had learned from their brief telephone conversation was that Patricia was a retired nurse and her husband still worked as a U.S. Forest Ranger.

"You have quite a green thumb," Susannah commented, glancing around. The profusion of fresh flowers made her heart quicken. Whoever was visiting Doug's grave had access to flowers, too.

Susannah was chagrined that she hadn't immediately thought of Patricia. She and Doug had been a couple from the time Patricia was a sophomore. Two years older, Doug had graduated and was working in town as a carpenter for a local builder. The war in Vietnam was in full swing then, and if Doug hadn't died in the car accident, it was likely he would've been drafted. Susannah remembered conver-sations between Doug and their father about the war. Her brother, who hadn't been academically inclined, had refused to apply for college, much to their father's disappointment. He'd wanted to enlist but Dad had been against it, insisting that Doug wait until he was drafted. The irony was that if Doug had gone into the service, he might be alive today.

"Actually, Tom's the one with the green thumb in the family," Patricia explained, breaking into Susannah's thoughts. She sat next to her and poured them each a glass of lemonade. Handing Susannah hers, she said, "I heard about your father. I'm sorry."

Susannah lowered her eyes and nodded. "It was very sudden."

"How's your mother doing?"

"About as well as can be expected. I just moved her into assisted living—she's having a bit of a problem adjusting. But I'm sure that eventually she will."

"Help yourself." Patricia leaned forward, pointing to the plate of cookies; Susannah smiled but shook her head.

"I take it this visit is more than for old times' sake?" Patricia asked.

Susannah appreciated not having to make small talk before she ventured onto the subject of her brother. "As I recall, you and Doug were dating at the time of my brother's death."

A sad, faraway look came over Patricia's face. "Your brother was my first love," she said softly. "It broke my heart when he was killed."

"I was out at Doug's grave recently." Susannah set her lemonade down on the pinewood table and studied Patricia. "There were fresh flowers on his grave." She eyed the flower garden, paying particular attention to the roses and peonies. "Would you know anything about that?"

"No," Patricia told her. "The only time I go to Calvary Cemetery is on Memorial Day. Tom and I put flowers on our parents' graves."

"So you weren't the one who put flowers on my brother's grave?"

Patricia shook her head. "Other than the day of his funeral, I've never visited Doug's grave."

This was discouraging news. Susannah had assumed it *must* be Patricia, who had once loved her brother. If so, it might explain who'd broken into the house, as well. "I thought for sure it was you."

Patricia shrugged. "Sorry, I can't help you. Make no mistake, I loved Doug, but that was many years ago." She stared into the distance, as if caught up in her memories. "Life goes on. I married Tom after I graduated from nursing school. Doug was dead, but I wasn't."

"I know." The tragedy had touched so many lives. In her heart Susannah believed Doug and Patricia would've been happy together. "I'm grateful you weren't with him that night," she murmured.

"Me, too," she said, sighing. "Actually, I might've been, but he called and broke our date at the last minute. I was plenty peeved with him at the time because I'd come home especially to be with him."

"Home?"

"I was at nursing school in Spokane by then."

"Oh, right." Susannah nodded.

"Doug and I were supposed to get together—it'd been planned for weeks—and then at the last possible second, he called and cancelled. Later, when I learned he'd been killed, I was devastated. Devastated," she said again. "And I felt so bad for arguing with him."

"I can imagine." As long as she lived, Susannah would never forget the phone call telling her that her brother was dead. Her father had tried to calm her. That day had been the most horrible of her life; being so far from home had made it even worse. Her parents had never understood how desperately she'd wanted to come home. Her father hadn't allowed it. In a few months, she'd be finished with her studies, he'd said, and it was too impractical and expensive for her to fly home twice in that short period. No matter how many years passed, Susannah could never forgive her father for being so heartless.

"My mother kept saying I could've been killed that night,

too," Patricia continued, "and she was right. If Doug hadn't called, I would've been with him."

"Life takes some odd twists and turns, doesn't it?" Susannah murmured, sipping her lemonade.

Patricia nodded, then grew still for a moment. "Afterward, I thought I'd die, too. I'd never suffered that kind of loss and I wasn't sure I could go on. I'd always assumed Doug and I would get married."

"I always thought you would, too."

She hesitated, and Susannah had the distinct impression that there was something the other woman wasn't telling her. She waited, hoping Patricia would reveal whatever it was.

"I was planning to talk to Doug that weekend," Patricia finally said.

"You were?" she asked softly, encouraging the other woman. "What about?"

"Well, when I first left for nursing school, Doug called me every night and drove up to see me at least twice a week. After a while, he started phoning every other night, and then just once the week before he died. I asked my friends who were still in Colville, and they assured me he wasn't cheating on me. According to them, he wasn't seeing anyone else. I didn't understand what was happening between us. Something was. I could feel it. Unfortunately, I never found out what. And I still wonder...."

Susannah wondered, too.

"All I know is that after I went to Spokane, nothing was quite the same."

"In what way?"

"I think there *was* someone else," she said softly. "I

was young and foolish, and I realize I'd romanticized the relationship, but that's the truth. If he was seeing another woman, then my guess is she's the person who's leaving flowers on your brother's grave." She sipped her lemonade and added, "Because it isn't me, Susannah. It simply isn't me."

Okay, so her brother might've been involved with someone else, although to Susannah it didn't seem likely that Doug would deceive Patricia that way. Granted, she'd idolized her older brother, she'd always turned to him for advice and had considered their relationship special. She'd counted on him. In fact, before she left for France, he'd promised to do what he could to help her work out the situation with Jake.

"I have another question for you," she began, "and I hope you don't mind my asking."

"Sure, go ahead."

"Did my brother ever say anything about my father?"

Patricia blinked as though the question took her by surprise. "Like what?"

"Well," she said, then exhaled slowly. "Did he ever say anything that might lead you to believe my dad wasn't the upstanding citizen everyone thought he was?"

"Never." Patricia sounded shocked. "Your father was a judge."

"He wasn't perfect. He had flaws like everyone else." Because she felt she needed to explain further, she said, "I'm going through my father's things, and I'm learning a lot about my family—stuff I never knew. If you remember *anything,* it might help me connect all the pieces." Of one thing she was certain; her brother would never have condoned paying off Jake's family. He would've been as outraged as she was.

Patricia's face went blank and she slowly shook her head. "Your brother never said a word to me about your father."

"Oh." She couldn't keep the disappointment from her voice. She'd hoped Patricia would have some answers to give her.

She finished her lemonade and set the glass down. "I'd better go and do some packing," she said, getting to her feet. "Thank you so much for seeing me."

Patricia stood, too. "I was happy to do it."

She walked Susannah to her car. "Listen," she said. "If you do find out who left those flowers at Doug's grave, would you mind letting me know? I'd be curious to learn who it was."

"I'll do that," Susannah promised and shut the door.

On the drive back to the house, she decided to stop at Safeway, since she needed a few groceries and didn't want to make a special trip later.

Walking into the store she felt someone staring at her and turned to find Sharon Nance, Troy's mother and her former classmate, a few feet behind her. The woman looked at least sixty. There was a hardness about her, evident in the wrinkled overtanned skin and heavily made-up eyes. She wore a short jean skirt that rode halfway up her thighs and a thin, purple sweater with lots of gold chains around her neck. She was smoking a cigarette.

"Hello, Sharon," Susannah said cordially.

"Well, if it isn't Susannah Leary." Sharon tossed her cigarette on the asphalt and crushed it with the toe of her flip-flops.

"It's Nelson now."

"Oh, right," she said in a bored tone.

"Your son and my daughter seem to have hit if off," Susannah said, not letting on how much she disapproved of the relationship.

Sharon's eyebrows shot up. "Is that right?"

Apparently Sharon didn't know, and Susannah was sorry she'd said anything. She nodded and as they neared the front of the store, she reached for a grocery cart.

"What are you doing in town?" Sharon asked, taking the next cart.

Rather than going into a long explanation, Susannah merely said she'd come back to move her mother.

"Really?" Sharon said with a sarcastic edge. "I thought maybe you were here 'cause of Jake. I saw Yvette the other day, and she told me you're thinking of looking for him. She figured I might know where he is."

Susannah didn't take the bait. "The subject of Jake did come up," she said, playing it low-key. And wouldn't Sharon love to know she'd actually paid a P.I. to find him?

"He came back to me, you know." She shoved the cart alongside Susannah's. "After you left for that hoity-toity French boarding school, he wanted to get back together with me."

Susannah let that comment slide and headed toward the produce aisle. She didn't trust Sharon for a minute.

"Can't say I blame him," Sharon added, following close behind her. She carelessly tossed a small iceberg lettuce into her cart. "I was here and you...weren't." She emphasized the last word.

"And I'll just bet you were available, too." Susannah didn't bother to disguise her scorn.

Sharon laughed. "I always knew he'd come back to me. You were fun for a while, but I was the woman he wanted. I will say he was bummed after you left, though. He showed me that St. Christopher medal you gave him."

Susannah made an effort not to reveal her shock. She'd almost forgotten about that. She had given Jake the medal and couldn't believe he'd shown it to Sharon.

"I heard from him not too long ago," Sharon said, pushing the cart past her. "I might still have his number if you want it."

Susannah's fingers tightened on the cart handle.

"Stop by the Roadside Inn some night and I'll see if I can find it for you," she said casually as she strolled by.

CHAPTER

24

Chrissie was already at the house when Susannah arrived. Hair flying, she ran out the front door the minute Susannah parked and surged down the steps with the energy reserved for the young.

"Where were you?" her daughter demanded.

That was an interesting question in light of the fact that Chrissie hadn't seen fit to enlighten Susannah about *her* whereabouts in two days.

"When did you get home?" Susannah asked instead, remaining cool and collected as she headed up the steps and into the house, carrying her groceries.

"You had a phone call." Chrissie, it seemed, wasn't planning to answer any questions herself.

"Who phoned? Dad?"

"No." Chrissie walked backward in front of Susannah,

her eyes flashing with irritation. "A private investigator. You're having Troy investigated, aren't you?"

That might not be such a bad idea. Susannah wished she'd thought of it earlier. "No, I'm not," she said bluntly. That denial appeared to mollify Chrissie—for approximately two seconds.

"Then what's it about?"

"Nothing." Nothing that concerned her daughter, at any rate. Although she realized she might have wasted a thousand bucks, since Sharon seemed to know where Jake was, and all she'd have to do was humble herself enough to ask for the information.

"Mom," her daughter cried, using the same voice she had as a five-year-old determined to have her way. "You can't keep this from me. *Why* did you hire a private investigator?"

Susannah set her purse on the kitchen table, then opened the refrigerator and put the pint of cream inside. While she had it open, she took out a cold soda. Closing the door, she leaned against it, frowning as she saw the ring dangling from a long chain around Chrissie's neck.

"Where'd you get that?" Susannah asked, reaching out to examine the ring.

"I found it in one of the bedroom drawers. It's kind of pretty."

Susannah sighed. "It belonged to my dad." The signet ring, bearing his law school crest, was the only jewelry her father had ever worn other than his wedding band.

Fingering the ring, Chrissie asked, "Is it all right if I wear it?"

"I guess. Just be careful with it." She pulled the tab on

her soda and took a deep swallow. "Now, what did the investigator say?"

Chrissie hesitated. "First I want you to tell me what this is about."

"No. This has nothing to do with you."

"Oh-kay…" Chrissie dragged out the word. "At least give me a clue."

"What did she say?" Susannah repeated irritably. The confrontation with Sharon was responsible for her mood. She hated knowing that Jake had gone back to his former girlfriend.

Chrissie paced the area in front of the kitchen sink. "She said you should call. You might not get her right away because she's going out of town, so she set up a two o'clock appointment for Tuesday, after the holiday."

Susanna had completely forgotten this was the Fourth of July weekend. Knowing that if she didn't catch Shirl Remington right away she'd have to wait, Susannah hurried to the phone.

Chrissie regarded her with a suspicious glare. "Are you sure this doesn't have anything to do with Troy?"

"I'm positive." As she picked up the receiver, Susannah discovered that she didn't have the agency number on hand.

"Where were you so long?" Chrissie asked again, this time without the defiant attitude.

Susannah sighed as she rummaged through her purse for the investigator's business card. "In Kettle Falls visiting my brother's old girlfriend and then I stopped at the grocery store."

Frowning, Chrissie mulled that over. "Any particular reason you looked up one of Uncle Doug's old girlfriends?"

"I thought I'd say hello. It was a social call. Why all the questions?"

"I just wanted to know where you were."

Susannah found the card and her heart slowed. She would rather have put off calling until Chrissie was out of the room, but checking the clock, she dared not delay a second longer.

"Are you going to tell me what the P.I. says?" Chrissie asked as Susannah lifted the receiver again.

Susannah ignored the question and punched out the number. After five endlessly long rings, Shirl Remington's answering machine clicked on. "I'm sorry I can't take your call. I'm either on the other line or away from my desk. Please leave a message and I'll get back to you at my earliest convenience."

Awash with disappointment, Susannah waited for the annoying sound of the beep. "Hi. This is Susannah Nelson returning your call. I'm sorry I missed you. I'll see you—"

"Shirl Remington." The P.I.'s voice broke in.

"Shirl, oh, hi." Susannah's heart rate soared. "I'm glad I caught you."

"I was on my way out the door. Your daughter gave you the message?"

"Yes. Were you able to find...my friend?" she asked, shooting a glance at Chrissie who was watching and listening intently.

"I'll be able to tell you more when I see you. Does Tuesday afternoon work for you?"

"Yes, perfect." Susannah hoped the investigator wouldn't keep her waiting until then. "Can you tell me anything now?" She hated to reveal how anxious she was.

"I managed to dig up one interesting bit of information. It's rather complicated so I'd prefer to explain later."

"Okay." The frustration was killing her. "I might have some information myself."

"Great. I'm putting out some feelers in Canada. Hopefully I'll have more to tell you when we meet."

"Canada?"

"I'll explain everything on Tuesday," she repeated.

"Right…have a nice weekend." Susannah's head was spinning. Did Jake live in Canada?

"Happy Fourth of July," Shirl said and, with that, the line went dead.

"What did she tell you?" Chrissie pried. "What was that about Canada?"

Still absorbed in her thoughts, Susannah shook her head. "She said we'd talk on Tuesday." Until then, her stomach would be in knots. Instinct told her she was close to finding Jake. She could feel it. Although maybe that was merely because she so badly wanted to talk to him.

"Dad doesn't know about this, does he?" Chrissie said, accusing her with a look of righteous indignation.

"Ah…"

"I talked to him this afternoon, and he said he didn't."

Susannah scowled at her daughter, furious that she'd mentioned this to Joe. "Thank you very much," she snapped.

Chrissie's jaw sagged as though she'd been the victim of a great injustice. "I beg your pardon. I thought my parents communicated with each other. Guess I was wrong. I suppose this has to do with that old boyfriend of yours. That's all you talk about, you know. Don't think I can't hear when you're on the phone with your friend—it's Jake this and Jake that. I even heard some of your phone calls to those other Jake guys. In case you've forgotten, you're *married*."

Susannah's face burned with anger and guilt. "For crying out loud—"

"You'd better call Dad," Chrissie cut in. "He wants to know what's going on and frankly I don't blame him." Chrissie stormed out of the kitchen and disappeared down the hallway to her room.

Susannah grabbed the icy soda. Her hand shook as she brought the can to her mouth. Sooner or later, she'd have to tell Joe about the thousand-dollar fee to the private detective.

After taking a few minutes to let her pounding heart settle down, Susannah tried calling Joe at the office. Her one hope was that he was in the middle of a complicated root canal and couldn't be disturbed. No such luck. He was between patients and eager to talk to her. He took the call in his office.

"What the hell is happening there?" he asked, clearly angry and worse than that, hurt.

Joe so rarely raised his voice that Susannah felt even guiltier. "Good afternoon to you, too," she muttered.

"Susannah, I only have a few minutes. Tell me what you're doing."

"If you're asking about the private investigator, I hired her to find Jake Presley." There, it was out with no embellishments, no explanations and no excuses.

The silence between them seemed to shout at her, echoing Chrissie's taunt. *You're married.*

"It didn't occur to you to talk this over with me first?" he finally asked. "How would you feel if I decided to look up Donna Terry? She was my first love, but you don't see me paying good money to hire someone to find her."

"This is different," she insisted.

"I know you're upset about what your father did," he continued, "and I get that, but this is carrying things too far."

"I want to talk to him."

"Fine. Why go behind my back?"

"Because...because I knew you wouldn't want me to and—well, okay, I knew how you'd feel. I don't expect you to understand, but this is something I have to do."

"So you went through with it even though you were well aware that I'd disapprove? My opinion doesn't count?"

"Ah..."

"You can't answer that, can you?"

"Joe, I'm sorry. I was wrong. I should never have handled this the way I did, but I didn't feel I had a choice. I was afraid you'd talk me out of it or make me feel guilty for wanting to track him down."

It was as if he hadn't heard her. "I would hope you'd trust me enough to discuss such an important matter with me."

"I know...." Her words faded. She wanted to explain what had led to her hiring the detective, but Joe wasn't listening. She certainly couldn't tell him that the money might well have been wasted.

"Why is it so important for you to find him?"

"It just is—for all the reasons I've already mentioned."

"He didn't bother to find *you*. Doesn't that tell you anything?"

It didn't, because Jake had to honor his father's agreement with hers. She was under no such obligation.

Another silence, filled with accusations.

"Did you talk to the detective?"

"Yes. She was on her way out the door so we didn't have a chance to say much. I've got an appointment Tuesday afternoon."

"You're keeping the appointment?"

Susannah frowned, feeling helpless in the face of her own regrets and his unyielding bitterness. "I intend to, yes. Please, Joe, don't be angry with me."

"Keep your appointment," he said, "but I don't want to hear a word about it, understand?"

Before she could agree or disagree, the line was disconnected.

25

Chrissie went outside and sat on the top step to think over what was happening to her family. Her hand curled around the ring. It seemed that her parents' marriage was dissolving in front of her. The minute she'd arrived home from college, she'd sensed that things weren't right between her mom and dad.

Now her mother was hung up on this guy she'd known as a teenager. Jake was on her mind 24/7. It was obvious. Hardly anything had gotten packed in the last couple of days because her mother was too busy doing her own investigative work, looking for her old high school boyfriend, talking about him constantly with Carolyn Somebody—whom Chrissie hadn't even met.

She couldn't worry about her parents, though; Chrissie had concerns of her own. Troy was exciting and fun and—she had to say it—dangerous. Almost every afternoon she made a run into Spokane with him. She didn't ask what that was about, but she had her suspicions. He left her in the car while he went inside a "friend's house." These visits took all of five minutes and then they drove back to Colville. A couple of times they'd stopped at Loon Lake for a swim. Once he'd taken her for ice cream next to a video rental place.

They spent hours at his friends' homes. These guys weren't the type who attended college, either. If her mom knew about Troy's friends, it would freak her out.

Chrissie brightened as the familiar sound of his truck came from the end of the block. She was off the porch and standing at the curb by the time he roared to a stop.

"Hi." He leaned out the window, elbow on the edge, and sent her a ready smile. "What's up?"

Chrissie shrugged. "Not much."

"Want to go for a ride?" he asked, with the lazy certainty that she would.

"Sure." She dashed around the front of the truck and climbed in.

"You don't want to get your purse?"

"Will I need it?"

"No, but I've never seen a woman who didn't drag her purse everywhere she went."

The problem was, Chrissie didn't want to go into the house. If her mother saw her with Troy, she'd ask where Chrissie was going and what time she'd be back. Chrissie could live without that particular form of harassment.

"I don't need it. Let's get out of here."

Troy responded with a throaty laugh and grabbed her bare thigh, his fingers creeping under the hem of her shorts. She didn't stop him.

"We going to Spokane?" she asked.

"Not today."

"Then where?"

"Ever been to Northport?"

"Nope." Chrissie had heard of the small town close to the Canadian border. Now she'd see it.

"It'll be fun."

Chrissie rested her head against his shoulder. "Everything with you is fun."

Troy released her leg, shifted gears and they were off. Normally he racked up the volume on his sound system and let the music blare. This afternoon, he seemed to notice her mood and kept the screaming pitch down to a more moderate level.

"What's wrong?" Troy asked as they pulled out of the city limits. "Is your mother on your case about me again?"

Chrissie shook her head. "What would you think if I moved to Colville?" she asked, testing the waters. She couldn't imagine going back to school after this summer. Not with the Jason mess and her current indifference to academics. Moving here made a lot of sense. Her grandmother needed her, and that way they wouldn't have to worry about packing up the entire house in a few weeks. She could live there and take care of everything.

Besides, she'd never had a relationship like this. With Troy, life was one big party and she was along for the ride and loving every minute of it.

"D'you want to live with me?" he asked.

That would definitely freak out both her parents. "I'll think about it," she said, but her parents weren't going to let *that* happen.

He laughed. "Your daddy would probably have me arrested."

"I told you I'm over twenty-one." It was a lie, one that slipped easily off her lips. So she'd exaggerated a little.

Troy chuckled and gave her a knowing look. "You're not twenty-one, are you." He didn't make it a question.

"I'm—"

"Just as long as you're not under eighteen."

"No way." Indignation caused her to straighten. "I'm not a kid!"

He stroked her thigh again and laughed.

Then, because she was curious, she asked. "Have you had girls live with you before?"

"A few. They generally don't last long." His eyes momentarily left the road and connected with hers.

Chrissie lost herself in the sexual intensity of his gaze, and her breath caught in her throat.

"I have a feeling that if *we* got together it'd be different, though," Troy murmured.

Chrissie felt as if her heart would melt at his words. "You make me so happy."

He cocked his head to one side. "Baby, you do the same for me," he rumbled in a low, sexy voice.

Chrissie ran her hand down his bare arm and smiled.

The highway curved, and Troy drove onto a little-used back road. "There's something else on your mind," he said, slowing the truck.

Chrissie stared out the window. "What makes you think that?"

Troy held her chin in one hand and turned her head so she couldn't avoid his gaze. "It's in your eyes."

She might as well tell him; he'd get it out of her sooner or later. "My mom and dad are fighting."

"I thought your dad's in Seattle."

"He is. They were on the phone when you arrived. My mom lied to him."

"They were yelling over the phone?"

"They don't fight like that. It's more these pauses when neither one of them's willing to talk, you know?"

Troy grimaced. "That's not how it was in my house. Fights meant throwing things. A couple of my so-called uncles got physical with Mom. More than once, Mom and I ran in the middle of the night so we wouldn't get the crap beat out of us."

Chrissie gasped with horror.

"Hey, I survived and I'm a better man for it."

Chrissie wondered about that. Her respect for his mother, whom she had yet to meet, wasn't high. She couldn't fathom any mother putting her child in that kind of situation.

"I'm afraid my parents might get a divorce," Chrissie told him. That was one of her worst fears. It happened to other families; it could happen to hers, too.

"Hey, my mom and dad never bothered to get married. Does that shock you?"

"No." From what she knew about his mother, very little would.

"My daddy took off before I was born. The bastard." Troy's hoarse laughter followed. "My daddy was a bastard and he made me a bastard."

"That's not funny."

"It's the truth, so get used to it." The humor left his eyes.

"I can't imagine growing up without my dad," Chrissie

said, wanting to wrap Troy in her embrace and give him all the love he'd missed as a child.

"Hey, don't go soft on me. There were plenty of men around," he said with a measure of irony in his voice. "My mother saw to that. She married twice before I was fifteen and after that she provided me with a series of interesting uncles—none of whom stuck around."

"Troy, that's terrible."

"Terrible? I'm a survivor because of it. No matter how bad things got, I landed on my feet."

"What about your mother?"

He glanced away. "She's all right. Her life hasn't been easy, but she's made the best of it."

"I'd like to meet her."

Troy didn't immediately respond. "Someday."

"Why wait?" Chrissie asked.

"You're a bit too—"

"Too what?"

"A bit too virginal."

Chrissie elbowed him in the ribs.

"I'd like to change that," he said suggestively. "Maybe you'll let me before the end of the summer."

"Maybe I will." Chrissie giggled. Troy made her see life in a completely different way. It was about surviving, and surviving meant not taking anything too seriously, not getting in too deep.

CHAPTER

26

By late afternoon, Susannah was beside herself with worry. Chrissie had vanished without a word, without even leaving a note. The last time Susannah had seen her was while she was on the phone with Joe. She didn't know where her daughter had gone or with whom.

Not that it was hard to figure out. Chrissie was more than likely with Troy Nance. The very least the girl could've done was tell her. She had a cell phone. Why didn't she call?

After an hour of pacing, she'd had it. She decided to escape the house. With a heavy heart, she drove to Altamira to visit her mother. Vivian was with friends, Sally Mansfield and two other women. Not wanting to interrupt her mother's visit, Susannah only stayed for a few minutes. When she returned to the house, she phoned Carolyn, hoping for a chance to get together.

"You sound upset," her friend said barely a minute into the conversation.

"I am," Susannah admitted. "I've had a horrible day."

"Come on over and I'll commiserate with you. My day hasn't been that wonderful, either."

Half an hour later, Susannah pulled into the long driveway that led to Carolyn's home. The scene was picturesque in the early-evening light; soon, the deer would venture down into the wide-open field next door. If she wasn't so agitated, she'd stop and appreciate the beauty of the countryside, with the surrounding hills standing guard. She envied Carolyn the tranquility of this lovely place.

The front door stood ajar, and after a courtesy knock, Susannah pushed open the screen door and let herself in.

"I poured the wine," Carolyn announced from the kitchen. "After the day I've had, I need something stronger than iced tea."

Susannah echoed that sentiment. They sat down in the family room, where the air conditioner blew cool air from the vent overhead. The afternoon had grown unpleasantly warm and it felt good to relax. Had she been in Seattle, she would've been preparing for a party to celebrate the holiday weekend. As it was, she'd probably join her mother at Altamira for a barbecue.

Carolyn sat at one end of the sofa and Susannah the other. After a sip of wine, Susannah gestured to her friend. "You go first."

Carolyn gave a weak shrug. "With me, it's a bunch of small things that added up to one disastrous day. I didn't set my alarm, so I overslept, which I almost never do. Consequently I was late getting into the office. My entire day was off-kilter. I was rude to Jim although I didn't mean to be and after that, everyone avoided me. I often stay late at the office, but not today. I wanted out of there the minute the whistle blew and frankly I think everyone was just as glad to be rid of me."

Susannah could sympathize. "I hate it when my day gets off to a bad start."

"I'll be checking my alarm clock from now on." Carolyn tucked her bare feet beneath her as she made herself comfortable on the couch. "All right, it's your turn."

"Anything else?"

Carolyn closed her eyes. "Okay, okay, I took the plunge."

"You and Dave?"

"I didn't tell you, but we made…sort of a date. For today." Carolyn sighed. "I ruined everything, though. He was weeding the flower beds this afternoon and I snapped at him and when I left work, I found a note on my windshield that said perhaps we should meet another night instead. Oh, Susannah," she moaned, "I'm so disappointed."

Hearing that her friend had acted on her desires was encouraging news. "You actually approached him? Is that how you made your sort-of date?"

Carolyn blushed. It was so wonderful to see Carolyn this excited that Susannah had to hold back a giggle.

"Dave and I…ran into each other," Carolyn explained. "At He's Not Here."

"What happened?"

"Not much… We danced one dance and talked a bit. We decided to meet here tonight and then I had to make a complete mess of things." She picked up her wineglass. "Enough about me. It's your turn."

Susannah wasn't sure what to tell her first. The most current crisis was her daughter, so she started there. "Chrissie took off…again."

"With Troy Nance?"

"That's my guess."

"Have you considered talking to Sharon about him?" Carolyn asked.

Chrissie would hate it if she went to Troy's mother, but Susannah was beyond caring. "I saw her earlier today at Safeway. She says she has Jake's phone number and that the two of them got back together after I left for France."

"And you believe her?"

Susannah didn't have any choice. She nodded. "She knew about the St. Christopher medal I gave Jake. I'd forgotten about it, but she hadn't."

"Do you really think she's telling the truth?" Carolyn asked.

Susannah shrugged. "I have to assume she is. Although she didn't seem to know that Troy's seeing Chrissie."

"She knows," Carolyn muttered. "Trust me, she keeps close tabs on her boy. If you want to find out where Troy and Chrissie are, she'll be able to tell you."

As much as Susannah hated talking to Sharon twice in the same day, she had to do it. This ridiculous situation with Troy and Chrissie had gone on long enough. "How old is Troy, anyway?"

"He must be around thirty."

Susannah frowned. Not only was this guy completely unsuitable, he was far too old for Chrissie. Sooner or later, she'd have to confront Chrissie about her relationship with Troy. When she did, she wanted her facts straight.

"Chrissie's got you down?"

Susannah ran her fingers down the stem of her wineglass and lifted one shoulder. "She's only part of the problem. Joe and I had an argument this afternoon."

"Any particular reason?" Carolyn asked, then rushed to add, "If it's none of my business, just say so, but if you want to talk, then I'm here to listen."

Feeling as wretched as she did, Susannah needed to share her dilemmas. "I didn't tell him I'd hired a private eye."

"Oh, oh."

Susannah sighed. "I know it's crazy. You can imagine how Joe felt when he heard what I'd done—from Chrissie, by the way, which just infuriated me. And yet it's my own fault for keeping it a secret. Joe was really angry with me, but he was at the office and couldn't very well vent with his entire staff listening in."

"He doesn't understand why it's so important for you to find Jake, does he?"

"I don't completely understand it myself. I wish I could just leave everything the way it is, but, Carolyn, I can't. It's too late." She bent her head, eyes closed. "Joe is my life raft, so why do I keep pushing him away? I can't seem to help it. I'm risking everything for this, and when I consider what's at stake, I have to admit it's crazy. I can't undo the past."

"So what happens next?"

Susannah wished she knew. "I have an appointment with the P.I. on Tuesday afternoon."

"So she didn't tell you anything yet?"

"Not really. She mentioned putting out some feelers in Canada. I don't have a clue what that's all about. She said she'd tell me on Tuesday."

"She must have some news, otherwise she wouldn't have asked for an appointment," Carolyn said.

"I'm hoping she does."

"If she *has* found him, what will you do?"

Susannah hadn't decided. Yes, she wanted to talk to Jake and apologize for her father's actions. But that could be done over the phone. Seeing him again was something else entirely. Despite herself, her heart raced with excitement at the prospect.

This was wrong, so wrong. She reminded herself forcefully that she was married. Joe was her husband and he was a good man who deserved better than to have his wife hungering after some high school boyfriend.

Yet Susannah no longer felt in control of what she'd set in motion. She couldn't stop the search for Jake now, even if she wanted to. And she didn't....

"Susannah?" Carolyn's voice broke into her reverie.

"What will I do?" Susannah repeated. "I'm not sure." She took another sip of her merlot. "Chrissie, Jake, Sharon, Joe—that's not the end of my hellish day, either."

"You mean there's more?"

"Yup," Susannah said, trying to sound lighthearted without much success.

"Go on. You might as well tell me."

"I found out something about my brother."

Carolyn straightened and leaned toward her. "Doug? What did you learn?"

"I went out to see Patricia Carney. Her name's Anderson now. You remember her, don't you? She and Doug were seeing each other."

Carolyn nodded, setting her wineglass aside. "I remember the two of them were dating, yes."

"Right, but Patricia seemed to think there might've been someone else in his life." She stared down at her wine. "In fact, the night he was killed, Patricia was going to confront him and then at the last minute he broke their date."

"The night he was killed?"

"Yes," Susannah said. "If he hadn't cancelled, Patricia would've been with him."

Carolyn's eyes widened at the implication and when she spoke her voice was soft. "She might have died that night, too."

Susannah nodded. "We talked about the twists and turns life takes. I promised I'd let her know when I find out who it might've been."

"Hold on, you just lost me. Who might've been *what?* Are you talking about this other girl he was supposedly seeing?"

"Yes, but in addition to that, someone's been putting flowers on Doug's grave. I thought it was Patricia, but she swears it isn't, so I assume it's whoever else he was involved with."

"She's telling you the truth," Carolyn whispered. She reached for her wineglass again and got to her feet. Walking back into the kitchen, she replenished her drink.

Susannah followed. "How would you know that?" she asked.

Carolyn stood on the other side of the counter, eyes downcast. "Because it's me."

"You?" Susannah asked numbly.

"Doug and I were writing to each other."

"What?" Susannah said, stunned by this revelation. "While we were in France?"

Carolyn nodded apologetically. "Soon after you arrived in France, Doug wrote to ask me how you were doing. He knew how upset you were with your father, and he was worried. I wrote back and he answered. Pretty soon we were writing regularly."

"And you never bothered to mention this to me?" Susannah asked, angry that the woman she'd considered her best friend had kept something so important from her. She'd told Carolyn all about her feelings for Jake; Carolyn obviously hadn't returned the favor. Now that she thought about it, Susannah remembered how eagerly Carolyn had waited for the mail. She had, too. It was what she'd lived for those months in France.

"I'm sorry." Carolyn shifted awkwardly. She didn't meet Susannah's eyes. "I never meant to keep it from you. But the first time he wrote, Doug asked me not to tell you, so I didn't and then, well...well, one thing led to another and I just never did."

"The two of you fell in love through the mail? Is that what you're saying?"

"I guess I am." Carolyn looked directly at her. "Don't you remember how frantic I was when Doug was killed?"

Susannah shook her head. She'd been so caught up in her own pain she hadn't noticed.

"In the last letter I got from him, Doug said he was going to tell Patricia about us. He planned to break up with her that night, I think."

"You still put flowers on his grave?"

They walked back and sat on the sofa again. "Every few

weeks I put flowers on my parents' graves and Lily's. I leave some at Doug's, too. I didn't realize you'd see them."

"When you were writing," Susannah asked, "did Doug—did he say Jake had gone back to Sharon?"

"No. But then, he didn't write much about Jake."

Susannah studied her friend. "What aren't you telling me?"

"I do know that Doug was mad at him about something—he just never said what it was."

27

Vivian had her good days and her bad ones, and today was good. Many of the bad days were before Susannah and Chrissie had come. Vivian had done her best to hide how defeated she'd felt. In fact, she hadn't realized how badly she was coping at home until she came to live at this prison place—or hospital or whatever it was.

Not that she was complaining. The food was all right when she had an appetite, and she noticed the meals had improved since her first week there. Granted, most days she *didn't* have much of an appetite, but she made an effort to eat. She was growing used to the way they did things here. It worried her some when she discovered that they locked the doors at night, but her friend George—not her husband, the *other* George—had told her why. The doors were locked to keep the crooks out. She could believe that. She already knew the world was full of people eager to swindle an elderly widow.

Barring the doors to thieves was fine with Vivian, but it kept someone else out, too—her George. She hadn't known locked doors were a hindrance to the dead, but apparently they were. He hadn't come to visit—at least not until today. When she woke from her nap, he'd been there, in her darkened room. Oh, he looked wonderful to her. Vivian had been overcome with joy. It'd been so long since his last visit that she'd nearly given up hope.

She asked why he'd taken all those weeks to find her. He couldn't answer, but that was all right. None of that mattered when he was with her. For a while they sat and looked at each other in silence. Tears had come to her eyes and although they didn't speak, Vivian felt his love for her and their children.

Once she'd composed herself, she told him how upset Susannah was, although she still couldn't recall exactly why. Poor George didn't know what to think. He'd frowned and shaken his head, and Vivian wished she'd kept it to herself. All too soon he was gone.

Invigorated by the visit, Vivian joined Sally and a couple of other women for dinner. Earlier in the afternoon, they'd also met for tea, which was becoming a regular occurrence, and one she had to admit she enjoyed. Then she'd had her nap, followed of course by dinner. Afterward as she started back to her suite, she felt disappointed that she hadn't seen her friend George, even though she knew he ate in his room. Vivian was proud of herself. She'd finished her entire salmon cake and small salad, but she didn't much care for the rice dish. No flavor whatsoever.

Leaning on her cane for balance, Vivian walked past the pool room. Sure enough, her friend was there, using his crutch as a pool cue just as he had the first night she'd met him. George glanced up when he saw her.

"I wondered if you'd swing by," he said in that gruff way of his.

"Well—here I am."

George made a dismissive grunt. "What's put you in such a good mood?"

"My husband visited this afternoon."

George lowered his crutch to the floor. "Did he now?"

Vivian nodded. "He stayed for a while, too."

The other man's gaze narrowed. "I didn't see him."

That made perfect sense to Vivian. "Of course you didn't. He only appears to me. He's dead, you know."

"Oh, right, I forgot. I don't suppose he talks much, either."

"Can't. He's dead."

George rubbed the side of his face, as if testing to see whether he needed a shave or not. "Did he let you know what he wanted?"

The question gave Vivian pause. "I think he was just checking up on me. I was mighty glad to see him, I'll tell you that."

"Did you mention that business with your daughter?"

"I tried, but it really bothered him."

"I thought I saw her here earlier."

If this conversation was going to take much longer, Vivian would need to sit down. She made her way over to the sofa and slowly sank into the soft cushion. "She *was* here."

"She didn't stay long."

Vivian frowned, clutching her cane with both hands. "Why not?"

"She didn't say, but she was here barely five minutes. I saw her when she was walking out the front door."

Ah, yes, Vivian remembered now. "My friends were visiting and then I lay down to rest."

"Did you sleep?"

Suddenly Vivian wasn't sure, but she must have. "Do you know who's looking after my roses?" she asked.

"Can't say I do."

"That's okay. Don't worry about it. I'll find out when the nurse comes with my pills."

"That's a good idea," George agreed.

Vivian started to get up, then changed her mind. She frowned. "Susannah stopped by like you said, and I think she was upset again."

"Does your daughter have a problem with anger management?"

Vivian took offense at that. "What a horrible thing to say about my Susannah," she flared.

"Don't get huffy. It seems to be a family trait."

This conversation was declining fast. Vivian tried to get up but found she didn't have the strength. "Somebody help me," she called out, ignoring George.

"I'm coming," George said, limping toward her with the aid of his crutches.

"Not you." George had insulted Susannah and she wasn't going to stand for it. Or sit, either.

"Who's going to help you up if not me?" George asked. He parked himself directly in front of Vivian, making it impossible for her to escape. "Guard," she yelled at the top of her lungs.

George hooted with laughter.

"This is no laughing matter," she insisted.

"Here." He offered her his hand.

A better woman would have refused, but Vivian wanted to get back to her apartment. She decided she'd be willing to forgive him this one slight against her daughter. But *only* this one.

Using her cane for leverage and holding on to George's hand, she struggled to an upright position, but it wasn't easy. Damn fools shouldn't put useless furniture in these rooms.

"I'm glad to hear your husband came by," George said as she headed toward the door.

"He was an important man, you know. A judge."

He nodded.

"George sent a lot of men to prison. They deserved it, too. He didn't tolerate crime."

"Good for him."

He sounded sincere, and Vivian was warmed by his approval. "He has to come during the day now."

"Why?"

Of all people, George should know the answer to that. "They keep the doors locked after eight."

"Oh, right. I forgot."

She snorted, not believing that for a second. Vivian was halfway into the hall when George stopped her. "I don't suppose you told him about meeting me, did you?"

Vivian shook her head.

"Is he the jealous sort?"

"My husband? Never—well, maybe a little."

Her friend followed her a short distance. "Do you play bridge?"

Vivian shook her head again. "I'm not much good at that sort of thing."

"Too bad. I could use a bridge partner. What about gin rummy?"

"I used to play that with the grandkids when they were little, but they outgrew it."

"Want to give it a try one afternoon?"

Vivian would've liked that, but she was afraid she'd lose track of the cards. "Maybe. You play Scrabble?"

George gestured with one of his crutches. "I'm not so good with words."

Perhaps they had more in common than she'd realized. "Me, neither."

George grinned and she smiled back at him. "The shuttle bus is taking a trip to the Indian casino in Spokane tomorrow afternoon," he told her. "How would you feel about going along?"

It would make for a long day but Vivian supposed she could manage it. "I think I'd like to go."

George seemed pleased.

"'Night," she said.

"'Night," George echoed. "Listen," he added, "the next time your husband stops by, you tell him he's got competition."

Vivian blushed. "I'll do that," she said over her shoulder.

Monday was the Fourth of July. After Susannah had attended the barbecue at Altamira, Carolyn accompanied her to the Roadside Inn five miles outside town. At first Susannah had dismissed her offer, but now as they approached the Inn, she was grateful not to be alone. One look at the seedy, run-down tavern was enough to convince her this was not an establishment she should walk into alone.

In fact, she had no desire to enter the Roadside Inn at all, under any circumstances. Had she been in any other mood, Susannah would have put this off, but she hoped to speak with Sharon, mother to mother, about Troy and Chrissie. And if Sharon had Jake's phone number, she wanted it.

When she picked Carolyn up, her friend was in a cheerful frame of mind—and it didn't take Susannah long to discover why. Dave! He'd come to see her on Saturday night. Carolyn hadn't described the visit in detail, but it seemed to have gone well.

"Would you stop," Carolyn muttered when Susannah reached the end of the driveway.

"Stop what?"

"Looking at me like you're ready to break into giggles at any moment."

"I can't help it," Susannah confessed. "You just seem so happy."

"You're such a romantic."

No question there. "So are you."

"I know… I wish Dave wasn't so concerned about appearances." She made a wry face. "I mean, I worried about it at first but I couldn't care less now."

"He doesn't want to embarrass you."

Carolyn shrugged. "He never stays anyplace long," she explained. "I told him I accept that. When he's ready to leave he should just go. I certainly can't stop him."

"What about the possibility of him being an ex-con? That doesn't bother you anymore?" Susannah felt she had to ask.

"I've been around men my entire life and I consider myself a decent judge of character," Carolyn said. "Dave's a good man. If he's ever been in jail it would surprise me…. Besides, I did a search in all the states he's mentioned and couldn't find any record of him in the justice system."

"You can do that?"

Carolyn smiled, nodding.

"You enjoy his company, don't you?" Susannah asked.

"We had a wonderful time. Dave barbecued steaks, and we sat and talked for hours. I've never felt this comfortable with any man. He's warm and funny and has this dry sense of humor that cracks me up. He's a completely different person when he's not on the job."

Susannah wondered if Carolyn understood the risk she was taking. And she wondered if she herself fully recognized everything she was risking in her quest to find Jake.

They were absorbed in their own thoughts as she drove the rest of the way to the Roadside Inn.

"There's a rough crowd here," Carolyn said once Susannah had pulled into an empty parking space.

The lot was full of trucking rigs and broken-down vehicles. One pickup actually had the passenger door missing. Loud music blared from inside, and a few disreputable types clustered near the entrance. Paying them no heed, Susannah marched resolutely toward the tavern, Carolyn at her side.

They stepped into the room and onto the sawdust-covered floor. Cigarette smoke hung in the air like a dense fog. It seemed that every pair of eyes was staring at the two of them. The one good thing about the wailing jukebox was that they couldn't really hear the catcalls and jeering remarks aimed in their direction. Ignoring her discomfort, Susannah strode over to the bar tended by Sharon Nance. Two men scooted down to make room and Susannah thanked them with a curt nod.

"Well, as I live and breathe, it's the Bobbsey twins," Sharon taunted as she strolled toward them from the other end of the bar.

"Hello, Sharon."

The other woman's heavily bleached hair was pulled tightly away from her face, leaving little to soften her sharp features. She planted both hands on the edge of the bar. "What can I do for you?"

"How do you know I didn't come in for a beer?" Susannah asked calmly. She chose to disregard the other woman's hostility.

Sharon snorted as if to say she wasn't that easily fooled. "You aren't the type. Frankly, I doubt you're here to have a good time, either, although any one of these guys would be more than happy to accommodate you."

Susannah had hoped for something a little friendlier. She tasted disappointment in the stagnant and smoke-filled air.

"What's the matter?" Sharon said, glowering at Carolyn. "Cat got your tongue?"

"Hello, Sharon," Carolyn said in the same cordial tone Susannah had used.

"How's Daddy's little girl doing at the mill these days?"

Several heads turned in their direction. A couple of the truckers picked up their beer mugs and left their stools at the bar, moving into the shadows.

Susannah didn't know what that was about. Were they protecting Sharon—or remaining uninvolved? She couldn't tell, but hoped it was the latter. This was uncomfortable enough without any further complications.

"I don't suppose you've met my daughter?" Susannah asked conversationally. Her voice trembled slightly, betraying her. "As I told you, she's spending a lot of time with your son."

Sharon's responding laugh was devoid of any real amusement. "What makes you think I'd *want* to meet your little girl? She ain't here, that's for damn sure, and if she was, it'd be of her own free will, now wouldn't it?"

Susannah nodded warily.

Sharon's black-rimmed eyes flared. "I bet that's got you worried. But guess what? Troy's never even mentioned her. What my son does is his own business. I will say this, though. He's got a weakness for sweet young things. If I were you, I'd keep your girl away from him."

"How old is Troy?" Susannah was furious that she'd allowed Sharon's attitude to get to her.

"Why do you ask?"

"Chrissie's only nineteen." She didn't add that Chrissie would turn twenty in another month.

"Are you trying to make trouble for my son?"

"No, but…"

"If Troy wants you to know how old he is, he'll tell you."

This wasn't getting them anywhere.

"Anything else?" Sharon asked, raising heavily penciled eyebrows. "Oh, yeah. This doesn't have anything to do with you, but you might find it interesting." She folded her arms and smiled at Susannah.

"What are you talking about?"

For an instant, the other woman seemed genuinely surprised. "You really *don't* know, do you?"

Confused, Susannah glanced at Carolyn. "Know what?"

Sharon's mouth twisted in a sneer. "Don't you think Troy looks a lot like his daddy?"

It took longer than it should have for the implication to sink in. "Are…are you saying Jake is Troy's father?"

Sharon said nothing more and went back to tending bar. "You tell me."

Now that she considered it, there *was* a resemblance between Jake and Troy. She felt sick to her stomach.

"Still want me to get his phone number for you?"

"Uh…" Reeling from shock, Susannah couldn't answer.

Sharon laughed. "That's what I thought."

Carolyn's hand clasped her arm. "Come on, let's get out of here."

"In a minute." Susannah didn't understand Sharon's animosity. She'd never been friends with the other woman, but they'd gone through eleven years of school together. While it was true that Jake had broken up with Sharon and started to date her, he'd apparently had a change of heart after Susannah left for France.

"Why are you so angry?" Susannah asked.

Sharon's laugh was hoarse from years of smoking. "The only time you come around is when you want something. Your brother did the same thing. Any other day of the week I'm not good enough for either of you."

That wasn't true. Susannah had never gone out of her way to avoid Sharon.

Crossing her arms and looking bored, Sharon muttered, "So, what'll it be? A beer or the door?"

"What can you tell us about Jake Presley?" Carolyn demanded before Susannah had a chance.

"Nothing," she returned flippantly. "You'll have to ask him yourself. If he wants to talk to Susannah, he'll find her. I'll let him know you were inquiring after his health," she said sarcastically. "Actually, I'm surprised you're not asking me about Doug Leary."

"What's he got to do with anything?" Susannah asked, incensed that Sharon would even bring up her brother's name.

"I always found it amusing that your daddy was the law-and-order man and his own son was dealing. Some family you've got there."

"My brother?" Susannah cried. "I don't believe that!"

"Believe what you want. I know what's true, and your brother was in big trouble."

"Let's get out of here," Carolyn said again, tugging at Susannah's arm.

She stumbled back a step. "Don't you *dare* say anything against my brother." Susannah was so upset she was trembling. Why Sharon would invent such fabrications, why she'd hurt her this way—it made no sense.

Sharon's gaze shifted to Carolyn. "I'm not lying."

Susannah shook her head furiously. The woman *had* to be lying.

"He was dealing," Sharon insisted. "Did you know that the night he was killed, he was running from the law?"

Too shocked to respond, Susannah stopped breathing. Sharon's story was more and more unbelievable. The only thing her father had told her about the accident was that Doug had taken the curve too fast and slammed into a tree.

"Sheriff Dalton was chasing my brother?" she asked, just so she'd be able to prove her wrong. She'd simply get in touch with the former sheriff and see what he had to say.

"Nope. Feds were the ones after him."

Sharon certainly had plenty of details, but whether or not they were true remained to be seen. They *couldn't* be! "The federal government?" This should be easy enough to disprove and once she did, she'd sue Sharon Nance for slander.

"Big mistake to mess with the feds." Sharon spoke in a somber voice.

"I don't want to hear any more of these lies," Susannah said. "We're leaving."

"Good," Sharon snarled.

Susannah glared at her. "I don't know what I ever did to you that was so awful, but whatever it is, I suggest you get over it."

"Let's *go,*" Carolyn hissed.

"Doug wasn't the only one, either," Sharon said loudly as Susannah stepped away from the bar.

"What does that mean?" she yelled back.

Sharon gave another of her guttural smoker's laughs. "You'll find out."

CHAPTER

29

"I don't believe a word of it," Carolyn said emphatically as she and Susannah walked out of the Roadside Inn.

"Sharon never even knew Doug."

"Did he ever say anything about this in his letters?" Susannah asked.

Carolyn hesitated.

"Carolyn?" she asked again.

"He didn't say anything directly," she told her. "But I could tell something was up, something he didn't want to discuss. I saved all his letters and on the anniversary of his death, I sometimes reread them."

"And?" Susannah pressed. The structure of her entire family was crumbling. Her father might've been having an affair and now she'd learned that her brother, whom she'd idolized, might have been dealing drugs.

"There were obscure hints in some of his letters," Carolyn continued as they neared the car. "Things I didn't understand. At the time I figured it had to do with Patricia. He was definitely uneasy—I assumed he felt guilty about breaking up with her. But then…"

"What?"

"There was some kind of…incident. I think maybe it involved Jake."

"No." Susannah shook her head. She would've known if Jake was doing drugs—or selling them. He couldn't have been.

"When Jake asked you to run away with him, did he mention finances?"

In an effort to remember, Susannah stood there in the gravel parking lot, trying not to be distracted by the din from the bar. She closed her eyes and the scene in the moonlit garden played back in her mind as if it had happened only hours ago instead of years. Jake had cupped her face with both hands and stared intently into her eyes. He'd asked her to run away with him and promised he'd marry her as soon as they found a justice of the peace in Idaho. Every time she asked a question about where they'd go after that, what they'd do, he'd cut her off with deep, probing kisses, kisses that comforted her and allayed her fears. She'd asked about money. She didn't have much; her father had made sure of that. Jake had told her not to worry, though. He'd take care of everything.

"He said I shouldn't worry about money," she whispered. Her heart ached as she looked at her friend. "What did he do?" she asked. "Where was he getting money?"

"I have my suspicions," Carolyn said in a low voice.

"But why would *Doug* get involved in anything like that?"

Carolyn's gaze met hers in the dim light outside the tavern. "I don't know and I doubt we ever will."

"Do you think that comment Sharon made about Doug not being the only one meant Jake was part of it, too?" she asked. "Jake *and* Doug?" Susannah broached the subject carefully, afraid of the answer. So many of the memories she'd nurtured were being destroyed. Everything she'd believed was turning out to be something else, and Susannah felt she no longer knew what was real and what wasn't. It gave her an unexpected insight into the kind of confusion her mother must feel.

"Sharon would say anything to upset you," Carolyn reminded her. "I don't know how much credit we should give any of the stuff she said."

"Right." Susannah agreed in theory. "Could Troy really be Jake's son?" she asked tentatively. When they'd started dating, Jake had been wild and undisciplined—the stereotypical bad boy. In contrast, she'd been the good girl, and the attraction between them was powerful. She'd made clear to Jake that if he wanted to be with her, he'd have to change, and he'd tried. He'd loved her, and had tried to prove himself to her and her father. Except that the mighty Judge Leary had refused to talk to Jake, had refused to have anything to do with him.

Everything she'd learned about Jake in these past few weeks had shattered the image she'd held of him and now, it seemed, her brother, too. For the first time since she'd arrived in Colville, she longed for her life in Seattle. Her summers there were peaceful, spent working in her garden and doing small projects around the house. The year before, she'd taken an upholstery class and reupholstered the dining room chairs and then, in a burst of enthusiasm, wallpapered the kitchen. A one-week jaunt to Hawaii with Joe had been an added bonus. By comparison, this summer felt like a nightmare with no escape and no end.

Once inside her car, Susannah gripped the steering wheel tightly. "I have to wonder exactly what the truth is. I have no idea anymore."

"Surely there's a way to find out."

Susannah wasn't convinced she wanted to dig up information that might best be left buried. She said as much to Carolyn.

But Carolyn shook her head. "You can't leave it there, especially if Sharon's implicating Doug in some kind of wrongdoing. And her hints about Jake—don't you want to know if there's any truth to them?"

"Oh, my gosh! Shirl Remington mentioned that she was inquiring about Jake in Canada. If he was in trouble, he might've fled there."

"So many young men went north to avoid the draft," Carolyn said.

"I might never find him, then. Especially if he changed his name." It was a possibility Susannah hadn't considered before. "At this point I don't even care. He obviously isn't the boy I remember or the man I thought he was."

Her friend shrugged. "You've paid the investigator. You might as well listen to what she has to say."

Susannah started the engine and turned onto the highway that led back to town. "I guess you're right," she said reluctantly.

They rode in silence for a while before Carolyn asked, "Listen, would you mind if I went with you to that private investigator?"

Whatever Carolyn's reason, Susannah was grateful for the company. "That'd be fine. But…oh, Carolyn, I don't think I could stand it if Doug did anything illegal. I mean, that's not what Shirl's looking for, but if he was involved with Jake in some stupid scheme, it might all come out. I'm really not sure I want to know."

"Not even if it's the truth?"

"I can't believe any of this is happening. I wish I'd never found that agreement between my father and Allan Presley. That's what got me into all this." In any case, it was what had intensified her need to search for Jake.

As Susannah drove the dark country road to Carolyn's home, she felt an overwhelming sense of discouragement. The road and the house looked much the same as they had when she and Carolyn were kids. And yet that sameness struck her as false. *Nothing* was as it seemed. Past and present seemed to blur, leading her to doubt the truth of her own history.

She turned down the long driveway and parked, and Carolyn climbed out of the car. "What time do you want to leave tomorrow?" she asked, sounding as casual as if they were meeting for some ordinary event.

Susannah bit her lip, calculating the distance. "About eleven-thirty."

Carolyn nodded. "I'll be at your house by eleven."

"Okay. See you then."

Susannah waited until Carolyn was inside and the lights were on before she reversed her route and headed back into Colville.

As she drove, she considered calling Joe, despite the lateness of the hour. She didn't blame him for his unhappiness with her. They rarely argued, and she hated this. The problem was, Susannah didn't know what she could say other than to apologize and she'd already done that.

When she reached the house on Chestnut Avenue, the lights weren't on, which told her Chrissie wasn't back from wherever she'd gone with Troy.

Still wondering about calling Joe, she hurried up the front steps and unlocked the door. She left her purse on the small hallway table and flicked on the light. Hoping for a phone message from her husband, she moved toward the kitchen, then paused midstep at a noise coming from the back bedroom.

Perhaps Chrissie had returned, after all. "Chrissie, is that you?"

Nothing.

Susannah froze. "Chrissie?" she tried again, less certain this time.

When there was no reply, Susannah grabbed her purse, raced out the front door and quickly located her cell phone. Scrambling, her fingers hardly able to function, she pressed 9-1-1.

An operator's voice answered. "9-1-1 emergency line. How might I assist you?"

"There's an intruder in the house," she whispered frantically into the cell. She gave them the address. "Hurry, please."

The operator immediately advised her to get away from the house and to wait for the squad car. By the time Susannah made it halfway down the block, her knees were trembling so badly, she sank to the ground. That noise hadn't been her imagination. There was someone in the house—but she was sure the intruder had heard her and would disappear before the police showed up.

Only minutes later, a squad car rolled down the street. Susannah jumped up and rushed to the curb as it parked behind hers. When two officers got out, Susannah jogged over to them. She read their name tags and didn't recognize either one.

"I believe someone's in the house—or was in the house." Her voice shook as she explained what she'd heard.

"We'll check it out." Shining a large flashlight, the first cop walked to the backyard and the other went through the front door, which Susannah had left open.

Susannah stayed where she was, grateful not to have to go back in alone. Standing by a streetlight, she couldn't help suspecting that all her neighbors were staring at her from behind their living room drapes. She resisted the childish urge to wave.

The shorter of the two officers joined her on the sidewalk. "The house is clear."

"Would you go in and see if anything's missing?" the other man asked.

She nodded and made her way toward the master bedroom. It was from this end of the hall that she'd heard the noise. The lights were already on, and at first glance nothing seemed to be disturbed. Naturally. Her fear was that she'd end up looking like an idiot. Or like one of those unbalanced people who called the police in a pathetic bid for attention.

The window beside the desk was raised two or three inches. She didn't remember leaving it open, but that was something she might easily have overlooked. Her father's desk appeared no different from when she'd left it. Large cardboard boxes, some sealed and ready to be delivered to the storage unit and others that were only half-packed, littered the floor. Nothing seemed out of place there, either.

"A cat might've come through the window," the short officer suggested.

"No," Susannah said quietly. "Someone's been here." She couldn't say precisely what was out of place or how she knew, but she did. "Someone was in this room and then left when I arrived."

"You're certain?"

"Yes…"

"What's going on?" Chrissie stormed into the bedroom, coming to an abrupt halt when she saw the two officers.

"We had an intruder," Susannah said. Feeling shaky, she reached for her daughter and hugged her.

"Mom, Mom, are you all right?"

Susannah shook her head and burst into tears.

CHAPTER

30

Carolyn got to the house shortly after eleven on Tuesday morning for their meeting with the investigator. After the events of Monday night, Susannah felt jittery and paranoid, certain that every creak of the floorboard, the slightest sound, was the intruder returning. None of the other break-ins had affected her like this—maybe because whoever it was had actually been in the house when she came home. Chrissie had phoned Joe, and he was furious with Susannah all over again, as though she'd purposely attracted their thief. On closer inspection, she'd found several things missing. Random papers, a tiny clock, an old fountain pen and— bizarrely—the small journal with the entries her father had made regarding trips and money. The burglar had obviously scooped up whatever lay on the desk.

Joe had insisted on ordering a burglar alarm. Susannah had argued that she wouldn't be there much longer. A week, ten days at the most. She was eager to get back to Seattle, to see Joe and talk to him face-to-face. The whole episode with Jake embarrassed her; the strength of her feelings about him now seemed like something from the distant past. She was sorry she'd pursued it at all. In fact, she regretted everything. At this point, all she wanted was to go home to her husband and family, to her safe and familiar life.

"You look dreadful," Carolyn said, standing at the foot of the steps.

"Thank you very much." But Susannah knew that wasn't an exaggeration. She hadn't slept all night. Dark circles shadowed her eyes. Whenever she'd managed to drift off, some noise would jerk her awake, and all morning she'd walked around in a sleep-deprived fog. Worries about Chrissie weighed on her mind, too. She hadn't said anything to Joe yet, but their daughter had dropped a bombshell.

"I'll get my purse." Susannah returned to the house, double-checked every window and door, then met Carolyn at the curb where her friend had parked.

Carolyn offered to drive, and Susannah was thankful. Because she was exhausted and in no mood to talk, she closed her eyes, unable to stop thinking about Chrissie. As soon as Susannah had calmed down last night and the police had left, Chrissie had announced that she was dropping out of college and moving to Colville.

Susannah was aghast. Her first thought had been to send Chrissie back to Seattle. She'd immediately realized that wouldn't work. Chrissie had managed to get to Colville on her own before, and she would again. She claimed she was moving here to be close to her grandmother, but Susannah figured that being close to Troy had more to do with it. The situation had to be handled delicately and she wasn't sure she was the best one to deal with it, considering the arguments she'd already had with Chrissie about that jerk.

Susannah felt Carolyn's gaze on her a few times, but neither spoke until they reached the outskirts of Spokane, when Carolyn needed directions to the detective's address.

Parked outside Shirl Remington's place, Susannah found that her palms were sweaty. She wasn't sure what she'd learn or if this was information she really wanted to hear. Enough of her illusions had been destroyed.

The front door was unlocked. Susannah and Carolyn rang the bell once, then, opening the screen door, they stepped inside. Shirl Remington was walking toward them. This time she wore her hair in a high ponytail.

Susannah introduced Carolyn, and the investigator shook her hand.

"Come in, please." She motioned toward the French doors that led to her office.

While Susannah and Carolyn settled in the two guest chairs, Shirl went to her desk. "Thank you for coming this afternoon," she said as she pulled the top file from her tray.

Susannah slid closer to the edge of her chair. The oddest sensation came over her—guilt and anxiety, dread and fear all at once.

Shirl opened the file folder, then leaned forward, hands clasped on her desk. All her actions seemed to be in slow motion. "I've done an exhaustive search," she said, meeting Susannah's eyes. "As far as I can determine, there is no record of Jake Presley beyond his life in Colville. There's no activity on his social security number. Nor has he filed income tax."

Carolyn frowned at Susannah.

"There's also no record of his ever having been incarcerated."

"Could he have gone out of the country?"

"Possibly Canada. No passport has been issued to Jake Presley. I did learn that he's got an outstanding drug trafficking charge against him. That's the reason I searched for him in Canada. But if he did move up there, it wasn't under the name Jake Presley."

"Drug trafficking?" she whispered. So Sharon had told the truth about that. Then perhaps everything else she'd said was also true. It made Susannah heartsick.

"What about the statute of limitations?" Carolyn asked when Susannah remained silent. "That crime took place years ago."

Shirl shook her head, the ponytail swinging as she did. "With federal crimes there is no statute of limitations."

"Oh."

"My guess is that he got into some kind of trouble with the law and fled into Canada, where he created a new name and a new life. Like I said earlier, I've put out some inquiries with a couple of associates, but it might take a while."

Susannah felt as if she were in a trance. This also explained why Jake was in and out of Sharon's life. Every time he entered the United States, he was putting his freedom at risk.

Carolyn looked directly at the P.I. "Susannah and I went to see an old schoolfriend of ours and Jake's. A woman called Sharon Nance. She claimed two things—that Jake's visited her in Colville, and that Susannah's brother, Doug Leary, might've been involved with him and…and the drug trafficking."

Shirl made a note in the file. "Let me find out what I can about all of that." She straightened and leaned back in the chair. "Did you learn anything else I should know?"

"Susannah interrupted an intruder in the house last night," Carolyn told her.

Susannah shrugged that off. "I don't think it's connected."

"At this point, everything that happens is suspicious," the P.I. said, writing that down, too. "Was anything taken?"

"A journal and some other papers. A clock and a pen. Of limited value to anyone other than family. Besides that…"

"What else?"

"Well, I'm staying in my mother's home," she explained, "and I had several boxes packed up, waiting to be moved. Without going through each one, it's almost impossible to tell." Everything in those boxes was of sentimental value. There was nothing of real monetary worth, but the intruder wouldn't know that.

"Has there been anything else out of the ordinary?" Shirl asked.

Nothing had been ordinary since the day Susannah had come to Colville. "I've had an intruder on at least three other occasions. Again, the only things taken were personal— some old track ribbons of my brother's, for instance." She paused. "I told you about finding that signed contract between Jake's father and mine in Dad's files. That was what prompted me to hire you."

"Yes." Carolyn bobbed her head. "We tried to locate Jake by ourselves but kept running into dead ends."

"Unfortunately I haven't had much success myself," the P.I. said.

"There's my daughter...." On all fronts, this was the summer from hell. "She's linked up with...with a young man of questionable character who may be Jake Presley's son." Susannah couldn't prevent a deep sigh. "The reason I came back was to get my mother settled in assisted living, and Chrissie joined me here."

Shirl nodded sympathetically. "Can you tell me about Jake and Doug's friendship?" she asked next.

Not knowing how to answer, Susannah and Carolyn glanced at each other.

"Doug and I were exchanging letters before he was killed," Carolyn began. "Last night I read through them again in light of what we've recently learned."

Susannah sat up straighter, hoping Carolyn had come upon some fact that would bring clarity to this whole sorry mess.

"Doug never spelled it out for me, but reading between the lines I believe he was trying to help Jake."

"*Help* him?" Susannah cried. "Help him how?"

"I don't know," Carolyn murmured. "What I suspect is that Jake got in over his head. We know now the FBI was on to him."

"You'd think he might've said something to me," she said. Both her brother and Jake had written in the beginning. Jake had written frequently for a brief time, and then less and less and soon not at all.

"How do you want me to proceed?" Shirl asked. "I can

keep looking for Jake Presley. With enough time and money, I can probably find him for you, if that's what you want. I can also look for a connection between your dead brother and Jake."

"No, stop now," Susannah said. "Sharon Nance, our, uh, friend from school, says she has a phone number for Jake." What Sharon hadn't told her was that Jake was living under an assumed name, most likely in Canada. Her preoccupation with him had been emotionally as well as financially expensive. At every curve in the road, she was uncovering information she'd rather not know, remnants of the past that shouldn't be exhumed.

"I don't care anymore. Jake doesn't want to be found, and that's fine. I'm content to leave it at that."

CHAPTER

31

When she returned from Spokane, Susannah wasn't surprised to discover that Chrissie was gone. Her daughter insisted she was moving to Colville. She'd left no room for discussion; she'd made up her mind and, as far as she was concerned, that was the end of it.

A quick check of Chrissie's bedroom revealed that her suitcase was still there. The last threat, when Susannah told Chrissie she couldn't live in the house after this summer, was a moot point. Apparently Troy had invited her to move in with him. Given no other option, she'd accept his invitation, Chrissie said. Susannah wasn't about to let her daughter blackmail her. Unsure how to respond, Susannah decided to bide her time and visit her mother. She hoped Chrissie hadn't mentioned the possibility of staying in Colville to Vivian, who would like nothing better than having her granddaughter nearby.

When Susannah arrived at Altamira, Vivian was in her room watching television, transfixed by the screen. As usual, she had on a cooking program.

"Hi, Mom."

Her mother finally dragged her gaze away from the TV and a smile lit her face. "Jean, it's so good to see you."

More and more often, her mother had been calling Susannah by her aunt's name. Her dead aunt's name.

"Mom, it's Susannah."

Her mother frowned. "I know that."

"Are you up to talking for a few minutes?" she asked, keeping her voice soft and patient.

Vivian picked up the remote control and muted the television. Sitting back in her chair, she tilted her head to one side in anticipation. "What would you like to talk about?"

"Mom, can I ask you a few questions about Doug?" This was hard.

Her mother blinked as if she didn't recognize the name. Then everything seemed to fall into place. Her eyes went liquid with grief, and a tear rolled down her cheek.

Susannah came to stand by her mother, bending to wrap one arm around her shoulders. "Mom, I'm sorry. I didn't mean to bring up painful memories."

She shook her head. "It happened a long time ago. I don't know how much I remember anymore."

"Just answer what you can, all right?"

"You want to know about Dad?"

"No, Doug." Her mother's short-term memory seemed to be declining, too. "Was Doug in trouble when he died?"

"Trouble?" her mother repeated. "With whom?"

"The law." She kept her voice devoid of emotion, as if

they were discussing something as mundane as the use of sea salt in a particular recipe.

"Doug was a good boy. Everyone loved him."

Knowing her father's penchant for keeping things from her mother, Susannah wondered how much she'd known at the time, let alone what she recalled now.

"No mother should ever have to bury her son." Vivian grew quiet. She stared into the distance as if lost in memory. "Oh, Jean, I'm so grateful you came to visit after Doug's funeral. Having you with me was all that kept me sane."

Again her mother had confused her with her aunt. Perhaps she resembled Jean more than she'd realized. She patted her mother's hand. It would be impossible to get any information from her; it'd been a mistake to try.

"Who were Doug's friends?" Susannah asked, making one last attempt. She crouched at her mother's side.

"There was Ronny Pedderson."

Ron and Doug had been in Boy Scouts together, Susannah remembered.

"Ronny lives in Portland now. His mother told me all about him and his family. Doug never had a chance to marry." Fresh tears brimmed in her tired eyes.

"Yes, Mom, I know."

"He and Scotty were good friends, too."

"Don't think about it anymore," Susannah murmured. "I shouldn't have said anything."

"Why did you ask about Doug?" Vivian was sobbing openly now. "George never let me talk about him, you know. Every time I brought up his name, he'd get angry with me." She pulled a tissue from the pocket of her dress. "I couldn't pretend we never had our son, but that was what George wanted. It was like everything gentle and good inside him died with Doug."

"I'm so sorry, Mom."

"You were my only joy." Vivian lifted her hands to Susannah's face. "I know you didn't get along with your father. I tried to make him see that his attitude hurt you both, but he wouldn't listen."

"Mom, please, let's not talk about it." Vivian was suddenly recalling things clearly, and that seemed even worse than her forgetfulness, because her memories brought pain.

Her mother nodded, sniffing a little.

Susannah left ten minutes later, filled with regrets. Every decision she'd made this summer had created disastrous consequences. Restlessness had led her on this quest to find Jake; her need had become a foolish obsession. Now she was paying the price, and it was far too high. For everyone.

Sitting in her car, Susannah got out her cell phone and after the briefest of hesitations, called Joe at his office. He was with a patient, but Miranda, the receptionist, said he'd contact her in about ten minutes.

Susannah parked in the shade at Colville City Park. The pool was at one end, with lawn and trees at the other. She sat and waited for Joe's call, watching mothers and young children at play, teenagers on bicycles, elderly couples strolling and holding hands.

Although she'd been expecting the phone to ring, she was startled when it did.

Call display told her it was Joe's office. "Hi," she said, knowing this would be a difficult conversation.

"I got your message." From his tone she could tell he was still upset with her.

Her nervousness made her stomach jumpy. "I saw the private investigator this morning."

He didn't ask for the results. He'd said he didn't want to know.

"She didn't track down Jake and, frankly, I don't care anymore. I've been such an idiot. Joe, I'm so sorry." Her voice cracked. "I've made a terrible mess of everything, and…and now Chrissie—" She couldn't finish.

"What's wrong with Chrissie?" he asked.

Susannah swallowed her tears and blurted out the ultimatum their daughter had given her. "Chrissie insists she's moving to Colville to take care of her grandmother and if we don't let her live in the house, then she'll move in with Troy Nance."

"What?" Joe exploded.

"I'm worried sick about this."

"You told her absolutely not, didn't you?" The anger in Joe's voice was so unlike him, so out of character for her normally even-tempered husband. "What the hell is going on over there?"

"I told her I'd talk to you about it. She's blackmailing us, Joe, and any argument I give her at this point will drive her straight into Troy's arms."

Joe was silent for a moment; he seemed to be mentally reviewing their options.

"Joe, I don't know what to do." She hadn't intended to tell him this way, but once she'd heard her husband's voice, she couldn't stop herself.

"How should we handle the situation?" she asked after a minute or so of silence.

"I know Chrissie's close to your mother," he murmured. "Maybe she really feels she can help."

"I'm sure that's part of it, but I don't want her around Troy. It's not a good relationship." She bit her lower lip hard to keep from telling him that Troy was almost certainly Jake's son. No need to add fuel to *that* fire. "He doesn't have any visible means of support."

"Which means he's probably doing something illegal."

Susannah didn't disagree. "You could talk to Chrissie, reason with her. She might listen to you," she told Joe.

"She stopped listening to me a long time ago," Joe said tersely.

"We *can't* let her quit college. Not only that, Troy Nance is completely wrong for her. This relationship could ruin her life." It didn't take much imagination to recognize trouble brewing. If Troy was a drug dealer, which everyone in town seemed to suspect, he could be arrested at any time, and Chrissie would be guilty by association.

"Well, what do you suggest?" Joe asked.

"I should've sent her home when she first showed up," Susannah muttered. "I'm the one to blame," she said wretchedly.

"We don't need to cast blame," Joe said. "Right now, we've got to concentrate our efforts on Chrissie."

Susannah pressed her palm against her forehead, thrusting her fingers through her hair. She heard voices in the background. Joe said something she couldn't understand.

"Suze, listen, I've got to go."

"Okay, but Joe—"

"I have to get back to my patient. I'll call you later, all right?"

"Of course."

The phone buzzed in her ear and Susannah shut it off. When she looked up, she noticed a couple in the park. She frowned as the man pushed the woman up against a tree and began to kiss her. His hands roved her body in what she could only describe as an X-rated manner; this display was completely out of place in public.

All of a sudden she recognized the man. *Well, well, well.* Darned if it wasn't Troy Nance—with another woman. Susannah strained her eyes to be sure.

This was the perfect opportunity to show her daughter that Troy wasn't to be trusted. If Chrissie wasn't with him, which she most certainly was not, she was probably still at the house. All Susannah had to do was get her daughter, bring her to the park and let her see with her own eyes what kind of man Troy really was. Telling her would never work, since Chrissie wouldn't believe a word she said.

Starting the engine, Susannah barreled out of her parking spot and headed for the house, praying all the while that Chrissie was home.

Of course she wasn't.

CHAPTER

32

Carolyn had dropped Susannah off at her mother's place after the trip to Spokane. From there, she'd returned to the mill, where she called Kettle Falls Landscaping and left a message for Dave Langevin to get in touch. She wanted to ask him to come for dinner.

He'd been to her house that one night, just that once, and it'd been the sweetest, most romantic night of her life. She hadn't told Susannah much about their evening together. Carolyn didn't know how to explain that she'd never felt more cherished. Yet Dave had hardly touched her.

Not for lack of wanting on either his part or hers. The attraction between them was explosive, and she knew his guardedness was no match for the pull he felt toward her.

Carolyn still had her own misgivings about an affair. By his own admission, Dave was a drifter. He'd never said why he moved around as much as he did or the reason he'd come to this area. Intensely private, he asked nothing of her, nor did he offer anything personal about himself. Nevertheless, she was drawn to him in a way she hadn't been drawn to any other man in years.

At the end of the workday, the whistle blew and the sound jolted Carolyn from her thoughts. Within minutes the men started out of the gates, their lunch buckets in their hands. Dave, too, would be getting off work and when he got back to the office he'd receive her message. He didn't have a cell phone, otherwise she would've contacted him directly.

But even if he did get the message, there was no way of knowing whether he'd accept her invitation. She waited at the office for an extra half hour, wondering if he'd get in touch with her there. When no call came, she decided to go home.

As she drove, Carolyn felt depressed. Needing a man in her life—a particular man—was an uncomfortable feeling. Dave had said that in the end he'd hurt her, although that seemed to worry him more than it did Carolyn. She felt a sudden and unaccountable conviction that he wouldn't show. That he'd already made his decision.

By seven she knew she was right. Barefoot and wearing red cotton capris and a sleeveless red-checkered shirt, she watered her garden, trying to focus on the sensual feel of the grass against her feet, the sun on her arms, the heavy scent of the old roses.

Two thick steaks sat on the kitchen counter, and the green salad made with lettuce from her garden and fresh tomatoes, green peppers and slivered carrots was in the refrigerator, ready for her green goddess dressing. The recipe had been her mother's and Carolyn hadn't prepared it in years.

Just as she was about to put everything away and make herself a peanut-butter-and-jelly sandwich, she heard a vehicle traveling down her driveway. Walking around the house to the patio, she saw Dave's truck.

She watched as he climbed out, noticed that he'd showered and changed clothes, wearing clean khakis and a black T-shirt. Standing beside his battered pickup, he didn't see her at first.

"I didn't think you were coming," she said.

He turned to her and his smile engulfed her. "I didn't think I was, either."

Her heart was racing. "I'm glad you did."

"I tried, but I couldn't stay away." He moved toward her then, his steps making short work of the distance. When he reached her, it seemed the most natural thing in the world to walk directly into his arms. He embraced her, holding her close.

Carolyn raised her mouth to his and brushed his lips with her own. The kiss was moist and sweet and filled with longing. Dave lifted her braid and ran his fingers down the length of it.

He kissed her again, and again. Finally, with a reluctance that equaled her own, he released her.

"I've got steaks ready to grill," she told him.

"Would you like me to cook them?"

"Please."

They dined on the patio, drank wine with their meal and savored a second glass. They talked little. It was enough just to be together. As the sun set and the deer grazed in the meadow, they held hands. Every now and then, Dave would kiss her knuckles.

"I've never spent time with a woman like this," he admitted.

"What do you mean?"

"It's difficult to explain." He shook his head as if he hesitated to say more.

"No, tell me," she urged.

"I should go," he said.

An automatic protest rose to her lips, but she swallowed it and stood up with him. He kissed her, his arms tightening around her waist.

Carolyn's body ached for him and she knew he experienced the same intense desire.

His gaze held hers, in it she read pain and regret.

"Does it bother you that I own the mill?" she asked.

"The truth is, I wish you didn't."

"Why?" The mill was part of who she was, her heritage. Bronson family blood flowed through that mill and she was the third generation to manage its operation. One day she'd be forced to sell it because the Bronson line ended with her, but she wasn't ready to think about that yet. She had too many goals left to accomplish.

He shook his head again, unwilling to answer.

"It doesn't bother me that you're who you are," she said, knowing she sounded defensive. "I'm sorry," she whispered. "It...it doesn't matter." She broke away from him and carried their empty plates into the kitchen.

Dave followed with the wineglasses. He took the dishes from her and set them on the counter. Carolyn's eyes locked with his and she nearly wept at the sadness she saw in him. Tentatively she raised her hand to his face. Her heart was pounding so hard, it felt loud enough to bring down the walls.

"I knew this wouldn't work," he said. "I tried to tell myself I'd do whatever was necessary to be with you. Damn the gossip, damn the speculation."

Carolyn was afraid of where this was leading. He was going to pull up stakes and leave Colville, and she couldn't bear it if he did. Her life had never felt empty until she'd met him. Now the emptiness was there anytime he wasn't.

Rather than allow him to continue speaking, she slipped her arms around his neck and brought his mouth down to hers. To her surprise and delight, she met with no resistance.

Dave took control of the kiss, his desire so strong it threatened to consume her. She grabbed his shirt collar, needing an anchor, something to hold on to while her senses went wild.

She gasped when Dave released her. They stood just inches from each other, their breathing harsh and ragged.

"The truth is, Carolyn, I am who I am and you are who you are. I'm basically an itinerant laborer, while you own the most important business in the area. I live in a second-hand camper, while you live *here*." He gestured around him. "People will talk. They are already. You think there's anyone in Colville who doesn't know about us? They all do and the things they say are going to hurt you. I won't let that happen."

"But—"

He gripped her shoulders to stop her. "I'll put in my two-week notice tomorrow."

"No!" Without a job, he'd do what he'd always done and simply drift away.

It seemed for a moment that he'd reconsider, but then he shook his head. "I'll find another job. Somewhere else."

"How will you support yourself until then?"

"I have very few expenses. I'll be all right."

"I don't care who knows about us!"

He touched her face gently. "I care. I won't have you talked about around town."

She knew he meant what he said. Throwing her arms around his middle, she hugged him. "I feel so selfish and guilty for wanting to be with you."

He stroked her hair and held her close. "I want to be with you, too. I won't leave you yet."

"Promise?"

She felt his smile against the side of her face. "Promise," he whispered.

When the time came, she'd let him go; she had no other choice. But she had to believe her love would draw him back.

CHAPTER

33

Wednesday morning, Susannah found herself wishing she could leave Colville, go home, be with her husband.

She'd done a lot of thinking since she'd talked to Joe. He'd called again last night, and they'd spoken for more than an hour. He'd reminded her of her feelings earlier in the summer, of her restlessness. She'd never divulged the dreams she'd had about Jake and how the memories had returned, haunting her sleep and then later her conscience. As for Jake, she hadn't found him and didn't care if she ever did. He was probably living under an assumed name. It was much easier to create a false identity back in the early '70s than it was now.

Never had she thought that in seeking Jake, she would learn what she had about her brother—if it was true. She still couldn't make herself believe Doug had been dealing drugs. That would have devastated her father. Devastated the entire family.

She could certainly visit the sheriff's office and ask a few questions. Although all of this happened more than thirty years ago, the county would have kept the records. Surely they'd be online.

Not wanting to interrupt Carolyn at the mill, Susannah decided to use a computer at the library downtown. She left without speaking to Chrissie. Her daughter had come home late last night. Susannah hadn't said anything about seeing Troy with someone else; she'd sit on that for a while and learn what she could about this other woman before confronting either Chrissie or Troy.

Susannah drove to the library and logged on to the Internet. However, even with the librarian's help, she wasn't able to get into the Colville sheriff's files.

Next she logged on to the local newspaper archives and did a name search for Jake Presley and found nothing. While she was there, she tried Doug's name; what came up was the article that reported his car accident. As she read it, tears filled her eyes.

If she'd seen it years ago, she didn't remember. The newspaper said Doug's neck had been broken and he'd died instantly. She breathed a sigh of relief that the car hadn't caught fire and burned. She hated the thought of anyone suffering that way. Self-consciously she reached for her purse and dug out a tissue.

Thanking the librarian for her help, Susannah left a few minutes later and crossed the street to the sheriff's office. The woman at the front desk, all too obviously watching the clock, seemed eager for her break.

"Hello," Susannah said as she stepped up to the counter.

The clerk was young and probably didn't remember her father, who'd retired a number of years earlier.

The clerk looked up, glanced at the clock again, and frowned. "Can I help you?"

"I hope so. I'd like to talk to someone about any charges filed against Doug Leary back in the early 1970s." She looked for any sign of recognition in the other woman's eyes but saw none.

"When exactly?" the clerk asked.

"1973."

The woman shook her head, her short curls bouncing. "All paperwork before 1978 is stored in the basement."

"Would it be possible to have someone get it for me?"

The clerk stared at Susannah. "You're joking, right? We're already short-staffed with two people on vacation."

"But they'll be back soon, won't they?" Susannah pressed.

"No one's got time to search through the archives unless it concerns a current investigation."

"This has to do with my brother. He was killed in a car accident and I recently learned that he might've been in some kind of trouble. I want to know what that was about."

Frowning, the clerk shook her head. "Sorry, I can't help you."

"Greg Dalton was the sheriff in 1973, wasn't he?" He'd been a good friend of her dad's.

The clerk turned toward the wall, where a row of photographs was displayed. "Looks like it. That was *way* before my time."

"Does he still live in the area?"

The clerk nodded and stood as another woman joined her. "I believe so. I'm taking my coffee break now. If you have any other questions I can call for a deputy—if there's one handy."

"Thank you, but that won't be necessary."

All Susannah needed to do was look in her mother's personal directory for the retired sheriff's address. He'd played bridge with her father at least once a week for as long as Susannah could remember. She drove back to the house and, without too much difficulty, located the address—Old River Road, a couple of miles out of town.

On the off-chance that he was home, Susannah drove there, then headed down the dirt driveway with the name Dalton printed on the rural route box. When she parked in front of the house, an older woman came to the screen door, holding it open. The house was small, the lawn green and well maintained. A creek flowed along the back of the property.

"Mrs. Dalton?" Susannah asked as she climbed out of the car. She didn't recall her first name.

"Yes. Can I help you?"

Mrs. Dalton was in her midseventies, a pleasant-looking woman with curled gray hair and a comfortably round figure.

"I'm Susannah Leary. My married name is Nelson."

"Susannah, of course. It's so good to see you! How's your mother doing? I wanted to get into town to visit after your father died, but I swear there just aren't enough hours in the day."

Susannah smiled, and they exchanged a warm handshake. "Thank you." It was difficult to accept condolences even now; Susannah was never quite sure what to say. They exchanged pleasantries, and Mrs. Dalton invited her into the house.

"Would it be all right if I asked Mr. Dalton a few questions?" she asked.

"Questions?" the older woman repeated.

"I've recently come across some information regarding my brother. You remember Doug, don't you?"

"Oh, yes, of course. I don't think your dear parents ever recovered from losing him."

Susannah swallowed hard.

Mrs. Dalton frowned. "Susannah, I'm afraid my husband's been ill for some time—a heart condition. I don't want to overstress him."

Susannah nodded. "I'll do my best not to."

Mrs. Dalton hesitated, as if gauging how much to trust her. Then she said, "Greg's sitting out back, enjoying the sunshine. If you'd care to join him, I'll bring us all something cool to drink."

Susannah followed her into the kitchen, slid open the glass door and stepped onto the patio. Greg Dalton sat with his shoulders slumped forward and his hands on his lap, facing the creek. He appeared to be napping.

Susannah didn't want to interfere with his rest, but when she reached for a chair, it made a slight scraping sound against the concrete. The old man's eyes opened and he glared at her accusingly.

"I'm sorry," she said softly.

"Who the hell are you?"

Susannah told him. His eyes widened when she mentioned Doug's name.

"You remember my parents, don't you?" she asked. "My dad was Judge Leary."

"'Course I do."

"And my brother? Doug died in a car accident many years ago."

Mrs. Dalton came outside carrying a tray with three glasses of pink lemonade. Susannah stood, taking the tray from her and setting it on the table.

"Who was it you were asking about again?" Mr. Dalton demanded.

"Doug Leary," his wife returned. "You remember Doug, Judge Leary's boy?"

"I wish you people would stop repeating yourselves. Yes, I remember Doug. He died—what?—thirty-some years ago."

Susannah caught Mrs. Dalton's grimace. "Would you like some lemonade, Greg?"

Her husband shook his head and closed his eyes, apparently resuming his nap.

"I'm sorry," Mrs. Dalton said, "but I was afraid this would happen. Greg naps much of the day. Perhaps I can help you."

Susannah wished she hadn't come. She should've left this alone. "I moved Mom into an assisted-living complex," she explained, without discussing her mother's problems. She briefly described what she'd unearthed that had led her to believe her brother might have been in some kind of legal trouble. Although it didn't seem possible, she explained, she wanted to check it out to be sure—if she could. "As you've probably guessed, all of this comes as a shock."

"That was so long ago," Mrs. Dalton said uncertainly.

Susannah agreed. "You might remember I was in France that year. I'm hoping to find out what I can about Doug and another friend I knew in high school by the name of Jake Presley."

Mrs. Dalton frowned sadly as she sat down next to Susannah. "I don't remember much, but I do recall something about Doug. My goodness, my memory's bad. It just isn't what it used to be."

"I understand," Susannah said. "Any information you have would be appreciated."

The old sheriff woke suddenly. "It was a crying shame," he mumbled.

"You remember what happened, Greg?" his wife asked.

"Huh." He scoffed at his wife. "I'm not likely to forget. Crying shame, that's what it was. I tried to help, but there wasn't a thing I could do. Those two young men stepped into a hornet's nest of trouble."

Susannah leaned closer, afraid any question she asked would break his train of thought.

"Doug wasn't a bad boy. The other one, either. They got in over their heads and couldn't get out. They were in the wrong game—hell, the wrong league—for a couple of small-town boys. One of the players was an undercover agent. The two of 'em were in Idaho at the time and managed to get away. Problem is, they ran back to Colville and in the process crossed state lines. Once they did that, it became a federal crime."

Susannah wasn't clear on all the legalities. "You mean the local authorities—"

"I mean," Mr. Dalton said, cutting her off, "that they'd be tried in a federal court with federal prosecutors. George was upset, very upset, and we talked it over. There was nothing I could do—or him, either, for that matter."

Susannah shifted toward him. "You remember all this?"

"Like it was yesterday," the older man concurred. "Your brother made a foolish mistake. His friend, too. Trouble like this wasn't just going to disappear. With the federal government involved, there wasn't much chance he'd escape prosecution, despite his father being a judge."

Greg Dalton stared into the distance. "I was the first one at the accident scene. He was already dead. Rammed into the tree. Smoke and steam coming from the engine. I pried open the driver's door and the boy slumped out, into my arms." The old man shook his head as if to say he didn't want to talk about it anymore.

"Greg went to plenty of accident scenes over the years," Mrs. Dalton said in a low voice. "But Doug was the son of a good friend. He phoned me. In all his years of working as sheriff, that was the only time I've seen my husband that distraught. He asked me to go and sit with Vivian while George identified the body."

A lump formed in Susannah's throat.

"I think it nearly killed George to bury his only son," Mrs. Dalton added.

"I know," Susannah whispered. She stared down at her drink. She hadn't taken so much as a sip and doubted she could swallow if she did.

"Out of respect for George and his position in the community, my husband did what he could to keep the federal charges out of the paper. The entire matter was as hush-hush as possible. Only a few people were aware of it."

"Do you know what happened to Jake Presley?"

Mrs. Dalton shook her head. "Sorry, no."

The sheriff cleared his throat and answered without opening his eyes. "He got away. Got clean away," he muttered.

This was what Susannah had suspected all along. She set down her glass.

"Did I help you get the answers you need?" the sheriff asked.

"Yes, you were most helpful."

"Good." He dropped his chin against his chest, eyes still closed.

"Thank you for your time," Susannah said and got to her feet. "If I have any other questions, can I phone you?"

Mrs. Dalton nodded. "We'll do whatever we can."

"Thank you." Susannah walked out to her car, surprised to find tears gathering in her eyes. She had the answers she needed, but they certainly weren't the ones she wanted.

CHAPTER

34

Chrissie wasn't home when Susannah arrived, which was just as well. Her head was full of what she'd learned and the idea of dealing with Chrissie right now overwhelmed her.

Although it'd been hard to keep quiet, Susannah hadn't mentioned that she'd seen Troy with another woman. It was doubtful that her daughter would believe her, anyway—and definitely not without proof. Chrissie made her feel a sense of powerlessness that bordered on desperation.

The house was warm. After opening the front and back doors to create a breeze, she sat down in a garden chair and closed her eyes, trying to think everything through carefully.

She found herself drifting off to sleep under the shade of a pine. It was little wonder, considering that she was functioning on less than four hours from the night before and even less the night before that. Her mind was clouded with worries. What was wrong with her, anyway? She'd always been levelheaded and sensible. It'd all started last year, after her father died, but she'd refused to believe Joe's theory that her depression was connected to his death. She was no longer sure of anything. Once she was home again, she hoped her life would return to normal.

Normal.

Normal meant that the way things *seemed* to be was also the way they were. No massive deceptions, no ugly secrets.

Normal would be a relief, despite her listlessness and her loss of enthusiasm.

Head back, eyes closed, Susannah could so easily picture the Jake of thirty years ago, dressed in his black leather jacket. Her heart sped up at that memory alone. As a girl, she'd risked everything to be with him. Her parents would've grounded her for life had they known how often she slipped out in the middle of the night. The garden was their favorite spot, hers and Jake's, especially the small rose arbor with its bench, hidden as it was from the house. He'd called it Susannah's garden.

As sure as she drew breath, she'd believed he loved her as deeply as she loved him. What he felt for her had been fleeting, however; she knew that now, and it stung. She'd believed in him and the power of their love, which had felt invincible, especially that last night before she'd flown to France.

Susannah had pleaded with her father, begged him not to send her away. She'd wept and shrieked, but he'd turned a deaf ear and insisted that one day she'd thank him.

He'd been wrong. She'd never forgiven him for what he'd done.

A car door slammed, and Susannah opened her eyes, her tranquility destroyed. She went to the front door as her daughter pranced toward the house, wearing tight blue jeans and a tighter top. Defiance flashed from her eyes. "You aren't stopping me, Mom."

"From what?" Susannah asked wearily, rubbing a hand across her eyes.

"From moving to Colville. I already talked it over with Grandma and she wants me here. She said she'd pay for my expenses until I can find a job. She needs me and I want to be here for her."

"Were we still discussing that?"

Her daughter cast her a furious look. "You talked to Dad, didn't you? That's why he's on my case now."

"Yes. Did you want to tell him yourself? I hope I didn't ruin the surprise." She could be as sarcastic as her daughter when the occasion called for it.

Chrissie placed one hand on her hip and scowled. "Nothing's changed."

Susannah sighed audibly. "I didn't expect it would. So you're determined to do this, despite…" She let her voice trail off.

"Despite *what?*"

"The fact that you aren't the only woman in Troy Nance's life." She was unable to stop herself. And once she started, she had to continue. "I saw Troy in the park with someone else."

Chrissie's eyes narrowed. "That is so lame."

Susannah raised her shoulders in an elaborate shrug. "Think what you want, but I know what I saw."

"You'd do just about anything to keep me from seeing Troy, but I didn't realize you'd lie."

"Ask him yourself," Susannah suggested, gesturing toward the kitchen phone.

Chrissie hesitated for a moment. "Fine, I will." She marched off with a righteousness fueled by certainty—or at least the pretense of certainty.

Susannah followed her, curious to hear what Jake's son would say. And yes, she'd reconciled herself to the truth of Sharon's claim that Jake was her son's father.

Her back to the wall, Chrissie sat on the linoleum floor. She rested her face against her knees as she held the receiver to her ear. When Susannah entered the room, Chrissie raised her eyes, sparking with indignation.

"Hi," she said when Troy answered.

Susannah sat at the kitchen table and folded her arms, patiently waiting. Not for a second did she believe Troy Nance would tell the truth.

"You weren't with someone else yesterday afternoon, were you?" Chrissie asked, purring the question.

He took his time responding. Chrissie kept her eyes lowered, then something he said made her look up suddenly and glare at Susannah.

"At the park," she said repeating his words. "Jenny Sandberg met you there."

Susannah's stomach tensed.

"She's an old friend. Uh, huh. A good friend from high school. Uh, huh. You hadn't seen her in a while." Chrissie was echoing his responses for her mother's benefit, and

Susannah sighed at her daughter's naiveté. Chrissie sounded so triumphant.

From the way Troy and this Jenny had been going at it, they were *very* good friends.

"Mom saw you and wondered," Chrissie said next. "She said you'd lie to me and I said you wouldn't."

Not a word of that was true. All Susannah had suggested was that Chrissie ask Troy herself. She felt disturbed by the fact that these two were lying to each other, Chrissie no less than Troy.

"Of *course* I believe you," she insisted, continuing to glare at Susannah.

Unwilling to listen any longer, Susannah turned her back and walked out of the kitchen.

"Why would I mind?" Chrissie was saying. She lowered her voice. "Yes, I told her."

This apparently had to do with her daughter's moving.

"She doesn't have any choice but to accept it," Chrissie said more loudly. "I make my own decisions."

Susannah felt sick to her stomach. She went into the living room and sat down in the one remaining chair. A few minutes later, Chrissie left the kitchen, and started down the hallway to the bedrooms.

"When did you talk to Dad?" Susannah asked her. "What did he say?"

"This afternoon." Her daughter paused, not turning to face her. "But it's more important what Troy told me. He said my parents would do whatever they could to break us up and I should be prepared for that."

Susannah arched her brows. "Did he?"

"Yes, and you just proved everything Troy said."

"I was telling the truth."

"So was Troy. Fine, he was with another woman, an old friend. I'm not the jealous type."

Susannah was far more interested in Joe's assessment of the situation than she was in Troy's. "What did Dad say?" She repeated her earlier question.

"I don't appreciate you running to him every time we disagree."

"You're our daughter."

"I would've told Dad when I was ready."

Susannah straightened, worried now. "Chrissie, we need to work this out."

"No, we don't. There's nothing you can say or do that's going to change my mind. You need to understand that I'm an adult and I have the right to decide what I want. If it's any of your business, I love Troy."

"You hardly even know him!"

"I know enough."

Her daughter was determined to make one of the biggest mistakes of her life.

Sick at heart, Susannah watched as Chrissie grabbed her purse and slammed out the door. A few minutes later, the distinctive roar of Troy's muffler and the blaring of his revved-up sound system rattled the windows. She looked outside to see Chrissie clambering into his truck.

The house was quiet again once her daughter had left. Susannah walked back to her room and sat on the edge of the bed, burying her face in her hands.

She didn't see the sheet of paper propped on her desk until she glanced up. Her eyes widened and she leaped up to seize it. Her breath caught in her throat as she read the message.

MEET ME IN THE CEMETERY AT 7 TONIGHT.

CHAPTER

35

"What's wrong?" Carolyn asked, closing her truck door and trotting toward the house. Susannah waited on the front steps.

She had frantically phoned, not knowing who else to call after finding the note. Whoever had broken into the house must have left it; maybe she just hadn't noticed it last night. Why that person wanted to see her remained as much a mystery as everything else.

Carolyn joined her on the steps. "I don't think I've ever heard you sound so panicky."

Susannah got up and led her inside, directly to her childhood bedroom. "Read that," she said, pointing to the small desk where the message still lay.

Walking slowly into the room, Carolyn advanced toward the desk.

"Do you know who wrote this?" she asked, glancing over her shoulder at Susannah.

"I have an idea." She'd considered nothing else in the ten minutes it'd taken Carolyn to drive into town.

Susannah sank down on the edge of the bed, her heart racing and her palms sweaty. She felt light-headed and realized she hadn't eaten since that morning. The thought of food, however, made her want to gag.

"The cemetery," Carolyn said. The mattress dipped as she sat down beside Susannah.

"At seven." Thankfully it would still be light then, although Susannah hadn't made a decision yet. Should she go? Or not? She tried to work out the consequences of each action.

"Do you think it might be Jake?" Carolyn asked in a hushed voice.

"I can't think who else it would be." Sharon had said she'd get in touch with him; apparently she had.

"It makes sense," Carolyn said. "We now know why he left and, more importantly, why he didn't come back to Colville when you got home."

Shocking though it was, all this information about Jake's problems with the law explained a great deal. After her return from France, the only address he had would've been the family home. Knowing what her father had already done to keep them apart, he might well have avoided any contact, for his own protection and hers. If, by chance, he had written, she could easily believe that George Leary had destroyed the letter.

"Jake must've heard that you've been looking for him," Carolyn suggested.

Susannah nodded. "Sharon told him. She said she would."

"Are you going to go?"

"I...I don't know."

Carolyn stared at her. "You've got to be kidding! I thought this was what you wanted."

"I did at one time. Now...I'm not sure." Indecision gripped her and she plowed her fingers into her hair. "Life can get very complicated," she said with a beleaguered sigh.

"If it is Jake, he's taking a tremendous risk."

"I know." If word of this got out, Jake would immediately be arrested and sent to jail. He could very well end up in a federal prison.

Feeling shaky, Susannah moved into the kitchen, followed by Carolyn. She put on water for a pot of tea.

"You look pale," Carolyn commented. "You're really worried about this, aren't you?"

"It's not just the note, it's Chrissie, too," Susannah said, dropping teabags into the two mugs still unpacked. "I saw Troy with someone else yesterday afternoon and confronted Chrissie."

"It didn't go well?"

Susannah snickered. "You could say that. I have no idea what Chrissie sees in him. I wish I trusted her judgment, but I don't." What bothered Susannah most was that she recognized how easy it would be to treat her daughter the same way her father had treated her. In fact, Chrissie's accusations were an eerie echo of the things she'd said to her own father. Here it was—her youthful rebellion staring her in the face, as though her teenage self was being channeled through her daughter. Susannah had a glimpse of the frustration her father must have felt. Even worse, even more ironic, the man in question was Jake's son....

The whistle blew as the water on the stove reached a boil. Susannah filled the mugs and set them aside to steep.

"Would you go with me?" Susannah asked. "The note didn't say anything about going alone." The prospect of going at all filled her with a mixture of excitement and guilt—the guilt because she'd be keeping this secret from Joe.

One meeting. Just one. She'd apologize for her father's behavior and leave it at that. The only other thing she needed to do was obtain some assurance that despite her father, Jake had had a good life. With all her heart, she wanted him to be happy. She'd ask about Troy, too; perhaps he had some influence with his son. Yes, Jake might be able to help her.

"You want me to go with you?" Carolyn shook her head. "Even if the note didn't say anything about it, I'm sure he expects you to go by yourself."

"I guess you're right," Susannah said reluctantly. "He'd probably figure it's safer for him if I'm there alone."

Susannah removed the teabags and took a carton of milk from the refrigerator. "I find the cemetery a curious choice, don't you? Like those Gothic romances we read in high school."

"Yeah," Carolyn agreed, stirring milk into her tea. "The ones with the heroine on the cover, wearing a nightgown and holding a candle. It's always dark and there's usually a cliff."

Susannah smiled. "And she's following the directions of an anonymous note."

"A note that leads her to the cemetery," Carolyn said

with a grin. "Perhaps this is Jake's way of telling you the relationship is dead."

They both sat at the kitchen table. Susannah suspected he'd chosen the site because it was unlikely they'd run into anyone who might recognize him at the graveyard. She told Carolyn this and they both laughed.

"Yeah," Carolyn said. "Dead men don't tell tales."

Briefly, Susannah wondered how many other chances Jake had taken over the years, risking imprisonment by coming down to the States. She assumed he'd come back for Sharon or perhaps she'd occasionally gone to him.

"You're sure you can do this alone?" Carolyn asked worriedly. "I'd offer to wait at the entrance but he hasn't said where you're supposed to meet him. It might be right at the gates, and if that's the case, he might disappear if he sees me."

"You're right. Anyway, I'll be fine." She *would* tell Joe about it, she resolved. Her husband deserved to know.

"I'll stay here at the house until you get back," Carolyn said.

"You don't need to do that."

"Yes, I do. Someone needs to know where you are. Besides, I'm dying of curiosity." She giggled then, sounding just as she had in high school.

At twenty minutes to seven, Susannah took time to freshen her makeup and brush her hair. Her nerves were on edge and she considered changing clothes, wearing something more feminine than her jeans and black cotton sweater. She examined herself in the hallway mirror, sucking in her stomach. No doubt about it, she wasn't seventeen anymore, but then Jake wasn't, either.

"How do I look?" she asked, twirling around for Carolyn to comment.

"You want the truth?"

"Of course I do." Susannah had already decided it must be bad. She tucked her hair behind her ears and realized she was trembling.

"You look like you're about to throw up."

Laughing softly, Susannah admitted, "That's exactly how I feel."

The phone rang, startling her. Susannah moved toward the kitchen with leaden feet, almost afraid to answer.

It rang again.

"Aren't you going to pick it up?" Carolyn asked after the third ring.

Susannah's instincts said to ignore it, but too much was at stake and she reached for the receiver just before the answering machine clicked on.

"Leary residence," she announced stiffly.

"Is this Susannah Nelson?" a crisp female voice asked.

"Yes, it is."

"I'm glad I caught you. This is Michelle Larson from Altamira. I'm sorry to tell you this, but your mother's taken a bad fall. We're transferring her to Memorial Hospital."

Susannah's heart leapt into her throat. "Is she all right?"

"I can't say for sure. It looks like she's broken her hip."

"Oh, no!"

"According to our records, you have power of attorney. Is that correct?"

"Yes." If they were asking Susannah this, it probably meant her mother was unconscious.

"We'll need you to sign the forms at the hospital."

"I'll be there in five minutes." Susannah banged down the phone and automatically headed for the door.

"Susannah!" Carolyn raced after her. "What happened?"

"It's Mom. She's fallen—they're taking her to the hospital." She scrawled a note for Chrissie, scooped up her purse from the hall table and had just opened the door when Carolyn stopped her again.

"What about meeting Jake?"

For a fleeting second, Susannah had completely forgotten. "You go."

"Me?" Carolyn flattened her hand against her chest.

"I don't have any choice. Mom needs me." She hated to ask this of Carolyn, but there was no one else.

Slowly, her friend nodded. "Okay."

"I owe you," Susannah said, and rushed out the front door.

"Yes, you do," Carolyn said, following her. "I'll meet you at the hospital."

The gate leading into Calvary Cemetery was closed.

"Oh, great," Carolyn muttered as she parked the car on the road and climbed out. There was space enough for her to squeeze through and walk onto the cemetery grounds, which she did.

Glancing around, she searched the area for any other parked vehicles and saw none. Being in a cemetery by herself was a little…well, scary—even if she wasn't a woman who scared easily. The note hadn't told Susannah exactly where she should meet Jake—or whoever her mysterious visitor was. Although Calvary Cemetery didn't have extensive grounds, it was large enough to hide in if someone wished not to be seen.

With her arms hugging her middle, Carolyn marched down the center of the paved roadway. The most logical place to wait, she supposed, was George Leary's grave. After a quick search, she located it. His marble tombstone noted his birthdate and the day he died and nothing else. Like her own father, he'd been a frugal man. Any added adornments, any words of comfort—a quote or a Psalm— were not desired.

Sighing, Carolyn looked up. The cemetery was dead silent. Carolyn grimaced at her unintended pun. No one, not even the groundskeeper, was anywhere in sight. There didn't appear to be any other visitors.

"This could be a very long night," she mused aloud, checking her watch. Five to seven.

Pacing up and down the row of tombstones, she glanced at her watch repeatedly. Each minute seemed to drag interminably. This was obviously a waste of time and she grew disheartened.

Walking over to the site where her own parents had been laid to rest, she crouched down and ran her hand over the large marble headstone. She'd last visited only a few days ago. The flowers she'd brought for them, for Lily and for Doug had gone limp by now and been removed.

Many of the grave sites were adorned with artificial flowers. She preferred a fresh-cut bouquet from the garden her mother had planted all those years ago. It seemed a fitting gesture.

By seven-thirty, she knew Jake wasn't coming. He'd probably seen her waiting and decided not to make an appearance. He didn't trust Carolyn, and there was no reason he should. She assumed he wasn't willing to risk his freedom for the opportunity to meet with her. It was Susannah or no one.

To be on the safe side, Carolyn waited another fifteen

minutes, then returned to her truck. She hated to be the bearer of disappointing news but there was no help for it.

When she got back to the house, she noticed that Susannah's car wasn't parked outside, which meant she was still at the hospital. Not bothering to park, she drove directly to Memorial.

The hospital, a three-story brick building two blocks north of Colville City Park, was the tallest structure in the county and the pride of Colville. Carolyn had only been five or six at the time of the ribbon-cutting ceremony, and she remembered every detail. The high school band had played and there'd been a tour of the facilities that included cookies and juice for the kids. That, in particular, had made an impression on her.

She parked and walked into the hospital foyer. The volunteer at the information desk directed her to the second floor, where Carolyn found Susannah in the small waiting room.

"How's your mother?" she asked, joining her friend.

"She's in surgery." Susannah chewed on the end of her fingernail. "It's a bad break—her bones are fragile and the doctor said he might end up doing an entire hip replacement."

"Oh, no." That kind of surgery wouldn't be easy on a woman of Vivian's age.

"Did he show up?" Susannah asked.

Carolyn shook her head.

Susannah shrugged. "I was afraid of that."

"But you'd hoped?"

She shrugged again.

Carolyn knew her friend had mixed feelings regarding this meeting, so perhaps his not showing was just as well.

"You feel someone's been in the house several times recently, isn't that right?"

Susannah nodded. "And some things have been taken." She pressed her lips together. "I don't believe anymore that these were random thefts, although at least one was made to look that way. It had to be Jake."

"Then perhaps he's hiding in the area. He might've come to the house, hoping to see you, and then realized you weren't staying there alone. He couldn't compromise himself by letting Chrissie see him."

"You're right." Susannah paused as she considered this possibility.

Everything was beginning to add up for Carolyn, and she guessed that the end of her friend's search was near. Susannah was paying the private investigator to track Jake down, but all this time he'd been practically under their noses.

Carolyn sat down on one end of the sofa and reached for a magazine—a six-month-old issue of *Reader's Digest*. It was hard to wait alone and although Susannah didn't appear interested in conversation, Carolyn had no intention of leaving her.

"Mom!" They could hear Chrissie's high-pitched voice from the elevator lobby.

So this was Susannah's daughter.

"Chrissie!" Susannah dashed out of the room, and Carolyn watched as mother and daughter hugged.

"Is Grandma okay?" Chrissie demanded, tears in her eyes.

"You got my note?"

"Yes—how's Grandma?" she asked again.

"Grandma's in surgery, but it seems to be going well." She glanced at her watch. "I don't think it'll be much longer."

"Poor Grandma."

Carolyn put aside the *Reader's Digest* and stood. Now that Chrissie was here with her mother, she wasn't really needed.

"How'd it happen?" Chrissie seemed to be badly shaken.

"I talked briefly to the nurse from Altamira. She stopped by the hospital and explained that Mom had been playing pool with one of the other residents."

"Pool?" Carolyn repeated incredulously.

A quick smile curved Susannah's mouth. "Mom was using her cane as a pool cue and lost her balance. She broke her hip, but Michelle, the nurse, seems to think she also hit her head on the edge of the pool table when she went down."

"Oh, no." Chrissie covered her mouth in horror.

"Whoever she was playing with was extremely upset and had to be sedated."

Carolyn knew Susannah hoped her mother would adjust to life in the assisted-living complex. In the beginning Vivian had been full of complaints; lately Susannah hadn't said much about her mother's dissatisfaction. It seemed to Carolyn that if Vivian was socializing with the other residents, that was surely a good sign. Now this.

"I think I should go back home," Carolyn said, preparing to leave.

"Oh—forgive my bad manners. Carolyn, this is my daughter, Chrissie. And Chrissie—this is one of my best friends in the whole world, Carolyn Bronson." Chrissie murmured a polite hello, but Carolyn saw the speculative look on her face.

"I can't thank you enough," Susannah said fervently as Carolyn started to leave.

"What are friends for?" she teased.

They hugged goodbye and Carolyn left the hospital. It'd grown dark—not surprising since it was now ten o'clock. On the off-chance that Jake might have shown up after all, she drove past Calvary Cemetery, which was in the opposite direction of where she needed to go. Just as she'd expected, the cemetery gates remained closed and there wasn't a car in sight.

Turning around, she drove back into town, reversing her route to get home. The evening was hot and humid. Carolyn preferred not to use her air-conditioning, so she kept the windows down. As always, she breathed in the scent of fresh-cut wood as she neared the mill, savoring it. Huge stacks of timber filled the yard, the sprinklers spraying them with water.

Carolyn wished she had a way of reaching Dave; she would've liked to talk to him, tell him what had happened. That wasn't possible, though, and she told herself not to count on his presence. He'd be leaving town soon. Leaving her.

Once past the city's outskirts and the mill, she increased her speed, but was quickly passed by another vehicle, driving well above the posted limit. She recognized the truck— and its driver—almost right away.

It was Troy Nance, and he wasn't alone.

Carolyn's headlights revealed two people in the truck's cab. The passenger was a woman with short blond hair, her head resting on Troy's shoulder.

Earlier Susannah had mentioned seeing Troy with some-one else. A blonde, she'd said. Not that it was any of her business, but Carolyn was curious. Maintaining a discreet distance, she followed Troy to the Roadside Inn. He parked, and the moment the blonde climbed out of the cab, it was abundantly clear that they were more than friends.

While Chrissie waited at the hospital for word on her grand-mother's condition, Troy was out with some other woman.

CHAPTER

37

"Does Dad know about Grandma?" Chrissie asked, sitting down on the waiting-room sofa.

Susannah shook her head. She'd tried to reach him but Joe wasn't home and apparently he'd turned off his cell phone. She'd left a message, and that was all she could do for now.

"Don't you think you should tell him?"

"He'll call as soon as he gets my message." She took out her cell, then noticed the sign on the wall warning against the use of cell phones in the hospital. Luckily there was a pay phone down the hall. Chrissie walked with her and stood by while Susannah called collect. Brian answered and accepted the charges.

"Hidy, ho," Brian sang. "How come you're calling collect?"

"Hi. Is your dad home yet?"

"Hey, Mom, what's wrong?" Apparently her son hadn't listened to the message.

"I need to talk to your dad," she said without explaining.

Her son asked, "Is everything all right?"

Susannah lowered her gaze and tried not to look at Chrissie, who was examining her like a biology specimen under the microscope. "Everything's going to be fine." And it would be once she spoke to Joe. He was her touchstone, and she needed him.

"Where's Joe?" she asked.

"Hey, Mom, hold on, I hear him in the garage. He was at some get-together with his dentist friends." Brian put down the phone with a clatter.

Susannah could hear her son talking in the background, and a minute later, Joe picked up.

"Hi," she said softly, loving him so much she wanted to weep. This time apart was wearing on her, wearing on him, too. "Mom fell and broke her hip," she said without preamble.

"How is she?" Joe asked, immediately concerned.

"Chrissie and I are at the hospital. Mom's in surgery now...." Susannah's voice faltered.

"Susannah?"

"She might need to have a hip replacement." Stifling a sob, she waited a moment before continuing. "Joe, she hit her head on a pool table, of all things, and was knocked unconscious. Altamira took care of everything. I can't imagine what might've happened if she'd been at home or by herself." These scenarios had played through Susannah's mind ever since she'd arrived at the hospital.

"Do you need me to come over and be with you?" he asked.

Susannah knew how difficult it was for him to get away at the last minute. "I...I think it'll be okay. I'll have a better idea once Mom's out of surgery."

"Of course. Needless to say, the more notice I have, the better, but I'll leave right now if you want me to."

His willingness to drop everything for her touched Susannah. She wanted him to know how much she appreciated this, appreciated him, yet all she managed to choke out was a simple, "Thank you, sweetheart."

"Anything you need? Anything I can do?"

"No. I don't think so." She felt oppressed by her worries—Vivian, the situation with Jake, the revelations about Doug, the conflict with Chrissie. Susannah was tired, so tired of feeling responsible for all of it. Tired of making decisions—and mistakes.

Soon afterward, the surgeon appeared, still in his green surgical gown. He explained what he'd done and the anticipated outcome. Her mother would likely spend several days in the hospital recuperating, and would be temporarily moved to a nursing home, where she'd receive the care she needed. Progress would be slow, but Vivian had come through the ordeal well.

Relieved by the news, Susannah and Chrissie drove back to the house.

"I'm glad you came to the hospital," Susannah told her daughter.

"I'm glad I did, too," Chrissie said. "When I read your note, I freaked. Troy drove me to the hospital, thank God. I asked him to come in with me, but he says he can't stand the smell."

Susannah bit the inside of her lip to keep from commenting. If Troy loved Chrissie as much as she believed, then wouldn't he want to be with her?

"I hate the thought of Grandma in pain," Chrissie added. "I don't think I realized how much I love her until I found out she'd been hurt."

"I know." But bad as it was, the accident could have been so much worse.

The house was dark and quiet when they got home. Chrissie immediately turned on the hallway lights, and they both listened, breath held, for any alien sounds. There was nothing. The only thing out of the ordinary was a real estate business card tucked in the screen door; this was the third one. She was nowhere close to getting the house on the market. Susannah tossed the card, as she had the others, annoyed by the aggressiveness of the agents.

She hurried to her bedroom and surveyed it carefully, looking, she supposed, for another message from Jake. He couldn't possibly know what had kept her away from their meeting.

"Mom, Carolyn's on the phone," Chrissie yelled from the kitchen.

Susannah hadn't even heard it ring.

"I understand you just got in," Carolyn said when she answered. "How's your mother?"

"She's going to be fine. She's out of surgery and in recovery. The hospital said they'd phone if there was any change."

"I'm glad to hear that." When Susannah murmured her thanks, Carolyn said, "Listen, I know this is absolutely none of my business, but I saw Troy Nance on my way home.

He's out at the Roadside Inn and he isn't alone, if you catch my drift."

"Really?"

"That was an hour ago, so I can't promise he's still there."

Susannah's eyes swung toward her daughter and then to the digital readout on the microwave. "I see."

Chrissie quickly noticed that the conversation somehow concerned her.

"What did Carolyn tell you?" she burst out the instant Susannah replaced the receiver.

"Would you be interested in a short drive?" Susannah asked instead. She wouldn't mention what Carolyn had said unless or until it was necessary.

"A drive, this time of night?" Chrissie stared at her skeptically.

"It isn't that late."

"You're not fooling me, Mom. This has something to do with Troy, doesn't it?"

"Why do you say that?" She got her purse and car keys and, without waiting for Chrissie, walked out the door.

Chrissie seemed about to stay behind, but after a moment stomped out to the car, resembling nothing so much as a pouting eight-year-old.

"This isn't going to work," she muttered when she climbed in beside Susannah.

"What isn't?" Susannah inserted the key and started the engine.

"I'm moving to Colville to be with Troy and to help Grandma, and nothing you say is going to change that."

"I haven't said a word," Susannah told her.

"Yeah, right." Chrissie gazed out the side window at the darkened street.

Silently they drove to the Roadside Inn. Susannah nearly clapped her hands with delight when she saw Troy's truck in the parking lot.

"What's this supposed to prove?" Chrissie demanded when Susannah parked next to it.

"Nothing. I feel like a drink. How about you?"

"Oh, please...."

"Fine, you go in on your own. I can wait here." Susannah leaned back in her seat, feigning a relaxed position.

"What do you expect me to find?"

Acting innocent, Susannah shrugged. "I wouldn't know. Why don't you tell me?"

"There's nothing to see here, so let's just go home. Troy and I had a long talk this afternoon, after you tried to discredit him. He doesn't like his women jealous. He said I was his girlfriend, and if I didn't believe that, I shouldn't be in his life."

Susannah sighed as if bored. "Check it out," she said and gestured toward the tavern.

Without responding, Chrissie got out of the car and slammed the door.

Susannah winced at the anger in her daughter. All she could do now was wait—and hope that Chrissie would actually see what should be right in front of her face.

Five agonizing minutes passed before the tavern door opened. Out strolled Troy and Chrissie, arms entwined around each other.

Troy yanked open the passenger door and leaned inside the car. "You've got a real problem, Mrs. Nelson," he said, shaking his head sadly. "Why are you so paranoid? Chrissie's the only one for me." He glared at her in unmistakable challenge. "Isn't that right?" Turning, he bestowed a smile on Chrissie.

"Yes," she reiterated. "My mother isn't going to break us up. I won't let her."

Great, just great. Susannah had gambled and lost. Now she just looked vindictive in Chrissie's eyes—vindictive, unreasonable and, as Troy had said, paranoid.

CHAPTER

38

In the morning, the first thing Susannah did was phone the hospital to check on her mother's condition, which had improved. After she'd spoken to the nurse, she made a pot of coffee, desperate for a caffeine boost.

Chrissie hadn't said a word to her during the entire ride home from the Roadside Inn. She sat there, arms crossed, shoulders back and her chin tilted as if being in such close proximity to her mother was more than she could endure.

Now, sitting at the kitchen table drinking her coffee, Susannah wondered if her daughter's attitude had softened. She didn't have to wait long to find out.

At eight, Chrissie came out of her bedroom, fully dressed. She entered the kitchen and stopped abruptly when she saw Susannah.

"Good morning," Susannah said in a neutral voice.

Her daughter ignored her.

"Chrissie, listen, this has got to end."

Her daughter scowled defiantly in her direction. "It's my life."

"Yes, I know, but…"

"No, you obviously *don't* know," she muttered. "Troy and I are in love."

That made Susannah feel like gagging. "You met him less than two weeks ago!"

Chrissie's eyes narrowed. "I thought you said you didn't want to argue. Then why are you starting off the day doing exactly that? You undermine every decision I make. Nothing I say or do satisfies you—or Dad, either. I'm constantly under your thumb and I hate it. I hate school. Meeting Troy's the best thing that ever happened to me. And now you want to take *him* away from me, too."

"Troy isn't the right man for you," Susannah began.

"You never even gave him a chance." Chrissie's voice quavered, and she sounded close to tears.

Susannah drew in her breath and slowly counted to ten before responding. "Give me one reason I should like Troy," she said as calmly as she could.

"Because I love him," Chrissie insisted, her hands in tight fists at her sides.

That wasn't a valid response in Susannah's opinion. She tried to point out some of his more blatant faults, in the hope that Chrissie would understand her position.

"Troy doesn't have a job, he's irresponsible, and on top of that he's too old for you."

"Oh, please…"

According to Carolyn, Troy was around thirty, but as Susannah had discovered, he had the maturity of a teenager.

Little wonder, she thought darkly, that the two of them got along so well.

"It wouldn't matter if he worked or not," Chrissie countered. "You'd make up an excuse to hate him."

"I don't hate Troy." Susannah didn't understand why it was so hard to talk to her daughter. Why wasn't Chrissie capable of seeing any point of view except her own?

Chrissie threw up her hands. "You're impossible!"

Susannah felt the same way about her. Her daughter hadn't been the easiest child in the world; that stubborn, willful streak had shown up at the age of two and grown stronger every year.

"I can't talk to you anymore." Chrissie bolted from the room, forgoing her usual morning coffee.

With a heavy heart, Susannah sat at the table, her emotions tangled. It didn't seem very long ago that she'd had the identical argument with her father over Jake. The results had been disastrous, and her relationship with him had been forever ruined. She didn't want that to happen between her and Chrissie. At the same time, she had a whole new appreciation of how her father must have felt toward Jake. Yes, he was a hellion and he'd had a juvenile record, but it had been expunged at age eighteen. She'd believed she was helping him straighten out his life, make a fresh start. But Susannah no longer knew if her faith in Jake would've been borne out in later years.

Her arguments with her father could've been Chrissie's arguments with her. It was a shocking realization, and although she now had a glimmer of her father's reasons— whether they were right or wrong—she saw that he'd made a critical mistake. George Leary hadn't given Jake an opportunity to prove himself. He'd been quick to find fault, eager to dismiss him as unfit for his precious daughter, despite the fact that Susannah loved him. Everything he'd said and done had only driven her closer to Jake.

Susannah refused to repeat those mistakes.

Swallowing her pride, she walked down the hallway to Chrissie's bedroom and knocked politely on the door.

"Who is it?" her daughter asked distractedly, as if it could be any one of ten different people.

Susannah rolled her eyes. "Mom."

Chrissie jerked the door open, keeping her hand on the knob, implying that with one wrong word, she'd slam it shut. "What are you going to tell me now? That I'm too young to know what I want?"

"No," Susannah said. "You're right—I haven't given Troy a chance."

Chrissie's eyes narrowed as though she expected this to be a trick.

"I'll do my best to make him feel welcome the next time I see him."

"You will?" Chrissie still sounded skeptical, but was visibly mollified. "He's really a great guy, Mom."

"If you love him, then he must be."

"I *do* love him. Troy's wonderful. He knows everyone in town, and everyone knows him. We can't go anywhere without people coming up and talking to him."

Her daughter was crazy about this guy because he was popular? The urge to walk away in disgust nearly overpowered her. The reason everyone was Troy's friend was that he was the local drug dealer. She suspected these so-called friends were looking for a hit of whatever Troy sold. Once again, Susannah was disappointed that her daughter could be so blind.

"Would you like to invite him to dinner tonight? We can order pizza and chat for a while." If Chrissie saw that she was making a serious effort, maybe, just maybe, her eyes would be opened to the truth about Troy.

Chrissie smiled brightly. "I'll ask, but you know, Mom, Troy isn't the kind of guy who enjoys sitting around the table and shooting the breeze." She offered her a tentative smile. "But I'll ask."

"I won't be offended if he refuses. All I really want is for him to know I'm trying." In truth, Susannah would be grateful if he declined. She didn't know if she'd be able to keep her mouth shut for more than five minutes.

"Thank you, Mom."

Susannah nodded. "You're welcome," she said as graciously as she could.

"How's Grandma this morning?"

Susannah repeated what the nurse had told her earlier.

"I was thinking I'd go to the hospital and see her," Chrissie said.

Susannah would've liked to go with her, but the home security company Joe had contacted was scheduled to install the burglar alarm between eight and twelve. "Tell her I'll be up this afternoon, will you?"

"Okay."

"They'll know more about her condition after the doctor visits," Susannah said, unable to conceal her worry.

"I can stay with her until he does and then report back to you," Chrissie said.

Susannah could see that her daughter was trying, too, and she appreciated it. "That would be great. Thanks, sweetheart."

Soon afterward, Chrissie left for the hospital, driving Susannah's car. Susannah returned to the kitchen to finish her coffee and gave herself an A for effort. Had her father done half as much, it might have changed the course of both their lives.

Chrissie had been gone only ten or fifteen minutes when the doorbell chimed. Susannah had begun to pack away pots and pans in the kitchen. She abandoned the carton she was working on and got up, assuming the home security people had arrived early.

But it wasn't the service company. Troy Nance stood on the doorstep, wearing a stained T-shirt, jeans and motorcycle boots. His hair was pulled back in a ponytail. He *was* Jake's son; she was sure of it. She saw the resemblance more and more.

"Hello, Troy." Susannah did her best to sound friendly and welcoming. If he was surprised, it didn't show. "Chrissie's at the hospital visiting her grandmother."

"Yeah, she told me. You're the one I wanted to talk to."

Susannah faltered a moment but recovered quickly. "Okay." She held open the screen door, but he ignored the invitation to come inside.

"Out here."

She shrugged and followed him down the steps to the walkway. "What can I do for you?" she asked, folding her arms.

"Chrissie phoned and said you'd had a change of heart about me."

That wasn't entirely true, but she'd keep her opinions to herself—for now. "Thanks for coming by, Troy." She wondered why he was here.

"Yeah." His eyes were like chips of ice.

"What will it take for the two of us to be friends?" she asked, moving forward.

"You don't like me," he sneered, "and pretending you do isn't going to help, so let's get that straight up-front."

At least they both knew where they stood. "I'm willing to try," she said.

"What for?"

Nothing less than the truth would satisfy him. "I don't want to lose my daughter over you."

He let the comment hang for a few moments and then smiled as if her answer had pleased him. "I might be able to help you out."

"That would be good," Susannah said, grateful they'd been able to find common ground.

He paced to the end of the walk, then turned on his heel. "Chrissie said if you don't let her stay in the house—" he gestured at the front door "—she'd move in with me." He paused. "Frankly, I'm not interested."

Susannah wanted to hug him, she was so thankful.

"I haven't told her, of course, but I figured you weren't that thrilled about the idea yourself."

"You could say that."

"The fact is, Chrissie's a bit of a drama queen."

Susannah sighed. "She does have a tendency to overreact."

"She's spoiled, too."

Again Susannah didn't have much of an argument, although she recognized how odd it was to be discussing her daughter's flaws with this man. The man Chrissie thought she loved... She studied him carefully. "Is there something you're trying to tell me?"

His mouth curled into a sarcastic half smile. "So you finally caught on, did you?" His cold eyes met hers. "If I asked, Chrissie would move in with me like that." He snapped his fingers as if she needed a demonstration.

"And your point is?" she said curtly.

"You just asked what it would take for the two of us to be friends, right?"

She nodded warily.

"I'm bored with Chrissie," he said bluntly. "She isn't much fun and she makes too many demands, but I could easily string her along—for however long it took."

A chill raced down Susannah's arms. "However long *what* took?"

He shrugged. "Whatever."

Susannah frowned, not sure she understood.

"What's your daughter's happiness worth to you?" he asked.

"What do you mean?"

"I could make her happy or I could break her heart. You choose."

"I beg your pardon?" Susannah could feel the outrage rising inside her. This had to be a distasteful joke, although she certainly wasn't laughing.

"Confidentially, I'm experiencing something of a cash flow problem. I was thinking you might be able to help me out."

"You want me to *pay* you?" Susannah couldn't believe what she was hearing.

"If you want me out of Chrissie's life, I could make that happen for as little as five thousand dollars."

Susannah's mouth flew open. He was serious. Five thousand dollars. The same amount her father had paid Allan Presley.

"This is a one-time offer. It won't be repeated and you have to decide now."

"Or what?"

"Or like I said, I string her along for a while and introduce her to a few of my friends. I'm sure you get the picture."

Susannah thought she was going to be sick. "You don't care about her at all, do you?"

"Not really. She was a nice diversion for a while." He grinned nastily. "Mom said you were a stuck-up prig in high school and it was fun getting a rise out of you."

Susannah stared at him, unable to say a thing.

"Well? Are you game or not?"

Game. This entire episode was a game. He was playing with Chrissie's heart and it meant nothing to him. Now it was up to Susannah to decide what to do.

"I don't have that kind of money here."

He lifted one shoulder in a half shrug. "Then get it from your husband and do it fast."

Susannah's mind raced. Joe would never give in to blackmail. She knew without even asking that he'd flatly refuse. "He won't agree to this."

"Then the deal's off." Troy started to walk away.

"No," she cried. She took him at his word—this was a one-time offer. "I'll find a way to get the money."

"What about your rich friend?" Troy suggested.

Susannah shook her head. "I'd never borrow money from Carolyn."

He raised his eyebrows in a cynical expression. "Not even for your daughter?"

"I—"

"I'll be waiting at the Roadside Inn tonight at seven. Either you're there with the money or no deal."

"But I might not have it by then," she began. "I—"

"That," he said, his voice as hard as steel, "is your problem."

39

Susannah paced the house, figuring out ways to come up with the money. She couldn't go to an ATM—there was a thousand-dollar limit on withdrawals. She and Joe had a joint account, and she doubted she could take out that amount, anyway, without his permission. A credit card advance? She went over and over the possible solutions until Chrissie returned with the car. Her daughter, in high spirits, was full of chatter and good will.

"Grandma looked great," Chrissie assured her. "She was almost like her old self, except..." She giggled. "She thought I was you. The nurse said that's common and I shouldn't worry about it. She'll be herself in no time."

"What did the doctor say?"

Chrissie stopped to think. "Not much, really, just that Grandma's making progress."

Susannah prayed her mother would make a full recovery.

Otherwise, they'd be looking at a hip replacement. From various friends she'd learned how serious that could be with the elderly.

Chrissie studied her. "Don't worry about Grandma, Mom. She's doing really well."

Nodding seemed to require a monumental effort.

"Is something else bothering you?" Chrissie asked with a frown.

"Not really… It's just that I've got an errand to run and I have to wait for the home security people." She'd decided to see Carolyn—to at least discuss this with her.

"Go," she urged. "I'll stay here."

Her daughter's willingness to help added a sense of urgency to Susannah's mission. Without a hint of regret, Troy would destroy Chrissie's life. Paying him off might solve the problem, but she wasn't convinced Troy could be trusted. She didn't dare give him all the money up front, or she'd have no insurance. But even half of $5000 was hard to produce on such short notice.

Carolyn was busy with a buyer when Susannah arrived. Waiting in the small reception area, she gazed out the window over the massive yard, stacked with row upon row of timber. The noon whistle blew, and the work crews broke for a thirty-minute lunch. The saws went silent.

Susannah watched as the men poured out from various places and congregated together. In the distance they looked alike, some short, some tall, but all dressed in the same style coveralls. These men were the fathers, husbands, brothers of many people in Colville, and Susannah was visibly reminded of the mill's importance to the community.

The door to Carolyn's office opened then, and Susannah heard her friend exchanging farewells with the buyer.

"Susannah?" Carolyn said behind her. "You wanted to see me?"

Tearing her gaze away from the window, she turned to her. "Do you have a few minutes to talk privately?"

"Of course." Carolyn led the way back into her office; Susannah followed and closed the door.

Carolyn's eyebrows went up as she rounded her desk and reclaimed her chair. "Is something wrong?"

Sitting down opposite her, Susannah nodded. "I had a visitor this morning." She swallowed hard, then continued. "Troy Nance came to see me."

"I take it this wasn't a social call?"

Susannah made a derisive sound. "Hardly. I took Chrissie out to the Roadside Inn last night, but it didn't do any good. He knows I'm on to him, so he came to tell me that for a mere five thousand dollars he'd break off his relationship with Chrissie."

"He'd what?" Carolyn yelped.

"That's not even the worst of it. Troy claimed the reason he got involved with her is because his mother thought I was—and I quote—a stuck-up prig in high school."

"What?" Carolyn sounded as shocked as Susannah had been. "We both know that Jake broke up with her because of you and she never got over it."

Susannah agreed. Sharon had been caustic the evening they'd driven out to the tavern, claiming that Jake had gone back to her. She'd taken pleasure in informing Susannah that Troy was his son.

"What are you going to do?"

"I'm not sure. My gut tells me to pay him the money and be done with it." It occurred to her then that she was doing almost the same thing her father had done. Another thought hit her and with it her stomach twisted.

"Are you okay?" Carolyn asked in alarm.

Susannah shook her head numbly. "What if...what if Jake's father approached *my* dad and demanded money?" she whispered. It had never entered her mind that Allan Presley might have done exactly that. Now she wondered. In her heart she knew it hadn't been Jake's idea, but she'd assumed her father was the one responsible.

Carolyn's eyes were wide. "I never thought of that."

The sinking sensation didn't leave her. Her mind whirled with the possibility and she didn't immediately realize Carolyn was speaking.

"What did Joe say?"

Susannah looked away. "I didn't tell him."

Carolyn frowned at that. "Why not?"

"Because I know my husband and he'd never agree to this. He's probably right, but I have to do *something*... I'm desperate. My daughter's future is at stake."

Carolyn's frown darkened. "Do you think keeping Joe out of this is a good idea?"

"I don't know. I just don't know." Her voice shook with near hysteria. That wretched man was risking Chrissie's future, without conscience, without regret and without a qualm. His threat hadn't been subtle—he'd introduce her to his friends. Susannah could easily guess what that meant. His friends had to be big-time losers. Even more disturbing was the implication that Chrissie would be hanging around with...with drug addicts and given cocaine or who knew what.

Now Susannah had no choice but to broach the subject of money with Carolyn. Drawing in a deep breath, she leaned toward her friend's desk. "There's a problem. I don't have five thousand dollars just lying around." She didn't wait for Carolyn to comment, fearing what she'd say. "I suppose I could get a cash advance on the credit card, but I'd rather not tell Joe about this if I can possibly keep it secret."

Carolyn's chest rose with a harsh sigh. "Troy is blackmailing you."

"I know."

"I think you should talk this over with your husband."

Susannah wanted Joe at her side more than ever, and yet she knew beyond a doubt that he wouldn't agree to this. She couldn't risk it, even at the cost of her marriage. When everything was settled, when Chrissie was safe, she'd tell him, but not before—otherwise they might lose their daughter.

"Going behind Joe's back *isn't* right," she agreed, "but for now and for Chrissie's sake, it's my only option." Opening her purse, Susannah set out the emerald ring Joe had given her on their twentieth anniversary. He'd paid twenty-five hundred dollars for it. In addition, she had her mother's pearls, which Vivian had given her for safekeeping. Taken together, she believed their value would total at least the amount she needed to borrow.

"I was hoping," she said, the words barely making it past the constriction in her throat, "that it would be possible to get a loan from you." Asking to borrow money was even harder than she'd imagined. Her face burned with mortification. "These are worth more but—"

"You want me to write you a personal check for the five thousand," Carolyn said.

Susannah hung her head. "The jewelry's the collateral."

After a short pause, Carolyn slowly straightened and opened a drawer, pulling out her checkbook. "I don't think you're doing the right thing in keeping this from Joe, but you're the one who has to make that decision."

Weak with relief, Susannah nodded. "Thank you."

"But I'd rest easier if at some point you told your husband."

"I will, I promise, just not yet."

Carolyn wrote the check and handed it to Susannah. Then she turned to her computer and typed up a simple IOU. "I don't want to take the jewelry. You keep it. The note is enough."

Susannah thanked her, signed the note and took back the ring and pearls. "I can't tell you how much I appreciate this," she said, on the verge of tears.

"I just hope Chrissie appreciates what you're doing."

God willing, she'd never find out. "I don't want her to know."

"You aren't going to tell her?"

Susannah shook her head emphatically. "No way! She'd never forgive me. Sure as anything, she'd blame me for this. I can't take that chance."

"What if Troy comes back for more money later on?"

Susannah had considered this. "I don't think he will. He said Chrissie's become a drag. He's bored with her."

The look on Carolyn's face was one of disgust. Susannah shared her opinion.

Before she left, she thanked her friend profusely.

Chrissie was busy packing up the hallway linen closet when Susannah got back to the house. "The alarm guy was here," she said, still on her knees, a stack of pillowcases in her arms. "It's the same alarm system we have at home. I gave him your birthdate, month and day, for the code."

"Good idea," Susannah mumbled. Now that the problem of finding the money had been solved, she should feel good. She didn't; if anything, she felt worse. Carolyn disapproved of the risk Susannah was taking, but she hadn't offered any alternatives, either.

"Mom? Are you okay?"

It was the second time that day her daughter had asked that question. Susannah forced a smile. "Of course I am."

Chrissie set the pillowcases neatly inside a carton. "This is about Troy, isn't it?"

The mention of his name startled Susannah, until she reminded herself that Chrissie couldn't possibly know what it was about Troy that had upset her.

"You're really trying, and Mom, I want to tell you how grateful I am."

"I'm doing my best."

Her daughter impulsively scrambled to her feet and hugged her. "You won't be sorry, Mom. I promise you."

Except that she already was.

Vivian was so tired. She knew she was in the hospital and she knew she was in pain. She couldn't tell what time it was. Afternoon, she assumed. She vaguely remembered a lunch tray, which she hadn't touched. It was all she could do to keep her eyes open. She thought George might come; that was why she had to stay awake. She felt certain her husband would know how badly she needed to see him.

Closing her eyes, she fought the waves of fatigue.

"Vivian?" a gruff male voice called to her.

Vivian opened her eyes to find George Wakefield from Altamira standing next to her hospital bed. He leaned heavily on his crutches and stared down at her, a look of worry creasing his face.

"George." He wasn't the George she'd been longing to see, but this George was good, too.

"How are you feeling?"

She gave a weak smile. Seeing him, she remembered she'd been with George playing pool when she'd fallen. It must've been quite a shock for him.

"I broke my hip."

"That's what they said. I *told* you not to take that shot with your cane. It's dangerous."

"You used your crutch. Fair is fair."

He nearly grinned, which would've been a first. This George was as stingy with smiles as her husband had been.

"How'd you get here?" Vivian asked. The assisted-living place kept close tabs on everyone. Getting away without one of the staff noticing couldn't have been easy.

"I signed myself out."

Vivian hadn't known she could do that. Anytime she'd left, it'd been with Susannah. "But how'd you get *here?*"

"Curious, aren't you?"

Vivian laughed softly. "I should find out, in case I decide to make a break for it."

This time he did smile and it cheered her immeasurably.

"Okay. I took the Altamira Shuttle. All you have to do is order it at the desk."

"Hmm." Vivian wondered if it was time for another pain pill.

"Any more visits from your dead husband?" George asked. Resting his crutches against the wall, he sank down onto the lone chair in the room and made himself comfortable.

Vivian shook her head sadly. "I thought for sure he'd come and see me, but he hasn't."

"It might be more difficult these days. They have restrictions on the other side, you know?"

Vivian had guessed as much. All she knew of heaven was in the pages of her Bible, and the descriptions there were somewhat limited. George hadn't told her anything, but then he'd never spoken. That apparently went against the rules.

"Did anyone ask about me?" Vivian inquired. "At Altamira?"

"Several folks. Your friend Sally. None of the nurses knew how you were doing, so I decided to find out for myself."

Vivian blushed; his attention flustered her. "I'm glad you did."

"Me, too." He gently patted her hand, and she felt herself grow warm. Oh, my. This George was a handsome man and she—

"Mom?" Susannah stood in the doorway holding a vase of roses. She wore the oddest look, as if she wasn't quite sure she should trust her eyes.

"Susannah!"

George struggled to his feet.

"George, this is my daughter, Susannah," Vivian said, rushing the words in her embarrassment. That look of her daughter's made her feel guilty, although she hadn't done anything wrong.

"Hello, George," Susannah said. "Have we met?"

"No, but your mother's mentioned you many times."

"I see." Susannah set the flowers down on the bedside stand and leaned close to kiss Vivian on the cheek.

"George isn't my boyfriend or anything," Vivian said

firmly. She wanted that understood right away. *Boyfriend* was such a silly word. In her day it would've been suitor. Or maybe gentleman caller.

"I'm not?" George said, and to her delight he sounded downright disappointed.

"We're *friends*."

"Right," George concurred. "Friends."

Susannah seemed to be in a good mood if that smile on her face was any indication.

"I suppose I'd best be getting back to Altamira," George muttered, reaching for his crutches.

"Please don't leave on my account," Susannah said.

"The shuttle driver's waiting. I told him I wouldn't be staying long." He patted Vivian's hand one last time. "You take care, you hear."

"I will," she promised and then because she wanted to be sure he wouldn't disappear the way her George sometimes did, she stretched out one hand and touched his face.

Surprise filled George's eyes. "Hurry back home," he whispered. "I miss you." Then, expertly wielding his crutches, he swung out the door.

"Mother," Susannah said. "You *do* have a boyfriend."

"I most certainly don't," Vivian denied hotly. She rolled her head to the side to examine the flowers. "It's very thoughtful of you to bring me roses."

"You're avoiding the subject."

Vivian sighed. "I don't want you to be upset with me."

Susannah stepped closer to the bed. "Why would I be upset?"

Lowering her lashes, Vivian felt it was time she told the

truth. "You were so angry with your father not long ago, although I don't remember what it was about...."

"I'm beginning to think I might have misjudged Daddy," Susannah said in a low voice.

It gladdened Vivian's heart to hear that. "I told you I'd ask your father, but he didn't come. I waited up half the night, and then I was afraid he didn't know I'd moved." She spoke quickly in her eagerness to confess what she'd done. "I wanted to talk to him so badly and he didn't come." She dared to glance up and to her astonishment, Susannah had tears in her eyes. This was what she'd feared most, that Susannah would be upset with her again.

"I'm so sorry," Vivian murmured.

"Sorry about what, Mom?"

"I told George—the George you just met—that you were angry with your father and that I was waiting for him to visit. When your father didn't show up, he suggested I tell you I'd spoken to George, which I had, of course, only it was a different George, and that anything your father did was because he loved you."

"He did love me, Mom." The tears in her daughter's eyes glistened. "I don't know why it took me so long to understand that."

"Do you understand now?"

Susannah nodded. "I've learned a lot in the last few days...."

"It wasn't a real lie. I did talk to George," she said, returning to the subject of her small deception. "It wasn't George, your father, but George my friend."

Susannah offered her a gentle smile. "It's all right, Mom. I'm not angry."

"Good." Vivian was tired then, really tired. After waiting most of the day, she had to assume her husband wasn't coming. Maybe tonight, but she wasn't holding out much hope.

"I think I'll close my eyes," she whispered.

"You go right ahead, Mom."

"Will you be here when I wake up?"

"Maybe," Susannah said. "But if I'm not, it's because I have an errand to run."

"That's fine, dear. Go ahead and do your errand."

"I love you, Mom."

Vivian smiled, glad she'd told the truth. She felt so much better now that Susannah knew.

She must have drifted off then, because when she woke, the room was dark and silent. The night-light shone from the bathroom.

She sensed she wasn't alone and turning her head, she realized she was right. George stood beside the bed.

Her George. Defying death, he'd come when she needed him most.

41

A raucous country-and-western song was booming from the Roadside Inn when Susannah drove into the gravel parking lot. She'd left her mother, who appeared to be resting comfortably; now she was about to meet Troy. She had the money to pay him off. It was with more than a little trepidation that she'd decided to play his game.

As before, the tavern was filled with truckers. The smoke was thick and the odor of booze and stale perspiration permeated the place. Troy sat at a table with the same blonde Susannah had seen earlier. He'd told Chrissie this "old friend" was named Jenny something. The woman looked adoringly up at Troy, her arm wrapped tightly around his waist. She wore a skimpy halter top and her breasts threatened to spill out.

Troy turned and stared at Susannah as she walked through the door. He said something to the blonde and disengaged himself from her embrace. His gaze holding Susannah's, he motioned with his head toward the bar.

As on her previous visit, Sharon was bartending. Susannah saw her former classmate stiffen at the sight of her. Susannah went rigid, too, still not sure she was doing the right thing.

Troy moved down to the far end and Susannah met him there.

"You have the money?" he asked coolly.

Clutching her purse close to her body, she nodded. "I have a few concerns we need to discuss first."

His eyes narrowed as he studied her. "Don't try to screw me over," he said in a heated whisper.

"I'm not. You're asking for a lot of money and I want some guarantees."

"Like what?"

"How do I know you won't contact Chrissie at a later date?"

"Forget it," he scoffed. "I've got other fish to fry."

"You mean you make a practice of this sort of thing?"

"No," he said as though her questions bored him. "I'm tired of her. What's that old saying—out of sight, out of mind? She'll go back to Seattle and that'll be the end of it."

This was what Susannah hoped would happen. "There's no guarantee Chrissie will leave Colville," she said.

Troy dismissed her concern with a shake of his head. "She will."

Susannah wasn't convinced. Her daughter was stubborn and might just decide to stay. In which case, everything could explode in Susannah's face.

"Are you changing the ground rules?" Troy asked, leaning one elbow against the bar.

"No, but I want Chrissie to go home where she belongs." She paused. "More precisely, I want her back in school."

Troy shrugged indifferently. "Works for me. I sure don't want her hanging around here. She'll go home, don't worry about it."

Susannah *was* worried. "She doesn't know anything about this, right?"

"You think I'd tell her?"

Susannah had the feeling Troy would do whatever it took to get whatever he wanted. If that meant disclosing the fact that Susannah had paid him off, she wouldn't put it past him. She couldn't help wondering if her father had experienced the same doubts when he'd paid off Jake's. Had he wondered if he was doing the right thing? Had he questioned his own judgment? Like her, she suspected he had. "I don't want Chrissie finding out I was involved in any way," she said sharply.

"Fine. Now give me the money."

"Not yet."

"Listen, I don't have time for this crap. Give me the money or I'll screw up your sweet little girl for the rest of her life."

Susannah didn't take his threat lightly. She sensed that Troy would derive real pleasure from hurting Chrissie out of spite.

Figuring any further discussion would do more harm than good, Susannah set her purse on the scuffed bar and unzipped it. Taking out a stack of twenties and fifties, she handed it to Troy.

He grabbed the money and thumbed through the bills. A minute later, he raised his hard eyes to lock with hers. "This is only half of what we agreed."

"The other half is at the house. You'll get it after Chrissie leaves for Seattle."

He clearly wasn't happy about it, but he didn't have any choice. Susannah wasn't about to give him everything at once and risk being cheated. This was the only recourse she had and she intended to use it.

He seemed to deliberate, then slowly nodded. "Fine. But you better come through." He stuffed the money in his wallet, which was connected to his jeans by a chain. Without another word, he walked back to the table where he'd been sitting and pulled on the blonde's arm. Hands linked, the couple walked out of the tavern. Jenny, if that was her name, swayed her hips provocatively. Susannah would've been embarrassed if that was her daughter.

"He's a handsome man, my son, isn't he?" Sharon sauntered up. "He looks more like his father every day."

Susannah ignored the comment. While it was true that Troy did resemble Jake, he lacked every other quality Susannah felt was important in a man—dignity, honor, character. All were missing in Troy and apparently in Jake, too. That made her more sad than angry. She'd honestly felt they'd shared something special. She'd been far too stubborn—not unlike her own daughter—to realize how right her father had been to get him out of her life. All the years she'd harbored this resentment against him and now…now she understood and it tore her apart. She'd wasted all those years, bitter and angry about the way he'd manipulated her life, and here she was, doing the same thing. She was doing it out of love, just as her father had.

"The minute you left for France, Jake came to me."

"That isn't true." For her own sake, Susannah wanted to believe otherwise—wanted to believe what his letters had implied.

Sharon laughed contemptuously, but Susannah didn't care.

"Jake was never interested in you. Not like you were in him." She held her ground, unwilling to let Sharon rattle her.

"Think what you want," Sharon said, as though it was of little concern. "Troy is all the proof I need."

The woman had a point, although Susannah would never concede it. "I'm sorry you have to lash out at others, Sharon," she said. "Jake must've hurt you very badly." Then she turned and walked out the door. By the time Susannah got to the car, her hands shook so badly it was difficult to push the remote that would unlock the vehicle.

Troy, of all people, had taught her one of the most valuable lessons of her life. She was her father's daughter.

As she inserted the key in the car's ignition, Susannah recognized that she'd risked her own relationship with her daughter in doing this. Her marriage, too. Having gone behind Joe's back again, she wondered how he'd react once he learned what she'd done and why. All she could do was hope he'd understand.

This summer she'd begun to view their relationship with fresh eyes. Through the years, Joe had proven himself. They'd shared hopes, made plans and borne each other's sorrows. He'd seen her at her best and her worst. Joe was the one who'd always been at her side. Not Jake. He was a fantasy, a long-lost love, a dream that had turned out to be false.

Considering all these revelations, Susannah drove home. The house was dark—did that mean Troy had already made good on his word? Was Chrissie with him? It struck her then that she'd paid this dreadful man twenty-five hundred dollars to break her daughter's heart. Just like he said he would...

Somehow, Susannah made it up the steps and into the house. Her eyes swam with tears and she could barely see. All those years she'd carried her anger toward her father, like a shield that could never be pierced. She'd held him off, refusing to let him close. Even recently, at the cemetery, she'd ranted at him, charging him with not loving her. But he *did* love her, more than she'd ever known, as much as Susannah loved her own daughter.

She'd been wrong about so many things.

Her father had loved her and she loved him. Joe had been right all along. As hard as she'd tried not to have any feelings for him, she did. Because of her anger toward him, she'd been unable to grieve normally. Instead, she'd revisited that time in her youth, reliving her outrage, her sense of injustice. Was that so she wouldn't have to deal with the emotions surrounding his death?

She missed her father, she loved him, and she was sorry. So sorry. Now she'd give anything, *anything,* to tell him how deeply she regretted her refusal to see his side. She buried her face in her hands and cried until there were no tears left.

When she felt she could speak again, she walked into the kitchen and reached for the phone. Thankfully, Joe answered.

"Susannah, what is it?"

"I—I need you. Please come... I can't do this without you anymore."

Her husband didn't hesitate. "I'll leave within the hour."

His simple acceptance of her need, not asking a single question, tore at her. "Joe, oh, Joe, I love you so much."

"I know, Suze. I love you, too."

"Joe, I've done something so foolish. Please hurry."

"I'm on my way. Don't worry. We'll discuss everything when I get there."

The road back to herself, to the person she used to be, *wanted* to be, led directly to her husband, Joe Nelson.

CHAPTER

42

Susannah had composed herself by the time Chrissie returned. As she expected, her daughter was devastated. Sobbing, Chrissie ran into the house and without a word flew into Susannah's waiting arms. With all her heart, Susannah prayed her daughter would never learn of her part in this.

"What is it?" she asked, cradling Chrissie's head against her shoulder.

"It's over," Chrissie managed between gasping breaths.

"With Troy?"

Her daughter nodded, hugging Susannah close.

"Can you tell me what happened?"

Chrissie shook her head. "I want to die."

"Oh, sweetheart."

"I loved him. First Jason, and now Troy. There must be something wrong with me."

"You can't honestly think that," she murmured soothingly. She stroked the back of her daughter's head and made soft reassuring sounds as she told Chrissie that she was a lovely young woman and would meet the right someone soon.

"Troy kept putting me off about helping if I moved to Colville and now I know why. Mom, oh, Mom," she cried. She leaned away from Susannah and covered her face with both hands. "He's got a woman living with him. It's that Jenny—the one he said was an *old friend*. She's been there all along."

This didn't come as any surprise to Susannah; foolishly the other woman was willing to ignore Troy's indiscretions.

"What am I going to do?" Chrissie sobbed.

"Everything will be better once you're home." Home sounded good to Susannah, too. A month earlier she'd been eager to escape. Her marriage had felt stale, her life in a rut. Now it would take several large volumes to list all her blessings.

"How will I get there?" Chrissie sobbed more loudly now.

"Dad's driving over tonight."

Chrissie wiped the tears from her cheeks. Her eyes were bright and moisture clung to her long lashes. "Dad's coming?" This was apparently the best news she'd heard in some time, because she gave Susannah a wobbly smile.

Susannah nodded. "Dad and I will finish the packing, and we'll hire Martha to do the cleaning. I'll go home with him, and you can drive my car back if you want."

"I do. Then everything's better between you and Dad?"

"Yes, much better. He was upset with me and rightly so. We all make foolish mistakes, Chrissie. The thing is, we need to learn from those mistakes and move forward."

"I'm going to," she vowed.

Susannah hugged her again. "Like mother, like daughter."

Chrissie's attempt to laugh sounded more like a cough. "That's not funny."

Susannah hadn't meant it to be.

Sniffling, Chrissie retreated into her bedroom. A short while later, Susannah heard her talking on her cell phone and was half afraid Chrissie had contacted Troy. She needn't have worried. Within a few minutes, she realized her daughter had called a girlfriend in Seattle.

At ten Susannah noticed the light was off in the bedroom and a quick check assured her Chrissie was asleep.

Susannah stayed up and waited for Joe to arrive, which he did at two-thirty in the morning. As soon as she heard his car pull up, she opened the door, clutching her house-coat around her.

Joe got out of the car and Susannah couldn't wait a moment longer. She raced barefoot down the steps, throwing herself into her husband's arms. As soon as she was safe in Joe's grasp, she spread kisses over his face, letting him know without words how grateful she was to see him, to be married to him, to love him.

Joe's arms tightened around her waist. "To what do I owe this warm welcome?" he asked, chuckling.

"I love you, Joe Nelson."

"I should hope so. We've been married for nearly twenty-five years."

"I mean, I *really* love you. I didn't even know how much until these last few weeks. Oh, Joe, I have so many things to tell you." Not all of them would please him, but Susannah vowed she'd hold nothing back.

Because he was keyed up from the long drive, they sat side by side on the sofa with a glass of wine and talked for another hour. Joe had been able to reach a retired dentist friend, who'd agreed to step in while he helped settle everything in Colville.

Susannah began to relate the events of the past weeks.

"You didn't!" Joe moaned when she told him about paying Troy the blackmail money he'd demanded.

"He's going to be looking for the extra twenty-five hundred in the morning."

Joe's eyes narrowed. "He's not getting it."

"But I—"

Her husband shook his head. "Don't worry, I'll take care of this. I have a few things to say to him, and if I have to bring in the sheriff, I will. Once I'm through with Troy Nance, he won't be bothering Chrissie or anyone in this family again."

The relief Susannah felt was instantaneous. It was a joy to rest on his support and his love. She should never have tried to deal with this on her own. They were a team and she shouldn't have forgotten that.

Joe wasn't finished. "First thing in the morning, return the rest of the money to Carolyn and give her a check for the other twenty-five hundred. I'll have the bank transfer the funds."

"Thank you," she whispered.

Joe put his arm around her shoulders. "I wish I'd come with you."

Drawing in a deep breath, Susannah bit her lip. "There's more."

"More?" He sounded worried and Susannah couldn't blame him.

"Perhaps I should save this for another time?" she suggested.

"Does it have to do with the P.I.?"

Susannah shook her head. "With Jake."

Joe leaned back on the sofa and slowly exhaled. "Ah, yes, Jake, the love of your life." There was a hint of irony in his voice, and she couldn't blame him for that, either.

"No," she insisted, holding her hands against his cheeks, "the love of my life is you. It's always been you and only you. For a while, I'd forgotten that." Tucking her legs beneath her, she laid her head on his shoulder.

"You'd better tell me."

For her, it really was the end as far as Jake was concerned. "Sharon Nance, Troy's mother, told me Jake is his father."

Her husband gave a low whistle.

"She seems to have been in regular contact with him. I don't think I can believe everything she says, but she knew about the medal I'd given Jake years ago, so I tend to believe her on this."

Joe frowned. "I'm sure she was trying to upset you."

"Yes, but I don't care anymore. I have you, and that's all that matters to me." And Susannah meant it.

"Are you ready for bed?" he asked, yawning.

Susannah nodded. "More than ready. I've been without my husband for a long time."

Joe chuckled and helped her off the sofa. With their arms around each other's waists, they walked to her bedroom, next door to where Chrissie slept.

Their daughter must have heard them talking, because the bedroom door opened and Chrissie appeared in the hallway. "Daddy?"

"Hello, sugar bear."

Chrissie hugged her father close and Susannah noticed that her eyes were red and swollen.

"I'm glad you're here," Chrissie said, looping her arms around her father's middle the way she had as a little girl.

"I am, too."

"How are you feeling?" Susannah asked, wishing there'd been some way to protect Chrissie from this pain.

"I'll be okay…. I just want to go home."

"You can leave in the morning."

"Good." Chrissie returned to her room, shutting the door.

Joe took Susannah's hand and led her into the bedroom. He made a disgruntled sound when he saw that she slept in a twin bed.

"We'll cuddle close together," she told him, nuzzling his neck.

"Really close," he said with a laugh. Then he abruptly went still.

Susannah lifted her head. "What is it?"

Joe released her and walked over to the dresser. "Someone's been here and left you a message."

Whirling around, Susannah noticed the single sheet of paper taped to her dresser mirror. It read:

MEET ME AT 10 A.M. IN THE CEMETERY.

CHAPTER

43

"You're going?" Joe asked the next morning as they held each other in bed. They'd slept that way for most of the night, as though they couldn't bear to be apart for even a moment. Their love was fresh and new and they'd rediscovered their appreciation for each other. Joe was her salvation, her constant, and she was horrified at what a dangerous thing she'd done.

"Yes. I have to."

"How the hell did someone get in here?" Joe had been brooding about this since the night before. "If it was that Jake guy…"

"Jake isn't important to me." All the desire she'd had to connect with him, to apologize for what her father had done, was gone. Whether he was Troy's father or not didn't matter to her. Jake belonged to the past, a past that couldn't be altered or relived. She'd idealized him in her mind, canonized him, but he was no saint, then or now.

"I can't," she whispered, hugging Joe, clinging to the husband who'd loved her and stood by her throughout her temporary insanity.

Slipping his hand beneath her chin, Joe raised her face so that her eyes met his. "If you don't, you'll always regret it, always wonder. Get this completely out of your system."

"Will you go with me?"

Joe's chest rose as he considered her request. Finally he nodded.

That changed everything. Susannah could face Jake with her husband at her side. With Joe, she could look her former boyfriend in the eye and tell him that her father's arrange-ment was the best thing George Leary had ever done for her. Only now did she understand that because of Jake, her father had lost both his children. Doug to whatever drug deal the two of them had been involved in and Susannah to anger.

By eight, Chrissie was up and packing. Susannah sat on her bed and they talked. "I really thought I loved him, Mom."

"I know, sweetheart." She bit her tongue to keep from re-minding her daughter how unworthy Troy was of her love.

"I guess I thought my love would change him."

Susannah had believed that about Jake, too. "What you loved was the man you knew he could be," she said, draw-ing up her knees and clasping her arms around them.

Joe brought them each a cup of coffee and seeing that they were talking, promptly left.

"I was so angry with you because you couldn't see Troy the way I did, and now I realize I should've been looking at him through your eyes."

This was a giant step toward maturity for Chrissie, and Susannah had faith that it wouldn't take her daughter nearly as long to recognize the truth as it had her.

"Everything I did was out of love," she told Chrissie.

Her eyes filled with tears as her daughter walked over to the bed and hugged her. "I know that now," Chrissie said.

At nine-thirty, Joe carried her suitcase to the car, and after a quick stop to see her grandmother, Chrissie would leave for Seattle. Once she'd spoken to her mother regarding the situation, even Vivian agreed that Chrissie's living in Colville wasn't a good idea. Susannah and Joe, arms around each other, stood on the sidewalk and watched their daughter drive off.

"She'll be fine," Joe said. "This has been a tough lesson for her."

"Yes…" Susannah murmured. Growth was a painful process—as she well knew.

"Are you ready?" Joe asked. "We should probably leave for the cemetery."

She didn't know if she'd ever be ready for this confrontation. "Promise me that no matter what happens, you won't leave my side."

"You don't have to worry," Joe assured her. "If this clown thinks he's going to walk away with my wife, he's got another think coming."

Susannah pressed her head to Joe's shoulder and smiled, amused that he could even consider it a possibility. The man who held her was everything she would ever want or need in a husband.

They took the road out of town, neither of them in the

mood to talk. The cast-iron gate leading into the cemetery was open when they pulled off the highway. As before, the note hadn't mentioned where they were to meet. Joe parked near her father's grave, which was close to the mausoleum, and they waited in front of the car, holding hands. It was still early; they had five minutes to spare.

Before, when Susannah had visited her father's grave, she'd felt nothing but anger, venting her frustration at him. Her attitude was vastly different now. She smiled down at the gravestone, her heart filled with renewed love for him, and a sense of loss for the wasted years.

Joe's hand tightened around hers. When she glanced up, she gasped. It seemed as if her heart had suddenly stopped. The world started to spin. No, this couldn't be right—she must be seeing things. It was because she'd been thinking about her father....

Stepping out from behind the mausoleum and walking toward her was...George Leary. Only he was younger, handsomer.

"Dad?" she whispered, her voice cracking.

"Susannah," Joe said softly. "It's Doug, your brother."

"Doug?" Tears flooded her eyes and her knees went out from under her. Her brother had been dead for over thirty years. She would have collapsed onto the freshly mowed lawn if Joe hadn't grabbed her waist and kept her upright.

"I'm sorry to shock you," Doug said, rushing forward, "but I didn't know any other way to do this."

"How...why...when?"

"Perhaps we should go back to the house and talk about this," Joe suggested.

Doug frowned, looking uncertain. "Your daughter's staying with you?"

"She's gone back to Seattle."

Doug nodded. "Good. I'll meet you there."

Susannah continued to tremble once they were inside the car. "He looks so much like my father." Then it came to her. "Oh, my goodness, Mom…" Her mother had repeatedly told Susannah that she'd seen George, and she *had* seen him, a younger version of her dead husband. Her son. With her mind befuddled by grief and disorientation, Vivian must have believed that George had come back from the dead to be with her. It explained so much of what her mother had told her. How quick Susannah had been to dismiss her claims.

Doug arrived at the house five minutes after Susannah and Joe, and surreal though it seemed, introductions were made. Susannah brewed a pot of strong coffee. She needed it. Had it been later in the day, she would've reached for a shot glass. There were times the body needed that kind of jolt to cope with shock.

Doug was about to take a seat at the table when Susannah began to speak. "I thought Jake was the one who left me the notes," she told him. "How did you get into the house the last time? I had the security alarm on."

Her brother smiled apologetically at her. "I turned off the alarm. The code was easy enough to figure out. You used your birthdate, and I had the key from inside the brick."

Of course. That was how Chrissie had gotten inside the house that first evening. Chrissie had put it back and neither of them had ever checked again. Susannah had forgotten all about it.

"I figured you'd think it was Jake," he went on. "Contacting you like this was a rotten thing to do, and I apologize."

"But...but if you're alive, is anyone buried in your casket? And what was in the house that you kept trying to find? It *was* you all these times, wasn't it?"

Doug put up his hand to stop her. "Maybe I'd better tell this from the beginning."

"Please," Joe said, gesturing toward the kitchen table. They all sat down.

Doug, who faced the window, stared sightlessly into the distance. "It started just before you went to France, Susannah, when Jake came to me. He needed money and needed it fast. He was desperate to keep you from leaving, and he'd gotten involved in a drug deal to make some quick cash. He ended up in Idaho, where he got into trouble with some not very nice guys, and asked me for help. I don't know what he thought I could do, but I went back with him in the hope of straightening everything out."

"Were *you* selling drugs?" Susannah asked.

"No," Doug returned adamantly. "I had no idea what I was getting into. Jake, either. By the time we knew, it was too late. We were part of a sting operation designed to catch the big-time suppliers, the guys Jake had gotten himself mixed up with. We were just some of the little fish caught in that net. But both of our names were on the arrest warrant."

"So you fled." Susannah didn't understand why, if he was innocent, her brother hadn't simply faced the authorities.

"Jake and I hightailed it out of Idaho, and it was the stupidest mistake of my life," her brother said. "I didn't realize that when I returned to Washington, a minor drug bust became a federal crime. All I could think of was to get to Dad and ask for his help."

Susannah nodded, but she still didn't grasp how the situation had gotten so quickly out of hand. "I was ready to give up, take my punishment," he said. "I even had a date with Patricia the night we got home, but then Jake panicked and went to Sharon Nance. Apparently she couldn't or wouldn't help him, so he stole my car."

"Did Jake resume his relationship with Sharon while I was in France?" Susannah asked.

"No," Doug said.

"Later then. He must have if she had a son by him."

"No," Doug told her again. "There wouldn't have been time. As I said, he stole my car and made a run for it."

"And got himself killed," Joe supplied, figuring that part out before Susannah did.

"Jake is...dead?" Susannah was having trouble taking this in. "But that's impossible! Sharon said he's Troy's father and that she's been in touch with him."

Her brother's smile was grim. "She lied."

"But...why?"

"She obviously resented you," Joe said, reaching for her hand and gently squeezing her fingers. "For some messed-up reason of her own. She refused to help him—and never saw him again. This summer, when she learned you were looking for Jake, she told you all those lies. She obviously wanted you to think the worst of him. And, Suze—it means he wasn't Troy's father."

Susannah could barely take that in, but her heart lightened. Jake had been true to her, true to the end of his life.

Doug sipped his coffee and went back to his story then. "With Jake dead, it all came down on me. Proof of my innocence had been destroyed. Dad had got hold of Sheriff Dalton before we learned about the accident. He knew he could trust his friend, but because everything had been turned over to the FBI, there was nothing the sheriff could do."

"Oh, no."

"It was Dad's idea to bury Jake in my stead." He spoke in a low voice. "He knew the chances of me getting off were slim, despite my innocence. After all the men he'd sent to prison, he feared it would be hell on earth for me there."

"What about Jake's father? Did he ever know?"

Doug shook his head. "To the best of my knowledge, he didn't. He took the money Dad gave him, and from what I understand, Jake and his dad had a falling out before the move. His father was living in Oregon, and Jake said he was finished with him." Doug paused for a moment. "Allan was the one who went to Dad, you know. When Jake found out, he was furious. Jake tried to be the man you wanted him to be, Susannah. Unfortunately, things didn't work out for him."

Despite Allan Presley's inadequacy as a father and a human being, she found it sad that he never knew his only son was dead.

"How did they ever manage to bury Jake and pass him off as you?" Joe demanded.

"Sheriff Dalton had Jake placed in a body bag at the scene of the accident, and he took him to Uncle Henry's."

"Uncle Henry?" Joe asked, frowning.

"My dad's brother owned the town mortuary," Susannah said. "He died years ago and it was sold."

"The funeral was closed casket," Doug went on, "and that was understandable with the type of accident it'd been. No one questioned any part of it. Jake was buried, and I was dead to my family." He paused for a moment. "Dad was able to get me new identification papers, and a social security number. He had the connections." He stared down at his hands. "Dad found out about a baby born the same year I was, a baby who died at six months of age. David Langevin. That's who I became."

"All this time Mom thought you were Dad."

Doug's sigh revealed his chagrin. "Yes, I know. But there was nothing I could do except let her assume that. I guess I do look a bit like Dad these days. Or at least the way he looked in middle age."

"She didn't know the difference," Susannah said.

"I never intended to show myself to her. I found her by the park one night, sitting on a bench, and she was clearly lost. I had to help her, but when she saw me she assumed I was Dad. I didn't speak for fear she'd figure it out. I didn't want to confuse her any more than she already was."

"You came back to see her again?"

Her brother nodded. "I visited her at the hospital once, and at Altamira. It seemed to comfort her. She never knew what really happened to me. Dad made the decision not to tell her I was alive. It would've been too hard on her, he said, keeping this kind of secret, so he felt it was best to cut all ties. I agreed at the time but later I wished I hadn't. He came to see me through the years and brought me money. I worked menial jobs in various states."

"Hold on a minute," Susannah said, stopping him. Once again she'd misjudged her father. "I found a small journal he'd kept of those trips. I thought Dad might've had a mistress and he was wining and dining her instead of our mother."

"I found it, too," Doug told her. "I was afraid of what you might think, so I took it. Apparently too late," he added ruefully.

"Oh, no." Susannah covered her eyes with both hands. She'd wrongly accused her father at every turn.

"At the time everything had to be decided quickly and I know Dad had his regrets after the fact. I did, too, but I couldn't set things straight because of what might happen to him. He was instrumental in setting this up and there would be ramifications for him because of it. I was trapped and so was he."

If the fraud had been discovered, Susannah realized, her father, her uncle and the sheriff would've been charged and possibly imprisoned. Naturally, her brother couldn't risk that.

"I didn't believe Mom when she told me she'd seen Dad."

"Don't blame yourself for that," Joe said, giving her hand another reassuring squeeze. Then nodding at Doug, he said, "Continue with what happened to you after the accident."

Doug looked sadly down at his coffee. "Dad gave me what cash he could and I crossed into Canada. I lived in British Columbia for a number of years under my new identity. I even worked in mills in a couple of B.C. towns. You remember I once had a summer job at Bronson's?"

"You never married, never had a family?"

Doug shook his head. "No. I couldn't drag innocent people into this mess."

"Oh, Doug."

"Eventually I came back to the States and worked at different places around the country. I drifted from city to city, state to state, never staying in any one place for long. I did what I could to make a decent life for myself."

"Why did you come back to Colville?"

Doug cupped his hands around his mug. "It was probably a crazy risk to take, but after all these years I figured everyone had forgotten about me. My appearance had changed quite a bit—as you can tell. Anyway...Dad and I had a complicated communications system and when he didn't respond last spring, I was afraid of what might have happened. I came to find out." His voice dropped. "I'm tired of running, tired of looking over my shoulder."

"Where have you been hiding all this time?"

"I haven't, actually. I've been working at Kettle Falls Landscaping."

Susannah stared at him. "David—what did you say? Langevin? Do you call yourself Dave?"

"Yeah." He gave her a puzzled look.

"*You're* Dave! Carolyn's Dave!" Susannah was hit with yet another shock. She gasped and leaned back in her chair to absorb this revelation.

Doug grinned, rubbing the side of his face. "When Carolyn didn't recognize me, I knew I was probably safe."

"Oh, my goodness—does Carolyn know?"

"No. I couldn't tell her before I told you."

"How long have you been in Colville?" Joe asked.

"About four months. Carolyn and I started seeing each

other recently…. It probably wasn't a good idea for either of us."

"I disagree," Susannah cut in. "She's crazy about you."

"I love her," Doug said simply. "All these years, I haven't allowed myself to feel about a woman the way I feel about her. She deserves far better than me, but she's hard to walk away from. I gave my notice and didn't intend on seeing her again, but… I'm not sure what to do."

"Why are you identifying yourself now?" Joe asked.

"Because of Carolyn and because of what was happening with you." He looked at Susannah as he said this. "She told me about your search for Jake and I was afraid you'd stumble upon the truth. I decided it was best to confront it now and be done with it. I have to trust you and Carolyn and make some decisions about the future."

"It's time she knew, don't you think?" Susannah said, eager for her friend to discover the truth. Before Doug could protest, she walked over to the wall phone and dialed the mill. In the past two weeks she'd called Carolyn so often, she'd memorized the number.

"Can you come to the house right away?" Susannah asked when Carolyn answered.

"Is everything all right?"

"You'll know when you get here." She could barely keep the excitement from her voice. "Just hurry."

Without hesitation, proving again what a good friend she was, Carolyn said, "I'll be there in ten minutes."

For the first time since he'd disclosed his identity, Doug looked nervous. He stood up and walked around the table. "Are you sure this is the right thing to do?"

"Very sure. I'd trust Carolyn with my life. Besides, she loves you."

Doug's head came up. "She told you that?"

"She didn't need to. It's obvious."

"You never did explain why you broke into the house," Joe said, distracting Doug with his question. "I can understand why you wanted to get the journal your dad kept of his visits but what about the other stuff?"

"It was stupid," Doug said. "But I'd given up so much, I was trying to collect small pieces of my former life—when I was still Doug Leary, when I still lived in this house. I took the ribbons I won in track and my letterman jacket, along with some of Dad's things. He had a ring I always wanted. I was looking for that."

"Oh, my goodness, Chrissie's got it! She asked if she could wear it around her neck and I said okay."

"No wonder I couldn't find it." Doug smiled, shaking his head. "Actually, I enjoyed going through the boxes of stuff you'd packed. You have no idea how good it was to look over the memories of my childhood. It gave me the connection I've been lacking all these years. I knew I was risking discovery every time I ventured close to the house, but even that wasn't enough to keep me away."

Susannah could only imagine what might have happened if she'd come across him. "Oh! You were the one tending Mom's garden, too."

Doug nodded sheepishly.

"What if I'd seen you? Or if Rachel next door had?"

"It was close the night you phoned the police," Doug admitted. "But I just couldn't stay away. Even when you installed the alarm, I returned."

They talked a few minutes more while waiting for Carolyn. Joe brought out the pictures he carried in his wallet, using them to update Doug on the family. Her brother was getting more nervous by the minute, and when the doorbell rang, he jerked to his feet.

"You might prepare her," Joe suggested.

Susannah agreed, and when she'd answered the front door, she kept Carolyn in the living room.

"What's all this about?" Carolyn looked terrible, her face pale and ravaged, as if she'd been crying for hours.

"What's wrong?" Susannah asked.

Fighting tears, Carolyn sat down on the one remaining chair and wiped her eyes. "I'm sorry, I'm an emotional mess. Dave's leaving. He gave his notice. I thought I'd try to reason with him. I tried to call him, but I couldn't get through. I'm sure he's already gone. I'm having trouble dealing with it. I'll be all right. It's just that I so badly wanted this to work…."

Squatting in front of her, Susannah reached for her friend's hands and held them in her own. "What I've got to tell you has to do with Dave Langevin."

Carolyn was instantly alarmed. "Has something happened?"

"He's here."

"Here?" Carolyn looked around and not seeing him, turned questioning eyes to Susannah.

"Dave is an assumed name."

"What?" Carolyn's gaze bore into hers.

"Hello, Carolyn," Doug said, coming to stand in the doorway.

"Dave?" she gasped.

He nodded. "You probably remember me as someone else."

"I remember you as Dave. What's going on?" she demanded, glancing from one to the other.

"May I introduce you to my long-lost, once-dead brother, Doug," Susannah said, slipping her arm around his waist.

The blood drained from Carolyn's face and she brought her hand to her mouth. "Doug?" she repeated in a hushed whisper. *"Doug?"*

He nodded again. "I wanted to tell you. I'm so sorry to let you find out like this."

Carolyn didn't wait to hear more. She rushed into his arms and soon they were locked in a tight embrace.

Joe stood next to Susannah, his arm around her shoulders. Jake was dead and that saddened her, but Doug, her beloved brother, Doug, was alive.

Susannah had returned to her childhood home, confused, uncertain and in many ways lost. Over the course of the last month she'd found her way home—to her true home, her true self. She didn't know what the future held for her brother and Carolyn, but she'd let them work that out themselves. Whatever Doug decided was fine by her; she'd stand by him. And, it went without saying, so would Carolyn.

"Are you still feeling shocked?" Joe asked, whispering close to her ear.

She had been at first, but the thing about finding your way home was that while the path might be familiar, it sometimes took unexpected twists and turns. Doug's return was one, the happiest of endings; her new knowledge of her father was another. And so was her rediscovered vision of Joe and their marriage.

CHAPTER

44

Now that she and Doug were alone, Carolyn couldn't stop crying. They'd driven to her home, where they could talk without the fear of constant interruptions. They'd barely made it to the laundry room off the garage when Carolyn broke down.

"I'm sorry, so sorry," Doug said, bringing her into his arms. "I would've done anything to spare you this shock, but I couldn't tell you before I told Susannah and her family."

"I know, I know." She buried her face in his shoulder, clinging to him. "You don't understand."

"What?"

Nothing felt as good as the way Doug ran his fingers through her hair, as if he couldn't get enough of the feel of her, as if he couldn't bring her close enough.

"I have always loved you…. I still have the letters we exchanged. When I found out you'd been killed, I wanted to die, too. If Susannah hadn't been in France with me, I don't know what I would've done."

"I'd come to love you, too," Doug whispered, kissing her temple. "I felt bad about what I was doing. Patricia and I had dated for quite a while and I hated the fact that I was writing to you and still seeing her. I felt guilty about both of you. I planned to break it off with her."

"I wrote you almost every day," she reminded him.

"And I treasured every letter." His hold tightened briefly. "At first I thought there might be a way for me to get to Paris, find you, convince you to go into hiding with me."

"I would've done it." She knew it was true. "But you didn't come...you didn't ask."

Doug shook his head. "I wouldn't do that to you or your parents. If I loved you, and I did, Carolyn, with all my heart, I couldn't do anything to hurt you. I couldn't take you into this hell with me."

Although she knew he was right, it was hard to forget about the years they'd lived apart.

"I told myself when I came back to Colville that I wouldn't get involved with you." She felt his smile against her forehead. "You don't know the hell I went through when I was assigned lawn care at the mill and then later at your home. The minute I saw you, I knew all the resolve in the world wouldn't be enough to keep me away."

Carolyn stroked his back through the thin T-shirt, so grateful he was with her and unwilling to relinquish even one moment with him. "This morning when I discovered you hadn't shown up for work, I was so afraid you'd left town. All morning I had the same horrible feeling I did when I heard that you—Doug—were dead. As if nothing mattered anymore."

"I couldn't leave you."

Emotion thickened her throat. "Oh…I don't even know what to call you."

"Dave. I'm accustomed to it now."

He'd been Dave far longer than he'd been Doug, she realized. Burrowing into his arms, she trembled with the joy of what she'd learned.

"What are we going to do?" she cried, panic taking over. No one must learn the truth. No one must suspect.

"I haven't got everything figured out yet," Dave admitted. "I know I can't leave you, though. I'm through with running."

That was reassuring but also threatening. They had to go someplace he'd be safe, where no one could possibly guess. That meant she couldn't stay in Colville. "I'll sell the mill and we can—"

"No." His response was adamant. "I won't let you. Don't even think like that. I've lived as Dave Langevin for the last few months without anyone in town suspecting. Doug is dead and buried. He's no longer a threat to either one of us."

"But…"

"It's a risk we have to take. None of this can come to light, Carolyn. There's Sheriff Dalton to consider and my mother, too. A shock like this might be more than she could handle."

"Oh, Dave, I feel so bad for your mother. I know we can't tell her but I promise you this—I will visit her and care for her on your behalf."

He raised her fingers to his lips. "Thank you. And if I *am* found out, then so be it, but I don't think it's likely. After Mom and Sheriff Dalton are both gone, I'll contact an attorney and see what can be done to straighten this out."

"No." Carolyn had strong feelings on the matter. "I won't risk having you go to jail."

"I've been there for the last thirty years one way or another."

"As your future wife, I should have a say in this."

Dave went completely still and stepped back, holding her at arm's length. "My future wife?" he asked hesitantly.

Her eyes brimmed with tears as she met his gaze. His wonderful face swam before her. Lifting her hands to his jaw, she smiled shyly and nodded. "I'm proposing, and if you have a lick of sense you'll accept."

"But…"

"I've waited for you my entire life."

"But…"

"Just say yes!"

"Carolyn, you're—"

"Didn't you hear what I said?" she cried. "I love you and I'm not taking no for an answer."

He frowned and a look of sadness settled over him. "I don't even have a pot to piss in. About all I own is that broken-down truck and my camper."

He was going to make this more difficult than she'd expected. So she did the one thing that might convince him. Wrapping her arms around his neck, she kissed him, using her mouth, her tongue, her fingers, her whole body to show this man how much she loved him. He was breathless by the time she'd finished, and so was she.

Dave placed his hand on the washing machine, as though he needed to hold on to something solid to maintain his balance.

"Do you have any other arguments?" she asked and marveled that she could have one of the most important conversations of her life in the laundry room.

Dave frowned and it looked as if he still had some fight in him. "Could you seriously leave me?" she asked.

A half smile lifted the edges of his mouth. "Probably not," he said.

"Next question. How much longer will we manage to stay out of the bedroom? Don't answer, because I can tell you right now, it won't be long. You know it and so do I."

Dave threw back his head, laughed and then swept her back into his embrace. "Carolyn, oh, Carolyn, I love you so damned much. There isn't a solitary reason on God's green earth that you should marry a felon like me, but if you *want* me…"

"Oh, I want you all right. I want you so much I wonder if I can last the three-day waiting period after we apply for the license." Only then did she start to laugh, too. Tears ran down her cheeks and she was laughing and crying at once. The man who'd been dead was now alive. No—that wasn't exactly right. Doug was dead, but *Dave* was alive. Alive and in love with her.

Joe and Susannah parked in the Memorial Hospital lot and went up to Vivian's room, where they found her eating lunch with every appearance of appetite. The color was back in her cheeks and she looked better than she had in weeks.

Susannah had been anticipating this visit. She'd had a long heart-to-heart talk with her husband, and together they'd reached a major decision. She'd begun to feel trapped in her job and now acknowledged that this phase of her life was coming to a natural end. A new one was about to begin.

"Should we tell your mother?" Joe asked.

"Yes. I think she'll be pleased."

"Hi, Mom," she said, coming all the way into the room and bringing Joe with her. "Look who's here. And look what I brought." She held a vase filled with white and pink roses from the garden and carefully placed it on the windowsill.

Vivian brightened and set aside her fork. "Joe!" She held out her arms for a hug. She sounded more and more like her old self. "Chrissie said you were in town. It's *so* good to see you."

Joe folded Vivian in his arms and gave her a gentle hug. "How are you feeling?" he asked.

"Better now that you're here." Her gaze went from Joe to Susannah. "The flowers are lovely, dear." She raised her eyebrows. "You have the same look you always did as a little girl when there was something you were dying to tell me."

"I do?" It wasn't any wonder; Susannah was giddy with excitement, giddy with joy.

"You might as well tell her right away," Joe said, sliding his arm around her waist. He smiled down on her, his eyes alight with love.

Susannah drew in her breath and blurted it out. "Mom, I'm going to buy a flower shop."

Vivian's eyes widened. "A what?"

"A flower shop. Joe and I talked almost all night. I need a career change. I'm burned out as a teacher. In fact, it's only been during these last few weeks that I recognized what was happening."

"A flower shop," her mother repeated as though testing the idea. "Where?"

"In downtown Seattle, on Blossom Street. Joe was there this week and he saw the For Sale sign at Fannie's Flowers. He stopped in to investigate and ask her some questions. I haven't talked to the owner myself yet, but the terms seem very reasonable. It *feels* so right, Mom."

Vivian looked at Joe. "That stubborn daughter of mine needs you, doesn't she?"

"I keep telling her that," Joe said, winking at Susannah. Susannah nudged him in the ribs with her elbow.

"Did you see the doctor today, Mom?" she asked quickly.

Vivian nodded. "He says I've got a ways to go, but I'll do it."

"I know you will," Joe said, "and Susannah and I will visit often."

"Good. Bring some of those flowers when you do." She reached for her napkin. "It wasn't easy giving up my home, but I realize now it was the best thing for me. Changing careers will be good for Susannah, too." Her mother sounded more clearheaded than she had all summer.

"I think so, too, Mom."

"I haven't seen you this happy in…in years, Susannah."

"I *am* happy, Mom. I feel wonderful." Her mother might be experiencing memory problems, but her intuition was in excellent working order. Although Susannah hadn't said a word about her father, she knew that Vivian sensed she'd made peace with the past and was looking forward to her future.

"Good." Her mother nodded once. Using the napkin to dab her mouth, she casually said, "George was by."

"Dad?" Susannah asked, sharing a secret smile with her husband.

"No, no, my friend George from Altamira. He didn't get to stay long, but it's nice to have company." Her mother blushed as she said it. "There's nothing romantic about it, mind you. George is my friend. He told me there's a big bingo pot building and I should hurry back before someone else gets it." Then she abruptly switched gears. "Fannie's Flowers? Will you keep the name?"

Susannah hadn't thought about that yet; the idea was still being born. "I don't know. Do you have a suggestion?"

Her mother nodded, eyes twinkling. "Call it Susannah's Garden."

"Susannah's Garden," she repeated slowly. She liked the sound of it.

"There's a yarn store next door," Joe added. "They apparently offer classes."

This was good news. Her mother had taught her to knit years ago, but Susannah hadn't picked up her needles in far too long. She'd love to take a class if she could fit it into her new schedule.

Vivian lay back against the pillow, looking tired.

"We'll let you rest now, but we'll be back later," Susannah said.

Her mother accepted Susannah's kiss on her cheek. Grabbing hold of her arm, Vivian whispered, "Joe loves you."

"I know, and I love him, too," she whispered back.

As they approached the elevator, Joe stole a kiss before he pushed the call button.

Stepping into the elevator, she moved into Joe's arms. "I hope you know how very much I love you."

Joe backed her into the corner and kissed her passionately. They hardly noticed that the elevator had come to a stop and the doors slid open.

"Look, Mom, newlyweds," a young girl squealed from the hospital lobby.

Embarrassed, Susannah and Joe disentangled their arms and self-consciously walked onto the marble floor.

"Are you newlyweds?" the youngster asked.

Joe chuckled. "In a manner of speaking, we are," he told her, reaching for Susannah's hand.

She'd found her husband again this summer—the summer that changed everything.

I want you to marry again...

On the anniversary of his wife's death,
Dr Michael Everett receives a letter Hannah had
written him. In it she makes one final request:
I want you to marry again – and she's chosen
three women he should consider.

Each of them has her own heartache, but
during the months that follow, Michael spends
time with and learns more about each of
them…and about himself.

www.mirabooks.co.uk